Milly Johnson was born, raised and still lives in Barnsley, South Yorkshire. A *Sunday Times* bestseller, she is one of the Top 10 Female Fiction authors in the UK, and with millions of copies of her books sold across the world, Milly's star continues to rise. Milly was chosen as one of the authors for The Reading Agency's Quick Reads 2020 campaign. *The Woman in the Middle* is her nineteenth novel.

Milly writes from the heart about what and where she knows and highlights the importance of community spirit. Her books champion women, their strength and resilience, and celebrate love, friendship and the possibility of second chances. She is an exceptional writer who puts her heart and soul into every book she writes and every character she creates.

Milly Johnson

The Woman in the Middle

SIMON & SCHUSTER

London · New York · Sydney · Toronto · New Delhi

First published in Great Britain by Simon & Schuster UK Ltd, 2021

Copyright © Millytheink Limited, 2021

1 3 5 7 9 10 8 6 4 2

Simon & Schuster UK Ltd
1st Floor
222 Gray's Inn Road
London WC1X 8HB

Simon & Schuster Australia, Sydney
Simon & Schuster India, New Delhi

www.simonandschuster.co.uk
www.simonandschuster.com.au
www.simonandschuster.co.in

A CIP catalogue record for this book
is available from the British Library

Hardback ISBN: 978-1-4711-9899-1
eBook ISBN: 978-1-4711-9901-1
Audio ISBN: 978-1-3985-0119-5

Typeset in Bembo by M Rules
Printed and bound by CPI Group (UK) Ltd, Croydon, CR0 4YY

In memory of my own Tanya – my pal
Tracey Cheetham who died aged 48 in 2020.
Brave, bold, beautiful and bananas. I was
beyond lucky to have her as my friend.

Sandwich

Noun: Food item consisting of two pieces of bread with a filling between them, eaten as a light meal, using the most appropriate bread that allows maximum enjoyment of the filling within.
'a cheese sandwich'.

Verb: To insert or squeeze (someone or something) between other people or things, typically in a restricted space or so as to be uncomfortable.
'the woman was sandwiched between her children and her parents on the bus.'

Prologue

Twenty-four years ago

Shay Corrigan stepped out of the limousine, holding on to her father's hand. The photographer freeze-framed the moment for the family album.

'Nice big smiles.'

The father of the bride did his best but the sight of his wife idling at the bottom of the church steps in her flowery hat was making that difficult because he knew why she was there and he'd warned her not to be. Not that Roberta Corrigan would be in the least bit cowed by her husband's disapproval, or be swayed from her mission by the bridesmaids, Tanya and Lesley, giggling as she held her hand up in front of the photographer's lens and said, 'And you can put that away for five minutes.'

'Roberta—'

'Be quiet, Harry, I want a word with my daughter.'

'Our daughter,' he corrected her. 'And you should be in church dabbing your eyes and showing off your frock after what it cost.'

'*Mu-um,*' appealed Shay as her mother grabbed her arm and pulled her far enough away from everyone else to give them some privacy.

'Shay.' Roberta looked her daughter square in the eye. 'I have to ask you, do you want to do this? Because we can get right back in this limousine now and go home, no questions asked. Your father can tell everyone it's off. Forget the expense, forget the cake, the flowers, forget everything. You can move back in with us. Now, are you quite certain, is this really what you want?'

Shay had thought at first it was a joke, but her mother had her deadly serious face on.

'Of course I want to marry Bruce,' she replied. 'Why would you pick now to ask me this?'

'Because your father said I shouldn't, so I held off,' said Roberta. 'But it's been going round and round in my head like a circling crow and it won't go away, and you should never deny a mother's intuition. So I'm asking you before it's too late, do you want to marry this man? Have you thought it through? Do you love him?'

'Yes, yes and yes,' replied Shay, without a pause, without letting thought have a chance to answer before her mouth did. She did love Bruce. She had wanted to and she had managed it. She stuck out a defiant chin. 'I'm old enough to know what I'm doing, Mum. So go and sit in the pew and let me get on with it.' Then she pulled her veil hurriedly over her face because she didn't want her mother staring into her eyes again, finding that shadow of doubt there that she'd forced into the 'wedding nerves' box in her head, even though it didn't belong there and was fighting its way out.

'Well, if you're sure,' said her mother, resignedly. She

helped adjust her daughter's veil so it was aisle-perfect. 'I love you.'

'I love you too. Now go sit.'

Her mother turned, went into the church and Shay let go the breath she didn't realise she was holding.

'Ready to be a wife?' asked her dad, holding out his crooked arm.

'Yep, I'm ready,' Shay answered him. Ready to be a wife and hopefully soon a mother. Not that she'd fall into the trap of ever letting any child take over her life; she wouldn't be Roberta mark II and have her identity buried under all her various personas: wife, mother, daughter. When a child came along, it would have to fit around her, not the other way round. She wouldn't sacrifice herself at the altar of family. And she would *never* lose her sense of self for anyone.

Falling

*Sometimes we need to fall to find out
where we stand*

ANON

Chapter 1

For as long as she could remember, Shay Bastable had felt
like the equivalent of a sandwich filling which had got more
and more compressed over the years until her once fresh and
jaunty ingredients had been squashed into a pâté by the two
fat slices of bread at either side of her. She didn't resent her
life, that was just how it *was*. Her presence was there to be
central in order to hold the sandwich unit together – to glue,
to serve, to bind. But she did feel somewhat relieved at the
outer slices relaxing their press upon her over the past year.
Her twenty-three-year-old son Sunny had left the family
home nine months ago to live with his fiancée Karoline,
and her daughter had packed up and moved out to flat-share
with her best friend six months later. Shay had expected her
back within twenty-four hours but nope, there was silence
on that front – and with Courtney, no news was good news.
She hadn't cried when Courtney had left home, but she'd
sobbed buckets when Sunny had, cried until the salt had
made her cheeks red and raw. Not because she loved her
son any more than her daughter, but because he was *easier*
to love. He'd been hard work, as all kids are, but his sweet,

easy disposition, his affection had been enough reward to sweep away the fatigue. Twenty-two-year-old Courtney was mercury personified, a shape-shifter. Her beliefs, hair, fashion, likes and dislikes changed with the wind and Shay had stopped trying to figure her out and had to stand back and let her find her place because – as she herself had once thought – parents knew nothing. They had grown out of the ways of the present world and were no longer in touch with it, their accrued wisdom of little value. Two very different children who had been raised exactly the same way and yet had turned out polar opposites. Shay knew, of course, that children were not the sum of their mothers' and fathers' influences, because she and her elder sister Paula had been brought up in the same household, yet apart from the equivalent number of limbs and head, there weren't a lot of other similarities between them.

Shay's parents had divorced only five years ago, in their seventies. Roberta Corrigan had settled well into single life, although she kept her (relative) independence thanks only to the amount of scaffolding her younger daughter supplied to hold it in place. Shay went to visit her mother every day: sometimes she'd bob up in the morning, but she was always there at teatime to cook her a meal, sort out her tablets for the following day and ensure she was warm and safe for the night. There was more and more memory slippage going on, but the doctor had said that as long as Roberta was remembering the important things like turning off hobs and locking doors, not to be too troubled by the fact that she couldn't remember who the prime minister was or her twelve times table. Plus she had wonderful neighbours who kept an eye out for each other. Their Neighbourhood Watch made the SAS look like a bunch of amateurs.

Shay pulled up outside her mother's house and noticed that building work had commenced next door. It had been expected, of course, why else would there have been a huge orange skip parked on their drive for the past two rain-sodden weeks? Odd couple, her mum's neighbours. Middle-aged and reclusive, they stuck out like a pair of sore thumbs from the sociable, elderly residents of Merriment Close. The close had always lived up to its name; it had been a happy cul-de-sac of ten bungalows; an outer circle of dwellings around an inner round of green which the pensioners themselves maintained to an impeccable stand-ard. Then last year Doris at 1A had died and her daughter had sold the bungalow to the dour Drew and Ann Balls who did not wish to engage with their neighbours on any level. Christmas cards to them had not been reciprocated, hellos in passing not returned, invitation to join the residents' asso-ciation ignored.

When Shay walked into the house it was to find her mother standing at the window, eyes glued to the skip as if trying to outstare it in a competition in the hope it would melt away in defeat. She had been strangely fascinated by it since it landed without being able to explain why, but it had obviously triggered something in her cloudy mind.

'What are they doing, do you think? All afternoon, they've been flinging bricks in that . . . orange thing. What's it called?'

'It's a skip, Mum. And I suspect they'll be having some building work done which is why people usually hire them. They'll fill it and then it will be gone, out of your way for-ever. Now, is there anything you fancy for tea?'

'You'll be able to see it from space, that thing,' said Roberta, ignoring the tea question. 'I can see it every time I look through the window, all shouty and orange.'

'Then don't look through the window at it,' said Shay. Her mum's brain chewed on minutiae these days, as if it were everlasting gum, the flavours refreshing every few minutes to encourage new mastication. Roberta was so much less tolerant of change than she had been even just a couple of years ago. Now, change and her mother were mortal enemies. One night they'd moved the broadcast time for *Coronation Street* forward by half an hour and it was right up there with the world's catastrophes: a volcano erupting in Iceland; a tsunami in the Philippines; Ken Barlow not being on screen at the allotted hour.

'Skip.' Roberta repeated the word over and over. 'Why didn't I remember the name? They tell you to do crosswords to keep your brain active and all they do is frustrate me. I used to learn a new word every day, now I forget an old word every few hours.'

It hurt Shay's heart when her mum said things like this. She never knew how to answer, didn't want to acknowledge it, brushed it under the carpet hoping it would wither and drop through the floorboards so she didn't have to face it.

'I thought baked potato and cheese for tea,' Shay said with a bracing smile.

'I'm not really that hungry.'

She always said this but she always ate what was put in front of her.

'You finish off your crossword and I'll get it ready.'

Her mum did the puzzles in the newspaper every day, but she wasn't getting the same pleasure from them as she used to. Too many holes had appeared in her vocabulary and her concentration levels weren't anything like what they once were.

When Shay bobbed her head around the door to

announce that tea was on the table, her mum was still standing at the window, lost in the view. 'Mum,' she called again
more loudly, and Roberta jumped slightly, dislodged from
whatever was occupying her thoughts, and wandered into
the kitchen, almost reluctant to leave her post.

'That looks nice. I haven't had a baked potato for a long
time,' said Roberta, sitting down to eat. Shay didn't say that
she'd had one only a few days ago.

'Good, well, enjoy it then. I hope I haven't put too much
cheese on it. I don't want you having bad dreams.'

'I've got plenty of time to digest it before bedtime,'
replied Roberta, picking up her cutlery in that delicate, cul-
tured way she had. She'd always had such a ladylike manner
about her.

Shay took some milk out of the fridge and checked the
date on the carton. Left to her own devices, her mother
would be eating mouldy bread and green bacon.

'What could they be doing in there that merits the need
for a . . .' Roberta shook her head impatiently.

'Skip.' Shay supplied the word again as she poured a
stream of tea from the old brown faithful pot that'd had
its place on the kitchen table since she was a young girl.
'Maybe they're having a new kitchen or a bathroom. You
said yourself that Doris still had the original 1970s fittings
in the house when it was sold.'

Roberta pressed her knife into the potato. 'They're up to
something. Everyone's saying they are.'

'I don't think so,' Shay replied, making less of it.

'Derrick at number five says he looks like a serial killer.
Christie. The one that young man was hanged for.'

Shay laughed at that.

'You'll have to put it out of your mind, Mum. Let them

get on with taking out the avocado bathroom suite or whatever it is they're doing because it's not going to affect you.
Live and let live, that's what your mantra was once upon a
time. Oh and guess what I've got for you – I found you a
DVD of *The Quiet Man.*'

'Oh, wonderful. Thank you, Shay.' Roberta was clearly
delighted by that.

'Yep. So now you and Dagmara can watch it the next
time you have one of your cinema mornings. You have
remembered that I won't be here for the next two days, hav-
en't you?' She asked the question but could guess the answer.

Roberta's jaw dropped open. 'Why won't you be here?'

Up until last year Roberta had always sent them a card
unprompted; now she couldn't even bring the date to mind.

'Bruce and I are going away to a hotel for a little treat.
We're driving there tonight, that's why I'm here early.' Shay
didn't mention the anniversary because she'd been taught
to try not to bring up the things her mother had forgotten, highlighting them, reminding her of her deterioration.
'Paula's coming to see to you. I'll leave her number by the
phone so if you need anything, ring her not me because I
won't be around.'

Roberta's face broke into a smile. 'Paula. That'll be nice.
I can't remember the last time I saw her.'

Neither can I, Shay said inwardly, and her mental faculty
was functioning perfectly. But then her older sister did have
a *proper job* that made driving twenty minutes to see her
mother – or father – on a regular basis very difficult.

Roberta's smile closed down then at the prospect of not
seeing her younger daughter for a couple of days. 'She's not
as patient as you though, Shay. She snaps at me.'

'Well, I'll have a word and tell her not to,' Shay said to

that. She'd have *the talk* that lovely Dagmara from next-door-but-one had had with her last year, the one that made Shay see things so differently she'd been shamed by it, though she'd been glad of the insight, grateful for the lesson. Shay used to get herself in a bit of a stew about her mother's failing memory, automatically correcting her at every turn when she misremembered facts until Dagmara, who had nursed her husband through dementia, had taken her on one side and given her a gentle, well-meaning, but essential, lecture.

'What does it matter if she remembers it that way, Shay? Who is it hurting, what does it change?' she'd said in her lovely Latvian accent. 'It's the new truth she remembers. Don't cause her stress by telling her she's wrong when her brain is telling her she's right.'

Dagmara was a bastion of patience, understanding and common sense and she was spot on with what she was saying. What harm was it doing to Roberta, remembering she was on a lovely holiday with her sister the day Princess Diana's car crashed, when Shay knew for sure her aunt had died the previous year? Being impatient with her, forcing her to try and remember the real truth when her brain wanted to reject it as a lie would not glue all the missing pieces back together and make her whole again. When coping with a loved one with the onset of dementia, it was necessary to acquire a new set of skills, one of them being knowing when to back off and shut up.

Roberta Corrigan had once been such a sharp cookie, an intellectually gifted woman fluent in five languages, with a working knowledge of at least two more; she absorbed them like a sponge. She'd been a teacher in a private school, then she'd become a self-employed tutor in order to fit around looking after her two daughters and her aged parents. Now, she couldn't even remember the name for a skip in her own native tongue.

'When are you back then?'

'I'll see you Monday.'

'That's a long time.'

'Just a weekend.'

Roberta scraped some potato away from the skin and then dumped the latter at the side of her plate.

'You should eat that skin, it's the best part,' said Shay, feeling, not for the first time, as if their roles had reversed. Roberta had made her daughters eat potato skins, stressing it was where all the nutrients were. Shay didn't like these moments; they were a pollution of world order.

'Nope, I've never liked it.'

But she had. Another tongue-biting moment. It was hard to watch a loved one lose her sense of self. Her mother's mind had always been so strong and here it was being chipped away at so cruelly.

Roberta had her usual small tub of ice cream after her tea. Tonight it was strawberry which triggered off a recollection.

'Oh, I had a phone call from Courtney this morning.'

'Did you?' *More than I've had*, thought Shay.

'She's changed her name, hasn't she?'

Shay rolled her eyes. Courtney had rechristened herself Strawberry Blue for whatever reason just before she'd left home. Bruce had refused outright to call his daughter Strawberry Blue, said the name that fitted her best was 'Wrecking Ball'.

'She sounded jolly,' said Roberta, speaking through her ice cream and spraying pink droplets. 'She's working at a clothes shop, isn't she?'

'That's news to me. Last I heard she was behind a bar in a nightclub,' said Shay. She didn't disbelieve it, because Courtney changed jobs like underwear and none of them seemed to fit. Shay respected that her daughter was just trying to work out who she really was and what she wanted and if it entailed a little exploration, then so be it. Bruce, who had always been perfectly content in his own skin, had never wanted to change his name to John Pliers/ Marvin Starface, and had known since he'd been a foetus that he wanted to be an electrician, was less understand-ing. When post started arriving at the house addressed to Ms Strawberry Blue, he'd had a mini meltdown, declared that she was an embarrassment and said that the sooner she sorted herself out the better. It was then that Courtney had made an accelerated effort to find an alternative place to stay and wouldn't be persuaded by her mother to change her mind.

'Not heard from Sunny though,' Roberta carried on. 'There's something not right there,' she added. 'It's not like him not to ring his grandma.'

It wasn't, Shay had to agree with that.

'I don't like her that much,' said Roberta, scraping the last of the ice cream out of the tub with the small plastic spoon supplied. She preferred that to a teaspoon, said it made her feel as if she was at the cinema having a treat.

'Who?' asked Shay. Her mother often flitted from one subject to another and it was hard to keep up sometimes.

'That Karoline our Sunny's with. Something not right about her.'

'There's something not right about everyone you know,' said Shay with a chuckle. The Balls, Karoline, her local MP, Chris – Paula's husband. Maybe she had a point with him though. He was so far up his backside, he could have sucked his own uvula.

'Not everyone. And you can scoff all you like, but I've always had a very strong intuition where people are concerned. She's not all she seems, that one,' said Roberta, disapproval shading her expression.

'You've only seen her once.'

'You only need to see someone once to *know*.' Roberta tapped the side of her nose.

'What's she done to make you think that?'

'Nothing, yet.'

'There you go then. Anyway, Sunny's happy with her and that's all that matters.'

He'd been bowled over by her from the off, she was like no other girl he'd ever met he said, and if Karoline was good enough for him, then she was good enough for Shay.

'I'm not changing my opinion,' Roberta sniffed haughtily. 'As I said, my intuition tells me otherwise.'

'Okay, Mum,' Shay smiled, amused by the mention of her mother's famous intuition.

After tea, Shay sorted out Roberta's tablets and did the washing up while her mother went to watch some TV, except she didn't because the distraction of the neighbour's skip proved too much to ignore. When Shay walked back into the lounge, Roberta was once again at the window, her lips moving over the words stencilled on the side like fingers working over the texture of cloth: SHARIF'S SKIPS.

'Mum? *Tipping Point* will be on in a minute.'

Roberta carried on staring at the skip with a faraway look in her eyes.

'I knew Omar Sharif once, I'm sure I did,' she said eventually. Her memory pool had been stirred by something and a recollection had popped to the surface like a bubble. A rogue one though, because her mother had never met the famous screen god. But, as Dagmara would say, what did it matter? It wasn't the worst false memory to have.

'Did you?' asked Shay.

Roberta's brow creased in thought. 'I think so. I wanted to marry him.'

'You and every other woman in the 1960s,' said Shay, giving her a gentle nudge.

But Roberta wasn't listening to her, she was lost in some other world, eyes closed, holding up her hand as if stroking the cheek of someone, feeling their skin beneath her fingers. Then she opened them and saw she was touching only empty air.

'Where did you meet Omar Sharif then, Mum?' Shay watched her mother's exit from wherever her reverie had taken her.

'What are you talking about?' came the scoffing reply. 'As if I ever met Omar Sharif.'

Chapter 2

Shay's father, it had to be said, looked nothing like Omar Sharif. Even in his heyday Harry Corrigan was heavy-set with thick sandy hair, muted blue eyes and pale skin, all of which Shay's sister Paula had inherited. Paula had never tried to make the best of the physical hand of cards she had been dealt: highlights and a different hair style would have flattered her face, make-up would have made the best of her full lips and long lashes. Instead she stuck to *au naturel* – even when she'd gone prematurely grey – and openly resented that her younger sister Shay was the pretty one with skin like amber honey, large brown eyes and long, shiny ink-black locks. Shay looked like no one in the immediate family except, so Roberta said, her aunt who was a fellow throwback to their Italian ancestry. Underneath her bleach-blonde hair, apparently, Roberta's sister Stella looked just like Sophia Loren. At least from the back with the light off, or so her dad used to joke.

Shay loved her father, though he hadn't been that much of a hands-on dad when she was growing up. He was either working or out watching football, playing snooker, having a pint with friends. He didn't go and see her act in plays or attend school prize-givings. He didn't take her to the swings or help her with her homework. He was just *there,* an affable presence who painted and wallpapered, tinkered about with his car and mowed the lawn. Then, when she was sixteen, he'd stepped up to the plate and become a dad, not just a father.

She'd never held his hand as a child, but now, here in the Whispering Pines care home, she was feeling the solid weight of it, the gravitational pull of his thick sausage fingers and it made her sad that even though he was a hollowed-out shell of himself, it had still taken her a long time to dare reach for his hand, to place it in her own as if expecting him to shake her off, embarrassed by such intimacy. She wondered if he knew she was there; she had to hope that he did. But then, would that mean he had sense of who didn't come and see him?

She'd checked the visitors' book, as she always did, waiting at reception for someone to give her an update on his situation. The book went back three months and only once did Paula's name appear – three weeks ago. She'd signed in and out within fifteen minutes and Shay wondered why she'd even bothered for so short a time, but that was Paula to a tee: duty over, so no one could say she hadn't done her bit. His wife Barbara tended to visit in the mornings, so their paths hadn't crossed for a long time. Out of respect for her mother, Shay had resisted getting overly close to the woman who had dealt the fatal blow to her parents' marriage. She'd always been polite and pleasant whenever she'd had to pick up her dad to take him to have his kidneys/prostate/ears/eyes looked at by medical professionals now that he didn't drive any more, but she'd desisted from any cosy chatty coffees in their kitchen. She had also been present at their small registry office wedding, though Paula hadn't attended, having been struck down with a convenient bout of shingles which gave her the excuse she'd wished for not to attend. It had been very weird seeing her eighty-year-old father so happy because he was marrying his mistress and she'd wondered what it did to children's heads in similar circumstances because it just about cabbaged hers as a fully grown adult.

There had been a lot of information for Shay to get her head around six years ago when seemingly out of the blue her seventy-three-year-old mother had filed for divorce on grounds of adultery. Shay's loyalties hadn't just been split, they'd been chopped up and mascerated.

It was only then that all the truth came flooding out with the force of the water behind an obliterated Hoover Dam: Harry Corrigan had been a serial adulterer for many of the years of their marriage, Roberta finally admitted to her daughters. She had forgiven him over and over to keep the family intact, and she'd mainly succeeded because neither Paula nor Shay had ever had the slightest inkling what had gone on behind the scenes of their parents' relationship. There were some years when Harry's priorities were focused first and foremost on the family unit but then, as the need for his command of the ship subsided, his faithfulness began to wane again. Harry's affair with Barbara had gone on for a long time behind their spouses' backs before they walked out of their marriages for each other. They enjoyed four and a half years of wedded bliss before a stroke clobbered him from left field, robbing him of everything but his breathing. Barbara had chosen, with care, a nursing home for him with a peaceful air and where the staff were kind and skilled.

He would have felt guilty to have people worrying over

him, Shay knew. He'd never liked a fuss, didn't want to put anyone out. This would be hell for him; it was hell for them all.

She'd never spoken to her father as much as she had since he'd been in this comatose state and she didn't know if he could even hear her; but she'd taken another lesson from Dagmara, that hearing was often the last sense to leave, and never to assume the father she knew wasn't still there inside, needing comfort and familiar voices. So Shay sat there for hours sometimes, reading the newspaper aloud to him, talking to him about what Sunny and Courtney were up to. Sometimes she gave him a shave because the nurses never quite gave him the perfect one his exacting standards required, and she'd splash some of his aftershave on for him. He'd always smelt lovely, her dad. Nothing expensive, but clean and fresh as pine trees.

'What's the point in going?' Paula had said once. 'He's not Dad any more, is he? He's more or less a vegetable.'

'How do you know what's going on in his head?' Shay snapped back.

Then Paula had come out with the classic, 'Well, I don't like to see him like that. It's upsetting.'

'Do you think I do, Paula? But I'm willing to take the risk he knows we're there and is comforted by it.'

Then Paula would let loose her final big gun. 'Well, he doesn't deserve us after what he did to Mum.'

In a past life Paula must have been an eel, Shay thought. She could wriggle out of anything. She'd have made a great politician. Shay didn't judge her dad as a husband, and as a father he'd been there for her when she needed him to be. He hadn't let her down; she wouldn't let him down either.

Sitting here with her father, just being with him,

breathing the same air, her mind unwrapped memories like sweets. Today, she remembered seeing her father come in late one night, head and shoulders covered in snow, carrying a bag that didn't quite cover the doll in a box, the doll she desperately wanted for Christmas. She remembered him painting Paula's bedroom ceiling black with glow-in-the-dark stars on it, so it would be a surprise when she got back from her school camping trip. She remembered him leaving a Mars bar on her desk when she was revising for her GCSEs, telling her it was 'brain food'. And that same summer, she remembered overhearing the conversation going on downstairs when she couldn't sleep. Her mother and father, a rally of heated voices: *We can't leave. We have to. It's totally the wrong thing to do. I won't have her living it over and over again. She's done nothing to cause this, and that's why she has to stay. No, we're leaving and that's that.* Her mother's will had won, and they'd moved from their home village to the city at what felt like breakneck speed. It meant her father had a little further to travel to work; it meant leaving behind everyone they knew; it had meant upheaval and cost and disruption but they'd moved, shed their old life like a skin. To protect her.

She didn't like to admit this, but Harry had seemed happier these past six years than he had ever been with her mum. His and Barbara's love for each other was clearly true and tender; they were always out having lunch or catching a bus to the coast and they'd been looking forward to many more years of the same, only for their hopes and dreams to be snatched away one Sunday morning when he was lazing in the conservatory. Barbara thought he'd died; maybe it would have been kinder if he had.

Shay placed her father's hand onto her face, moulding the

fingers around her cheek, wishing they'd stay there when she let go, but they didn't. She spoke into his palm, in the hope that the soft whisper would sink into his pores, join his bloodstream, drift into his brain.

'I shan't see you for a couple of days, Dad, because I'm going to a nice hotel in the Dales for the weekend with Bruce. It's my twenty-fourth wedding anniversary tomorrow. Next year we get all the silver, like you and Mum did. Do you remember? I sprayed my hair silver for your party and then I couldn't get it all out for weeks.'

She willed him to respond with a facial tic, a bend of the finger, a blink – anything. But there was nothing. Just a breath in and then out again: life, without living.

Chapter 3

Shay picked up the satiny scrap of underwear, put it in the case, took it out again. She had shaved off a few pounds to fit into these knickers that she'd bought in the spring sales so she could take them with her, but suddenly she felt rather silly and a teeny bit nervous. She couldn't remember the last time she'd worn such a blatant flag of availability, although there hadn't been much point because she and Bruce hadn't been intimate for months, he'd been totally off it. He hadn't touched her in bed and on the couple of occasions she'd tried to initiate anything, he'd told her he was too tired and she'd respected that and not pushed it. He seemed to be working longer and harder for less and less return. Electricians were ten a penny these days, he'd grumble, and people seemed to want cheap prices before quality work.

She wished her best friend Tanya were still around because she would have opened her heart to her about it, asked her advice on what to do. Les would have made a joke of it, told her to jump on Bruce and not take no for an answer, but Tan would have been more sympathetic and constructive. Tanya, Lesley, Shay – the Yorkshire Charlie's

Angels, as Les's dad used to call them. The three of them had been a tight, solid band since sixth form but Tan and Shay were just a little bit closer. Not even Bruce knew the full story of why Shay's family had suddenly upped sticks to the other side of Sheffield when she was sixteen and he didn't know anything about the year of her life spent in darkened rooms, hospitals, pill-induced sleeps and with doctors who couldn't slice bits out of her brain with knives but tried to do it in other ways. But Tan knew it all. It had been three years since she died and Shay still struggled to believe she wasn't there any more, that she'd never hear her voice on the phone again pretending to be a scam call or a dodgy salesperson. She was mad, bonkers, beautiful, loyal, fabulous and it was the finality of it that had hit Shay the hardest; that someone so alive and vibrant could somehow not be there any longer, that they would never meet again, that there was a hole inside her where only Tan could fit.

Shay lifted up the scrap of pants and stretched the sides. Once upon a time Bruce would have torn them off her with his teeth, but she wasn't sure what his reaction would be this weekend. Their sex life sat like a big fat lazy elephant in the room, silently condemning. It was their anniversary and expectation hung heavy that they should indulge in more than a peck on the cheek and a 'sleep well'. She felt not unlike a virgin anticipating her wedding night. They shouldn't have let things get this far, become an issue as sensitive as a gout-riddled toe.

Shay's thoughts were interrupted by the noise of the letterbox flap. She dropped the pants into her case, went downstairs and retrieved the post from the mat. Cards, judging by the stiffness of them. She ripped open the first with a smile at the large swirly writing on the front, unmistakably

Courtney's hand. She took it out of the envelope and a spray of metallic confetti fell out with it. A sweet, traditional *Happy Anniversary Mum and Dad* card. Inside:

> Shit card alert – this was all they had in Tesco. Happy Anniversary you two – hope you have a great weekend away, Lots of love and see you soon – Court xxx

Courtney never failed to send cards and they were never late either. Odd, considering how much her focus was on herself, that she had a real thing about cards: the choosing of them, the sending of them. But Courtney was a mass of enigmas and contradictions. She likened herself to a salmon, swimming upstream because her nature dictated it. But not even Mother Nature was infallible: the effort it took the fish to do that knackered them, ultimately destroyed them. But then, all mothers made cock-ups.

Another card from Great Aunt Freda whose handwriting became more spidery with every passing year. The last envelope bore the unmistakable loopy style of Lesley. Inside, a card with two swans on the front, their necks entwined, and the words: *'Did you know that swans mate for life?'* Once opened, a drawing of those swans bleeding as they pecked at each other, along with the caption, *'No wonder they're so f***ing bad-tempered'.*

It was a card that said more about Lesley and Morton Jagger's marriage than hers and Bruce's. Tan always said that if Les and Morton hadn't rowed they would never have spoken to each other. Les moaned constantly about her husband, in fact she'd been threatening to leave him since their honeymoon. But despite her many whinges about him, they were still together twenty-three years on and were on course for Les to be nagging him about his shortfalls through to their diamond anniversary. It wasn't Shay's notion of an ideal set-up, but whatever happened behind closed doors was pumping plenty of oxygen into the lungs of their relationship to keep it going.

Short and sweet: 'Love, Les' and a single kiss. They hadn't been in touch for ages. Too often, life got in the way of living, and after Tanya had died, Shay had been determined not to let that keep happening. Easier said than done, though, when you were snowed under with work and family commitments.

There was no card from Sunny; it might arrive tomorrow when she was away, but she had a strange feeling that it wouldn't and that would be very out of character for him. She hadn't expected him to come back and visit them every week, but since he'd left home to go and live with Karoline, they'd only seen him once in the last six months.

He'd texted a few times to check all was well and said that he was busy and would call in soon, but he hadn't. Bruce said he had left his old life behind and was enjoying being in his new one and if she couldn't accept that then she was just jealous that she'd been supplanted as number-one female in her son's life, which was ludicrous because she wanted him to be happy with a nice woman like Karoline. She couldn't rationalise why she felt just a teeny bit anxious about not seeing her son for such a long time, nor could she shake it off, it was just intuition. Just as her mother had blamed intuition for trying to press-gang her into jilting Bruce on her wedding day.

Stop worrying and finish your packing. The voice of reason in her head these days sounded just like Tanya's.

'Okay, I will,' Shay answered it aloud. This weekend

was about her and Bruce for a change. There was no point in leaving everyone behind only to take them all with her in her head.

*

Birtwell Manor was a crumbly old mansion which had been converted into a hotel after the war. It stood in acres of grounds with cultivated gardens, a woodland walk and fishing rights attached to the bordering river, so said the online blurb. Shay had booked the grand Buckingham Suite with its surfeit of wood panelling, imposing four-poster bed and heavy red tapestry drapes at the windows which afforded a stunning view of the estate. Coming to places like this always reinforced to Shay that she was a country, not a city, girl at heart. She liked to have greenery, fields, rivers and farms on her doorstep. Bruce preferred the anonymity of bigger places; villages were always full of nosy bastards, he said. He'd been brought up in one and couldn't wait to leave it.

There was a bottle of champagne waiting for them in a silver ice bucket and a tray of handmade chocolates. Bruce strutted around the space, checking out the en suite, testing the day-bed sofa in the corner for comfort, opening the wardrobes, poking about in the drawers, all the while nodding approvingly.

Bruce was a good-looking man, one of those enviable types who grew sickeningly more attractive with every crinkle to his eyes and those handsome genes had been passed down to their son. Sunny had his father's mouth with its generous lower lip, the strong square jaw, the height and broad shoulders, but he'd inherited his mother's dark eyes instead of his father's blue ones. Also, like his mother, his skin tanned when the sun merely brushed it, whereas Bruce had to work at getting brown. Father and son may have looked like each other, but in temperament, they were very different. Sunny was much more gentle in his manner and he had a kindness of spirit that hung around him like an aura. Bruce saw the world in blacks and whites, Sunny saw the greys. Sometimes Shay found herself wishing her son were less sensitive like her, more resilient like Bruce. It was a hard world and the Bruces fared better in it.

'Let's get the lid off this, shall we?' said Bruce, pulling the champagne out of the bucket and tearing off the foil. She'd picked this place for him more than for herself, something old-grand, caviar and champagne, sophisticated and civilised. He would have liked the high life twenty-four-seven, she knew. If they ever won the Euromillions, he'd have put a down payment on a Ferrari as soon as he'd checked the Lucky Stars numbers. A soft pop as the cork jumped from the bottle, then a small wisp of gas escaped like a genie. Bruce poured it out too eagerly and the champagne frothed up and over the rim of the flutes. He handed one to his wife but it was she who made the toast.

'Here's to the next twenty-four.' Shay chinked her glass gently against her husband's.

'Yep,' he said and Shay found herself waiting for more words that didn't come.

As Shay sat at the dressing-table mirror to put on her earrings, she watched Bruce behind her, checking himself in the full-length mirror with the thoroughness of James Bond before a mission. She liked that he had pride in how he looked. He'd gone a little metrosexual over the past year, because he'd definitely had his eyebrows attended to and those greys at his temples had been reversed. Personally, she thought both detracted from his handsomeness rather than added to it, but she hadn't said so. Rather that than be like Morton Jagger, who wasn't averse to using string for a belt and needed surgical intervention to remove his steel toe cap boots.

Bruce's suit was black, slim-fitting, his shirt snow-white, shoes patent shiny. He was hot property, even more so since he'd cut out the fried bacon and egg breakfast sandwiches and pasty lunches and hit the gym a couple of years ago after one of his overweight mates, 'Jabba', had had a fatal heart attack at the age of forty-two. Bruce worked hard because he wanted to retire early and live somewhere sunny near a taverna and he wanted that retirement to be very long. They used to get holiday brochures and look for possible places where they'd settle, design their perfect villa on a notepad, though they hadn't spoken about it for ages. Maybe tonight over dinner was the perfect time to reinject some energy into their joint project, she decided. It was also something for them, not about her parents, their children – just them.

I wonder how he's aged.

The thought came into her head from an unseen direction and she felt the impact in her heart as it launched a trio of pounding beats. Twenty-nine years had passed since she'd last seen Jonah Wells and yet the memory of him was as clear and shiny as if it had been polished daily. She leaned on the door in her mind to keep him out; his boyish fresh scent, the dark chocolate colour of his hair, the bright hazel of his eyes, the press of his mouth against hers . . . none of it had any right being there; she'd had to bury everything: the sweet and the sour. She'd even picked her wedding date specifically to stamp over that portion of her life, to give her something in June to smile about, to blast the shadows into oblivion with some sunshine. But the date never held up to close inspection because she could still see him there in the background, never quite disappearing because the roots were too deep to dig out; he would always be part of her. *The sweet and the sour.*

Chapter 4

The dining room of Birtwell Manor was textbook classic elegance. Ridiculously high ornamental ceilings with just the right detail of cracked plasterwork to suggest age and authenticity, upmarket shabby chic. The tables were dressed in crisp heavy white fabric with a satin sheen, the cutlery old silver. Shay wouldn't have been surprised to see Hercule Poirot dining among them.

'Blimey, this is a bit posh, isn't it?' said Bruce, not quite trusting the waiter who tucked him under the table, as if he expected him to whip the chair away at the last second.

'We deserve posh today,' said Shay, smiling at him because she knew she'd chosen well. For the next forty hours, Bruce could imagine this life was his norm and he'd play it to the beat. Once upon a time, their plans for their house in the sun were much grander and featured his and hers dressing rooms; his with rails of suits and shirts – all designer names and a secret compartment for his many Rolex watches. He liked 'names'; it wasn't her thing but she respected it was his.

Shay was wearing a black velvet dress, only a high-street

purchase, and she'd worn it before, but she felt lovely in it. Coupled with heels, it lengthened her medium height and gave shape to her slim, curveless figure. She'd piled her long, thick hair into a half up-do, a style that suited her oval face, made her look every inch the Italian of her ancestors. In short, she felt as glamorous as she was ever going to get and she was so looking forward to this evening – with her handsome husband.

The waiter gave them both a leather-bound menu and Bruce's eyes almost popped out of his head when he opened it.

'Jesus Christ, look how much for a fillet steak. You could buy a bloody yacht for . . .'

Shay threw him a look that withered Bruce's words on his lips.

'Okay, okay, I'll not look at the prices,' he relented. Bruce wouldn't have thought twice about paying ridiculous money for clothes, but he didn't splash the cash so easily on more transient pleasures.

From the food menu, Shay chose the lobster-tail salad with Thermidor butter starter, then a fillet steak with Bearnaise sauce. Bruce chose the creamed mushrooms and a sirloin. She knew he'd ask for it rare because it sounded classy, but he'd eat around the edges and leave the red-oozing middle section – happened every time.

'Well, this is nice, isn't it?' said Shay, when the waiter had taken their choices to the kitchen and they were settled with a large glass of Chablis each. Bruce had chosen it. He hadn't a clue about wines but pretended he did. He'd peruse the descriptions, and the prices, at length then pick the second or third cheapest.

'It's fantastic,' replied Bruce. He sighed in the way he

did when he was relaxed and she smiled at that. He'd been working too hard recently and needed this break.

She picked up her glass. 'Here's to a lovely couple of days. I can't remember the last time we went out for a meal, can you? We haven't done it nearly enough in our marriage, just having you and me time.'

'Well, we've both had too much on, haven't we? Kids, my parents, your mum . . . then your mum and dad, then your dad . . . then your mum again. You really should put your foot down where that sister of yours is concerned and tell her to pull her weight a bit more.'

'I know. But then she has a *proper job*, unlike me.' Shay loaded the two words with all the sarcasm they could carry. She didn't expect Bruce to say, 'Well that's as maybe, but it still doesn't excuse her not going to see your mother more. She doesn't exactly live in the Outer Hebrides, does she? It's less than a twenty-minute drive with a fair wind behind her.'

Shay's jaw dropped slightly open.

'What do you mean by "that's as maybe"? Don't tell me you don't think I have a proper job either.'

'Well it's not a *proper* job in the true sense of the word is it?'

'Because I work from home at the kitchen table, you mean and I don't have a swanky plaque on my door that says "Paula Houston, Financial Services Manager"?'

'Well I don't either, do I?' said Bruce.

'Yet you'd class what you do as a proper job?' She started bristling so much, she was in danger of popping out spines like a hedgehog.

'All I'm trying to say is that it's convenient for Paula to see you as a mug, isn't it?' said Bruce. 'You're always going to be first call for going to your mother's when you only live around the corner.'

'Well I'm not going to be a mug this weekend,' said Shay. She couldn't turn off her phone in case her dad's care home rang, but she'd put it on silent and she'd promised herself that she would not open any texts Paula sent because there were bound to be plenty of them: *Where's the salt/bin-liners/ Tenaladys? Is she allowed the sherry she's just asked me for? How do you turn on the DVD?* It would do Paula good to think for herself, tread a couple of days in her shoes.

The waiter arrived with their starters. They looked beautiful, like pieces of artwork on plates.

'I wish we could go out more often than we do,' said Shay. 'We should make it at least once a month . . .'

'You what?' said Bruce, scooping some mushrooms up with his fork and trying to balance them on a miniature slice of bruschetta. 'We'd be bloody bankrupt.'

'Let's talk about selling up and splitting. I know you want to.'

Bruce's eyes bugged out and he stopped chewing, as if a giant pause button inside him had been depressed. It seemed to take an age before he spoke.

'What do you mean?'

'What do you think I mean, Bru—' Her brain caught up with her mouth then and the penny dropped. 'Splitting as in going away, not splitting up. Don't tell me you've forgotten the master plan. Us, villa, sunshine?'

A beat. Then Bruce started chewing again.

'Well, that's not going to happen, is it? It's all right planning that tripe when you're twenty, but as the years go on . . . well . . . you see it for the pipe dream it is.'

'I'm not asking you to pick an exact date to go, Bruce. It's just talk. We used to love to talk about it.'

'What's the point? Your mother would never leave her

house and she'll most likely outlive us all. You'll probably drop dead making her dinner one night. Then there's your dad . . .' His voice trailed away, as he saw the look of horror his wife was giving him across the table.

Shay wished she hadn't brought up the subject of a life in the sun. It was all becoming a bit bogged down in reality, more of a nightmare than a dream. They ate in silence for a few minutes, Shay trying not to be cross, trying not to think horrible thoughts about death and medical states of limbo. She didn't want this evening spoiled, tried to get it back on track, forced some jollity into her voice as she speared the last piece of lobster.

'I suppose the next occasion for dressing up in our best bib and tucker will be Sunny and Karoline's big day in September,' she said.

'I can't wait to be related to that lot,' replied Bruce with a grumble, launching into an impression of Karoline's mother with her affected accent. 'We h–absolutely h–insist on paying for h–everything because we h–are loaded and like to lord it over h–everyone.'

Shay grinned. 'Very good,' she said.

'It would have been more realistic if I'd got a few more chins.' He shuddered at the thought of Karoline's mother, Angela Stannop. 'That's what Sunny's got to look forward to, because Karoline will turn out exactly like her mother in a few years and Sunny will end up like Simon, squashed underfoot. What a pathetic little man. I bet he has to ask his wife's permission before going for a waz.'

Shay was just about to protest that not all patterns repeated themselves, but her own marriage and that of her parents had too many similarities to discount. A thought best not dwelled on today.

When the waiter brought their mains, Bruce asked for another bottle of wine. He was knocking it back a bit, thought Shay, who was just at the bottom of her first glass.

'We should go out with Les and Morton somewhere for a meal. I don't mind being designated driver,' said Shay.

'God, do we have to?' Bruce rolled his eyes. 'He's a pain in the backside.'

'It would give me a chance to see Les, because I haven't seen her for yonks. She's been really busy at work,' said Shay. 'The last time we spoke, she said she had a new boss who was cracking the whip. She's had to do a lot of unpaid overtime.'

'More fool her then,' mumbled Bruce.

'It's what you have to do in some places. I know because, if you remember, once upon a time I had a *proper job* where you were expected to earn your salary by working far more than the hours you were contracted to do without overtime pay.'

'Anyone who does that needs their head looking at,' said Bruce, cutting slices of steak from around the more well-done edge. 'That's why I like being my own boss. The only person I'm a slave to is myself.'

'Do you remember when I was getting in at all hours and hardly saw the kids? I would never have got a parking space had I set off for Leeds later than six in the morning and there was no point setting off home before six in the evening or I'd have been stuck in traffic.' Looking back, she'd no idea how she'd managed it.

'All for a shit wage, too,' said Bruce, with a shake of his head.

'It wasn't exactly a shit wage, Bruce. I was paid quite well.'
Very well, as it happens. She'd enjoyed the admin job and

ended up being drafted to becoming PA for Colin Parks-Davis, the chief exec, not that she'd sought the promotion; her quiet diligence and pleasant personality had done all the work for her. Then the firm upped sticks from Sheffield to Leeds and she'd had to move with them. They were two years she wouldn't have wanted to repeat, hardly seeing the children, getting in at stupid o'clock – thank God her mum and dad had been on hand to help. She'd either been working, travelling or knackered and something had to give. She had her letter of resignation in her pocket when Colin summoned her to his office. He was leaving the company, he said, starting up his own from his home in Lincoln. Would she consider working for him remotely: managing his diary, organising travel, compiling expenses and whatever else he might need? It was the perfect solution. She charged him by the hour for her services and earned a reduced, but not bad, wage without the nuisance of commuting. She could do the job and work around the household, shop, clean and tend to everyone's needs as they arose, including having a hot meal on the table for her husband when he came home every night. She knew that Bruce would say that what he did was a proper job and what she did was a few part-time bits in between washing things. He was basically right, but it felt so much more.

'So . . . a night out with Lesley and Morton then,' said Shay, herding the conversation back to them.

Bruce lowered his head, shook it slowly from side to side. 'Put me off my dinner, why don't you?'

'He's not that bad. He's quite funny when he's on form.'

'I really don't want to, Shay. Not after the last time.'

He read the blank expression on her face. 'The Taj Mahal,' he reminded her. 'When he got plastered on Cobras.'

Shay nodded, cringing. 'I'd forgotten about that.'

'How could you? It's seared on my brain. Forever. Mort telling his "famous fart jokes" in his loud voice. And let's not talk about him going off to the loo and coming back with soaking wet trousers because his flies had got stuck and he "couldn't stop the flow happening".' Bruce's shoulders juddered with revulsion.

Lesley had been mortified. She'd spent the whole taxi journey home railing at him, telling him she really was divorcing him this time.

Shay hooted, without meaning to and covered up her mouth after Bruce gave her a disapproving look. 'I'm sorry,' she said, 'I don't know why I'm laughing, because it's not really funny. It's just that I've always had a soft spot for Morton. There's no harm in him at all and he adores Les. If they ever did break up, it would be so hard on him.'

She knew there was little chance of it. Les would have done it years ago if she were serious. And they still had a lot of glue holding them together in their marriage. Lesley was very open about what sort of glue it was too.

She raised her head and found Bruce staring at her with such emotional intensity that she gave a little embarrassed laugh.

'What's up?' she asked him.

'You're so beautiful, Shay. I've never said it to you enough, have I? What a truly lovely person you are – inside and out.'

Her first instinct was to dismiss his words as a wind-up, dash them away, but that look in his stunning blue eyes implied he really meant them and they came from a very deep place.

'Thank you.' She wasn't sure what else to say. It had been a long time since he'd given her a mushy compliment.

Actually, she wasn't sure when the last time was. He wasn't exactly the gushy type.

'I don't want to talk about them when we're here to celebrate our anniversary,' Bruce went on. 'I don't want to talk about anyone but you and me.'

There was a shine of tears in his eyes. Or maybe it was all the alcohol he'd drunk making a bid for freedom.

'Yes, you're right,' she said. 'It's too easy to get distracted.' She cut a piece of steak; it was perfection. She chewed it until it was gone, and then opened up her mouth to ask what he thought about Courtney working in a shop now but stopped it just in time. It was ridiculously hard to talk about things that didn't expand into a wider circle of friends, kids, work . . .

Bruce surprised her by ordering a sweet. He never had dessert usually. Shay wondered why he'd asked for a giant slice of cake when all he did was pick at it in between large glugs of wine from the second bottle. She could tell he was getting a bit hammered but that was fine. She wanted him to let his hair down, plus it might unloosen his inhibitions, which, in turn, would unloosen hers.

After dessert, she ordered a coffee; he had a brandy, which he necked like a shot then ordered another – a double this time.

'You okay?' she asked him, starting to wonder if he was trying to anaesthetise himself.

'Yes, fine. It feels like ages since I had a good drink and this' – he lifted up the brandy balloon – 'is *very* good stuff.' His words were slurring now. 'Have one with me. Go on, let's sit in the lounge and mellow.'

'Okay. If that's what you'd like us to do.'

Bruce waved over a waiter, gave him an order for two doubles.

They went into the lounge, sat on a beautiful antique sofa in front of the massive unlit fireplace. The waiter followed with the brandies and Bruce hurriedly downed the one he had carried through with him to start on the new one. He was travelling fast from a bit tipsy to totally bollocksed. His eyelids had started to droop and he'd settled in a weird angle against the corner of the sofa, like an abandoned Victorian doll.

'So, we'll get up tomorrow and have a lovely breakfast and then mosey around the village, that work for you?' she asked him. She'd checked out the area before she came and there were shops, a pub, nice walks, a cheese factory.

His brow creased in an attempt at concentration. 'Yep,' he replied eventually. 'Let's just . . .' he flapped his hand like a seal's flipper '. . . see where we are when we are.' This seemed to make perfect sense to him. He leaned forward, scooped up a few complimentary Japanese crackers from a bowl on the coffee table, then pressed his back into the sofa again.

'Isn't this great?' he said, smiling like a benign, well-dressed, arseholed scarecrow. It might have amused her at another time but now, it narked her a little because it crossed her mind that he might be deliberately sabotaging any possibility of intimacy by drinking too much. Then she felt mean for that thought: it wasn't a trait of hers to think the worst of someone before the best.

She watched his eyelids drop completely down and she pondered in the silence if she had changed as much as he had in the years since they'd met. In looks, neither of them had, really; both were still easily recognisable from their younger selves. But yes, she reckoned, they'd both changed a lot, not just him.

For her twenty-year-old self, just being with Tanya and Lesley was enough. She didn't want to open her heart to anyone, she'd just wanted to go dancing and get ratted and snog people with whom she had no intention of taking things any further. But then Tanya had met someone and fell hook, line and sinker and Lesley met Morton and though their friendship never broke, it had stretched and changed to allow for new priorities. Shay was the last of them to meet her life partner and maybe that had its part to play in softening her resistance to Bruce's cheeky persistence when, in a nightclub, he wouldn't take no for an answer. He had a killer grin, eyes like a Caribbean sea and a cracking line in patter. Tanya used to say they were the best-looking couple she'd ever seen and then would pretend to stick her fingers down her throat. She and Bruce used to laugh loads together in those days; she couldn't remember when they'd stopped.

He'd worn a black suit to their wedding, similar to the one he was wearing now. Yellow tie, to match her bridesmaids' dresses and all the flowers. Tanya looked stunning in her frock, Lesley looked like one of those dolls that sat on a bog roll. She couldn't think of that day though without recalling her mum waiting outside the church to give her the eleventh-hour option of pulling out.

'I'm asking you before it's too late, do you want to marry this man? Do you love him?'

And she'd answered yes because she did love him. But she hadn't told her mother that she loved him enough to chase a boy called Jonah Wells out of her thoughts, out of her heart, because that would have been a lie; though she'd try and keep on trying, because she couldn't have Jonah Wells and that was that.

The sound of Bruce snoring pulled her abruptly out of her memory pool and she leaned over and nudged him. He stirred; looked around him, the way drunk people do trying to remember their bearings. Time for bed, she reckoned. Time for sleep. Not time for scraps of pants and long-overdue sex.

Sure enough, when she came out of the bathroom after brushing her teeth, Bruce was laid out on the bed in a fully-dressed crucifix, dead to the world. She left him there and slept alone on the day bed in the corner.

Chapter 5

Shay was awoken the next morning by the tortured sound of retching coming from the bathroom. A flush, then Bruce emerged, looking on the dead side of white.

'I feel shit,' he said, clambering into the giant bed, holding his head. 'I think it must have been something I ate last night. I'll be okay after a little sl . . .' Then he tumbled back into sleep with the ease of someone falling off a chair.

There was no way Bruce would rally this morning and she had the gut feeling that if she so much as mentioned the word 'breakfast' he would be hanging over the bowl again by the time she'd got to the 't'. Shay lay in the narrow, single daybed staring up at the ceiling, trying not to feel cross or resentful but failing dismally. She gave up the ghost of enjoying a lie-in, showered, dressed and went downstairs for breakfast by herself. A maître d' showed her to a table set for one because she hadn't even attempted to lie that she'd be joined by her husband. He laid a complimentary newspaper down for her to read then waved over a waitress who took her order for coffee and told her to please help herself to any of the continental breakfast items laid out on a long trestle table where nothing had been omitted. There was every kind of fruit, seed, yoghurt, bread, cereal, ham, or cheese one could imagine. Bruce would have loved this, she thought, battling down the vortex of annoyance spiralling inside her.

The à la carte menu was a foot long and included everything it was possible to have for breakfast: from a full English to grits, huevos rancheros, Caribbean French toast, steak, kedgeree, warm waffles. She chose poached eggs, crushed avocado on rustic bread with a side order of buttered potato scones. Then she lifted up the paper with a pretence of reading it while she spied on other guests. There was an old couple – he very tall, she tiny with a hunched back – by the cereal station. He was dressed casually but smartly in short-sleeved shirt and slacks, she had pearls at her throat and pink lipstick that extended beyond the lines of her mouth. She watched how the man filled up two bowls and carried them because the old lady's hands shook and she listened to how he spoke to her: 'If you don't like it, I'll come back and get you the cornflakes, darling,' and something inside her warmed at the tone of respect and love in his voice.

That's what she wanted to have in her marriage and it wasn't there but it should have been because it had been promised to her. For all their plans, for all the flannel Bruce had given her, she had ended up in exactly the sort of relationship her parents had (give or take the serial adultery) where the man went out to work and earned the bread and the woman was left to do everything else and it was a skipful of duty more than he had to fulfil. It wasn't 'his thing' to go and see the kids perform in school plays or meet the teachers at parents' evenings. And he worked so hard during the week, surely he should be allowed to 'blow off steam at the weekend watching a football/rugby/cricket match with the lads'. Even Morton had never missed watching Little Mort perform in the school pantos, even if he was usually cast as the back half of a horse and not seen until he took his bow at the end. At least with her dad, when push came to shove he'd changed, lifted his share of the family burden and more onto his shoulders; but Bruce never had. He'd left everything to her unless it involved electrics or a lawnmower.

He'd said all the right things to her in their courtship; they'd planned to lump all their dreams together and then lump all their energy together to make those dreams come true. They were both united in wanting a family, a big house, his own business, a good job for her, nice cars, savings, a villa in the sun. They'd started out walking a path at the same pace but somehow she'd slipped behind him and couldn't catch up because she'd to stop so many times to pick up rubbish that had fallen in her way or navigate around obstacles that had risen up to hamper her. He'd carried on, without a break in his stride, not caring to look back, assuming all was well. Somehow they'd become two people who shared a house, kids, a duvet, but not laughter and lazy Sunday breakfasts in bed any more and she didn't know where or when that had started and why they'd let it go on. Now the kids had flown the nest and her mother was relatively free of ailments, her father looked after as best he could be, this should herald a time to get her and Bruce back on track. Time for the bread slices holding the sandwich to peel away and let the filling breathe. Before it was too late.

As she was waiting for her cooked breakfast to arrive she made the mistake of taking her phone out to double-check there were no calls from the care home. There weren't, but there was a log of six missed calls from Paula and a text in shouty capitals.

RING ME, URGENT. ABOUT MUM!!!!

No kiss. Paula didn't do them.

She put her phone away, then got it out again. It would hang over her head all day if she didn't find out what was so 'urgent'. Paula picked up after two rings.

'Oh, you're alive then,' Paula said in that permanently exasperated way of hers.

'Yes, I am,' said Shay in a low voice. She didn't really like having phone conversations in public places as some did, revelling in forcing their one half of the dialogue upon others. 'What's up?'

'Did you know the people next door to Mum were converting their garage into a lounge? She's going absolutely bonkers. She asked the builders what they were doing this morning and they told her so she rang me in a right old state. I was supposed to be going shopping and instead I've had to come here at stupid o'clock.'

'They can't do that, can they?' asked Shay. The bungalow in Merriment Close was a link detached. The Balls's garage was attached to both their bungalow and Roberta's, but if it was converted, that would make the two houses semi-detached instead.

'When we come to sell it, it'll be worth much less if they go ahead,' Paula went on, clearly focusing in on the money side of things.

'How's Mum, did you say?' asked Shay. She didn't want to think about selling the house, because then she'd have to think of why her mother wasn't living in it any more.

'Driving me insane. I've only been here half an hour and my brain's already fried. She doesn't know what day it is.'

Shay felt a shot of anger speed through her.

'I asked how she was.'

'I told you.'

'No you didn't, you told me how you were.'

Paula ignored that. 'When are you getting back?'

'I'm away all weekend, you know that.'

Paula gave a long outward breath of annoyance. 'Can't you cut it short?'

Had Shay not been in a dining room full of people, her answer might not have been as measured.

'Would you, had it been you on your anniversary weekend, Paula?'

Paula swerved a direct answer. 'I don't know what to do with her. If she mentions that bloody skip once more I'll scream.'

'Have a cup of tea with her, Paula. Snapping at Mum won't—'

'Oh wait, there's that woman from next door but one. The foreign one, she's knocking.'

Dagmara – she'd calm Mum down. Good.

'Right then, I'm going to enjoy the rest of my weekend, knowing that Mum is in your capable hands,' Shay said and ended the call before Paula could get another word in.

She reached for the coffee pot, tipped it over her cup and added milk. But it was no longer the relaxing, carefree interval she had hoped it would be. It had been spoilt, by those who continued to see her only as the middle of a sandwich, something to be squashed out of existence.

When Shay returned to the bedroom, Bruce was still sleeping soundly, his breath steady, deep. There was no way she was sitting in a darkened room waiting for him to rouse, not on a beautiful day like this, so she brushed her teeth, reapplied her lipstick and grabbed her cardigan. She propped the anniversary card she'd bought for him up against a complimentary bottle of water on the dressing table together with a note saying that she'd gone for a walk, and exited the room after hooking a 'do not disturb' sign on the door handle – a small act of kindness she wasn't sure he deserved.

There were no clouds in the bright blue sky and Shay was glad she'd packed clothes in line with the weather forecast on Metcheck. She had on a sleeveless dress, yellow cotton, with small blue flowers and a swishy skirt. She'd found it on a sale rail the previous autumn and had snatched it up because it had reminded her of a dress she'd had when she was seventeen and loved so much she'd worn it all that long, hot summer. The year when she rejoined the world again after missing a whole twelve months of her life.

She took a right, saw the welcome sign for the cheese factory in the near distance and joined the small queue at the entrance. She tried her best to put her mum's neighbours, her overbearing sister and her hungover husband out of her mind and instead concentrate on the origins of Birtwell cheese but it was hard.

There was a gift shop and a café tucked in the corner. She bought too many cheese rounds from the first and a pot of tea and a slice of apple pie with Birtwell cheese baked under the top crust from the second. She wasn't hungry really and still a tad too annoyed to enjoy it. She hoped Bruce's headache was relentless. She hoped it felt like a hammer-drill in the side of his skull because his sabotage was deliberate at worst, thoughtless at best. Everyone else in the café was in a group or a couple; she was the only saddo by herself and it was her twenty-fourth wedding anniversary. She took a tissue out of her bag to blow her nose and surreptitiously dab at her eyes to push any tears back before they made an appearance because they were close to the surface. She felt very alone, sitting in a café on such a beautiful day surrounded by people. She never wanted to be alone on this date, it was too dangerous. It was the date when the present and the past were separated by a film as fine as gossamer. It was too easy to travel back there, to remember how it all was, how happy she'd been once upon a time. In another life.

After she had eked out her tea for as long as she could, she left the cheese factory and walked on into the heart of the village. There were a few gift shops there, selling the usual mass-produced tat that such places sold, plus a lovely gallery featuring works by local artists. At the back were shelves full of blank canvases, paints and brushes and her eyes fell on a wooden art box crammed to the gills with tubes of oils and acrylics and everything a budding artist would need. Her hand reached out to it instinctively to sweep it up and take it to the till for Sunny in the way she used to buy him drawing materials whenever she saw something she thought he'd like. Since he was a toddler, he'd loved to draw and she'd encouraged him with pens and pencils as well as praise. Art had become his passion; he'd gone to York to do a degree in Fine Arts and had come out with a first. Then he'd met Karoline just after he graduated and somehow his ambitions and plans had been altered by this relationship, reduced until they had been stifled out of existence. She couldn't understand why, because Karoline was an ambitious woman, a manager in some financial institution, a sort of prettier, softer version of Paula and definitely someone who would spur Sunny on to fulfil his potential. But he was now working for an insurance firm in Leeds, a 'proper job' at a desk, with a pension and holiday pay, a position which was as much of a mismatch for him as life in a convent would have been to Courtney.

Shay wandered outside into the sunshine then, not quite brave enough to go into the quaint-looking pub, intriguingly called The Grey Mouse, by herself for a drink. Instead she sat on a bench, soaking up the sun, people-watching: families, couples, a group of teenagers laughing as they walked along, enjoying being young, mortgages and responsibilities years away. She'd been like that once, carefree, her only worries being the forthcoming GCSEs and having enough money to buy make-up and clothes, her head so full of Jonah Wells it was wonder it didn't burst.

She tore her thoughts away from where they were determined to lean. It was this time of year; it always happened, she'd learned to accept that and always tried to keep busy, distract herself from the past with lovely things of the present, but this present had little to offer her.

She wished she were here with Les and Tanya instead. They'd have swept up breakfast together, eaten too many cheese samples in the factory and then sat in the beer garden of The Grey Mouse and drunk cold white wine while soaking up the rays. She imagined Tanya sitting here with her now, keeping her company, telling her that Bruce was a cock for leaving her to celebrate her anniversary alone. Les would have told her to count her blessings that she was by herself and how she wished she could spend all her anniversaries without Morton being there to make a show of himself with his corny banter to waiters, terrible impressions of Hollywood actors and general vulgarity.

The old couple at breakfast drifted into her eyeline, heading towards the cheese factory, hand in hand. That's what she wanted for her and Bruce, that sweet intimacy again. Surely he wanted it back too?

When Shay returned to the hotel room, Bruce was in the bath, lounging there in a vast volume of scented water.

'Hello, love,' he called meekly. 'Where've you been?'

'Out,' she replied.

'Right. Thank you for your card, it was smashing.' He was in suck-up mode, clearly.

'No problem.' Her tone clipped.

'I'm sorry, I think I left my card for you in the van. I could kick myself.'

She thought about offering to kick him instead and save him the job. She answered him with her silence.

'My headache's gone.' His voice was soft with a whee-dling quality to it.

'Has it now.' Her mood couldn't have been clearer.

There followed a plug-gulp, a getting-out-of-the-bath noise. A minute or so later, Bruce emerged, wrapped in a complimentary white towelling robe. He smiled at her; a small smile of apology coupled with the hope of forgiveness.

'Shay, I'm so sorry I overdid it last night,' said Bruce. 'I feel really bad about it. I ruined today for you, didn't I?'

I'll say, she concurred inwardly. She couldn't wait to see what he had lined up for later; was he going to throw him-self out of the window to avoid getting too close to her? Feign an anaphylactic shock from being near a bowl of peanuts in the bar?

'Actually, I've had a lovely day,' she lied, sitting at the dressing table to twist her hair up and fasten it with a claw.

'What did you do?' He sat on the bed. She didn't turn

to answer him but spoke to his washed-out reflection in the mirror.

'Had a superb breakfast, a walk in the sunshine, then I visited a cheese factory.'

'Sounds really nice.'

'It was. It's a gorgeous day. Not to be wasted.'

'I was going to ask if you wanted to go to the pub we passed on the way here and have some lunch.'

He was making an effort to mend the broken bridge between them; she very much needed it to be mended today.

'I suppose so,' she replied.

The Grey Mouse was every bit as pretty inside as it promised to be from the outside. It had a low ceiling with beams, a large inglenook fireplace, dark wooden wall panels, horse brasses, a vast selection of craft beers and locals sitting on stools at the bar counter. There were a few tables free in the large beer garden and Shay claimed one in a far corner while Bruce got the drinks: two chilled white wines – his small, hers large. She wondered if his modus operandi might now be to get her drunk in the hope that she would pass out instead.

'This is great, isn't it?' said Bruce, settling into the chair, tilting his head back, letting the sun warm his face.

'Yes, it is.' Shay took a sip of wine, which tasted a bit of paint-stripper. She wouldn't be knocking it back in one, if that was Bruce's plan.

'Has it been like this all day?'

'Yes.'

'Lovely weather. Was it cool in the cheese factory?'

Shay gave a small snort of laughter and covered it up with a cough. They'd been together for over twenty-five years and this was his line in patter. She wouldn't have fancied his chances on the singles market if they ever divorced.

'Ambient,' she answered him. 'Neither cool nor warm – just nice.'

Bruce nodded, nursing his wine with both hands as he continued basking in the glory of the sun that seemed as though it was treading water in a sea of blue sky.

Shay left it a few minutes before she asked him the big question, which was growing too much to hold in any more.

'So, are you going to tell me why you got completely hammered last night?'

He opened one eye, looked at her in the manner of someone who thought he'd got away with a crime only to find Columbo at his shoulder.

'What do you mean?'

'I'm not stupid, Bruce. You got blotto on purpose.'

'No, I didn't.'

'Yes, you did and you know you did.'

Bruce put his glass down on the table, hard, like a gavel. He was incapable of putting anything anywhere without a clang, a scrape or a bang. 'No, I was just enjoying being with you, forgetting about work, about the job, about everything outside us' – he made a rapid to and fro movement with his finger between them – 'and I haven't got drunk for so long that I didn't realise I was tipping over the edge. I used to be able to drink a lot more than that and stay . . .'

His words died on his lips as he saw that she wasn't buying it. They'd watched enough crime documentaries between them to know that those who protested too much were trying to deflect the police with overly detailed accounts and too-practised answers.

He swallowed, and his eyes dropped away from hers. He

lifted up his glass again and took a long swig from it, and another, then he said very quietly as he bowed his head, 'I'm sorry.' He sniffed and drew his fingers under his eyes; she saw a drop of moisture flick through the air, heard him issue a salvo of swear words under his breath, clearly embarrassed by such a show of emotion.

Shay leaned in, any remaining annoyance segueing instantly into concern. This wasn't like Bruce at all. He was a fully paid-up member of the 'big boys don't cry' club. 'Bruce, what is it?'

He gave his head a quick vibrato of a shake. 'I can't.'

'Can't what? What's the matter, love?'

Bruce lifted his head to check how far away the next people were from them, deduced it was probably far enough.

'I can't ... you know ... get ... it up.' He didn't leave space for her to comment but carried on. 'I don't want to talk about it other than to say I'm going to make an appointment at the doctor's.'

Shay hadn't been expecting that at all and she felt awful that he'd been carrying this burden without saying anything. And there she was, presuming he just couldn't be bothered.

'Oh Bruce, it's nothing to be ashamed of.'

'I thought it was a temporary hiccup,' said Bruce. 'What man wants to admit he can't ... do that ...' He shifted in his seat, his discomfort clearly visible.

A sympathetic wave of such magnitude overtook Shay that she was surprised it didn't physically gush from her and wash Bruce into the ornamental beer barrels in the far corner of the yard. She put her hand on his to comfort him and it was as if her fingers were curled around a hard, unrelenting stone.

'I'll sort it, I promise,' said Bruce, pulling his hand away and picking up his glass with it.

'I'm glad you told me,' said Shay. She wished he'd opened up before.

'I've been putting off saying it until I had to. I thought it might sort itself out. I knew you'd want to . . . you know . . . for our anniversary. I mean, I want to as well. I even tested out a Viagra but it didn't work. I just . . . there was nothing . . .'

She rescued him from his stuttering. 'Bruce, it's fine.'

'No, it's not. When a man's got stuff on his mind it doesn't . . . stay only on his mind, that's the problem.'

'What's on your mind?' Shay asked him, as a cold shiver rippled down her spine. 'You're not ill or anything, are you?'

'No, nothing like that. I think it's just a mix of work and . . . getting older. Jabba's been on my mind a lot recently. Maybe I'm having a mid-life crisis. I'm a bit down, that's all, don't worry.'

She didn't like the vocabulary he was using, and Bruce would be the type to underplay it even to his own wife, to struggle on alone, equating seeking help with weakness.

'You know you can talk to me about anything.'

'I know, I know,' he said. 'Just let me sort it in my own way. Let's not talk about it, please, because I'm on it.'

She nodded, but her senses were already up and arming themselves. She didn't want to overreact but it was hard not to, especially when someone she'd once been close to had been swallowed up by the darkness of depression and she hadn't seen it happening.

Shay pressed a Paul Smith shirt for Bruce to wear for dinner that she'd just taken out of its packaging. He'd been on a recent spend then, not that she minded. They didn't have the sort of relationship where each had to account for what they bought with the money they'd earned.

The shirt was pale-blue and it fitted him perfectly when he put it on. He looked gorgeous and he smelled gorgeous – his usual Dior Sauvage, which complimented his skin chemistry to a tee. When she was helping him with his tie, she wanted to press her lips against his and kiss him hard, but she was afraid to bridge the distance. Now she knew what was wrong, she had to be patient, not make him feel inadequate. Or *should* she kiss him, her mind argued back? Shouldn't she be showing him she still loved him and wanted him? She didn't know. This was the sort of question that cropped up on problem pages in magazines and she wished she'd read one recently and learned what the best course of action was.

They had another exquisite meal in the restaurant and a brandy and coffee to follow in the lounge. A pianist was playing old-style music of yesteryear, entertaining the guests who were mostly elderly. They didn't go to many places where she and Bruce were the youngest, thought Shay as she sat and sipped her drink. Actually, they didn't go many places these days full stop. Bruce looked relaxed and she envied him that, because she wasn't. This weekend had been an expensive disaster and all she had to show for it was a big bag of cheese and a head full of anxiety. She'd hoped her batteries would have been recharged because she was close to flat, but they'd drained even more because she'd spent most of her time being narked with, then worried about, Bruce, and Paula had fly-tipped their mum's neighbour problem into her brain. And there wasn't a chance that her sister would say, 'Shay, do stand back and let me deal with this.'

In the huge four-poster bed that night, with Bruce's back facing her, she listened to his contented snoring and wondered why he hadn't touched her, recognised her needs even if his own couldn't be satisfied. Her brain rolled until it eventually found sleep and dreams took her back twenty-four years, where she turned left and back into the limousine instead of right and forward into the church.

Chapter 6

Bruce ate the equivalent of two breakfasts the next morning, making up for the one he'd missed. Shay didn't feel that hungry but she chose eggs Benedict to keep him company. The egg yolks were sticky and orange under the creamy hollandaise sauce, the ham thick-cut and lean, the muffins toasted to perfection but every bite seemed to cling to the insides of her mouth as if she had forgotten how to swallow.

She'd checked her phone to find another six missed calls from Paula and a couple of angry texts demanding Shay ring her immediately. Paula, she decided, had got her mixed up with one of the minions who worked for her and she didn't take well to being ignored. Shay, however, was annoyed enough to snub her sister's foot-stamping. Plus, she rather hoped Paula had gained a little insight into what she had to do for their mother when need arose above and beyond putting out some tablets and making sure she ate a hot meal. Roberta wasn't hard work to anyone with a bit of patience, she just required some routine, company, care and therein lay the problem because Paula had neither tolerance nor warmth.

They'd never really got on. Paula was seven years older, a cavernous seven years. She'd resented having her status as an only child revoked, been jealous of the attention a perfect, pretty baby had drawn. Then when Shay was eleven, Paula had gone on to poly and never came back home to live because after she'd graduated, she married her arsehole boyfriend Chris whom she'd met there.

Paula considered herself a bit of a lady and had reconfigured her past to accommodate her self-delusion, painting it and herself in portrait colours. Her 2:2 degree from Leeds Polytechnic had become a 2:1 at the university. Their mock-Tudor, three-bedroomed detached, on an estate with many more of the same was referred to as a 'manor house'. Chris, with his string of failed business ventures, was a wildly successful entrepreneur. She'd even worked hard to drop all traces of her Yorkshire accent and round her vowels to such effect that she sounded as if she was auditioning for one of the posh parts on *Downton Abbey*. She had, however, worked her way up the ranks into a very important 'proper job' with holiday pay and BUPA and a bonus funeral plan. This gave her carte blanche to declare she had too much responsibility to the financial world to keep breaking off to take her mother for new glasses at Specsavers/a scale and polish at the dentist/a cut and blow-dry at Rita's salon.

Paula would not have been able to stand having to repeat everything three times because Roberta insisted she was not deaf enough by half to have a hearing aid. And Paula would be driven up the wall by her mother's repetitions, by her getting her words muddled. Her frustrations would be heavily weighted against the sadness that their mother, who had helped hundreds of children – and adults – through their Spanish, French, German or Italian exams, who read

Dostoyevsky and Pushkin in native Russian, couldn't now remember the English words for vinegar, hedgehog and skip. Paula would avoid putting herself out for the woman who had put herself out for them, reducing a promising teaching career to home tutoring to fit around her family, protecting them from anything that would upset their stability when they were young, shielding them from their father's infidelities, covering up his shortfalls, forgiving him over and over to keep them all together as a family.

Bruce made yet another trip to the breakfast buffet and Shay's eyes followed him. He was head and shoulders above the little old ladies on either side of him. He had new stone-washed jeans on – Armani, an expensive pair she hadn't seen before and they made his bum look lovely. When they'd first got married, they were so skint, the idea of him ever owning a pair of Armani jeans would have been laughable. But they'd laughed more when they were poor than when they had money in the bank.

They'd had a lot to deal with in their twenty-four-year marriage – mainly other people. They'd planned to have time to themselves before any children came along, but Sunny was a honeymoon baby and pregnancy was one of the happiest times of Shay's life. Her son had been an easy birth despite being nine plump pounds and was smiling as soon as his mouth worked out how to curve. It was so easy she couldn't wait to do it again but her second pregnancy turned out to be a much harder ordeal. Courtney had to be winkled out via an emergency C-section, nearly killing them both. She never seemed to sleep, either, preferred screaming to smiling. And thereby set the template for the rest of her life to date. If there was a tide to swim against or a reason to rebel, Courtney would – and did.

Shay was pregnant with Courtney when Bruce's father decided he wanted to be part of his son's life after being absent for most of it. They put him up in the spare room for a while because he had nowhere else to go but he borrowed money he couldn't pay back, turned up drunk at the house at all hours, and ran up debts in their name. Just before he was pushed, he jumped, and buggered off back to the off-grid hole he'd crawled out of, never to be heard of again. Bruce's hypochondriac mother was always in the background with her various aches and pains needing doctors or hospital investigations. She moved in with them when she became properly ill. Brenda Bastable idolised her son and grandchildren but didn't extend the same pleasantries to the daughter-in-law who became her main carer. Fittingly Brenda died in her sleep still holding the little bell in her hand that she rang every half-hour to summon someone to her aid.

After Brenda died, they could enjoy family life as a four for a while before her own parents started falling to bits with increasing health niggles and their eventual divorce bombshell. Things were relatively stable at present but with Harry being very poorly and Roberta's memory dissolving, the sands would shift soon enough. Plus Shay couldn't quite trust that Courtney's life would stay all quiet on the western front and then there were these irrational niggles about Sunny to contend with. Then throw into the mix Bruce's recent disclosure. She wondered how her hair hadn't blanched white overnight sometimes.

As Bruce walked back towards her with a plate piled with breakfast buffet food she smiled. Despite everything that had been flung at them, they were still together and that had to count for something. She didn't want to be one of those couples who realised, when the kids had gone, that they had nothing to say to each other. She had to concentrate her efforts on making sure she was giving Bruce and her marriage as much of herself as she gave to everyone else. The years that lay in front for them had to be easier than those in their wake. They had achieved all they set out to do, had their nice cars and big house, his successful business, children. Now it was their time to enjoy the fruits they'd earned and she would make sure they did.

'Have you actually left anything for anyone else?' she asked him as he sat down. He smiled at her.

'Couple of grapes and some Marmite.'

She poured him a coffee from the cafetière.

'I'm so sorry I ruined this weekend, Shay. I know you did everything to make it special. I was thinking about it all as I was picking up my ham and cheese.'

She laughed at that. 'I can't quite see the correlation but I'm glad you appreciate my efforts.'

'I do, I really do.'

He reached over the table, stroked her cheek with the back of his fingers. 'I do love you, Shay.' Again that overflow of emotion in his voice, sadness rather than tenderness. She chalked it up to the off-kilter weekend and said that she loved him too.

As Bruce drove home, a text came through from Lesley.

Hope you've had a nice anniversary. Fancy meeting for lunch? Tues? Got something I can't tell you over the phone.

Shay texted back immediately.

Intriguing. Yes, I'm free. Tell me where
and when x

'Ooh,' said Shay, to herself more than anyone but Bruce questioned it.

'What's up? Who are you texting?'

'Les. We're going out for lunch on Tuesday. She says she's got something to tell me that she can't tell me over the phone.'

'Like what?'

'I don't know, seeing as she can't tell me over the phone, you numpty.' She mused then. 'Must be something big if she has to see me in person.'

Another text from Les came through, advising her when and where.

'When was the last time you spoke to her?' asked Bruce as Shay was writing her response.

She did a quick calculation in her head.

'Must be about four months. We were supposed to go out for lunch but she cancelled at the last minute with a sick bug and we never rearranged it.'

They had sent a few texts since then though, generic 'Everything okay? Have to get together soon' ones from Shay, replies from Les saying she would 'love to but really busy at the mo'.

Silence for seconds, then Bruce said:

'Don't bring me up in conversation.'

Shay's head zipped around to him. 'What?'

'You heard. I know how women talk and I don't want you gossiping about me and . . . you know what.' He sounded deadly serious.

'I won't. What do you take me for?' replied Shay, careful not to swear or promise. She needed to talk to a friend she could trust and there was only Les now. No subject had ever been out of bounds between them; they knew more about Morton's willy than even he did. 'I'll be talking about jobs and kids. Last time we spoke I think Little Mort was buying a house and doing it up. I'd like to know how that's going, and if he did move out, how often he calls his parents.'

Bruce let out a long, exasperated breath. 'Are you still going on about Sunny not being in touch? He's a young man with his own place and a drop-dead gorgeous girlfriend. He'll probably be having sex twenty-four-seven.'

'Not something I want to picture my son doing, thank you, Bruce,' said Shay with a little shudder. 'Wonder what it is she has to tell me. Maybe she's finally left Morton.'

'What makes you think that?' Bruce asked.

'It was a joke, Bruce. They'll never split up. They'll be drawing their pensions together, those two, whatever she says to the contrary. There are worse men out there; he's never cheated or gambled, never raised his hand to her. I know he's far from perfect but he absolutely idolises her.'

Bruce didn't answer. She stole a glance at him to see he was staring ahead, his jaw clenched. He probably wasn't even listening to her; he was wrapped up in thoughts she wasn't party to and she suspected he was about to disappear into a mental man-cave. He'd been forced to give up his secret, show her his soft underbelly and she could tell he was already regretting it. Plus they both knew that as imperfect as Morton Jagger was, he was the personification of a horny stag high on rampant bull jelly and comparisons were bound to be made in Bruce's brain. She sighed; the landscape of the near future stretched before her like a field full of eggshells. Not for the first time.

*

Back home, Shay checked through the post that had arrived
in their absence: a winter holiday brochure, a postcard from
the energy company asking for meter readings, a couple
of brown envelopes for Bruce, no anniversary card from
Sunny. She didn't mention it to Bruce for fear of provoking
him, but it hurt a little and stayed with her, though she tried
to put it out of her mind. After a cup of coffee, she rang
her sister. The phone was snatched up at the other end as
soon as it connected and Paula's brittle voice coursed down
the earpiece.

'At last.'

Shay pictured her elder sister's downward arc of a mouth.
Paula was already getting marionette lines. In less than five
years she wouldn't look out of place sitting on a ventrilo-
quist's knee saying 'gottle of geer'.

'Nice to know you care so much about your own mother's
welfare,' Paula went on, seeing as Shay left her a big enough
gap to shovel some blame into. But Shay had long been
armed, waiting for this sort of cheap shot.

'Are you really going to play the dutiful daughter card,
Paula? You've stuck about three meals for Mum into a
microwave in the past year and a half and you dare to—'

Paula cut her off. 'I was eager to get hold of you because
Mum is really shaken up about what's happening next door.
She was still very upset when I left last night.'

'Maybe you should have stayed over, then,' said Shay.

'I stayed as long as I could,' said Paula. 'I can't sleep
there, can I?'

'Well you could, seeing as there are three beds in the
house. I've had to plenty of times. The bed in my old room
is always made up ready just in case.'

'She would have only said she didn't want me to.'

That was true. Roberta didn't like to inconvenience her elder daughter who was always very busy. She only felt safe to ask her younger one for help, the one who didn't pick apart for mistakes everything she said.

'Have you been to see her this morning?' Shay asked.

'No. I've had work to catch up with.'

'On a Sunday?'

'Yes on a Sunday, Shay, so there's only so far I can stretch myself.'

A concrete block had more stretch in it than Paula. Shay, however, was expected to stretch herself to her limits and then beyond. Breaking was not an option.

'Besides, it's you she wants with her, not me,' Paula went on. 'And actually I did ring this morning to see if she needed me and she told me her neighbour was going round and they were having a cinema day.'

Dagmara Mitic should have been bottled and given out on prescription. There was no one, apart from Shay, that Roberta would rather have sit with her in a crisis than Dagmara.

'I'm back early, so you don't have to go round tonight if you don't want,' said Shay. She'd better find out first-hand what was going on with the neighbours.

'Oh, well, that's good,' said Paula. She didn't fight it, but then Shay never expected her to anyway.

Shay unpacked her suitcase, putting her new satin pants in her drawer, the one she kept all the things in that were special or out of season, like woolly winter tights, Spanx and fleecy PJs. She put the cheese in the fridge and wondered who on earth was going it eat it all because Bruce didn't even like crumbly cheese. Courtney would have scoffed the lot in a single sitting. Like Shay herself, her long coltish daughter had always been able to eat what she wanted and not put any weight on, something that had always infuriated Les and Tanya about her. Did she know how lucky she was? The pair of them put on a pound watching Shay wolf down a doughnut. Shay batted back that maybe it was a payoff for all the flack she took from the school playground bullies who called her skinny, sticky names; Theresa Briggs being the worst culprit. There was a lot that Shay could have said back to her, but she knew, as young as she was, that Theresa was just trying to make herself look big and clever because she didn't have that great a home life. If it wasn't one brother in the local paper for drug-dealing, it was another for shoplifting or her dad for affray. She'd often wondered what Theresa Briggs was doing now, though she'd probably intimidated someone into marrying her and giving her ten kids. She didn't think about Theresa Briggs that often, because then she'd think about Jonah Wells jumping in to tell her to sod off and do one. And she'd think about Denny who made her feel better by buying her some chocolate in the shop. And she didn't want to think about Denny because her heart grew a new crack in it every time she did.

Chapter 7

After loading up the washing machine, Shay drove around to her mother's house and couldn't quite believe her eyes when she saw what had been going on next door since she'd last seen her mum on Friday night. The garage door to 1A had been removed and was leaning heavily on the hedge that her dad had planted, which annoyed her for a start-off. A breeze-block wall was half-built where the aperture had been, while lots of large white bags and more bricks on pallets had been delivered and were sitting patiently at the side of the Sharif's Skip.

She called ahead of her as she walked in to the bungalow, pushing open the lounge door to find Dagmara sitting in the armchair, newspaper on her lap, finger against her lip and her mother fast asleep on the sofa.

'She didn't have very good night,' whispered Dagmara. 'She just dropped off about ten minutes ago. We were watching a film together.'

There on the TV was a paused frame: three conjoined people kneeling on the floor.

'What on earth . . . ?'

'*The Human Centipede,*' said Dagmara. 'I've always wanted to see it and Derrick at number five found me copy in a car boot sale. We've had quite a cinema day. First we watched *From Russia with Love* and then this. I can't wait to see how it ends.'

'I'll give you a clue: not well,' returned Shay.

Dagmara pushed herself up from the chair. 'Let's go into the kitchen and I'll tell you what's been going on,' she said and so Shay followed her in and they both sat at the table there.

'Derrick says maybe you need to speak to the planning department at the council,' said Dagmara, thumbing towards next door. 'That's a party wall. They can't touch it without permission.'

'I'd better go round and speak to Mr Balls tonight and—'

'No point, they're out. They're always out on Sundays. Nagraj went to ask them yesterday what they were doing, on behalf of your mama and that . . . that horrible man pushed him off the doorstep and he fell backwards on the ground.'

'You're joking,' said Shay, although Dagmara obviously wasn't.

'He's going to have a big bruise on his *dibens,*' Dagmara went on, rubbing the side of her bottom. Nagraj lived at number three and was a retired plant machinery driver, a gentle, quiet Indian man in his mid-seventies.

'That's assault, surely,' said Shay. 'Isn't there any CCTV around?'

'No CCTV, no witness, only Mrs Balls who would say accident of course,' said Dagmara with a lift and drop of her shoulders.

'I'll ring the council first thing in the morning,' said Shay with conviction, then her eye caught sight of something out of the kitchen window.

'What the hell is that?' she said, standing at speed.

'They're also building at the back, Shay. Look, extension. With hole for a window that will let them see straight into your mama's garden.'

'No way,' said Shay, feeling a flush of anger heat her cheeks. 'Absolutely no way is that happening. What are they thinking of? How have they got the . . .' She was going to say 'balls'.

'Shhh, now,' said Dagmara, trying to calm her. 'You know, Shay, the man who built Merriment Close, he vas greedy. There were only supposed to be nine, but he squash another house in. That's why this and next door are link-detached, not proper detached like the rest. That's why my house is 1 and Mr and Mrs Balls are 1A. I'm always getting their post when we have new postman.' She gave a little laugh and leaned forward to impart a secret. 'I'm not going to put anything I get through their letterbox any more. I'm going to burn it.'

'Don't get into trouble. I think that's illegal.'

'I don't care,' said Dagmara. 'After all I've been through in my life, I'm not easily scared.'

Her history was testament to that. When she was a little girl, Dagmara lived a privileged life in a country house near Riga at the side of a lake with maids. But her anti-communist father refused to let the Russians take over the house in 1943 and was shot. Dagmara and her mother had to flee, eventually ending up in the UK where her mother cleaned floors for a living. Dagmara met her husband dancing. He was also a refugee, a once equally privileged boy from Yugoslavia who'd fled the communist takeover. Dagmara's mother did not think this young man was good enough for her daughter to marry, So Dagmara got pregnant in order to force her mother to relent. She'd been a spirited minx then and still was now.

'The noise yesterday was terrible,' said Dagmara. 'And cars and vans everywhere. So many of them.'

'Well that can't be right at all,' said Shay. Surely you were supposed to tell neighbours when you were doing work that might affect them. 'I'll sort it.'

'I will leave you now with your mother,' said Dagmara. 'She has kept asking when you are back. Paula is . . . different from you, isn't she?'

Which was one way of putting it.

'I hope so,' replied Shay.

Dagmara smiled at her. 'You are good girl. Your mama is lucky to have you.' She sighed then. 'It's not easy when someone starts to lose bits of their mind. Your mama has been a little mixed up today. She thought I was her sister Stella. I wish.' She chuckled. Stella was the reported stunner in the family, with her beautiful long legs and Italian film-star looks, yet Shay always thought her mother was the prettier of the two, with her strawberry blonde hair, killer smile and curvaceous figure.

'Thank you, Dagmara, I'm so glad she has you,' said Shay at the door.

'She has all of us on the close,' replied Dagmara. 'Apart from *them*. We look out for each other.'

Shay went back into the kitchen to put out her mother's tablets, trying to avoid looking out of the window and seeing the building work. Her mother had always loved this house, thought it was much cosier than the draughty Old Rectory they used to live in. Shay, however, had missed their previous house a lot when they moved here. She'd had the whole attic floor there, with its sloping ceiling and a reading nook.

By comparison, her bedroom in the bungalow was square and characterless, although her father had done his best to make it a 'girl-den' for her. He'd painted it in cool pastels and built her a cosy corner with bookshelves that had secret drawers. Some of her old annuals remained on the shelves, the bed still had her Beastie Boys duvet cover on it, the dressing table that her dad had found in an antique shop and rag-rolled in cream paint for her stood in the window. She kept a few toiletries, brush, comb, a spare nightie and underwear in the drawers for whenever she needed to stay over, as she'd had to do quite a few times. There was a poster of Edward Scissorhands on the wall next to her wardrobe and another of Brad Pitt on the back of the door. The room was like a shrine to her teenage self. She'd wondered why her parents had never redecorated it or cleared it out. Then her own children left home and she realised it was harder than it looked to dismantle the end of the era.

The clock on the kitchen wall was stuck on ten o'clock so Shay replaced the battery then emptied the kitchen bin which was about to overflow. Paula wouldn't have thought to do it, she'd have just seen to the basics.

'Hello,' called a voice croaky from sleep. 'Shay? Is that you?'

'Yes, Mum,' she answered and went into the lounge.

'Oh, it's nice to have you back, Shay. I have missed you,' said Roberta with feeling, as if Shay had been away for weeks.

'Nice to be back.'

'Have you seen what they're doing next door?'

'Yes, Mum,' Shay replied and put on her best headmistress's 'no nonsense' voice. 'I'll be on it first thing in the morning, so don't you worry.'

'Oh, thank goodness,' said Roberta, physically sagging. That sag said everything: she could relax because Shay was on the case. 'I'm going to give them a piece of my mind when I see—'

'What have you eaten today, Mum?' Shay said, diverting her attention away from the Balls duo. Even small problems tumbled in her head as if they were items in a washing machine, round and round on an eternal cycle.

'I haven't felt like anything to eat,' Roberta replied. '*They* put me off any food.'

'Well that's not going to do you any good. What shall I make you?'

'How can they do this, Shay? I've lived in this house since your father and I were first married without any trouble and then this.'

Paula would have corrected her, said *No, you haven't lived here all that time, Mother* but Shay didn't.

'Shepherd's pie?'

'They're going to be spying on me when I'm in the garden through that window. I'll have no privacy.'

'What about chips, egg and beans, white bread and butter. Some comfort food, eh?' Her mum used to make great chips, the real ones out of potatoes. Somehow, the world always seemed a bit brighter after one of her mum's chips, egg and beans teas.

Roberta thought about that for a moment, then nodded. 'If I must.'

'Good,' said Shay. 'Let's sit in the kitchen and I'll make us a big pot of tea.'

'We were watching a very interesting film, Dagmara and I,' Roberta said, getting to her feet. 'Have you seen it? *The Hungry Caterpillar.*'

Shay had an inward chuckle at that.

'Yes I have, and it's revolting. Whatever made you both want to watch that?'

'I used to love a good horror,' said Roberta. 'Your father and I used to go to the cinema all the time when we were courting. The grislier the better for me.' She gave a trill of laughter. 'Harry preferred Dracula but he was a bit too tame for me. We used to make a night of it. He'd buy me a quarter pound of chocolates to take in and we'd walk home with fish and chips.'

She was smiling, splashing around in a sea of old memories. Shay smiled too; she liked to hear that her mum and dad had had good times.

'We had such hopes and dreams when we met. I wanted to open up a private school to teach languages and he was going to head up the biggest plumbing company in the north.'

'Then you had kids,' said Shay, sprinkling some frozen chips on a tray and slotting it into the oven.

Roberta's eyes flicked up rapidly to her daughter and she said quickly, 'It wasn't the girls' fault. Any of it. Something had to give because I couldn't have it all so I chose what was most important.'

Shay's heart gave a bounce in her chest, as if it was attempting to leap out and towards her mother to comfort her. She loved her dad but he really hadn't shouldered his fair share where the family was concerned. When he came in from work, he relaxed. There was no such luxury for his wife, who had to bend her life around her teaching, looking after their children, cleaning, cooking and checking in on her parents. She couldn't call in to the pub after work and chat up the barmaids, she couldn't presume that all she had to do was tip up her wage and the house would run automatically like a well-oiled machine, clothes would be washed, sheets would be changed, bills would be paid. Give or take the barmaids, the template of her parents' marriage was too familiar.

As if her mother were party to her thoughts she asked, 'Do you remember when you got married, Shay?'

'I do indeed.'

'Not the ceremony, I mean when we were standing outside the church. Just you and me and I asked you if you wanted to get back in the car.'

Shay gave a little laugh. 'Yes, I remember.'

'I wish you had.'

'Mum, what a thing to say.'

'Don't get me wrong, I like Bruce, but I never thought he was the man for you.'

'Well I'm glad I proved you wrong,' Shay said, buttering some bread.

'Did you?' asked Roberta. 'I wouldn't have missed you having Courtney and Sunny for anyone, but . . .'

That *but* hung in the air like a balloon, fattening with air by the second until Shay popped it with the obvious question.

'What do you mean "but"?'

'I was frightened for you, Shay. Frightened that you were marrying someone you didn't love enough. You were too *precious*.'

'Precious? Me?' Shay scoffed.

'I wanted you more than I've ever wanted anything before,' said Roberta, her grey-blue eyes shining.

'Why's that, Mum?'

'You wouldn't have met him if I hadn't got it so wrong.'

Shay was getting more and more baffled by the second.

'Got what wrong?'

'You'd have shone. You were so clever at school, on course for university; instead here you are looking after everyone but yourself and I saw all this coming. That's why I wanted to bundle you into the car and take you home. I'm so sorry, love.' Roberta's head fell, as if bowed by the weight of thoughts within it, sad thoughts with a bulk to them.

Shay put down her buttering knife and came to sit at the table.

'Mum, it all worked out fine.'

But Roberta was wrapped up in a confusion of memories, knotted as old wool.

'I never wanted to be the one who split up the family, you know. I didn't want you and Paula to be spending a weekend with me and then a weekend with him, us arguing about where you'd be at Christmases. I forgave him the first time, it was only fair that I let it go and I tried so hard to mend it, every time it broke but I couldn't.'

Roberta was agitated now. Shay took her mum's hands in an effort to calm her.

'I nearly asked you if you'd take me to see him, you know, but I couldn't face it. I'd rather think of him happy with *her* than like that. He should have had his chance, I held on to him longer than was fair and I can't forgive myself for that. I've made so many mistakes. I've messed it all up.'

'You haven't messed anything up.' Shay grabbed the kitchen roll from the work surface and tore off a square to give to Roberta, who was sniffling now.

'Oh, I have,' insisted Roberta, pressing the tissue against her eyes to blot the tears that were coming. 'If only I hadn't gone, it would have been all right then. I wouldn't have known any different.'

'I don't know what you mean,' Shay said gently.

'He was right, we should have stayed. That would have been best for her. We shouldn't have taken her away,' Roberta explained impatiently as if Shay was dense for not understanding.

'Best for who, Mum?' asked Shay. It was hard to watch her mother in this mode, her frustrations apparent as she tried to put the pieces together in her head. It seemed as if she had two different jigsaws going on here, though.

'Her. Best for her.'

'Who's "her"?'

'Shay,' said Roberta, at volume. Then realisation shone through the clouds in her mind that she was talking to the person she was talking about. She shook her head. 'Oh, I'm getting mixed up. I don't know what I mean. I'm all over the place. Those builders next door have done something to my brain. I'll end up in the funny farm, I will.'

'I hope not,' said Shay, relieved that her mother was back in the room with her again, away from whatever thoughts were torturing her.

'If I do, I won't get Paula coming to visit me, I know that much,' said Roberta, after blowing her nose on the kitchen roll. 'She told me that it upsets her to go and see her father in that place,' Roberta huffed then. 'So we can safely assume that if anything happened to me, she wouldn't come and see me. I don't know how she grew to be so unfeeling. She doesn't get that from Harry and I'm pretty sure she doesn't get it from me either.'

'She doesn't,' said Shay. 'She's another family throwback, one who howled at the moon.'

'I caught her going through my drawer when she didn't think I was looking.'

Shay bristled. 'What drawer?'

'The drawer in the dresser, the one with all my documents in it. You know, bills and bank statements.' Roberta paused before adding, 'I thought to myself, I bet she's looking for my will. I expected it.'

'Surely not,' said Shay, though she wouldn't put it past her sister.

'My old will's in there but not my new one. I changed it.'

'That sounds very mysterious,' said Shay. 'Are you leaving everything to the local dogs' home?'

'The old one has you both down as executors and everything halved.' Roberta was deadly serious now and not in the mood for joking. 'I left it in there to avoid trouble.'

Shay braced herself for an answer she wouldn't be able to make sense of but her mother's brain had switched track to her once sharp self.

'My new will is lodged with my solicitor David Charles, you do remember me telling you?'

'Yes, I remember,' said Shay.

'Dagmara has a copy as well, as surety. All my funeral arrangements are written in it. I want Mr Goodchild to handle it, he does the best buffets.'

'Mum, don't talk about this stuff,' Shay waved her hand to fend it off.

'I want you to listen, Shay, while I remember. I left that old will in the drawer to appease Paula if she went looking for it, because there will be trouble after I've gone and I'm sorry that I'll be leaving it with you to sort. I haven't told you this before but I've given Paula money over the years. She was desperate to bail out that halfwit she married but that's up to her what she does with her inheritance.'

Shay blinked heavily in astonishment at that revelation. She'd taken over her mother's finances two years ago and every penny was fully accounted for from then on, so this must have happened before that.

'She's had a lot from me up front until I finally said no more,' Roberta continued, 'and my new will takes that into account. I kept track of it all and I know she'll be expecting half of what I leave as well and that won't happen, because it wouldn't be fair to you. It's a terrible thing to say but I don't trust her as much as I trust you, so I've stipulated that you take charge of making sure my final wishes are followed to the letter. You promise you'll do this for me?'

Shay gestured at her mum to stop.

'Please don't talk about wills and final wishes, Mum.'

'I need to, while it's straight in my mind because not a lot is these days, so listen to me, Shay.'

There was a tone of desperation in her voice that Shay couldn't ignore.

'I'm sorry I've had to resort to tricks, leaving that will there like cheese on a trap. It made sense at the time when I did it.' The look on her face suggested it didn't make the same sense now, but Shay understood her motive. Roberta didn't want to fall out with her daughter and the new will would cause a small war. Shay found herself wishing she were in as much blissful ignorance as her sister.

'Anyway, that's all I wanted to say on the matter. I'm not planning on popping my clogs any time soon, so you needn't worry.'

'Good, I'm glad to hear it.'

'You will stop them doing all that building next door, won't you, Shay?'

'I absolutely will,' came her daughter's assured reply.

*

At home, Shay filled in Bruce on what was happening with her mother's neighbours. He looked at length at the photos she'd taken of the building work in progress – front and back and then shrugged his shoulders.

'Dunno,' was his pronounced verdict.

Shay huffed. 'Can't you go round to see them and ask what they're doing?'

'No, I can't. They'd tell me to piss off, as is their right,' said Bruce grumpily, 'as I would have told Dave and Sylvia if they'd come round to ask us what we were doing when we built the porch.' He inclined his head towards their own neighbours.

'That's totally different, Bruce. Our porch didn't turn their detached house into a semi.'

'You'll have to talk to the council, Shay. If the Balls are acting illegally then they'll stop them, won't they?'

'Will you at least just ask any builders on site to have a look at the photos I've taken if I WhatsApp them to you?'

He mumbled something by way of an answer and carried on reading the newspaper, then something jumped into his mind and he snapped the paper down to speak over the top of it.

'Do NOT ring Courtney and tell her. She's bound to march straight round there fists flying and get herself into trouble.' Then he added pointedly, 'Again.'

'I won't, I'll sort it myself,' said Shay. That's what usually happened anyway, why change the habit of a lifetime?

Chapter 8

As soon as she awoke the next morning, quarter to six, Shay was on her laptop researching neighbour disputes. It was crystal clear that permission had to be sought from next door if you were planning on buggering about with a party wall. 'Always instigate a civilised chat to head off acrimony' was the advice one site offered. There was an accompanying graphic of two people talking over a fence, laughing, both holding cups of tea and chomping on biscuits. Neither of them looked like a vulnerable old lady or a psychopath who pushed old men over, though.

'Why did you get up so early?' asked Bruce, coming downstairs at seven-thirty.

'There wasn't much point in staying in bed when I was wide awake,' she answered him truthfully.

'Oh well that's nice,' Bruce replied, clearly affronted. 'Very nice.'

'What?'

'Thanks a bunch.'

How the hell could he have derived an insult from that? She decided he was spoiling for a fight and she wasn't going to give him one. She pasted on a smile and tried to reset the morning.

'Coffee and a slice of toast?' she offered.

'No thanks. I shouldn't be too late home.'

'Okay, have a nice day,' she said, like a cheerful American waitress at a burger joint. Even that seemed to offend him because he slunk out like a kicked dog. She heard his van revving out of the drive as if making a statement about his present mood, which she suspected wouldn't even have been lifted by finding Nigella Lawson waiting for him in the passenger seat.

In college, all the girls had the book, *Men Are From Mars, Women Are From Venus*. She, Tan and Les would read out passages to each other in the common room. She remembered the revelation that men disappeared into caves to avoid things they'd rather not address, or stretched away from you like rubber bands. And she remembered Tan saying, 'Except they're not really rubber bands are they, they're just twats,' because she saw straight through that bullshit. It was no excuse to blame it on innate behaviour, she declared. It was just a cover for rudeness and inadequacy. But what the book did get right, Tan conceded, was that women had to suppress their own urges to mope over and mollycoddle men. They should use the time while the man was sullenly dragging his knuckles all over the floor of his cave to concentrate on themselves and their own needs. That way, when he did emerge into the sunlight with his club in his hand, the woman would feel better about herself and he'd be grateful that his wishes were respected. Win-win – everything tickety-boo. Shay couldn't in all honesty remember her dad being in the slightest bit moody like Bruce. But then, there was a lot in her dad's life she didn't know about, so maybe he wasn't the best comparison.

She had quite a few assignments to do for Colin that morning too, trains to book, a car to hire, expenses to tot up, invoices to send. She got as much out of the way as she could because she wanted to devote the week to sorting out what was going on with her mother and if that involved physically lobbying someone at the council or chaining herself to a railing, then so be it. First stop, though, the 'civilised chat' with Mr and Mrs Balls. Well, first stop after chasing up her mother's recent blood tests, booking her in for her check-up at the dentist and calling in at the supermarket for her weekly shopping. Her mum needed a PA every bit as much as Colin Parks-Davis did.

When Shay got there that afternoon, Merriment Close was once again overflowing with surplus vehicles, all of them servicing number 1A. She parked up, pasted on her best 'friendly neighbour' smile and knocked on Drew Balls's door, waiting a respectable interval before knocking again. This time, the front door opened slightly and there stood a slice of man, pasty, lineless face, small round glasses, wearing a knitted brown sleeveless cardigan.

'Mr Balls?' she enquired politely.

'Who wants to know,' he replied, his voice reedy and nasal. He opened the door a touch wider and behind him Shay could see a woman hovering, whip-thin with a concrete grey block of hair just like her sister Paula's, which biased her still further.

'Hello, I'm the daughter of Roberta next door,' Shay introduced herself.

Drew Balls didn't reply, just stood there waiting for her to continue.

'Can I ask what work you're having done here?'

'Do you mean "can" or "may"?'

She tried not to bite at his smart-alec reply.

'Well . . . may I ask?'

'What's it got to do with you?' he answered, his voice a curious mix of bolshy and nervy.

'Well, that's my mother's party wall and you're not really allowed to touch it without asking permission for starters.' She kept it polite but she could feel her blood begin to heat.

'I've knocked on her door a few times and she's never answered.'

That was an obvious lie and Shay hated liars with a passion. Lies had a potency far greater than the mere content of their words. Lies destroyed.

'She would have answered if you'd knocked, Mr Balls. But I'm here now so you can tell me what you're doing.' She widened her smile but it didn't reach her eyes.

Balls nudged his glasses up his nose with a pointy finger. 'I don't need to ask anyway and I don't need to tell,' he replied. 'It's nothing to do with you. It's all above board.'

'Don't need to?' Shay questioned. 'Not even as a matter of courtesy? To let an old lady know that your workmen are going to be banging against her property at all hours of the day?'

'Can't do anything about the noise, sorry.' It wasn't an apology.

Shay felt her smile too heavy to hold up now. 'Do you have planning permission for that extension at the back?'

'Don't need it.'

'You've got an aperture for a window in it. You'll take all my mother's privacy away if she sits out in her garden.'

'Is she, then?' Balls asked, now aware of eyes on him – the

builders working on the garage roof, neighbours on their doorsteps.

'Is she what?' asked Shay, confused by the question.

'Is she going to sit out in her garden?'

'I beg your pardon?'

'I said,' Drew Balls replied, using a tone one might use to address a village idiot with no powers of comprehension, 'is she going to sit out in her garden?'

'Well, what difference does it make if she is or isn't?' Shay's volume button was cranking up now. 'The window will not only look onto her garden but directly into her house.'

'That it?' asked Balls and went to close the door, but Shay hadn't finished with him. Her hand came out to keep it open. The look on Balls's face was priceless; his mouth a stunned long 'O'.

'You're going to turn my mother's house into a semi-detached, Mr Balls, and I'm not going to let you do that, I'm afraid.'

'You can't stop me,' he replied. 'Permitted development. I can change my garage, I can build at the back, I can add another storey on without having to ask you jack shit.'

Shay's breath caught in her throat. 'You're building on another storey as well?'

'What's it got to do with you what we do?' He tried to shut the door again but Shay's hand didn't budge.

'What it's got to do with me is that you're taking away my mother's privacy, her light, you're spoiling her house, you're devaluing her home.'

A nasty smile bloomed on Drew Balls's mouth.

'Oh I see, that's what this is all about now,' he said, his grin wide and quite horrible. 'The senile old cow's ready for croaking and you're worried about your inheritance.

Fuck off, you greedy bitch.' The door then slammed hard in her face.

The strength left Shay's body, as surely as if someone had pulled out a stopper in her heel and let it drain away at speed. Her head was prickling with anger, shock and shame that such an untrue accusation could be levelled at her. She couldn't move for a long moment, then she jumped, feeling a warm arm placed around her shoulder. Nagraj. She had no idea he was nearby. As he led her back down the Balls's path, she could see all the residents of Merriment Close, bar Roberta, on the pavement. They'd all heard the exchange, if the looks on their faces were anything to go by: a spectrum of quiet, stern-faced rage through to sympathy.

'I should have warned you that the voice of reason was not going to work,' said Nagraj.

'Surely no one thinks that about me?' Shay said. Her voice was shaking, her whole body was shaking. The accusation that money was at the forefront of her worries, before her mother's welfare, had scored a brutal bullseye.

'Of course no one does,' said Nagraj firmly.

Inside Shay, adrenaline was busy transforming her upset to anger. *How dare they*, she thought, how dare they think they could ride roughshod over a vulnerable old lady.

She turned to the building site that was the Balls's house then and screamed at it, hoping her words would penetrate the walls and assault his eardrums.

'Get ready, Balls, I'm coming for you. Do you hear me?'

A hand patted her arm. She looked to her side to see the smiling face of Dagmara.

'Go and see to your mama, Shay. Don't you worry. Leave it to Lady Karma, she's a bitch.'

Shay hoped Dagmara was right and that Lady Karma

would come and bite the Balls on the backside. But she also knew she didn't always come and mete out what she could. That's what made her the biggest bitch of all.

Roberta was sitting on the couch, reading from a pile of books beside her, oblivious to the floorshow that had just happened outside her house. Shay tilted her head to read the title but it was written in Cyrillic.

'Russian novel?' she ventured, trying to sound normal and not as someone reeling from a very public humiliation.

'Russian love poetry,' Roberta corrected her. 'My favourite of the languages and the one I would be most sorry to lose.' She tapped her head then before continuing. 'Listen to this, Shay.' She read a poem aloud; Roberta Corrigan, who wittered about skips, reading poetry flawlessly and beautifully in perfect Russian. Shay couldn't understand a word, yet it brought a lump to her throat and that was because her clever, erudite mother was back with her, whole again, as Shay would always want to remember her: reading books, notepad at her side, leaping around in words that fired up her heart.

'Pushkin,' said Roberta at the end of it. 'Such strength of expression, glorying in excess. In my opinion there's no better language for poetry, no richer vocabulary.' There was a brightness in her eyes that Shay had not seen for a long time, and it cheered and saddened her in equal measure for its transience.

'What's it about?' asked Shay.

'A past love,' Roberta answered with a smile. 'A hope that though it was not to be for them, another would love her as tenderly and sincerely as he did.' She closed the book slowly. 'It's ridiculous how much Russian I retain when more and more of my own language is eroded every day. Dagmara and I sometimes speak it and I never stumble over words. Why is that, do you think? No doubt some professor somewhere will have done a paper on it. And if they haven't, then they should.'

A whirring drill started up, as irritating as nails down a blackboard. It sounded as loud as if it was on her mother's side of the wall rather than the other. Roberta's fingers pressed against her ears.

'Oh, not again. That's been on and off since this morning. It's relentless.'

'You don't need to worry, Mum. I'm on it. I'll get it all stopped. I'll fight them for you.'

Shay would give it everything she got, but then she was used to fighting harder for others than she'd ever fought for herself.

'What did Paula cook for you when she came?' Shay asked at the kitchen table where her mother was sitting with her favourite post-tea dessert, one of the huge éclairs from the local Potterworth's bakery.

'Nothing. I wasn't hungry. I told her not to go to any trouble.'

'Nothing?' Shay's lip curled. She'd expressly told Paula that she must make sure she put some food down in front of her mother because she was bound to say she wasn't hungry, but would eat it anyway. Her sister really was a lazy hound.

'Did she leave out your tablets for you?'

'I think so,' replied Roberta. Her face and fingers were covered in chocolate.

'I wish I had a camera,' said Shay, smiling. She reached over for the swivel mirror that stood on the windowsill and held it up so Roberta could see herself.

'Oh my goodness – the state of me,' said Roberta laughing. 'I look like that day I was with your father eating an ice cream and someone bumped into me on a pushbike and it went all over my face.'

'You never told me about that one before,' said Shay.

Roberta chewed her lip as she tried to dredge up the memory. 'They needed Russian language teachers you see. I volunteered. I was away from home for months.'

'Right,' said Shay; but this was a false memory, stirred up by her reading Russian poetry.

'Yes. Your auntie Stella and your father looked after Paula between them. She was only a little girl.'

Shay was confused now. 'So Dad ... wasn't ... with you then?'

Roberta closed her eyes, tried to solder together the missing electrical links in her memory chain. 'No, he wasn't there. I got that bit wrong.' She made a noise of frustration. 'Why can't I remember this, because it's important?'

'Who was it that needed teachers?' asked Shay. Usually when her mum got confused, there was some truth to be picked out from the chaff in her stories.

'The government. They needed people with Russian language skills. It was very exciting, very hush hush. It was the time of the Cold War, you see. Yes, yes I remember now.' The look on her face said that her mind had secured a floating memory and was hauling it in for closer inspection. 'We lived in a huge building, old with ivy growing all over the walls. There were iron gates at the front. So many wonderful people from around the world. It was top secret, we were told we could be put in prison if we ever talked about it.' Another recollection popped to the surface like an air bubble in water. 'We caught a train

to the seaside. It was chocolate ice cream,' Roberta went
on. 'Why would I remember that when I've forgotten so
much else?'

'I have no idea, Mum,' replied Shay, wondering if her
mother was mixing up some memories with the films she'd
been recently watching with Dagmara. She waited for mention of a centipede but none came. 'Was this in Russia?'

Roberta's head snapped round. 'Russia? When have I
ever been to Russia, silly girl? No it was here in England . . .
somewhere. Chelmsford – that rings a bell. There was a
famous headquarters there.'

'You don't mean Cheltenham do you? GCHQ?'

Roberta's lips curved into a face-splitting smile. 'That's
it. That's the place.'

Paula, at this point, would have told her mother not to
be so daft, but what harm was it doing, letting her mother
think she had an important role in the Cold War, even if it
was taking romancing to another level.

'We should go for lunch, I know a place that serves the
best ice-cream sundaes. Maybe that would help jog some
more memories.'

'I don't want to leave my house at the moment in case *they*
know I'm out.' Roberta pointed at the wall.

'You haven't been out for ages, Mum. You'll start to get
stir crazy.'

'I will soon. Just give me a bit of time.'

Shay didn't nag her to go out if she didn't want to.
Roberta's hips were often sore and she'd had a slip in the
snow in January which had scared her. Shay had suggested
before that they borrow a wheelchair, but that had been met
with a deeply scornful response. Roberta's world was presently the home she loved and the extent of her universe the

safe, quiet circle of Merriment Close. The fact that it was presently under threat had shaken her considerably.

'I'm going for lunch tomorrow,' said Shay. 'With Lesley. You remember her, don't you? My friend from college. She was one of my bridesmaids.'

Roberta licked the chocolate from her fingers. 'Is that the nice one or the other? Who's the tall girl?'

'Tanya.'

'Ah yes, Tanya, the nice one.' Roberta smiled and nodded. 'Do you see much of her?'

Her mum had even forgotten that Tanya had died.

'Now and again,' said Shay.

'I didn't like that other one very much,' said Roberta. 'There was something not right about her.'

'Oh no, not another one on the "something not right about them" list,' Shay chuckled. She had never heard her mum say this about Les before. Perhaps she'd got her mixed up with someone else – Paula, maybe.

'I always thought she looked like someone who'd be all smiles to your face but wasn't so nice behind your back. Sly.'

Shay's features creased in consternation. 'Are we talking about the same person?'

'Yes. The one who could barely fit up the aisle when she got married.'

'*Mum.* She did give birth about two weeks after the wedding.'

'And she picked the most hideous bridesmaids' dresses for you and . . . Tanya that I've ever seen in my whole life. She didn't want you to outshine her.'

Shay laughed. 'You're biased.' But still, she was right about the dress. Angelina Jolie would have looked a munter in it.

'Three will always be a crowd where friends are

concerned,' Roberta said then. 'And the odd one out always knows who she is.'

Her mum was wide of the mark there. They were an equal three. Shay might have confided in Tan more but she loved them both the same. She'd never questioned their parity. It made her wonder, though, if the other two ever had.

Chapter 9

Shay walked into the restaurant and saw the woman stand up at a far table and wave but it wasn't Lesley. The woman waved again. A double-take. Yes it really was Lesley, but not Lesley as Shay knew her. This Lesley had a waist and thick caramel hair falling down to it; she looked like something off *The Only Way is Essex*. Close up, after she had weaved her way through the tables to get to her, there were even more differences from the old Les: fuller lips, enormous black lashes and a tan that suggested Lesley must have spent the time between Shay seeing her last and now skewered on a rotisserie spit. She even smelt differently as they greeted each other. Gone was the Poison she had worn since she was a teenager and in its place was something spicy and exotic and very overpowering. Shay imagined it would act like mace if it were sprayed in someone's eyes.

'My God, Les, I didn't recognise you.' Shay's eyes fell onto the bag that sat on the table, focused on the upturned triangle motif. 'Wow, is that real Prada?' she mouthed.

'Don't be daft,' said Lesley, 'it's a good copy from Turkey.

Someone from the office brought it back for me. It was still dear, mind.'

Lesley whipped the bag off the table and put it under her chair. Shay noticed her nails as she did so, like eagle talons, painted pearly white with swirly patterns on them. They'd be impossible to type with and Les did a lot of keyboard work in her job.

'You look absolutely fabulous,' said Shay, trying not to stare too much at the many differences between this version of Les and the one she'd seen four months ago. She'd been dieting hard and had lost two stone, but this was one hell of a serious update since then.

They sat and before Shay could even ask what Les's big news was, she revealed it.

'I might as well tell you, I've left Morton.'

Shay's jaw dropped; she really hadn't expected that. Not after all those years of threatening to but never doing it and 'No . . .!' was all she could articulate by way of response.

'Choose what you're having in case the waiter comes and then I'll fill you in.'

Shay glanced at the menu but her brain was far from engaged. She picked the first thing she saw that sounded nice because food was secondary at this lunch and she just wanted to get quickly to the juice.

As Les was relaying her salad niçoise and Shay's buttermilk chicken steak choices to the waiter, Shay tried not to scrutinise her face but couldn't help it. She'd definitely had something done to it apart from the poutier lips. Her forehead was smooth enough to ski down and her eyes didn't move when she flashed a smile; it looked a bit odd if she was honest. Her client Colin used to have lovely crinkles around his eyes before he went to Poland and returned looking as if he'd been dipped in wax. Shay wouldn't have been surprised to find a wick protruding from the top of his head whenever she saw photos of him in trade magazines.

Lesley, who would have ordinarily ordered a pint of lager at this point, plumped for a sparkling mineral water. When the waiter melted away, Shay could hardly wait for her to begin.

'I bet you thought this day would never come,' said Les.

'Well, I'm ... I'm shocked,' replied Shay, which was an understatement. 'What made you finally do it?'

Les dabbed the corners of her mouth delicately with her napkin. Les and delicate fitted together as much as Les and salad did.

'Nothing I can put my finger on. I was woken up by his pig-like snoring, as happens most nights, but this time instead of ramming my elbow into his back, something in me snapped. He went out to work and I packed my stuff, got in the car and booked into a hotel. Simple as that.'

The waiter arrived with the water and a small Pinot Grigio for Shay, who wished she'd ordered a large one now. The ice rattled cheerfully in Les's glass as she lifted it to her inflated lips which looked as if they might pop at any moment.

'Then?' asked Shay, intent on hurrying her along.

'Let me just say, it's surprising what you choose to take with you when you're in the zone; your brain goes into a very strict essential/non-essential mode. Two suitcases full, that's all I took. I filed for divorce the same day and that's that.'

'When did all this happen?'

'Two weeks, five days ago.'

'Blimey.'

'He thought all this was for him.' Les smoothed her palms down her body. 'It wasn't, it was for me and it was long overdue.'

Mid-life crisis, it had to be, thought Shay. Or early menopause. It was a well-known fact it made some people have epiphanies – and breakdowns.

'I'm gobsmacked,' said Shay. 'Where are you staying?'

'I'm renting somewhere at the moment. It's fully furnished so that's good.'

'What about your job?'

'I walked out of that as well. I didn't want Morton turning up and causing a scene. I know how he operates so I needed to disappear totally.'

'Just like that?'

'Just like' – Lesley clicked her fingers – 'that.'

Shay blinked her eyes in disbelief. Lesley had worked as a legal secretary for the same firm since she'd left college.

'What are you living on?' Shay was starting to get a little worried now. This surely hadn't been thought through if she'd acted so impulsively. 'Are you okay for money, Les? I can help you out if—'

'Don't worry, I've been saving for this for years. I'll figure it out as I go on,' came the reply.

'What's Little Mort said?' asked Shay.

'Mort's a grown man now, it's none of his business.' There was a slight snap in Lesley's voice. 'I wish people would stop calling him Little Mort. He's six foot six for a start and living his own life . . . and it's high time for me to live mine.'

Lesley didn't even sound like Lesley, never mind look like her. But then she had always been the hardest one out of the three of them. The one who kept her cards closest to her chest. Still waters.

The waiter arrived with their food. Shay's looked enormous compared to Les's salad.

'Do you think that Li . . . Mort leaving home might have had something to do with you—' *flipping* '—leaving too?'

'Why should it?'

'I mean if you missed him and it altered the dynamic in the house.'

'I didn't miss him. I was glad when he went. Surely you're glad that yours have sodded off.'

'No, I miss them terribly.'

'They haven't exactly emigrated to Australia, have they, Shay? You can still see them, you just don't have to do their washing any more. What's Sunny up to these days?'

'He's still selling insurance.'

'I see all that money was well spent at university then,' Les said with a single note of hollow laughter.

'I'm hoping it's only temporary.' Shay gave a strained smile. 'I hardly hear from him. I've only seen him a couple of times since he moved in with Karoline,' she said.

Les looked surprised enough by that to try and raise her perfectly threaded eyebrows, even though the Botox opposed the attempt.

'When Mort left, he rang every couple of days, if not every day, to check in. I had to tell him not to. The apron strings are cut as far as I'm concerned and I don't want them retying.'

Lesley plunged her fork into the salad as if she didn't have a care in the world.

'Does he know about you leaving?'

'I haven't told him yet and I suspect his father hasn't either because he'll be in a state of denial. I know how his mind works. He'll ignore the divorce papers in the hope that I've thrown a hissy fit and when I calm down I'll' – Les drew two wiggly apostrophes in the air with her fingers – '"come to my senses", even though I already have. I'm expecting him to pull a few stunts, but he can't stop the divorce happening whatever he has up his sleeve. But, if he plays ball, gives me a decent cash payout and lets me have a quick divorce, I'll not go for half the house and I'll leave his pension alone. You'll know when the penny's dropped because he'll contact you in the hope you can talk me round.' She gave a one-sided smile at that with her new lips.

'Have you spoken to him since you walked out?'

Lesley tossed her Miss Piggy hair back over her shoulder and cleared her mouth of Lollo Rosso before answering.

'He's left a lot of voicemails, I haven't listened to them. I never do. Anyway, what's the point when the conversation would only consist of him saying "Come back" and me saying "No". I'm paying a solicitor to do all the talking for me. When you hire a dog you don't bark yourself, do you?'

Shay had her friend's back, of course, but Morton must be in a proper state, she reckoned. Just walking out without any explanation was a terribly cruel way to end things.

'He must be ...' Shay picked her words carefully. Les could be combustible. '... a little confused, maybe?'

'Oh come on, Shay. If he doesn't know by now why I'm divorcing him, he never will. I've tried for too many years to polish that particular turd.'

'What reasons are you citing?' asked Shay, figuring that the inability to polish a turd was not acceptable grounds for divorce.

'Unreasonable behaviour,' replied Lesley, wrinkling up her nose, as if it was obvious. 'Never again do I have to listen to him burping like a warthog and watch him savouring his own farts; oh, you have no idea how blissful my life is now. I've seen better-dressed scarecrows in fields than him. He's a crude, repulsive, embarrassing . . .' She made a shudder of disgust but ended the list there before she put herself off her anchovies. Then she held up a perfectly white palm which contrasted sharply with the teak-sideboard shade on the back of her hand.

'And if you're about to say that I'm a bitch, save your breath.'

'As if, Les,' Shay deflected that accusation, though it had to be said, she did feel sorry for Morton because Les was being really harsh. Morton idolised her and wouldn't have seen this coming. He might been more Boris Karloff than Liam Neeson but he'd always been a hard grafter, faithful, generous and was a more hands-on father than Bruce had ever been. He'd taken Little Mort fishing every Sunday and, when Mort was feeling a bit crap about himself and blimpy, he'd whisked him off to a boxing gym to help knock his lad into some shape. Morton had also relished that his son was as much a dyed-in-the-wool builder as he was and was set to join the trade. He'd enjoyed teaching him all his skills but, unlike his own builder father, he'd still made sure he buckled down at school. Little Mort had singlehandedly built Courtney a wooden summer house in their garden when he was fourteen and she a year younger. Rather surprisingly her queen-of-cool daughter had always had a massive, sisterly soft spot for the big gauche lad. She'd even been known to bash people for saying he was thick.

Les gave the remainder of her salad a rousing twist of black pepper.

'I've only ever been out with one person and so now I'm going to make up for lost time and see what I missed. You're only here once, after all,' she said with an emphatic nod. 'I wish I could turn the clock back. I'd have an abortion and stay single.'

'Lesley!' Shay was horrified.

'Oh, you know what I mean.' Les's expression said she knew she'd gone too far with that admission. 'Look, much as I wouldn't harm a hair on my son's head, I think a part of me has always resented him, you know, because I wouldn't have married Morton if I hadn't got pregnant. And I know it takes two to tango, but I've thought a lot about this over the years and I'm totally convinced he put holes in the johnnies deliberately with his teeth when he tore them out of the wrapper. He was always going on about having babies and a family and doing it all properly, not like how his parents dragged him up. I'd have been permanently up the duff if I hadn't gone on the pill. I know he trapped me is what I'm saying.'

'But you loved him when you got together, I know you did.'

'I thought I did. You and Tanya were so much prettier than I was and spare me any tripe to the contrary because you bloody know you were. No boy ever looked at me twice except Morton who wouldn't take no for an answer. He made me feel . . . desirable, like you must have felt hundreds of times. It was very intoxicating.'

'Slight exaggeration,' Shay laughed that off.

'I don't think so.'

Shay didn't try a further denial. It was embarrassing sometimes how much attention she and Tan got from boys in and out of college. In Tanya's case because she was stunning, in Shay's case – she reckoned – because she just wasn't interested in anyone and that pandered to their male desire to conquer. Not that Lesley helped herself. She'd had a strange pudding-basin haircut and thought make-up was stupid. She wouldn't wear skirts because she said her legs were too thick then wore tops that were too tight and showcased her puppy fat. She'd had eyebrows like woolly bear caterpillars when they first met, until Tan had attacked them with her tweezers. Les was the clown in their group, funny, sharp-witted, a wicked mimic, but both Shay and Tan knew Les would have traded her personality for looks any day of the week.

'Anyway, enough about me. How's things with you?' asked Les. 'How's your mum?'

Shay had been going to ask Lesley today if she could pop over to the farmhouse and talk to Morton about the Balls and their building work but she could hardly do that now.

'She's . . . doing okay. Bit forgetful and gets things mixed up. She was telling me she was a Russian spy yesterday. She believed every word of it too.' Shay gave a little laugh, half-fond, half-sad.

'Oh, bless her. Do you still go over every day?'

'Yep, at least once. Sometimes I have to stay overnight.'

'Jeez. I don't know how you manage to do that.'

'You just do, Les.'

'And how's your dad?'

'No change.'

'That's a shame,' said Les. 'I was lucky, if you can call it that, that my parents didn't have lingering illnesses. Mum was there one minute and gone the next and Dad followed her so quickly that I'm sure he must have died of a broken heart. I don't think he ever got over losing her so I cheer myself up by thinking they're together now. I have to say though I do like the feeling of freedom. Unlike you, I don't have any other person to worry about. I can properly breathe for the first time in years. No parents to worry about, no husband, no kid.'

'Little Mort never gave you any trouble though, did he?' said Shay.

'What?' Les pulled as much of a face as she could. 'I was always having to go down the school because he'd thumped other kids.'

'Yes but he thumped kids for other kids as I remember it.'

'Just like your Courtney.'

'Not quite. Mort thumped bullies; Courtney thumped anyone who got in her way, including a few bullies,' replied Shay. She shook her head as a memory bloomed of having to do the walk of shame yet again to the principal's office. Courtney always had a cast-iron excuse why she'd laid someone flat and her arguments were so feasible, the principal told Shay her daughter should consider becoming a barrister. Mort, however, was a big lad with fists like hammers and if he ever used his size, it was to stop trouble happening for others – fighting fire with fire. He'd once given a black eye to a boy for picking on Sunny and that was only because Courtney was at home with chicken pox, otherwise he wouldn't have got a look in.

'As for worrying about Sunny,' Les continued, 'you shouldn't. He's away doing his own thing, living with his girlfriend. It's only right that you're way down on his priorities. He'll be filling his boots full of Karoline, before the rot sets in.'

'You sound like Bruce,' said Shay.

'That's two of us talking sense, then. Did you have a nice time on your anniversary?'

Shay puffed out her cheeks by way of an answer.

'What?' prompted Les, when she didn't add any actual speech to the gesture.

'I'm not supposed to say,' said Shay, staring at her half-eaten chicken.

'Fuck that for a lark. You can't leave me hanging. What?'

There was no way that Shay could keep it to herself. She needed help and for that, she needed to talk.

'We had a stunning hotel, the weather was fabulous. We had dinner on Friday during which Bruce got totally arseholed and passed out in bed and was too hungover to do anything the next day so I went off to a bloody cheese factory by myself and ate some pie.'

Les's face split into a smile which she covered up with her hand and apologised for. 'Sorry, Shay, but you're not selling it to me. Why did he get so hammered?'

Here we go. Ready to launch.

'Bruce . . .' She looked to the side as if expecting to see him materialise, 'He . . . admitted to me that he's been having . . . problems. Downstairs.'

'By which you mean . . .' said Les, making a circle of her thumb and finger and slipping a finger from the opposite hand into the space.

Shay nodded. 'We haven't had sex for months. Not even an attempt. I thought he was just tired. I didn't realise that he couldn't . . . you know . . .'

Les thought about this for a few long moments, then asked.

'Are you still sharing a bed?'

'Yes, of course. But he's at one side and I'm at the other. We might as well have barbed wire down the middle.'

'Right,' was all Les said to that and took a breadstick out of its wrapper.

'Now, it's just got stupid because he had to tell me but

he didn't want to and he's obviously embarrassed and is in a really odd mood. One minute he's all moony-eyed at me and the next he's snapping like a crocodile. Did Morton ever have that problem?'

Lesley answered with a hoot of laughter. 'You are joking. Mort had a permanent stiffy. And he defied all the theories because boozing made him even harder. I will give credit where it's due, he was fantastic in bed.'

Lesley used to make them laugh with tales about her bedroom shenanigans. She might have been permanently annoyed with Morton, but they had a very robust sex life and she used to say that only in the throes of passion could she ever forget he was a twat.

'As for Bruce,' Les went on, 'well, you can't pressure him, can you? You'll have to be patient and back right off. Is he going to see a doctor?'

'He said he was. I wondered about getting hold of some herbal tablets. I was reading about Horny Goat Weed and Red Ginseng. Holland and Barrett sell them so they must be okay, yes?'

Les wagged the breadstick at her friend, like a conductor's baton. 'No, Shay, you can't. Let him do that. Don't emasculate him further. So was there *any* bedroom activity?'

'A peck on the cheek. And he told me that he loved me. He got a bit tearful as well, which was really odd.' An unbidden thought entered her brain then, like a worm sneaking in from the side. 'Oh my god, what if he's having an affair?'

Les gave her a disapproving look. 'That's just stupid. One, this is Bruce we're talking about and two, impotent men do not have affairs anyway. What would be the bloody point?'

'What if he'd lied about it, just to put me off?'

'Bloody hell, Shay, don't you know anything about men?' Les laughed as if she were a world authority. 'Men don't lie about stuff like that to put a woman off a scent. Far too ego-damaging.' She lifted up her glass of mineral water, pinky finger stuck out. 'How's he been since you got back?'

'In a proper funk. You could cut the atmosphere with a knife.'

Bruce could keep up a sulk for days when he wished to and she'd discovered over the years that the only way to deal with it was to ignore it until he got bored. It was a very unattractive trait and as a consequence, she'd come down hard on both Courtney and Sunny if they ever veered near such behaviour. Sunny, however, wasn't the type to and Courtney couldn't keep quiet for long enough to sulk.

'Maybe he's under pressure here.' Les tapped her temple with one of her Wolverine-length fingernails.

'He says business isn't what it used to be and—'

'There you go then,' cut in Les. 'If a man's got anything on his mind, it makes its way instantly to his genitals. Unless you're Morton, because even that would have the tendency to fire him up. Give him some stress and you might as well have doused him in powered rhinoceros horn.'

'Won't you miss the sex?' asked Shay, which was a fair question.

'Haven't you heard of Rampant Rabbits?' Les replied.

Outside the bistro Shay said, 'Please let's not leave it so long until the next time.'

'Absolutely,' said Lesley, 'but bear in mind I have a lot on at the moment.'

'Of course,' said Shay, looking around for her little Toyota. 'Where are you parked?'

'Over there,' said Les, pointing to a red sports car.

'Bloody hell,' said Shay. 'That's gorgeous.'

'It's only on hire, I got rid of the Aygo. Knowing Morton, he'd be driving around looking for it. I've had to more or less go into witness protection to avoid him.' She looked at the car and gave a sigh, as if it were Justin Timberlake. 'I have to say, it's a fabulous drive so I just might buy myself one when my divorce settlement comes through.' Les rubbed her hands together gleefully. 'Maybe I should go for half the farmhouse because it'll be worth a small fortune.'

The farmhouse had been in Morton's family for generations. He'd been born and raised in it and renovated and changed it over the years to Lesley's exacting standards but it was still much more his nest than hers. Making Morton sell it would be the equivalent of castrating him.

'I think it's incredibly generous of you to tell him that you won't force him to sell up,' said Shay. It was actually, as Les to money was like a magpie to shiny things.

'Only if he plays ball, I said,' replied Les. 'That should tell you how much I want out and how fast.' She pointed her zapper at her car door with a perky gesture that indicated she was very much enjoying her little illusionary taste of the high life.

'Oh Les, it's been so lovely to see you and you know where I am if you need an ear, or anything else,' said Shay.

'Course I do. Take care, you.' They embraced but there was none of Les's customary squash, just a stiff, brief forward tip from her and an air kiss at the side of Shay's ear. *She doesn't even say goodbye the same*, Shay thought.

Chapter 10

If Dante didn't have a council planning and building regs department and a Party Wall Act of 1996 in his inferno, it couldn't have been proper hell. Over the next few days, Shay lived in a nightmare world of trying to cut through jargon and not lose her rag with people whose standard mantra seemed to be, 'We do not get involved in party wall disputes. This is a civil matter. Shall I send you a link to the Party Wall Act of 1996?' It was less legislation than it was a maze intended to send one insane for its author's pleasure. Meanwhile the building work carried on and Roberta got more and more upset with every brick that was cemented in.

The internet advised finding a solicitor who specialised in such disputes. She rang one, who told her she needed a surveyor. She rang a surveyor who told her she needed a solicitor. Shay got a first-hand insight how tennis balls at Wimbledon must feel. Eventually she found a legal expert willing to give her a free half-hour's consultation. He scared the bejaysus out of her, using words such as: *barrister, injunctions, court, four thousand pounds up-front fee* to start off with. And for that he couldn't guarantee any success. This was not going to be as easy to battle as she'd thought. She was learning fast how unconcerned the law could be about people's moral rights as well as their legal ones.

Shay had just got home from her mum's on the Friday night and poured herself a large shiver-cold white wine, when her mobile rang with an assigned ringtone she hadn't heard in too long.

'Hello, you,' she said, trying to strip her voice of the tidal wave of relief she felt at hearing from her boy.

'Hi Mum. Look, before you say anything, I'm so sorry I missed your anniversary.'

'It's fine, really, love, I'm just glad to hear from you.' She felt stupidly like crying, not helped by the knackering week she'd had. She took a deep breath because she was in danger of pouring herself down the phone to her son. 'Everything okay with you?'

'Yep. Nothing to report.'

'How are the wedding plans going?'

'Oh, they're ... happening,' said Sunny. 'I'm staying out of it really.'

'We still would like to pay something towards it, your dad and me. It doesn't feel right that we're not.'

'Oh Mum, trust me, I've tried but it's an absolute no. Karoline's parents insist. It's awkward, I know.'

'Should I talk to them?' asked Shay.

'It wouldn't do any good. Anyway, how's Dad, how's you? Did you do anything special for your anniversary?'

'Oh, he's fine, working too many hours; I've forgotten what he looks like.' Although a bear with a sore bum would be a good comparison at the moment. 'We had a couple of nights in the Dales over the weekend which was ...

nice. Your Auntie Paula looked after your gran while we were away.'

'Right.'

The way he said that one word summed up exactly what he thought about his Auntie Paula. Mind you, she'd never much bothered with her niece and nephew, had never sent cards or presents for them. The children had felt her *froideur* since they were little. Courtney had only been about four when she'd asked her aunt why she had had 'miserable lines painted down the sides of her face', which hadn't been received too well.

'Have you been really busy at work, then?' Shay asked him.

'Yep. I've changed positions and there's been a lot to learn to get up to speed. My brain doesn't retain those sorts of facts very easily.'

'I'm not really surprised. It's not you, is it?' She winced at her words then because they sounded overly judgemental.

'It's okay for now, Mum. It's steady and they're nice enough people. How's Gran?'

'She's a bit fragile. The people next door are making her life miserable with building work. It'd cheer her up to hear your voice.'

'Surely Dad knows someone in the building trade who could help.'

'He said he'd ask around.' *Even if he did keep saying that he hadn't had the opportunity yet*, she added to herself.

'I went to see Grandad last night. There's no change, is there?'

'No, love. He's hanging on in there.'

'Look, I'm planning on bobbing over to Gran's on Monday morning if that's okay. Be nice to see you too if you're free.'

Shay tried not to sing the Hallelujah chorus.

'That'll be lovely,' she said. 'She'll be delighted. And so will I.'

'I'll aim for ten, that work?'

'Perfectly.' She gulped. 'I miss you.' She couldn't help herself.

'I miss you too, Mum,' said Sunny. 'Got to go. I'll see you then. Love you.'

She could barely say it back, her throat was too clogged with tears.

She topped up her glass right to the rim. The way she felt today, she could have sunk the whole bottle but then she imagined Tanya, the voice of reason, telling her that she'd have a crap sleep and have to get up in the early hours and forage for headache tablets. Tanya would also have told her that she was proud of her for standing up to those pieces of work next door to her mum's. She hadn't told Bruce about the altercation because she knew he'd tell her she was a prize idiot for going round to confront Drew Balls, and she didn't want to give him any further excuse to be more neanderthal than he already was.

He'd been grumpy all week, stuffed in his cave, so she'd called in at the local farm shop that morning and bought a couple of fillet steaks for tea, hoping to draw him out of it. She planned to team them up with some potato dauphinoise made with some of the cheese she'd brought back from her weekend in Birtwell. She'd had to give some away to the neighbours at either side to get rid of it rather than waste it. Her dad would have eaten the rounds whole; instead, he was lying in a clinic being fed through a tube in his nose and for what end? He loved to eat and drink and laugh and sing karaoke down at his local – these were the things that gave his life its worth and he would never be able to do any of them again. She wished he'd just let go, not hang on in there because his determination insisted he didn't abandon those he loved. How could he be so weak and strong at the same time?

Bruce came in just after half-past six. If ever there was a dish that would thaw his mood, it was steak. The air of the kitchen was thick with the aroma of fried onions and garlic and she could almost hear his stomach keen in anticipation of the feast to come.

'Hi,' she greeted him chirpily.

'All right,' he returned, catching sight of the steaks on a plate, waiting to be fried. 'Steaks, eh?'

'Yep. Are you having a shower first?'

'No, I went to the gym after I'd finished and had one there so I'll only be five minutes.'

'Okay, I'll throw them in the pan now then.'

Bruce nodded and trudged upstairs. She caught his scent as he drifted past her, manly and clean and she felt desire rise up inside her. Or was it desperation because she couldn't have him and needed the confirmation that he still wanted her? She wondered if the smell of her skin, her perfume still triggered chemical changes within him. They were far too young to have a celibate relationship; she needed to get them back on track and if that meant trying every trick in the book and bending any way possible to make it happen, then she would.

He arrived downstairs just as she was putting the warmed plates onto the table. The steaks looked every bit as good as those they'd had at Birtwell Manor, with the added bonus that all his favourite must-haves were catered for:

cheesy potatoes, caramelised carrots, onions, buttered sugar snap peas.

She poured a glass of Chablis and handed it to him.

'Oh, that's good,' he said, appraising the first taste. 'I'm ready for this. I've had a pig of a day, I'm absolutely knackered.'

'You should have given the gym a miss then,' she said.

'Yeah . . . I probably should have.' He sat down at the table ready to be fed. She didn't say that she was pretty tired out herself after a hard week filled with translating Party Wall Acts into decipherable English, chasing council members for answers, having arguments with neighbours, doing admin for her bosses, cleaning two houses, washing, ironing, trying to calm down a distressed mother, shopping, ordering tablets, picking up tablets, fixing roller blinds, changing beds because all that heaped on a scale would not weigh heavier than Bruce's tasks. His was a job, hers was just 'stuff of life'.

'Sunny rang earlier on,' she said, sitting down opposite him. 'He's going to visit Mum on Monday morning so I said I'd pop round. He sounds okay.'

'Course he's okay,' replied Bruce, picking up his cutlery.

'He said he'd given up asking Angela and Simon if we could contribute to the wedding costs.'

'Good,' said Bruce. 'Snotty bastards.'

Shay knew there was a bit of jealousy there. Bruce would have killed for their his and hers Range Rovers and holiday villa in Cyprus. They'd only met Sunny's future in-laws once, at the ridiculously over-the-top engagement party held in the garden of their ten-bedroomed (and ten-bathroomed, as they took immense pride in flaunting) house with orchard, orangery and sauna suite. They were an odd couple: Angela, wobbly and round, loud – a typical nouveau-riche show-off; Simon, so dull and quiet, a walking shade of grey. It was his business brain that had brought in the revenue but his wife who held the purse-strings.

'I hope we don't have to see them before the wedding,' said Bruce. 'Please tell me they're not having one of those rehearsals in church.'

'I haven't heard anything.'

'And I'm not wearing a top hat either and looking like Little Lord Fauntleroy just for their bleeding amusement.'

Shay wanted to laugh at that but didn't. 'Then don't wear one.'

Bruce speared a carrot.

'I hope she doesn't get pregnant quick either. We've enough on having to deal with your mother and your father and no doubt Courtney's gearing up for a new disaster.'

Shay's brain questioned the use of that 'we'. Bruce had done very little for her parents and it was always she who'd had to deal with Courtney's escapades over the years. He'd just roll his eyes and withhold her pocket money for a week. Now he'd hold up a flat palm to it all, turn his head and say, 'I don't want to know. She's old enough to sort herself out.'

'We don't have any control over that, do we?' Shay replied, though she secretly hoped the same. 'And as for my parents, well, I can't not look after them, Bruce. They looked after me for long enough.'

'Yeah, I get that. I just mean I don't want to be a free babysitter any time soon on top of everything else.'

'Well, Karoline's a career woman isn't she, so I expect they'll wait a while to have any children,' Shay said. Something else she didn't want to think about because Karoline's mother was a textbook monopoliser – another battle waiting up the road for them.

'Steak's nice,' said Bruce, mid-chew.

At home she cooked it medium for him, so he'd eat it all. She sometimes wondered if he imagined the chefs in hotel kitchens reading his order chit and saying, 'Wow – what a man, he takes his steak rare' and doffing their toques in reverence.

'I'm working all weekend,' Bruce said then, eating at speed like Oliver Twist on his first bowl of gruel.

'Really?'

'Sooner I finish the job, the sooner I'll get paid, so yes.'

'Did you manage to show any builders the photos of Mum's house yet?'

Bruce shook his head, an exasperated slow movement.

'As I've said to you before, there are no builders on the estate now, just sparkies and plumbers doing their thing, so no, I haven't.'

She wasn't sure she believed him but she could hear the stirrings of annoyance in his voice and so she backed off.

'I went for lunch with Les on Tuesday,' she said. She thought he might have asked about it during the week, but he'd been in too much of a strop to initiate that sort of conversation.

'Oh yeah. She okay?'

Something shot into her brain and shot straight out again before she could register what it was. Something unsaid, something that didn't make sense. Beyond annoying.

'You wouldn't recognise her. She's had hair extensions, lip fillers, Botox, she's about five stone lighter than when you saw her last and . . .' a dramatic pause to secure his full attention, 'she's left Morton.'

'Has she?' Bruce speared a pea. He didn't miss a beat.

'You don't sound very surprised.'

He dropped a hard note of laughter. 'Well, I'm not, are you?'

'Yes, very.'

'It's been on the cards for years, hasn't it?'

'She didn't even tell him, just moved out of the house. She's renting somewhere apparently.'

'Oh yeah? Where?'

Shay gave her brain a squeeze for the answer to that. 'I don't think she actually said.'

'Wise. If you don't know you can't tell Morton if he asks.'

Morton. It was something to do with Morton. Something small but significant. She gave herself a mental shake; it would come back to her if it was important.

'Yes, I suppose so. Les said that when he realises she really isn't coming back, I'll be his first port of call and I'm dreading it because I don't know what to say to him.'

That derisive laugh again. 'Well, if you don't know anything you can't tell him anything can you? Has she left him for someone else?'

'No, not at all. She just upped and left and sounded very happy to be by herself.' Shay recalled the line about Rampant Rabbits. 'I hope she's okay, because she seemed . . . different. There were . . . too many changes to get my head around in one sitting, if I'm being totally frank.'

Bruce's fork clattered onto the plate. 'Well, that was nice, cheers.' He got up still chewing, his chair scraping across the tiles.

'Don't you want a coffee or anything?' Shay was only half-finished.

'There's a match just starting on Sky, that okay?' he said, wiping his mouth with his fingers.

'Yeah, course, you go and watch it and unwind. I'll clear

your plate away,' she replied, and with permission granted, he was off to their lounge, like a kid rushing to meet his pals.

Shay lifted up another chunk of steak to her lips and then put it down again. She wasn't that hungry really. She'd only cooked it so they could eat something together, talk, break down the barriers which he'd put up against her in the past week. And what was it about Morton that was buzzing around in her head like a fly refusing to be caught?

Chapter 11

Shay had an unexpected visitor the next day; well not entirely unexpected because it was only a matter of time before someone from Lesley's family got in touch, but she presumed it would be her husband before her son. She was just trawling the internet for more information about neighbour disputes when there was a thud on the door of debt-collector proportions. Through the frosted glass, she could see a gargantuan bright orange figure and edged forward down the hallway with caution.

'Hello,' she called tentatively.

A face pressed up against the glass, a dear face she recognised. 'It's me, Auntie Shay.'

Little Mort. Although when Shay opened the door, she thought what a ridiculous misnomer that was and she must get out of the habit of saying it. It had been a long while since she'd seen him last and he'd changed almost as much as his mother had. There was nothing of the boy left about him now; Little Mort was every inch a man, a powerfully built one at that and she marvelled that they even made high-vis vests in his size. He wasn't carrying an inch of puppy fat any more, he was pure lean muscle. What hadn't changed that much was his face; he had his mum's smiley mouth – pre lip-inflation – and his dad's thick, wild hair and kind brown eyes.

'Hello love, come in,' she said.

Mort stepped over the threshold and enfolded her in a hug. She instinctively compared it to the 'hug' she'd received recently from his mother. Mort's hug could have crushed bones if he'd applied even a little pressure.

Mort slipped off his boots and put them next to Bruce's size eleven slippers, dwarfing them.

'Coffee?' asked Shay.

'Please, if you've got time. I don't want to disturb you.' He had such impeccable manners, she thought. So, oddly, did his father. Morton never failed to excuse himself after he'd farted in a public place.

'Always got time for you,' Shay said and meant it. Mort was her godson and she had a great fondness for him. So did Sunny, for that matter, and Courtney but in her case, where it was obvious she thought of Mort as a second brother, he revered her like a goddess on a pedestal.

'I'm working just around the corner and so I thought I'd pop in and say hello.'

'It's lovely to see you, Mort. You sit down and I'll put the kettle on.' It had not long been boiled so took no time at all.

'We're doing a loft conversion. Really enjoying it as well. Nice people, cups of tea every half-hour and you don't get that on many jobs. And biscuits. Oh, that wasn't a hint by the way. I don't want any so I'll save you offering.'

'Milk, sugar?' Shay smiled but inside she was bracing herself for the niceties to be out of the way and for the questions to come.

'Strong and black, no sugar, please. I told Courtney I was calling. She said to tell you that she'll see you soon.'

'Oh, you're still in touch with each other, then?'

'Yeah, we go to boxing classes together.'

Shay nearly dropped the mugs she'd just picked up and was carrying to the table. 'She's boxing?' *Great*, she thought. Not just any old chaotic Courtney then, but a Courtney trained to kill.

'I dragged her along to Tommy Tanner's gym with me – you know, the current welterweight champ. I thought the discipline would be good for her. She's a natural.' He grinned and Shay thought what a handsome lad he'd turned out to be, a proper gentle giant, too. 'I wouldn't like to get on the wrong side of her, that's for sure,' he went on.

'Would anyone?' asked Shay, picturing her daughter in boxing gloves, standing victorious over a flattened body in the ring.

'I didn't tell her why I was coming, though.' Mort rubbed the fresh stubble on his chin, a gesture that smacked of nerves.

'Oh?' Shay handed him a mug and it looked half the size sitting in his great paw.

'Auntie Shay' – a long, loaded sigh – 'do you know about Mum and Dad splitting up?'

Of course that's why he was here. She nodded. 'I met your mum this week for lunch. I haven't seen her for months and well . . . it was a shock, I have to admit.'

'Did she say where she's living? Will you tell me?' Mort looked agitated, desperation in his voice.

'Mort, I honestly don't know. She didn't say.'

'She's left Dad and filed for divorce. She just walked out and left him; he's in a right state. I've had to move back in with him for a bit because I was that worried about him. He thinks she's got someone else, that's what's tearing him up.' Mort's eyes were shiny and he blinked rapidly to settle rising tears.

'That's not the impression I got at all. And she would definitely have told me if that was the case,' said Shay. At least she could put that rumour to bed.

'But . . . do you have that much work done to yourself *for* yourself? Is that normal?' Mort asked.

Ah, that's what had made him think like that.

'Of course you do, love, sometimes; it's not necessarily for another person. Women at our age might start going through the menopause early and it can do strange things to your hormones, make you want to change all manner of stuff before it's too late.'

'She won't pick up her phone if I ring and I've been worried sick that she's not well, you know, in the head. Sorry.' Rogue tears escaped, he dashed them away with his large cigar-fingers. When he made the summer house for Courtney, those big fingers had been capable of such delicate touches, the fretwork windowsill, the perfect dovetail joints, the tiny carved falcon above the door.

'She looked perfectly well when I saw her, Mort. I didn't get any vibes from her at all that she wasn't sure of what she was doing, which may or may not be what you want to hear.'

'I suppose that's something,' said Mort with a heavy breath out. 'I got a text from her last night, one line, "I'm okay, stop worrying and give me some space". I'm really having to bite my tongue, Auntie Shay, because if she *is* well, then I'll be so angry at her for what she's doing to Dad. I mean she's always treated him like muck, but this is taking it to another level. It's cruel.'

Mort had always been closer to his dad than his mum, but then Morton put more of the time and effort in than Les. Shay didn't like to think this of her friend: that she was disappointed in Little Mort because he would rather put bricks together than pursue a more intellectual path. Tanya had once said that she'd told Les off for measuring Mort unfavourably against Sunny. Tan thought it was because having a brickie for a son didn't give Les half the opportunity to show off that a son at uni would have.

'It's a big change for your mum,' Shay said softly, hoping she could cut Les some slack. 'She probably just needs to recalibrate. Maybe give her the space she asks for, Mort, and see what happens then.'

'Dad's been driving all over the place to see if he can see her car parked up anywhere,' said Mort. Shay remembered Les saying he'd try that.

'There's no point in him doing that,' said Shay, combining some truth with omission to save Morton torturing himself. 'She's got rid of it and was driving something else but I didn't take much notice what it was. I had no reason to.'

'She's thought of everything, hasn't she?' Mort shook his head slowly. 'She must have been planning it for ages. That's what hurts, really. She didn't have to do it like this, she could have been decent about it.'

Poor Mort, thought Shay. And poor Morton. But she couldn't judge Les too harshly; maybe cutting and running was the only way she could leave. It didn't smack of too much forward planning to her.

'She's jacked in her job as well,' Mort went on. 'I went there to try and talk to her and they said she'd just rung and told them she wasn't coming in any more and that was that. They didn't seem very happy about it.'

As big as Mort was, at that moment he just looked like a little boy in need of a cuddle. Shay's heart gave a sad bounce in her chest and she reached out, squeezed his arm.

'Mort, all I can do is ring or text her and tell her I've seen you and that you're in a bit of a state. Do you want me to?'

'Thank you. I appreciate that. And if there's anything I can do for you building-wise, I hope you'd come to me and Dad,' said Mort. 'I know I'm young but I've been at this game since I could hold a drill, so I know what I'm doing.'

Shay seized the chance. 'Actually, there is. Have you got time for a top up?' she asked.

'The stupid government has relaxed all the planning laws, Auntie Shay. People are knocking up extensions and extra floors for a laugh and there's nothing you can do to stop them,' said Mort, looking at the photos of her mum's house. He pulled his phone out of his pocket. 'Send me those photos and let me make a call. I know a bloke who's a chartered architectural technologist. What he doesn't know about this sort of thing, you can write on the back of a stamp.'

Adam Appleby, Mort's contact, picked up immediately. Shay could hear his voice through the phone; he sounded delighted that Mort had rung him and of course he'd help him if he could, he said. Mort forwarded him the photos and gave Adam time to peruse them, then he told Mort to put him on speaker so Shay could listen in.

'No, they wouldn't need planning permission for that extension at the back and yes, they can have a window looking out onto your mum's garden because, quite frankly, the council can't stop them. And yes, they can change their garage into a living area, all in the scope of permitted development. And sorry to say, they can build another storey onto their bungalow.'

Shay's heart sank. 'I rang a solicitor who said we had a case, though,' she tried.

'You rang a solicitor who said he'd take your money off you,' Adam parried. 'I can't tell you how many boundary disputes I've been involved with over the years. I wish, I really do, that I had good news, but you might as well throw your money down the toilet than try and raise a legal challenge because you won't win.'

'So we've no chance, then?' Shay asked for absolute clarification. She could tell it pained Adam to respond.

'None, because what they're doing is the new legal. Chalk it up to the idiots in Whitehall who altered all the regs without thinking of the implications. They're causing wars between neighbours. I'm really sorry.'

'But it's so wrong,' Shay replied with a frustrated growl.

'You can put up a two-metre fence, that'll block out that window overlooking the garden and pee on their bonfire,' Adam suggested.

Shay raised the smallest smile – a smile she didn't feel inside. She felt the army of resolve inside her down tools, go back to their wives and children. How on earth was she going to tell her mum that the Balls duo had won?

'Thank you anyway, Adam,' she said.

'I wish I could have given you better news, but I can at least save you a fortune in legal fees,' Adam replied, sounding every bit as glum about it as Shay.

Mort put down his phone after he'd rounded off the call. 'Soon as I saw the photos I knew you didn't have a leg to stand on, Auntie Shay,' he said. 'But you're better hearing it from a building specialist, then you're in no doubt. I'll put the fence up for you. Just pay me for the materials. I'll paint it a lovely shade of fluorescent yellow on the side facing them.'

Shay smiled. 'Thank you, Mort.'

He stood up and knocked his head on the low-hanging light fitting, laughing at his clumsiness as he reached up to straighten it.

At the door, his arms closed around Shay as he said thank you for listening and goodbye. It was like being in the clasp of a bear, and yet she could feel the fragility coming off him in waves.

Shay rang Lesley as soon as he'd gone. She didn't pick up so she texted instead, since she'd said at their lunch that she didn't listen to voicemails. She wrote that Mort was worried about her and had been in touch. She also asked Les to let her know she was okay and when she was ready for another lunch. Out of the three friends, Les had always been the most likely to reply quickly to messages so Shay knew, without any doubt, she'd hear from her soon.

Shay supposed she ought to ring Paula and let her know what she'd just learned about their mother's house.

'It'll have to be quick,' Paula said. 'I'm having my hair done in a minute. I'm gowned up and waiting for Mr Peter.'

Shay's eyebrows rose. Mr Peter owned *the* salon in Sheffield. His prices were astronomical and yet he still managed to make her sister's hair look as if it was carved out of concrete. Shay, however, knew her sister and what buttons to press for her attention. She was as easy to work as a child's toy.

'It's about the devaluation of Mum's house.'

Unsurprisingly, Paula was all ears then.

'We haven't got a leg to stand on,' Shay went on.

'Rubbish,' replied Paula. 'Have you been in touch with a solicitor?'

Have you, Shay wanted to throw back at her. She would complain and grizzle but she wouldn't put herself out to help.

'Yes I have. And an expert on planning laws. I've exhausted every avenue. What they're doing is completely allowed so no court is going to find in our favour. It would cost a fortune to fight and it would all be for nothing.'

'I see,' said Paula, after she'd digested that.

'I daren't tell Mum, she's going to be heartbroken.'

'I know. You forget I was there at the weekend having to endure her talking about it on a continuous loop,' said Paula to that, making herself sound like a sadly lacking Mother Teresa. 'Can't you go round and speak to the people next door and try and reason with them?'

'I did. And it didn't go well. He was vile.'

Paula sighed. 'I suppose it works in her favour that she's getting more deaf by the day and won't hear much of their noise through the wall.'

Shay's jaw hit her shoe. 'Did you really just say that?'

'Look, Dad should never have gone for a link-detached in the first place,' said Paula, a snarl in her voice. 'I never liked that house anyway. They bought it in haste and so eventually comes the repentance.'

'Mum's always been happy in that house. She loves it.'

The volume in Paula's voice rose as much as it could without attracting attention in the salon. 'They wouldn't have had this problem with their old house.'

'They'd have had other problems. Do you think Mum could have managed all the stairs as she is now? It was draughty and freezing in winter and the garden was way too big.'

Paula ignored that because it didn't fit her narrative.

'They should never have moved from Millspring. It was a lovely village.'

'Well, they did.'

'Yes, because of you,' hissed Paula. 'Because you couldn't keep your fucking legs shut and a boy died, didn't—'

Shay pressed the disconnect button and crashed her mobile down onto the table with such force it was a wonder it didn't smash the screen and land her with a two-hundred-quid repair bill.

Paula really was a genius at firing bullets, especially ones packed with bile. She'd pierced Shay hard in the tenderest part with that one, releasing a flare of guilt from a motherlode she had been carrying with her for twenty-nine years. The grass had long grown over what had happened, reduced it to a sad episode in history, but never inside herself where it churned at every point of settling. The lies that had been told about her had stained her indelibly, caused scarring bone-deep; they had forced her to live another life, a smaller existence, one where she feared moving out of the safe shadows and worried too much about the well-being of loved ones. It was a life built on a pretence of foundations and as much as she'd tried to move on in the way that counsellors had guided her, to accept a lot she could not change, she had not found her peace.

She'd had such a wonderful childhood, solid and secure. She'd had a school she enjoyed going to, teachers she liked. And she'd had Denny Smith as a best friend, and she'd had Jonah Wells. Her mum had said it was young love and that never lasted anyway. But here she was twenty-nine years later still unable to think of either Denny or Jonah without pain and knowing that, despite time, despite distance, despite every effort she'd ever made to forget the past, she had never got over losing either of them.

Chapter 12

Bruce was working the next day as well and though it would have been nice to have relaxed together, gone out with him for Sunday lunch in a country pub, Shay was quite glad he was out of the way with his present mood of gloom. The house was growing more like a powder keg with every day that passed. There had to be more to it than he was saying. She'd thought about it at length and concluded that she didn't really buy his job worries. He had a solid reputation, he was turning work down because his diary was full. They didn't have money problems either. They had healthy savings, they'd both put money into private pension pots, enough to retire early, and they drew revenue from a couple of houses which they'd bought when the prices were low and rented out to long-term tenants. She'd followed in the footsteps of her parents there who had banked quite a sum of money over the years by successfully investing in rental properties. No, there was something else he wasn't telling her and she would get to the bottom of it. This couldn't go on with him shutting her out, sulking, then the next minute getting all gooey and gushing how much he loved her and how beautiful she was. It was like living in a Fun House at Blackpool Pleasure Beach with constantly shifting floors, although without the 'Fun' and the 'Pleasure' parts.

Shay was just reading the Sunday newspaper, bored witless, when her phone rang and she saw Courtney's number flash up on the screen. She felt a mixed shot of emotion at hearing her daughter's voice, consisting mainly of joy and trepidation. Courtney courted disaster the way Casanova had courted nubile young women.

'Wotcher, Mum.' Courtney's voice was brimming with her customary cheerfulness.

'Hello love, how's it going?'

'Fine, I'm great. How are you? How's Dad and Gran?'

Better to be slightly economical with the truth where the latter was concerned. 'Your gran's neighbours are having some building work done which is annoying her a bit, but with any luck it'll be finished soon.'

'Is Dad okay?'

How to answer that one. 'Yes, he's working today.'

'Right.' A beat. 'Are you very busy at the moment?'

There it was, that change of tone that Shay knew so well, too well. The sweep on the ice before the curling stone came into play.

'No, I'm only reading the newspaper, why?'

'I could just . . . do with a chat.'

'I'm never too busy for a chat.'

'I'm parked around the corner. Okay to come in?'

'Of course. You don't have to ask if you can come into your own home.'

'I'll see you in a minute then,' said Courtney and ended the call.

Shay got up to look through the front window and saw her daughter's powder-blue Fiat roll into view from up the road. They'd bought it for her twenty-first birthday, a safe, immaculate, little car. As it drew nearer, Shay noted the crunched bumper and the ugly black impact marks scrawled along the side panel. Courtney got out of it, her hair now flamingo-pink, a colour that would be visible from Mars. A weight of dread landed with a bump in Shay's stomach and she thought, 'Here we go again.'

'You heard from Sunny recently? Because I haven't,' said Courtney, as her mother brought two mugs of coffee over to the kitchen table.

That surprised Shay because her children had always been close, despite infuriating each other with their many differences.

'I hadn't heard from him in ages, then he rang on Friday and he's coming over to your gran's tomorrow morning, so I'll see him there.'

'He's blown us all out for *her*,' Courtney crinkled up her nose as if a bad smell had just drifted past. 'What's that thing they say about a son only being a son until he takes a wife' – she grinned – 'but the good news, Mum, is that a daughter is a daughter all of her life.'

Shay raised her eyes heavenward and Courtney hooted.

'He's okay, Mum, don't worry. He'd say if he wasn't. He's just getting on with a new phase of his life.'

'So everyone keeps saying to me,' replied Shay.

'Bit annoying though when you ring and he doesn't answer and then he sends you a text as if he doesn't want to actually talk to you.' Courtney slurped her drink while she mused on that.

Shay, however, was presently more concerned about her daughter than her son.

'What happened to your car, Courtney?'

Courtney flapped her hand with a casualness that belied the words that followed the gesture. 'Well, Dingo borrowed the car to go into town. Honestly, Mum, he was only gone ten minutes and he managed to damage it in that time. I was so angry. We had a proper fight. In fact, I ended up finishing with him, you'll be relieved to hear.'

Shay would have been if she could have believed it. Dingo would have been better named Boomerang, on account of him always managing to thud repeatedly back into Courtney's life.

'What do you mean by "fight"?' asked Shay.

'Oh Mum, you don't have to worry about me, I'm quite capable of defending myself.' Courtney winked and clicked her tongue. 'I've been having boxing lessons. I've developed an excellent jab.'

'Yes, I heard.'

'Mort? Yeah, he said he was coming to see you. What is Auntie Les on?' Courtney threw her hands up in the air. 'I mean, you did know she's just buggered off and disappeared without so much as a kiss my arse?'

'I didn't know before last Tuesday,' replied Shay. 'It was quite the surprise to me too.'

Courtney got up from the table to pillage the biscuit barrel. 'Mort didn't tell me until last night. I think he was hoping it would all blow over and there would be nothing to tell. She's being a bit of a cow in my opinion, but that's nothing new.' She brought a handful of Jaffa Cakes over to the table.

'What do you mean?' asked Shay.

'She puts him down a lot,' said Courtney, throwing herself heavily onto the chair which creaked in protest; she'd inherited her father's inability to do anything unannounced and gracefully. 'She thinks because he's got brawn he can't have brains as well and he really has. He reads all the time and just because he hasn't got A-levels doesn't mean he's thick. His dad's much nicer than his mum, if smellier,' and she laughed.

'I didn't know you were still close to Mort.'

Courtney looked shocked by that. 'I've always been friends with Mort and I always will. Why wouldn't I be? Plus he's really handy if you need anything mended. And before you say it, no I don't use him. I like him. Obvs not in *that* way.'

If only she did, thought Shay. If only her daughter liked nice boys like Mort and not knobheads like Dingo Shaw.

'So, tell me about the car,' said Shay, herding emphasis back to that.

'I'm insured. It's fine. It's going into the garage tomorrow. Though I've had to lie and say it was *mea culpa* because Dingo wasn't insured to drive it. Or anything for that matter, because he's banned.'

Shay rubbed her forehead, hoping it would help her make sense of her daughter's reasoning, but it didn't.

'Why would you let anyone drive your car who wasn't insured for it? And then lying that—'

'Chillax, Mum. If it makes you feel any better, I'm not happy about doing it. One-off, promise, pinky swear.'

'Well thank you for that, it really helps,' Shay replied, with no small dose of sarcasm. 'I thought you'd treasure your car.'

'I do,' replied Courtney.

'You've only had it a year,' said Shay, temper bubbling now. 'And I thought you and Dingo were already over.'

'Well, he rang and apologised and we gave it another shot. But that's really it this time. Anyway, Fiona doesn't want him staying at the flat any more. Not after he kicked the TV stand and broke it. I paid for a new one, obvs because Mort couldn't even mend it.'

Courtney's typical disclosures were coming out like handkerchiefs from a magician's sleeve, one awful one after the other.

'Which brings me to ask you a favour, Mum. I'm only working part-time at the moment because the shop isn't that busy so I could really do with a cash injection to help me. The rent's due and I owe Fi some for last month and I lent Dingo some and seeing as the last time I saw him his nose was bleeding profusely and he told me to eff off and die, somehow I don't think I'm going to get it back.'

'How much?' asked Shay with a laboured sigh. Her daughter was constantly in debt. Shay had lost count of the times that she had sat down with her in an effort to organise her finances, and paid off her overdraft behind Bruce's back, only for Courtney to dig her head in the sand and the whole cycle to begin again. It was beyond frustrating.

'Six hundred if you have it,' said Courtney with an expression of pain. 'I'm really sorry. I will get it back to you, somehow.'

Her daughter usually did pay her debts off, if only in dribs and drabs, earning her one brownie point out of a possible five hundred.

Shay picked up her phone, went into her online banking and pinged it across.

'Thanks, Mum,' said Courtney, leaping out of her chair

to give her mother a hug of gratitude. 'I really appreciate it. It's a shit job. No one ever comes into the shop so it's really boring but I'm on the lookout for something better. Totally hate being skint and unchallenged.'

'Why are you working in these dead-end jobs with crap pay, Court? I want more for you than this.' She was a bright girl, brilliant with computers, clever at the written word and ballsy enough to sell bottled water to fish.

Courtney made a face. 'I don't know what I want to do with my life yet, Mum. Nothing's jumping out at me. You're worrying about it more than I am.'

'Well do your best to try and sort yourself out, Court,' said Shay. 'And stay away from Dingo. Fiona really shouldn't have to put up with things like that . . . and you should not be in a relationship where you're raising hands to each other.'

Quiet, sensible Fiona, Shay secretly hoped, would be a steadying influence on her daughter and knowing that Courtney would be sharing a flat with her made it bearable that she'd left home. Dingo, however, was a curse of an individual, rough, rude, no redeeming features that she could pinpoint, plus he reminded her too much of a boy called Glynn Duffy she'd known once.

Now Courtney had her money, she was off. Outside, on the pavement, she looked around.

'Is it in the garage then?' she asked her mum. 'He's not taking it to work I presume.'

Shay hadn't the slightest clue what she was on about. 'What?'

'Your new car.'

'What?'

'I saw Dad driving it last week down the Parkway. I blasted the horn but he didn't notice me. Brand new black Audi.'

'He wishes. Sorry to disappoint but your father's still driving his trusty van.'

Courtney's brow furrowed. 'Are you sure?'

'I think I'd know.'

'Must have been tripping then,' said Courtney.

Shay reared. 'Please tell me you aren't on drugs.'

'Back in your box, Mum.' Courtney laughed. 'I'm hardly Keith Richards.'

'Courtn—'

'God Mum, really, I'm winding you up. Tell Dad I said hello, but don't tell him I borrowed any money.'

'I will and I won't in that order,' said Shay, and stood on the step until her daughter had gone, waving while wondering if she'd ever cease being the compressed filling in the family sandwich.

Chapter 13

Roberta was delighted to see Shay call in that Monday morning bringing a coffee and walnut cake with her. That flavour made her think of Sunny for some reason, maybe it was his favourite. It frustrated her that she didn't know why coffee and walnut and Sunny were together under the same bracket, in the same way that she couldn't remember why that gaudy, buckled skip on next door's drive held a significance. It perturbed her, poked something long buried in her head, something that sat like an unexploded bomb couched in thick padding but never relinquishing its potential to maim and destroy.

The house was dark because she'd had to close her back curtains so the builders couldn't see in. Masonry dust had blown all over her usually immaculate front windows after she'd just had them cleaned. The sight out of them was best occluded anyway: a massive white builder's van blocking her usually lovely view of the green and, to the side on next door's drive, the Sharif's skip. For the first time, her home felt more like a prison than a sanctuary.

So when not only her daughter but her grandson rocked

up Roberta's spirits took a well-needed soar upwards. Shay knew he'd arrived as she heard her mother's shriek while she was in the kitchen hanging a few bits of washing on the airer; it was too dusty outside to put them on the line.

'Shay, look, it's Sunny.' The delight in her voice was as evident as the Prodigal Son's father's must have been when he turned up on the doorstep. Well, there was no fatted calf, but there was a coffee and walnut cake ready sliced.

Shay tried not to run into the lounge but to no avail.

'Hello darling,' she said, half-launching herself at him, filling her arms with him. He felt different, too lean.

Never one for subtlety, Roberta said, 'There's nothing of you, Sunny. Are you eating?'

'Yes, Gran,' he said with an embarrassed smile.

'It'll be the wedding,' Roberta diagnosed. 'Dagmara's ordered me an outfit from a catalogue on the computer which should be here any day now. I can try it on and if it's not right we can send it back. Dress, coat, hat and some shoes. I'll be resplendent in violet.'

'Sit down and talk to your gran. I'll bring the tea in,' said Shay, fighting the urge to hug him again. In the kitchen she loaded a tray and brought it through. Her mother was in full flow, filling in Sunny with the escapades of next door.

'. . . He calls himself Drew but his real name is Andrew, because Dagmara gets his post all the time. Your mum is going to get the building work stopped. I have to laugh sometimes when I see them putting bricks up because I know they'll be coming down before long.'

Oh God, thought Shay.

Roberta was holding Sunny's hand and the smile on her face was that of a small child who had just been given a monster bag of sweets.

'Here, Mum, take a breath and have some cake.' Shay pushed a plate into her hand. Then she passed her son a plate too. She wanted to take him home and fatten him up.

'It's so lovely to see you, Sunny.' Roberta sighed. 'I wish I could see you a bit more.'

'I'm sorry, Gran,' said Sunny.

'Oh Mum, don't guilt-trip him. He's busy,' Shay admonished her, feeling a hypocrite because inside she was thinking exactly the same as her mum.

'Busy painting you mean? You should bring me one of them up so I can put it on my wall.'

'I work in an office, Gran. I don't do any painting these days.'

Roberta's fork stopped before it got to her mouth and she looked from Sunny to Shay for clarification. They'd had this conversation before and each time, Roberta was astounded anew. Shay moved on quickly on before her mother gave Sunny a lecture about it. He was a grown man capable of making his own decisions and she'd had to step back and accept that, bite down hard on the question that wanted to leave her lips every time she thought of him doing that job: 'Why would someone with your obvious talent for art not be throwing everything you have at it, son?' How could he have lost his love for it when it was all he'd wanted to do, ever since he'd been big enough to hold a coloured pencil in his hand?

'How's Karoline? Is she all right?' asked Roberta, for once managing not to imbue the name with venom.

'Yeah she's . . . she's okay.'

'You don't sound very sure,' said Roberta, having one of her moments of astuteness. 'Is she or isn't she?'

'Well, she's off work at the moment for . . . a couple

of . . . weeks.' He pulled his ear lobe absently and Shay remembered how he used to do that as a little boy, when he was nervous.

'What's the matter with her?' Roberta asked.

'Just a bit of stress. It's nothing, I shouldn't have mentioned it really.'

Roberta, however, was on it like a rat on a pound of Edam.

'What's she stressed about? Nerves, we used to call it, not that they'd let you have any time off with it. Not unless you were bad enough to be locked away,' Roberta sprayed cake crumbs as she spoke. 'She should have come here with you today if she's off. She'd have been made very welcome.'

'I know.'

'How long's she off for and—'

'Mum, stop giving him the third degree.' Shay interrupted her mother's Gestapo-like interrogation. 'Are you managing for money, son?'

'We're fine for money, thanks. Karoline's parents throw it at her. It can be annoying if I'm honest.'

'Yes, I imagine,' said Shay. Sunny wasn't a freeloader. He'd always paid his own way. He would be hating that his in-laws were the ones financing a wedding too big for him to afford. Unlike his sister, he had always preferred to live within his means and be solvent.

'You still playing rugby?' Roberta asked him.

'Yep.'

He didn't look big enough any more to play, thought Shay, trying not to stare at her son too intently. He'd be snapped like a twig on the pitch. He lifted his head and caught her eyes and she saw something there she didn't like. They weren't the big brown eyes shining with a love of life that she was used to. She felt suddenly odd, as if on an exclusive mother and son wavelength that existed with placenta-like strength and was tuned with insight.

'Are you *really* all right Sunny?' she asked him, unable to stop herself.

He opened his mouth to answer but it didn't come out, whatever it was he was about to say wouldn't budge further. Then a rasping pulse broke the moment as Sunny's phone went off in his pocket and he scrabbled to take it out as if it were programmed to self-destruct unless it was answered within three rings.

'I'd better just get this. 'Scuse me.'

Shay had caught sight of the screen and the large name written at the top, *Karoline*.

Sunny got up and walked into the kitchen, closing the door behind him.

'Who was it?' asked Roberta.

'Shh, Mum,' said Shay, creeping to the door, listening through it to his half of the conversation.

'. . . I'm at my gran's . . . yes, of course I'm here . . . she's not been well so I took the morning off . . . last-minute decision, that's why I didn't say . . . Karoline, let me speak . . . do you want me to put her on the phone to prove it? . . . Okay, I will then . . .'

Shay just managed to assume her position on the sofa before Sunny returned, holding his phone out to Roberta.

'Gran, Karoline would like to say hello.'

'Hello Karoline.' Roberta pressed the speakerphone button inadvertently and so they were all party to the conversation.

'Hello Roberta. Sunny tells me you aren't well.' Karoline's voice was soft, sympathetic and Roberta, despite her misgivings about the woman, was touched by her concern.

'Oh I'm perfectly fine,' she cooed, making a lie of her grandson's words. 'It was a lovely surprise to see him. It's a shame you couldn't come too. It might have done you good having a drive over if you've got problems.'

Shay watched Sunny's face fold into an instinctive cringe, quickly corrected.

A trill of laughter from Karoline. 'I don't know what Sunny's been telling you, I'm just a little under the weather, nothing for you to worry about.'

'I've got a violet outfit for the wedding. I hope that doesn't clash with anyone.'

'Sounds fabulous,' replied Karoline. 'You have full permission to wear whatever colour you like, Roberta. Anyway, I'll let you carry on chatting. You take good care of yourself and I'll see you soon, I'm sure.'

'You're welcome any time, dear.' Roberta's smile was presently the size of a crescent moon.

She waited then for a response, but none came. 'Hello . . . hello?' she called into the phone, then she shook it. 'She's gone. Did I press something I shouldn't have? I haven't broken it, have I?' She handed it back to Sunny. 'Well, that was short but sweet.'

But the coin had flipped, because her mother might have been temporarily charmed but Shay's senses had pricked up. What was going on there? Why was Sunny lying to his fiancée that coming here had been a last-minute decision? And why did it feel somehow that visiting his family would be such a big deal?

Sunny finished off his cake and his coffee but he didn't seem at ease however much he tried to give the impression he was; micro gestures gave him away, another pull on his ear, a tapping foot. That phone call had unnerved him and it wasn't an over-active imagination telling Shay that, as Bruce would have scoffed.

Roberta's old grandmother clock chimed the hour and Sunny seized on that as a sign to go. 'I'd better get back, it was just a flying visit to check in. Thanks for the cake, it was delicious. My favourite.'

'I knew it was your favourite,' said Roberta with an emphatic wag of her finger. She was delighted she'd half-remembered that.

Sunny bent to give his gran a hug then.

'Aww,' said Roberta, not letting him go. 'I could have sat and talked to you all day. Come and see me again soon, Sunny. You don't know how long I've got left.'

'Oh, stop that, Mum,' said Shay with a reproving chuckle.

'Those ... idiots next door will kill me off, I tell you,' Roberta shook her fist at the party wall.

'I promise I will, Gran.'

'Come on, I'll see you out,' said Shay.

She walked with him to his car, took his arm, savoured the feel of him. The temptation to inundate him with questions was almost too much. Then he headed her off at the pass.

'Before you say anything, Mum, because I know how your mind works, we're just having a rough patch. It'll pass. Karoline's got too much time on her hands, being at home and she was cheated on by her last boyfriend, so she has a few trust issues.'

'I see,' replied Shay, not liking the sound of this at all. She couldn't stop herself asking the question that came out of her mouth next, even though she could hear Bruce's voice in her mind trying to censure her for it.

'Should you be getting married if you haven't sorted those trust issues out, love?'

'My fault. I haven't helped by taking the morning off work and not telling her. She'll have read all sorts of things into that.' He smiled ruefully at his own stupidity.

'Why didn't you just tell her, then?'

He shrugged, shook his head as if it was a deeper matter he didn't want to get into, then he put his arms around his mother.

'See you soon, Mum.' He held on to her just a smidgeon more than a goodbye length, she noted.

'You know you can talk to me about anything,' said Shay, when he had let her go.

'Course I do, and I would,' he replied. And she knew that, once again, he was lying.

Roberta was still twittering about Sunny's visit that evening when Shay called around to make her dinner. Not only that, but Courtney had rung and asked if she could bob over and see her that week; also her outfit had arrived from Dagmara's catalogue and it fitted her like Cinderella's slipper apparently, though Shay wasn't allowed to see it until the big day. In short, Roberta's spirits were sky-high for a nice change. Shay wished her own spirits were as lofty, because seeing Sunny had troubled her. And who could she talk to about it? Les still hadn't responded to her text message from the weekend, so was obviously off grid and she felt as if there was a fence between her and Bruce. Nor could she work out if he was just being rude or was putting up a wall of bluster to hide behind because he was sinking into an abyss. Depression took many forms, she knew that and she needed to know what was really happening in his brain so she could help, and for that he had to let her in.

*

'I meant to tell you,' she said at dinner that night. Overdone lasagne, because Bruce was very late home and Shay hoped the heavy snow of Parmesan cheese disguised the burnt bits. 'When Courtney came over, she said she saw you in a brand new Audi driving in Sheffield.'

Bruce momentarily stopped eating and looked up.

'Is she mad? No, don't answer that, she's barmy – and blind.'

'She seemed convinced it was you.' Shay smiled. Once upon a time he'd have made a joke about it, said that the surprise was spoiled because he'd bought it as a gift for her and was giving it a test drive. Now, he just carried on eating, stabbing his fork into the pasta as if he was stabbing it into whatever was irking him and chewing like a bolshy teenager chewed gum.

'Sorry about the burnt offering,' she said then.

'I suppose that's my fault is it?'

Yes, actually, she thought, but wriggled out of it with a lie to skirt any altercation. She would not load the gun he was pointing at her head with bullets.

'No, mine. I put the heat up too high so apologies, though I quite like it a bit crusty. Oh and Sunny called in at Mum's today.'

'Oh yeah.'

She waited for him to ask how he was, the son he hadn't seen for months. He didn't.

'Karoline's off work with stress apparently.'

Bruce laughed at that, a humourless *humph*. 'What's she know about stress?' he said, in a low voice that probably wasn't meant to be overheard. Shay's senses ruffled.

'It affects people in different ways though doesn't it? Some fold, some work through it, some project and try and blame others for it, some pretend it's not happening.'

Bruce looked up slowly. 'This directed at me, is it?'

'What?'

'You heard.'

Shay huffed. 'I was talking about Karoline.'

'Yeah, course you were.'

Enough now. She couldn't be a human dartboard for him any more.

'Why are you being like this, Bruce? You've been off with me since you told me about you-know-what. I haven't put you under any pressure, I haven't even mentioned it.'

'You don't think you do, but you have little digs all the time, *Some pretend it's not happening.*' He imitated her, giving her a whiney voice which incensed her, and that told in the rising volume of her response.

'I can't help you if you won't let me in.'

'I don't want your fucking help,' Bruce retorted.

'Then tell me what you do want because I don't know,' she implored, at the end of her tether with it all now. 'I don't understand what's going on between us. Do we need to go and see a counsellor—'

'Counsellor.' He repeated the word, scoffed at it.

'Is there someone else?' She blurted it out without meaning to because she didn't believe it anyway.

Bruce screwed up his face in disgust. 'Are you really asking me that? What sort of relationship do we have that you'd say that to me, Shay?'

'I don't know what sort of relationship we have at the moment, that's the point. We are off track and I don't know what's caused it. If I try and talk to you, you won't. I'm walking on eggshells around you in case I upset you, I'm filtering through things I say in case I inadvertently mention something you can take the wrong way. I'm worried about you, Bruce. I love you.' She threw the last words at him, hoped they'd stick like hot sugar, brand onto his skin so he accepted them, believed them. She felt them bounce back, unwanted.

'I think I'm going to move into the spare room for a bit, Shay. Don't read too much into it. I just feel as if my brain is going to explode' – he lifted his hands to his head, jiggled them in the air at either side of his ears – 'and you lying . . . beside me, makes me feel inadequate. Just . . . give me some space, will you? No counsellors, no heavy talks, I need to work things out my own way,' he said wearily. 'Please.'

Shay swallowed before speaking. 'Just promise me that you're *okay*.' Her meaning was clear. Bruce knew the sketchiest details about her childhood friend. He closed his eyes and let loose a long breath of veiled impatience.

'Shay, I'm not going to do anything stupid if that's what you're thinking so you don't have to hover over me and fret every time I walk out of the house.'

Shay nodded, relief blooming in her chest. She didn't speak. What could she say anyway that hadn't already been said?

Chapter 14

Shay had been sleeping alone for two weeks now. The bed hadn't shrunk around her in that time, it felt as cavernous every night. She'd never minded sleeping alone when Bruce was working away from home, but there was so much more that was separating them now than a mere plasterboard wall.

She tolerated it because it had warmed up his mood towards her. He was civil now, less snappy, but she still didn't know if he'd contacted a doctor and she remained on the begging end of information. It was an interim measure that couldn't last; they weren't brother and sister and she didn't want to live as if they were, but she had enough to occupy her mind for now and there were only so many fronts she could fight on.

She was worried about her mother most of all. She'd had to tell her eventually that there was nothing they could do about the Balls's building work, and then wished she could have grabbed the words in the air and crammed them back into her mouth after seeing the effect they'd had.

'I will keep trying though, Mum, so don't lose hope,' Shay had added hurriedly, a reverse thrust that came across as an obvious lie. That conversation signified the moment when Roberta packed up the ashes of hope into a suitcase, climbed on a slide and prepared for the descent.

'Have you got time to wash my hair, Shay? My shoulder's a bit stiff and I can't reach over,' asked Roberta when she'd finished her meal. She hadn't eaten much, just moved most of it around on the plate as if she hoped it would shrink away.

'Course I have,' replied Shay. 'You've not made much of an impact on your dinner, Mum, would you like an éclair?' She'd checked the food stocks in Roberta's cupboards and they were hardly going down. Not even the chocolate digestives that she liked to mainline with coffees.

'No thank you, love. I'm not in the mood.'

'Why don't you come and stay with me for—'

'No, Shay, I'm not budging from this house and that's final.' Roberta was adamant. '*They* won't drive me out of my home. I'm sticking my heels in and staying strong.'

She didn't sound strong, she sounded beat and she'd already let slip to Shay that she hadn't been sleeping well. Shay took her plate and emptied the uneaten meal into the bin.

'The builders are nice, no one's blaming them. They've promised to put the grass in the circle right for us when they've finished.'

'Well, that's decent of them.'

'They're good lads. They don't like *him*, you know, they don't like how he talks to people. He called Derrick "an old swear word coffin dodger" yesterday when he asked him if he'd stop blocking his driveway. He deliberately parks across them so you have to ask him to shift his car and then he can shout abuse. He laughs about it to the builders, but they don't like him. Derrick gets to know what Balls says because his nephew is friendly with one of the bricklayers.'

What a piece of work, thought Shay.

'Apparently Balls has told the builders to insulate the wall between us last.'

Shay nearly dropped the plate she was washing. 'What?'

'I'm sorry, I shouldn't have said. I don't want to worry you any more. You do enough. You never stop. Are you all right, love? I forget, you know, you've a lot on.'

'I'm perfectly fine, Mum, don't you worry about me.'

'You're such a lovely woman, Shay, I do love you,' Roberta said with a tender smile. 'People don't say that enough in this world, do they?'

Shay chuckled. 'What's brought this on? Have you been watching *Little House on the Prairie*?'

'No, I just love you, that's all.'

'And I love you too. So don't keep things from me. I can't do anything about them if I don't know.'

'I won't do it again,' said Roberta, but she knew she would. She hadn't told Shay that Balls had started playing a radio next to the thin adjoining wall all night at full blast, and if she could find Harry's big hammer she'd bang hard on it and give him a taste of his own medicine. She hadn't told Shay either that she'd learned two days ago that the converted garage between them was going to be Drew Balls's party room and since she'd found that out she'd had a headache screwing into her brain that refused to abate. She relied on her daughter so much, she was ashamed to admit that she never asked her if she was all right, never said thank you enough, took for granted that she had no problems of her own to deal with. Shay held everything together, but who was there to hold her together if she needed it?

Shay massaged the shampoo into her mother's scalp as she leaned over the sink.

'That's nice,' Roberta sighed; the sensation was far outweighing her headache and the relief was wonderful. 'I could let you do that all day.'

Shay gave it an extra shampoo; why not, if her mum was enjoying it? As she rinsed off the foam, she saw her mother's baby-pink scalp underneath the thin white hair that had once been such a shiny golden shade of strawberry blonde. Roberta had always worn it in a chic French roll, though it had tumbled almost to her waist when she released it from the pins. When had all the colours faded? When had it become so fine and wispy, like the down of a baby bird? Shay lifted it in her hands, felt the small weight of it. It seemed to embody how fragile the whole of her mum was, her strength and colour ebbing away a little more with every tide of time, and she felt suddenly tearful. She pushed some conditioner through it, her throat full of emotion.

Her father too was waning; a cruel double-whammy. These once strong people who had sacrificed so much of themselves for her benefit were being washed away by life, reduced to shadows, ghosts of their past selves. Last night Shay had been up to Whispering Pines and given her dad's eyebrows a trim. The barber always used to do it for him with his haircut, because they grew wild and long if left and he never liked to look unkempt. Part of her attraction to Bruce was that, like her dad, he made the best of himself. She'd never understood why girls like her own daughter found scruffy, sour-smelling males attractive.

She wished her dad had opened his eyes. He'd had eyes that smiles swam in, kind blue eyes. She'd been jealous of Paula when she was younger because she had the same colour eyes as their father. She didn't want to look like some old great great grandmother who came from Naples, she wanted blue eyes like her dad and sandy eyebrows. Paula would have asked her why she was bothering to trim them for him, what difference did it make; and she didn't know the answer, only that she was doing it out of love, because she needed to do something for him to assure him that she was there, caring. It was a small task, like washing her mum's hair, but it meant so much more than it was.

Shay blotted Roberta's damp hair with a towel and then fetched the round styling brush that she kept in her old teenage room, curling the feather fluff of her mum's hair around it as she blasted it with the still-working 1970s Vidal Sassoon dryer she had in the cupboard. Her mother's head felt like a fragile shell in her hands.

'I feel much better for having it done, thank you,' said Roberta, as Shay was finishing it off with some hotbrush curls.

'I'll wash your hair any time if you can't manage it yourself, Mum. You only have to ask me.'

'I wish I could ask Paula the same way I can you,' said Roberta. 'I think I cursed her calling her that name. Your dad's mother. Can you remember her?'

'She died before I was born, Mum.'

'Did she?' Roberta seemed surprised by that. 'You were saved that ordeal then. Paula Corrigan wasn't just cold, she was frozen solid. He didn't have any love growing up, your dad – yet he cried like a baby at her funeral. I still, to this day, think he was crying for the mother he wished she'd been rather than the one she was. Poor Harry.'

Her dad had said to Shay once, when they were in an empty hospital waiting room, that he'd wanted to be a better parent than his own but he hadn't been. He'd got himself in a proper loop about being a rotten dad. And Shay had told him that she'd grown up warm and safe and well fed and happy. And that when she needed him most, he was there for her and he'd brightened to hear that. She said she loved him and he'd said he loved her but he had a block about telling her because he'd been brought up never hearing those words. Then he'd been called into the consulting room and that was the first and last conversation they'd ever had on the subject, the first and last time he said he loved her.

'I've been thinking about before a lot recently,' Roberta said then.

Shay knew what she meant by *before*. They never talked about it; there was no point in moving away from it only to revisit it.

'It was that skip next door, Shay. I felt it was trying to tell me something, as if it had been put there for a reason. It's taken me a long time to work out what it was.'

'I'm all ears.'

'That I was wrong and your father was right,' said Roberta.

This was turning into one of her mum's puzzles, which made sense to her but meant nothing to anyone else.

'We shouldn't have come here. Harry said we needed to stay and I said we had to go and I won. We both wanted to protect you in our own ways, but I thought my way was better. I tried to pretend it hadn't happened, you see, but you can't rewrite the past just because it's easier. Not when you see people getting hurt by the lies.'

Shay clicked off the hotbrush and sat down at the table, let her mum talk uninterrupted.

'I thought of that boy, the one who died. You brought him for tea, do you remember? He ate as if he'd not eaten for months. His little face came out of nowhere into my head, covered in buttercream he was.' She smiled and Shay felt a flare of pain deep inside her, a dormant scar reminding her of its presence.

'We left because I didn't want them to hurt you any more but you never properly healed, did you? I saw that over the years, even though I tried not to. We should have stayed and braved it out like Harry said. But a part of me at the time was scared . . . because . . . I wasn't sure what the truth really was, Shay. I'm ashamed of that, because Harry never doubted you.'

'It was the absolute truth,' replied Shay, feeling the rate of her heartbeat increase, the blood heating her cheeks.

'I'm sorry. When I got that letter I realised I was wrong, I should—'

Shay's head jerked. 'What letter?'

'From the Smith boy.'

'A letter from Denny?'

'Yes, I'm sure . . .' Roberta's voice tailed off into a groan. 'But I can't have got a letter from him, can I, Shay?'

Shay shook her head. 'No, Mum. Denny was long gone by the time we moved here.'

'Oh, I wish I'd written this down when it came to me.'

'Mum, don't get yourself in a state. It doesn't matter.'

'It does matter, Shay.'

Roberta knew what she wanted to say mattered a lot and she foraged deep into her brain to try and recall the letter, because it had to be real, it came with too many feelings of confusion and guilt and regret to be a mere trick of the mind. She tried to keep hold of the memory and pull it towards her because it was important, but she felt it slipping away into the fog and she growled, frustrated at herself, pressing her fingertips into her forehead. 'Oh, I don't know what I'm saying. It's gone.' The shards of glass in her head, which the sight of the big orange skip had briefly brought together to form a whole clear picture, crashed down to the ground into an indecipherable jumble.

'I called my daughter Shay because it was his mother's name,' she said then.

'Who, Mum?'

'Omar Sharif,' said Roberta.

Shay stayed longer than usual with her mum, until she was settled, until the only thing she was nattering about was making sure that she didn't miss the feature length *Poirot* that was coming on TV. Shay left her calm, warm, content with a pot of tea and a plate of biscuits on her coffee table. After she'd closed the front door behind her, she stalled for no discernible reason, turned on the step, went back inside and gave her mother an extra kiss, although Roberta was too engrossed in David Suchet by then to even notice.

When she got home, Shay checked Omar Sharif's mother's name only to discover it was, in fact, Claire. She wasn't quite sure why she'd bothered or what it would have meant had she found that she and Mrs Sharif shared a name. But there was an end to it anyway; let her mother remember her affair with Omar Sharif and the ice creams they'd had strolling down the prom for the manufactured truth it was.

Chapter 15

The call came at two a.m. Derrick had got up to let his little terrier out and noticed that Roberta's light was still on and her curtains weren't drawn. He'd looked through the window to see her prone body on the carpet and he'd both rung 999 and had roused Dagmara to ask her for Shay's number.

Shay and Bruce arrived at the same time as the ambulance. They hurried in and found Roberta still with the hammer in her hand that she'd used to batter gouges out of the party wall to stop the noise of the music still playing through it at full blast. Motörhead – *Iron Fist*, Shay recognised it, the riotous soundtrack to her mother's last breaths as the paramedics worked on her. Then the track cut off abruptly and in its place was a charged silence which was equally deafening.

One day, Shay would find a small comfort that she was there with her mum at the end; she would even begin to believe that Roberta had been hanging on for her. But there was no solace at the time, just a cold, all-enveloping numbness.

Rock Bottom

When you hit what you know can't be anything other than rock bottom, someone is sure to hand you a shovel so you can keep digging

LINDA FLOWERS

Chapter 16

The hours that followed were a blur. Shay couldn't remember what order she'd rung people in, or what she'd said to them. Courtney had been nigh hysterical at the news. 'There's nothing you can do, don't drive over in a state,' Shay had warned her, but it hadn't stopped her. Sunny arrived next at the hospital, looking gaunt and grey. Courtney couldn't face seeing her gran, she didn't want to remember her like that but she wanted to be near her so she sat outside the private room where Roberta lay. Shay and Sunny sat in with her, their hands on top of Roberta's, above the blanket and though Shay's eyes were on her mum's dear face, her thoughts were a tumbling mass of blinding rage. All she could see in her head was her mother hammering chunks out of the wall as a desperate protest against the noise, probably falling over the fire companion set, catching her head on the corner of the display shelf in a terrible and tragic choreography because the markers of the fatal collision were clear. How long had Balls been doing that for? Is that why her mother said she couldn't sleep at night? Is that why he'd asked the workmen to insulate that wall last so he could torment her with an endless racket? Balls had as much killed Roberta as had the knock she'd incurred from her fall. Shay wanted to march straight from the hospital to kill him.

Sunny was crying hard, berating himself for not seeing his gran enough these past months. What was it about death that plunged people into a cold bath of guilt? She recalled feeling the same when Bruce's mother passed away, the crippling recriminations that she hadn't done enough for her, that she'd not been there with her when she had slipped away in her sleep.

Only hours ago Shay had been washing her mother's hair, nagging her about not eating her dinner and trying to tempt her appetite with a Potterworth's éclair. They'd had that confusing conversation about skips and Omar bloody Sharif and her mother had said that she loved her and she'd never hear those words again from her. She'd turned around after saying good night , gone back inside just to give her mum an extra kiss, as if on some subliminal level she'd known what was going to happen; such a little act which had grown into proportions of epic size now. None of it seemed real, yet it was and it was horrible.

The door cracked open and Paula walked in, ashen-faced, but hair brushed, clothes chosen with care rather than just thrown on because they were the closest to hand. Sunny relinquished his chair and went outside to leave the sisters alone.

'What happened?' Paula asked, sitting down. Her hand came out to touch her mother's briefly over the blanket before recoiling. But Shay wouldn't hold that against her; this wasn't their mother any more and she couldn't get her head around that either.

'One of the neighbours saw all the lights on and the curtains were open and rang me. It looks as though Mum was banging on next door's wall and toppled over and hit her head.'

'What on earth was she doing that for?' asked Paula.

'Because the tosser was playing heavy metal at full blast. You can't imagine how loud it sounded. He must have seen the ambulance because it suddenly switched off.'

Shay needed to change the subject quick because she wanted to feel grief for her mother, not anger for the Balls. They could wait; she would give them no place in her head at the moment.

'What happens next?' asked Paula after a few moments of silence.

'The nurse said she'd take me through what I need to do. There's a list of people to inform and forms to fill in and an order to do things in. I'll work my way through it,' said Shay.

'When do we arrange the funeral?'

'I don't know. I'm sure it'll all be on the list.'

'I imagine there's quite a lot of paperwork. Plus there'll be the house to put up for sale—'

'Jesus Christ, Paula,' snapped Shay. 'She's barely gone and you're ready for erecting a for sale sign?'

For once Paula didn't retaliate like for like.

'It's just how my mind works,' she answered quietly. 'Practical first, emotional second. It's not really hit me yet.'

She sounded so uncharacteristically meek that Shay felt immediately guilty for snapping at her. She knew what Paula meant. She hadn't cried yet; if she cried it meant it was real and something in her brain was trying to repel accepting that fact.

'I don't mind doing the paperwork side of things if you like,' said Shay then.

'Well it makes sense if only one of us does it, we don't want too many cooks spoiling the broth,' Paula replied, then adding quickly, 'we can sort out the terms of her will together after the funeral. I imagine we'll have to apply for probate. Didn't she have some property in Millspring?'

'Just the one cottage. She and Dad sold the others and the monies were all apportioned in their divorce settlement so Mum could fully own the house she lives in—' she swallowed as the present tense rang out as wrong, but she couldn't say 'lived' instead of 'lives'. One small change of letter, one giant change of circumstance.

'Yes, I seem to remember that happening,' said Paula.

They sat quietly in a dreadful vacuum, Shay in a whirl of denial and confusion that they could be here, that the woman in the bed between them was her mother and not her mother at the same time.

'You definitely won't need me for the next few days then?' Paula reaffirmed. 'Because I can be here if it's necessary.'

'I know you're busy, Paula. I really don't mind.'

An awkward trill of laughter, Paula rubbed the back of her neck. 'Well, it's not ... really that ... it's just that it's Chris's birthday tomorrow and we were going up to the Lakes for two nights with friends. I've booked a log cabin and—'

Shay spared her the discomfort of further explanation.

'You go. There's no point in you cancelling it.'

Paula's outward breath of relief. 'Of course if I had to ...'

'You don't. It's fine. You go.'

Shay couldn't think of anything worse than going on holiday the day after her mum's death, unless it was going on holiday the day after her mum's death with Chris Houston, but who was she to judge.

'I was going to call up last weekend and see her,' said Paula with a regretful sigh and a sniff. 'I had a bit of a cold though and I didn't want to pass it on. I wish I'd risked it. If only I'd known.'

Was that true? Who knew. But Shay couldn't be bothered to question it. What good would it even do?

She stood. 'I'll leave you for a few minutes with Mum so you've got some privacy.'

'No, I don't want to be left alone,' said Paula, standing quickly. 'It's not really Mum now, is it? Not any more. I'll go. I've got a taxi waiting outside on the clock. I said I wouldn't be that long; I just wanted to say goodbye and I've done that.'

It wasn't worth Shay's energy being surprised at Paula, it really wasn't.

It was odd to have their family reunited back at the house, albeit just for a short while. Shay made some tea and many rounds of toast which sat on a dinner plate uneaten.

'You been losing weight?' Bruce asked his son.

'I've just cut the crap out of my diet,' Sunny answered. 'I feel better for it.'

'You don't look better for it,' said Courtney with her usual directness. She didn't, however, mention the angry cold sore on the side of his lip, so she did have some sensitivity.

Sunny's phone started vibrating in his pocket. He took it out.

'It's Karoline, I'd better let her know what's happening.' He walked into the hallway to take the call.

'Anyone want a proper drink?' Shay didn't wait for an

answer but went into the lounge for the bottle of malt; she needed something to numb her from the inside out. She could hear Sunny in the snug talking into his mobile.

'I'll be home as soon as I can . . . I'm not leaving them . . . an hour maybe . . . For God's sake, Karoline, my grandmother has just died.'

It didn't sound right, but there was no room in Shay's head for anything else to fret over. Not tonight.

Chapter 17

Shay called at her mother's house just once before the funeral, to pick out something for Roberta to wear. Courtney offered to come with her but she said she'd do it alone. Her daughter, she knew, wouldn't have been any use at all; she'd have cried as soon as she'd opened the wardrobe and seen all her grandmother's colourful clothes lined up, her shoes denoting her age when she wore them from the vintage pin-heel stilettos to the low blocked heels of recent past. Roberta Corrigan was never one for flats; even her slippers were heeled.

How could you choose? But it mattered that she got it right. Courtney would have picked something cosy, slippers and her gran's fleecy dressing gown, but Shay just felt that would have been the wrong choice. There was the red dress her mother had worn for Courtney's twenty-first party; the blue trouser suit she said made her bum look nice; her psychedelic top with the batwing sleeves. There was the turquoise suit with flared trousers she'd only worn once, for Sunny's engagement party. She'd teamed it up with a long string of pearls and a totally over-the-top fascinator. Bruce had asked her if she'd got mixed up and thought she was off to Ascot and they'd all laughed about that in the taxi. And hung up in a plastic suit-cover was the gorgeous violet outfit she'd bought for Sunny's wedding. She'd been so excited about wearing it. Yes, this was what she would want; something elegant and smart, a statement colour. Roberta had always loved clothes, the braver the shade the better, so meeting her maker in violent violet seemed appropriate.

Paula wouldn't have thought of that, she'd have lifted the first thing that came to hand, something mumsy probably because 'what did it matter what she wore'. But it mattered a lot to a woman who had always taken pride in how she looked.

Shay had rung Paula to ask if she wanted anything specifically said in the eulogy.

'Just that she was very clever and kind . . . I don't know, you're better at putting words together than I am.' She'd asked then, 'Are you sure you're okay doing it all? It would upset me too much. You'd think someone would do it for us, wouldn't you?'

'What, like a death fairy?' Shay couldn't resist. Her sarcasm was lost on her sister though.

'Someone from the council maybe. I'm only just beginning to process how much there is to sort out and it's really quite a burden, isn't it? Anyway, when Dad dies, it'll all be taken care of by me so you won't need to be involved. I'll perform my filial duties to the full, I promise.'

The self-sacrifice was thick as syrup in Paula's voice, along with something else that Shay couldn't quite identify; something sour, sly even, but she couldn't give it any energy now. She didn't want to think about their father passing but she hoped that Barbara would take command when the time came because she'd do a loving and sensitive job. For now, Shay was just grateful that her sister had left all the arrangements to her for their mum so that she could go in peace, because there wasn't going to be much of that around when Paula saw her most recent will.

She didn't feel comfortable knowing something about it that Paula didn't because it was sure to cause major ructions – the younger daughter telling the older one how it was, turning the chain of command on its head but what choice did she have? She'd promised her mum she'd carry out her wishes, and she wouldn't break her word, but what a task she'd been left with. She only hoped she could hold the showdown off until after the funeral. Even now, with her mum no longer here, Shay felt as compacted in the middle of that sandwich as she ever was.

She sat at the kitchen table having a cup of black coffee. The whole house felt too empty to try and imagine that her mum was merely outside in the garden or having a natter at Dagmara's. Roberta was gone and her home couldn't make any sense of it.

Everything else could wait, but she needed to throw the perishable food in the cupboards away, the loaf in the bread bin, the milk and cheese, the yoghurt and the bacon in the fridge. But it was the lone Potterworth éclair on the shelf in there that brought the tears fast to her eyes. Her mum's favourite. It never crossed Shay's mind when she bought it for her that she would be dead before she managed to eat it and that realisation made Shay's thoughts spin. How fleeting and fragile life could be, like spider thread. One minute someone was there; the next gone, leaving a space that felt so much bigger than the physical one they had occupied. Tanya's death had punched her heart so brutally, she had felt the bruise for a long time, still did occasionally. It never hurt less, it just hurt less often and she supposed it would be the same with Roberta, because people were hardwired to survive the ongoing circle of existence. But it hadn't been that way when Denny Smith died because that defied the natural order. It had changed the fabric of her down to the DNA; she was not the same Shay Corrigan after it as she was before. The canvas that had grown over the gaping hole he had caused in her kept splitting and as much as she'd tried to stop herself staring into the rottenness in the chasm, she couldn't help herself.

There was a knock at the front door, followed by the sound of it opening.

'Shay? Hello?'

Dagmara Mitic wandered into the kitchen, her smile pinned on as usual, but a different smile today; one of sadness and sympathy. She was carrying a large brown envelope in one hand and a packet of malted milk biscuits in the other.

'Oh my darling Shay,' she said, putting her arms around her, flooding her with the perfume she and her mother both used. It was almost too much, too easy to imagine it was her mother holding her, arms tight about her.

'Would you like a coffee, but I've no milk?' Shay said when she let go, wiping her tears away with the heel of her hand.

'No, I just saw the car and came to see if you were all right. And I brought you these.' Dagmara put the biscuits on the table then sat down, reached for Shay's hand and held it fast.

'I came to get an outfit for Mum,' Shay said. 'I don't want to be here for too long. It feels awful.'

'I know, I know,' said Dagmara. 'What have you chosen?'

'The suit she ordered from your catalogue.'

'Ah.' Dagmara reached into the envelope and took out a photo. Roberta posing in the wedding ensemble, hat on her head at a cheeky tilt, hand on her waist, proud bow of a smile on her face.

'I ran off copy for you. Doesn't she look lovely? She tried it on but it was all creased, so I pressed it and we had fashion show. Perfect fit. She looked like duchess in it.'

Shay's vision blurred, she rubbed at her eyes to clear it. 'It's beautiful, Dagmara. Did she pay you for it?'

'Of course,' said Dagmara. 'From the purse at the back of the drawer where she keeps all her documents. You have to pull it out because it's lodged behind it for safekeeping.'

'Oh, that's why it doesn't shut properly.' Shay gave a small smile, shook her head at how methodical her mum could be at the same time as so muddled.

Dagmara took a hankie out of her pocket and wiped her own eyes.

'She was the best friend I ever had. I will miss her. Who am I going to plan the murder of the pair of Balls with now?'

They both laughed, a well-needed spurt of jollity.

'It's too early I know to talk of things but when you come to sell, Derrick's son Errol would be interested. I hope you don't mind I mention it, Shay, because it will be one less thing for you to have to worry about.'

'I don't mind at all, tell him thank you for me, please. I would like it to go to someone who fits in with you all,' said Shay. Unlike her sister wanting to slap up a for sale notice straightaway, Dagmara's motives were based on thoughtfulness, not greed.

'Are you coping? There is so much to do when your heart

is breaking and your head just wants to lie down until it all goes away.'

'The one thing I can do in my sleep is paperwork, Dagmara,' replied Shay. She wasn't good at delegating and had told Sunny and Courtney and Bruce that she could – and wanted to – handle it all alone, which was why she was exhausted.

Shay drank the last of the coffee in the mug. She'd always enjoyed the cheapish brand her mother preferred, but it didn't taste the same without the warmth in the kitchen, her mother twittering that she wasn't hungry and didn't want anything for tea and Shay insisting she eat: the often frustrating familiarity of their interchanges. A chaos of emotion welled up within her, needing an out.

'Was I a good daughter, Dagmara? You know, when the weather was bad or work was piling up at home or my own kitchen needed cleaning, it felt like a chore when I had to break off and come here sometimes. But I'd give anything to see her again with a list of her to-dos: replace that light-bulb, dust the top of the wardrobe, put that stupid handle back on the cupboard that kept dropping off. I should have forced her to come home with me, not just let her stay here with that monster Drew Balls playing loud music through the walls. Did I let her down, Dagmara?'

'Shh,' Dagmara squeezed her hand tightly. 'You are not a saint, Shay. It's been hard, I know; pressed from all sides. I've been there too. You would not have overruled her and forced her into your car and taken her away because it was important to both of you that she was the mama and you the daughter for as long as you could be like that.' She sat back in the chair, took in the distressed woman opposite her, the child of her dearest friend. 'You were wonderful daughter,

you did *everything* out of love for her so don't doubt yourself. But even the most perfect daughter would hunt around
inside herself now to find something they had not done,
something they had missed, it's what happens when someone you love dies. But no daughter is perfect, no mother is
perfect. We can only do our best, and you always did your
best. You never let her down.'

Shay nodded. Dagmara's brain was just like her mother's
had been when it was bright and sharp and incisive and yet
her body had crumbled so much more than Roberta's. Shay
would have picked the mental advantage every time.

'Did she tell you why we moved here? From Millspring?'

Dagmara gave a small nod.

'Twenty-nine years ago,' replied Shay, 'and it's all as fresh
in my mind as the day it happened. I try to pretend it's not
there in my life, but it never goes away.' She reached behind
her and tore off a square from the kitchen roll. 'I don't think
Mum knew how deeply I felt for Jonah. She thought it was
just young, first-love stuff, innocent, forgettable. And that
one day I'd get over what happened to Denny, make my
peace with it. She admitted to me this week that she thought
I might have done what I'd been accused of, twisted the
truth to make myself come out of it better, but I didn't.'

Dagmara studied this woman in front of her, felt her pain.
She'd heard her friend's version of the story years ago but it
had never been mentioned again, until the past few weeks.
Something about it all had sat unquiet in Roberta too.

'So tell me, Shay. Let me hear what happened from your
own lips.'

Oh, where to begin.

'I can't remember a time before Denny Smith was in my
life. He was the sweetest friend anyone could have. I think

even when I was small, his vulnerability called to me. There was something, I don't know ... pure, ingenuous about Denny, as if he was too good for this world. Jonah said the same once. He had an awful home life. He lived with his pig of a grandfather Bradley, his mum and older sister Rachel on a smallholding. There were rumours that their grandfather was actually their father as well. Rachel had learning difficulties, his mother Ella was odd, his grandfather was vile but Den ... Denny was lovely. He was picked on a bit at school because he was soft, not really the football type if you know what I mean. He liked nature, he liked collecting leaves and sticking them in books. I stood up for him a lot.'

Shay laughed then, because it came to her – right then, and it never had before – where Courtney might have inherited some of her traits from.

'Then one day, not long after my fourteenth birthday, we'd gone to the cinema and were walking home and there was a group of three older boys coming towards us. One was a real nasty piece of work called Glynn Duffy. He had this really flat nose, like an unlucky boxer. They blocked our way. Glynn started pecking at Denny, asking him if he was that kid whose grandad was a pervert. Denny just tried to shrug it off but Glynn was relentless until I couldn't stand it any longer. So I said, "Get lost, nose" which was a really stupid thing to say because you just didn't mention Glynn Duffy's nose. I waited for him to hit me. And then from round the corner came Jonah Wells.'

Shay's face lit up with a smile, remembering it all so clearly. She couldn't have felt more relief if the A Team had turned up. '... I'd been in love with him since I first saw him. He was one of the cool kids, lanky limbs, bright hazel eyes, dark hair that fell where it wanted and a smile that could melt butter at fifty paces. He'd just come from rugby practice and he was with six other players.'

Shay closed her eyes, she could not only see them but feel that glow inside her again as if someone had switched on a light in her heart.

'Jonah looked at us, then at them and said, "Evening, ladies, is there a problem here?" Glynn backed off. And Denny and I went home. I think I floated home if I'm honest. Then a few days later, Jonah came up to me at school when I was at my locker and asked me if I was okay and' – Shay put her hands to her cheeks – 'I can feel myself blushing now because this "It" boy was talking to me. In fact, everywhere I seemed to go, he was there as well, as if we were gravitating to each other. And not just me because he'd say "all right" to Denny and Den got some street cred for that, because if Jonah Wells had time for him, it was the best endorsement. And I have no idea how it happened, but the three of us starting hanging around together. Obviously we weren't Jonah's only mates because he had his rugby lot and everyone wanted to be in his orbit, but he liked us and we'd go for walks and sometimes we'd pitch tents in the wood and have a barbecue, stay out there all night.'

'It sounds lovely,' said Dagmara. Roberta hadn't gone into a lot of detail with her version of events, until recently, when she was desperate to remember everything but couldn't.

'It was. But then things began to change. We were getting older, hormones kicked in. Denny always used to tease me about me fancying Jonah but it was much more than that, I was falling in love with him, and I felt bad about that because I knew how much Denny felt for me. Then one night Denny couldn't get out to go camping with us and it was just us two. I don't think Mum or Dad would have let me stay out if they'd thought it was just going to be Jonah and me, because having Denny there added . . . an innocence to us, if you know what I mean. So . . . needless to say, I didn't tell them.' Shay swallowed hard. 'How can I remember this so clearly after all these years?'

Dagmara gave a small chuckle. 'I too remember everything, when we had to leave Latvia: the sounds, the fear that can still make my heart race, and how my lungs burned when we ran. I remember it all.'

'You can guess what happened when we were alone, under the stars. We were sixteen, we weren't too young, we were ready and it was wonderful. I thought I was going to burst I was so happy. I loved Jonah and I know he loved me and it was real, proper love. The only worry was telling Denny. We didn't want him to feel squeezed out.'

'That was kind of you,' said Dagmara.

'We were a three and we didn't want it to alter our friendship. He seemed fine about it when I told him, I was so relieved when he said he was happy for us. Then suddenly he wasn't any more; he just cut us off. He didn't call at my house, he didn't ring for a chat. We should have been going camping together, the last time before our summer jobs started and I went up to the farm for him, but he was really odd. What I didn't know then was that his grandfather had run off and I've often wondered if that had a part to play. But then again, he could only have felt relief because the man was a beast.'

'A big responsibility for a young boy if he had to take care of his mother and sister,' said Dagmara.

'Denny would have though, he was that kind of person. I know it wasn't that. He said he wasn't coming camping with us. He said that I had Jonah now and not to worry about him and I told him not to be such a dick because we were a three and we always would be. He didn't want to talk to me and Denny talked to me about everything so I knew something was really wrong. I said I wasn't leaving without him and he screamed at me to go away, swore at me, he even pushed me. That wasn't him. He'd never been like that with me before, but I knew he was upset so I took it on the chin, I didn't give him a single reason to fight with me. I said I'd be back tomorrow. But I never got to speak to him again.'

Shay let out a juddering breath; the heat of a real, physical pain flared up inside her.

'Denny went missing the day after I'd last seen him. When we heard, we went searching with everyone. I don't know what made me think of it but I had a horrible feeling where he might be and I was right. It was Jonah and I who found him in Millspring woods. He'd hanged himself from our tree, where we used to camp. And the only possible explanation for that at the time was that he'd done it in that particular place because he was so upset about Jonah and me and he wanted to spoil it for us ever meeting there again. That's what people said and it made perfect sense, but then again it didn't because Denny would never have been so bitter.'

'I'm so sorry, you poor girl.'

'The police interviewed me; they said they'd been told that I'd gone up to the farm the day before and shouted at him, told him that I didn't want to see him any more because I had Jonah. They said that's what his mother had overheard, but I swear on my life, Dagmara, that's not what happened. But who were people more likely to believe, who would they want to believe, a sixteen-year-old girl protesting her innocence or a grieving mother who said I'd broken her son's heart?'

Shay's head fell into her hands. If only she could lay physical hands on the part of her brain where all this had stayed, festered, she would have cut it out with a knife.

'It was in the newspaper with some lurid, sensationalist headline; they didn't name me of course but everyone knew who I was, this callous cow who'd driven her friend to take his own life. The gossip machine cranked up and a few people really had a field day, adding bits on, spicing things up. They'd have burnt me as a witch if they could. I was blamed entirely; cancelled, before it even became a thing.' Large teardrops tickled down her cheeks; she dashed them away, only for them to be replaced by more. 'I didn't want to see Jonah any more, I couldn't think about him without thinking about what we must have done to Denny. Not that he tried to contact me anyway, which said everything.

'I was a mess, I was terrified to leave the house, I daren't even go outside into the garden, I felt as if the top layer of my skin had been peeled off and everything hurt. I just wanted to die. That was when Mum decided we had to leave. It all seemed to happen so quickly. I dropped a year of my life. Then I picked it up again. Went to a sixth form where no one knew me or my history, met new friends, rejoined the world. But I've never felt as if I was on the track I should have been on and I never got the chance to try and get back on it. Does this make any sense?'

'Oh yes,' said Dagmara. 'I know. My life also. A different life but mine has been very happy ...' She reached out to Shay, smeared away a fresh tear from under her eye, '... you have a lot of open wounds.'

'And they won't heal, Dagmara, because there's so much inside me that's unresolved. I've never been back to Millspring, yet sometimes ... I think I should, because I feel as if I was pulled out of it, like a bee from a sting, and I left too much of myself behind.'

'So you never heard again from the boy you loved?' asked Dagmara.

'No, never.' She knew she never would either. So there had been no point in keeping her heart open for Jonah Wells.

Dagmara smiled at her, a wise, sympathetic curve of her lips. 'Shay, I'm sure you have thought over the years that there must have been much more going on in that young man's mind than you knew about, for him to have done what he did.'

'Yes, Dagmara, but I can't work out what it was. I know ...' – Shay pressed her fist into her heart – 'I *know* that what I remember is the absolute truth. I'm not my mum remembering eating ice creams with Omar Sharif when it never happened.'

Dagmara was silent, thoughtful. She had to be careful what she said next, let out just a little of what she knew. Her old friend had left her with a burden that was already too heavy to bear, secrets that weren't hers to keep.

'What if I told you that ... that your mother regretted leaving Millspring. That she acted only out of love for you.'

'I know she did.' A sigh came out of the very deepest place in Shay. 'I don't blame her, Dagmara.'

'She didn't want you to get hurt any more,' said Dagmara.

'I was just whisked away though, and she tried to plaster over it and I let her think she had, but she hadn't.'

Dagmara remained silent, but she knew that Mr Sharif's skip had made Roberta face the things she had run from: and even in her confused and muddled brain she'd had to finally admit that some truths could never entirely be covered by lies. They would fight and claw and bleed and leak and do everything they could to find their way to the surface, however long it took.

'I'd better go,' said Shay. 'I'm sorry, none of this was meant to come out.'

'I think it was ready to come out,' replied Dagmara.

Chapter 18

Shay sat beside her father, gently holding his hand as she clipped his fingernails, then filed them so there were no rough edges. Harry had been a plumber and his hands were roughened but he'd used industrial-strength hand cream to try and undo some of the damage and he hated dirty fingernails with a passion. He said it was because they reminded him of his father's unkempt hands, and they had been cruel, unkind hands to him.

'I have some news, Dad,' said Shay and then took a breath. 'Mum died. I know you'd want to be told.' She looked at him: if ever there was a time when he would manifest a response, it would be now – but there was nothing. Shay swallowed hard, not sure why his lack of reaction upset her so much when she could expect nothing else. 'I did think about not telling you for a while. I know that whatever has gone on between you in the past, you'd still be upset. You were together a long time, weren't you?'

She'd wondered a lot since her mum had died about what had really kept her parents together for so long. She knew that her mum had forgiven her dad for his infidelities, but what was it that he tried to find in other women that he didn't get from his wife? Shay hadn't felt it her place to ask, and now she'd never know.

When they moved from Millspring, both Harry and Roberta had worked as a single unit to support her, heal her. Their new home in Merriment Close was full of warmth and it had made her realise, only by comparison, that it hadn't quite been like that when they lived in the Old Rectory. But then she'd left home to be married to Bruce and her parents had stayed with each other for another eighteen years before finally splitting. Who knew what the glue was in people's marriages? Take Les and Morton, there had to be more than the wild sex. Or was it just that the other sorts of glue that bound people together pretended too well to be love.

'She's going to be wearing a very vivid, violet suit,' Shay went on. 'Do you remember her wardrobe, Dad? There wasn't a black or navy thing in it. I wonder if that's where Courtney gets it from.' She hadn't thought about it before, but it made perfect sense, if such things can be passed on through generations. Maybe that's how her children had been gifted their artistic talents, from some throwback ancestor. The Italian one, maybe.

'Do you remember when she had that animal-print suit and the matching shoes, Dad, and you said she shouldn't go out in public like that in case someone thought she'd escaped from a zoo and shot her.' She chuckled and then it somehow segued into sadness because her dad wasn't laughing along with her. They'd both ached from the pains in their stomachs when he'd said it all those years ago, the humour exacerbated by Roberta standing there with her arms akimbo, face frozen, waiting for them to stop. She'd never hear the boom of his laugh again, see the smile that was so wide it almost reached his big ears. Her daddy was here and he was gone, the worst sort of paradox.

There was a small knock at the door then and Shay scrabbled to compose herself before it opened.

'Is it okay to come in?' It was Barbara.

'Of course,' said Shay; her father's wife didn't need her permission.

'Hello, my darling,' said Barbara, leaning over Harry, giving him a kiss, stroking his hair back tenderly before taking a seat at the other side of the bed and addressing Shay. 'Oh, you're doing his nails, that's lovely. My hands aren't very good these days or I'd have done them for him.' She held out her hand which was lumpy and twisted from arthritis. 'I used to play the piano every day but no more, sadly,' she added.

She'd aged since the last time Shay had seen her, when they'd brought her father here all those months ago. Her face was a portrait of tiredness and helplessness underneath the make-up but she was smartly dressed and her blonde hair styled. Her father's fashion sense had sharpened being with her, though strangely it never had being with her mother.

'I shan't be long,' said Shay. 'I don't want to leave any sharp bits.'

'I used to massage his hands, he loved it,' replied Barbara with a smile, before remembering who she was talking to and twittering an apology.

'You don't need to say sorry, Barbara. You're his wife.'

'Well you're his daughter and you don't need to rush off on my account,' came the reply. 'He'll be enjoying you being here telling him your news.'

'Maybe not my news today. I just came to tell him that Mum died.'

'Oh Shay, I am so sorry.' Barbara's response was immediate and genuine. 'That's so sad. I know Harry would be heartbroken about that.'

'I didn't know if I should tell him,' replied Shay, touched by Barbara's words. 'It didn't seem right to and it didn't seem right not to either.'

'He never bad-mouthed her once, you know,' said Barbara. 'He always gave her full respect as the mother of his children.'

'That's nice to hear,' replied Shay, with a lump of emotion in her throat as big as a dwarf planet. She put her dad's hand carefully down by his side and slipped on her jacket. She'd leave her father with his wife now.

'I don't think your sister comes here. Paula. Is she all right?'

How to reply to that; with the standard answer that flowed too easily from the lips: *She's busy.* Instead she plumped for: 'Paula and I see things very differently.' Barbara nodded, gave a small sigh, read the meaning in her words.

Shay leaned over and gave her dad a kiss on his cheek. His skin was smooth and soft and strangely youthful.

'He loves you both,' Barbara said then. 'But I could always tell that he liked you much more.' She smiled. 'You look after yourself, Shay.'

'And you, Barbara. I know how hard this is on you.'

Both women reached out simultaneously and squeezed each other's hands, communicating something complex, but shining through was their mutual love for the man they had both come to see.

Chapter 19

The funeral procession left from Merriment Close, the home her mother loved; her sanctuary for so many years, the place where she felt safe and happy among neighbours, friends. They were out in force today, all of them – bar two contemptible exceptions – in their finest suits and dresses, standing outside in the pouring rain under umbrellas in a respectful line, ready to join the cortege of cars.

'The sky's crying for Gran,' said Courtney, dressed in traditional black and playing the dress code down to the black lacy gloves and black lipstick and nail polish. Her hair was neon violet, to match her gran's outfit, although she'd toyed with dyeing that black too. Like Sunny, her head was full of self-recrimination that she hadn't been to see her gran as much as she should have over the past year. She'd presumed she'd be there forever, or at least give plenty of advance warning before leaving them. A brutal life lesson notched up.

'I hope you're going to behave,' said Bruce. 'No dramatics. This is your gran's day.'

Courtney wrinkled up her lip at him. 'As if. I know, Dad.'

Karoline was there with Sunny, stylishly and respectfully dressed in black. They'd greeted each other warmly and Shay was glad that Sunny had her to hold him up because he looked a wreck. She'd filled out a little since Shay had seen her last all those months ago at the engagement party, her cheeks had grown plumper but it suited her. She really did have the prettiest face: large blue eyes, long dark lashes, small tip-tilted nose, full rose-pink lips. She looked like a perfectly-iced cake, as if a sweet vanilla sponge lay underneath that flawless skin. Her figure, though, was less curvy and more blockish now. It was almost as if she was putting on some of the weight that Sunny had lost. Shay hoped that Bruce's prediction was wrong and Karoline's fate wouldn't be to morph into her mother Angela, who had jowls that shuddered in a light breeze and mean, pinched facial features that a pound of Botox, a bottle of Lenor and a heavy flat iron wouldn't have been able to soften.

There were no builders' vans on the Close that day – probably rain had stopped play, but in the centre of the green a large digger sat like a smug metal spider, a portent of more disruptive work to come.

As the limo pulled away from the house, Shay noticed Drew Balls standing in his window, grinning, waving. She'd never loathed anyone as much in her life. She turned her head from him sharply because today was about her mum, not him. Today was about love, not hate.

Bruce held her hand tightly. The morning of her mum's death, after Courtney and Sunny had driven home, she'd crawled into bed and been surprised that Bruce had slipped in beside her. And every night since. He'd just held her, been there for her. He'd come back from work early, forgoing the gym and he'd asked her if she wanted cups of tea, coffee, a glass of wine which she couldn't remember him doing for ages. He'd helped her with some paperwork, he'd even forced her to have some toast when he thought she hadn't eaten and the last time she recalled him doing that was when Courtney hadn't been sleeping as a baby and she was constantly off her face with tiredness. He'd been kind and she'd felt a shift in their relationship, a change of course back to what they should be.

Shay scanned the crowd waiting outside the crematorium chapel for Les, but there was no sign. Shay had rung her twice, left a voicemail and followed it up with a text: once to let her know about her mum's passing, then to tell her the date of the funeral because, whatever was going on in her own life, Shay would have put all her savings on Les being there for her at this time, when it counted.

The service went perfectly. Dagmara read a poem she'd written, about love being everlasting; Shay stood up to do the eulogy, about how special a person their mum was, too special for just a short speech, but she hoped to do Roberta proud. She thanked the people of Merriment Close for being so loyal and considerate and affirmed how much their mother thought of them all. She told everyone how Roberta had always been there for her daughters whenever they needed her and how she and Harry had looked after their grandchildren when Shay had had to go out to work and about the activities they'd done together. She said how clever Roberta was at languages and had planned to run her own school, but she'd put her family commitments above any of her lofty ambitions.

Shay had written plenty of humour into her speech because she knew it would keep her strong enough to deliver it. She related how Roberta couldn't remember the English word for skip and yet had never lost a word of Russian, and after watching a James Bond film recently had declared that she'd had a short career as an international spy. She made the congregation laugh by saying how, before she died, Roberta remembered having chocolate ice cream with Omar Sharif at the seaside and how happy it made her. She did not say that her mother had been a rock when Shay was accused of being responsible for the death of a boy, had sat by her daughter's bedside praying that she'd be okay, had done everything in her power to bring her daughter back from the edge of a very dark brink.

They listened to Roberta's chosen song, 'The First Time Ever I Saw Your Face' and Shay wondered why she'd picked that. She couldn't imagine the passion that song evoked being directed at her dad. But then she thought all children must think that of their parents, forget they were once youngsters with carnal desires who snogged and groped each other in cars. As the song played, a succession of photos that Shay had chosen flashed up on a screen: grainy black and white ones of Roberta as a chubby child in a frilly hat; a teenager with her long strawberry-blonde waves, linking arms with her dark-haired, Sophia Lorenesque sister Stella; as a bride in a frilly white dress, her waist tiny. As an exhausted, beatific mum holding her first newly-birthed daughter, as a smiling, contented woman holding her newly-born second child; all stages of her life, but her smile never ageing. A photo of her and Dagmara peering around a tree in the park, looking like naughty children trapped in pensioners' bodies; wearing a bright pink wig at her seventieth birthday party; photos of her with Courtney and Sunny, every inch the proud grandmother. One of her dazzling in her violent violet suit that she'd intended to wear at Sunny's wedding; the same photo stood in a frame on her coffin.

Shay felt the creak of the closing curtains make an echo in her breast. She wanted to rip them open, tear her mother out of her casket, see her one last time, kiss her goodbye. She wasn't ready to let her go; she would never be ready to let her go. It was as if someone had pulled the floor from under her feet and there was nothing to grab hold of to stop the fall.

As they left the crematorium, the family lined up outside to say thank you to everyone and reiterate the invitation to join them for a bite to eat. Shay looked again for Les but there was no sight of her. She said as much to Bruce as they were being driven to the community centre in the limo.

'I don't know why she's not here,' was his answer to that, accompanied by a shrug. 'Funerals aren't for everyone are they?'

'Mort says that Les still hasn't been in touch properly with him either, just a text here and there to tell him to stop bothering her, the old cow,' said Courtney.

Chris, Paula's husband, cleared his throat in such a way as to express disapproval of his niece's language, without being brave enough to actually voice his opinion in words.

Paula's hat took up a huge proportion of the car. It was as wide as a flying saucer with a veil expertly draped over her sad expression.

'That went well,' she said.

'Yes, very nice service,' added Chris. His shirt was straining over his gut and if one of those buttons popped off, it would spring like a bullet and shoot someone, Shay thought. Funny what the brain conjured up at such times. She imagined her mum noticing the poor buttons' valiant effort to do their duty and saying something inappropriate like, 'There's no shame in buying bigger shirts, Christopher, if there's comfort to be had,' and she dropped her head to hide an inappropriate smile.

'Funny song choice, I thought,' said Paula.

'That's what Mum stipulated she wanted.'

'Not be long until Sunny's wedding, will it?' Paula asked. 'Eight weeks I think I worked it out as. Are you a brides-maid, Courtney?'

'Good question, Auntie Paula. I haven't had the official request so I reckon it must be lost in the post.' Courtney's reply gave every indication that this subject was a sore point, especially as it was accompanied by a few under-breath mumblings which may or may not have been expletives.

Paula turned back to Shay. 'I've got the rest of the week off so if you want to meet me at Mum's tomorrow we can discuss what happens next.' She meant dish out the money of course. Paula wasn't the type to start packing things in boxes and organising what to do with all her mother's effects, she just wanted to bank the cheque.

'Yes, of course,' said Shay, her small smile disguising her great dread.

'How's business, Chris?' asked Bruce.

Chris replied in his smug, toady voice, 'Couldn't be better.' He considered himself a cut above a sole-trading electrician, at least until he was chasing some invest-ment: then he'd open up like a book with a broken spine to anyone.

'Is this really July?' Paula looked out of the window at the clouds which were the same miserable grey shade as her hair.

'Sunny's doing well for himself,' Chris remarked, as the silver Porsche bearing Karoline and Sunny over-took the limo.

'It's Karoline's car,' said Courtney. 'Hence the personalised number plate.'

'Very nice.' Chris was virtually salivating.

'Karoline's parents are loaded,' added Courtney with relish. 'Always making clever investments.'

You little minx, thought Shay.

'There are two lots of people who have personalised reg plates, I always think,' Courtney continued. 'Total show-offs and those trying to cover up how old their cars are.'

'Courtney.' A warning from Bruce.

'Not necessarily, Courtney,' said Chris. 'Both your Auntie Paula and I have them on our cars.'

Courtney's ensuing silence spoke volumes. Shay would have words with her daughter when they were alone, unless her father got in first.

'Awful weather,' said Paula as the rain suddenly increased, as if someone had twisted a tap in the clouds. The limo driver upped the speed on his wipers.

'I went to tell Dad about Mum,' said Shay.

'Well that was a wasted trip,' said Paula.

'That's a bit harsh, Paula,' said Bruce, stepping in.

'I think Paula means he can't have registered the information,' Chris immediately came to his wife's defence.

'You can't know that for sure, Chris,' said Shay.

'I could take an educated guess,' replied Chris, adding, 'Sadly', in an attempt to head off causing offence.

Shay opened up her mouth to remonstrate but today was not a day to butt antlers, especially not with a pig-headed, stubborn, 'I'm always right even when I'm wrong' blubber mountain such as her brother-in-law. He'd been an arrogant piece of work when Paula first started going out with him and Shay could never figure out if her sister had been responsible for forming him into this finished model or if he'd formed her or if they'd both grown naturally into a pair of galvanised, self-serving shits.

The designated room in the community centre was full of people either in knots talking or queueing at the bar in the corner by the time the limo arrived there. Waitresses were ferrying cling-filmed plates of buffet fare from the kitchen to a long table. There was a lot of food.

'Bet this cost a pretty penny,' said Chris, who referenced money a lot.

'Yes, it did,' replied Shay. 'My mum would want there to be plenty for everyone.' Roberta had been to a few funerals over the past years and she always took great delight in telling Shay what the post-service refreshments were like. The buffet reflected the respect in which the family held the deceased, was her philosophy. By that measure, no one was going to talk about them penny-pinching today. Shay also knew as soon as that cling film came off, Chris would be elbowing pensioners out of the way to get to the pastry. She heard him mutter the word 'excessive' at his wife and was tempted to knee him in the balls. Bruce bought a round of drinks; it wouldn't have entered Chris's brain to offer first. Shay guessed he'd have conveniently disappeared by the time it came to reciprocate.

She felt a tug on her sleeve and turned round to see Dagmara dressed in her black finery, including a cloche hat with a large bow at the front which made her look very vintage and sweet.

'Dear Shay,' she said. Tear lines had cut through the thickly applied powder on her face. 'That was a beautiful service. You said all the right words, your mama would be so proud of you. I know how hard it is to stand up and say them when your heart is crying inside.'

Shay squeezed her tiny hand.

'Thank you for coming, Dagmara. I think everyone from Merriment Close is here. Apart from you-know-who.'

Dagmara leaned in close.

'Roberta will have last laugh, don't you have any doubt about that.'

After talking to a few more of her mum's neighbours, Shay then managed to head over to her son who was standing with his fiancée. She noticed Karoline's hand coiled around Sunny's arm and an image came into her mind of a snake which was ridiculous. Maybe Bruce was right and there was some underlying jealousy there that she had been supplanted in her son's heart as number one woman.

Sunny had met Karoline just after he'd finished his degree, when he'd been working through the summer in a farm shop in Wakefield. She was seven years older than him, confident and assured, intelligent and forthright with a cracking figure and blonde hair out of a bottle, but expertly done. She had been a totally fresh taste of mature woman for the 'geek-chic' Sunny, who had more than a touch of the Clark Kents about him. He'd never wanted to go hardcore clubbing or to foam parties in Ibiza or ride on giant bananas, quads or jet-skis, much to his mother's relief. He was a quiet, decent kid with a love of rugby, a passion for art and a fire in his belly, even though he hadn't been sure what for. Shay had hoped he'd find the path that suited his talents, not have his ambitions so easily extinguished by one squirt of a woman's seductive perfume.

'Very sorry that we're meeting again for such a sad occasion,' Karoline's words were slow and spaced, each one perfectly enunciated. She'd been privately educated, her Yorkshire accent exorcised.

'Yes, it is. How are the wedding plans going?'

'Very well, thank you.'

'If you need any help . . .' Shay offered.

'Thank you, I have it under control.'

'I', not *'we'*, Shay noticed.

'Did I hear wedding talk?' Courtney crashed in from nowhere, knocking her brother forward and almost sending his drink over the rim of the glass. Bruce's description of her as a wrecking ball was disturbingly accurate sometimes.

'So when do I need to make myself available for my bridesmaid's dress fitting?' asked Courtney, with a mile-wide smile. She looked up at her brother adoringly then. 'You are having me, aren't you? I mean, I am the only sister of the groom.'

Shay gave her daughter a withering look, even though she did have a point.

'I'm sorry, Courtney, but we've decided not to have grown-up bridesmaids. I hope you're not too disappointed,' replied Karoline with a regretful smile.

'Sunny?' Courtney ignored her and continued to flutter her eyelashes at her brother.

Shay watched the colour creep into her son's cheeks. Then as if he was an animal caught hopelessly in a trap, his sister took pity on him, sprung the lock and released him.

'Yeah, well it's your nuptials so you know where I am if you change your mind.' She put her arm around her brother and squeezed him, though Karoline was still clinging to his arm at the other side. 'You still playing rugby, bro?'

'Yes, I am.'

'Well, be careful because you could puncture the ball with those ribs. Karoline, are you feeding this boy?'

'Court, pack it in.' Sunny was at the end of his patience with her now.

'Actually, Sunny's been on a diet to fit into his suit,' said Karoline.

'Should have just bought a bigger suit. He looks more like a clothes prop than a prop forward.'

Sunny made a noisy outward breath of irritation.

'I think we will be heading home soon.' Karoline pushed out another smile. 'I hope next time we'll be together in happier circumstances.'

'Have you met our Auntie Paula?' Courtney said to her. 'You'd get on like a house on fire.'

'Thank you for inviting us.' Karoline leaned forward to give Shay a kiss on her cheek.

'Are you really going so soon?' asked Courtney. 'Sunny, stay longer, *pleeease*. I hardly ever get to see you. I might just turn up at your house unannounced one day to check up on you.' She grinned as angelically as one could with black lipstick. 'You can take that as either a promise or a threat.'

'I hope you all stay well,' Karoline said, managing to make it sound like a papal blessing. 'I'm sorry, I need some air, I'll let you say goodbye to Sunny. Sorry, have to . . .' With that she turned, cut through the people around them while fanning her face with her hand.

'Let?' commented Courtney, when she'd gone. 'That's big of her.'

Sunny rubbed his ear, that nervous gesture again, his mother noted.

'She didn't mean it like that so stop picking fights. Especially here, today. As if things aren't bad enough.'

Courtney was shamed sufficiently by that to say a sub-
dued, 'Sorry, bro.'

'She's not well, Courtney. You're lucky she made it today.'

'She still stressed and off work?' asked Shay.

'Yeah. Mum, do you need me to do anything for you?'

'No, darling, but thank you for asking.'

Sunny bent to his mum, put his arms around her, kissed
her cheek. Shay held her lovely boy tight. Courtney was
right, he was all bone and no flesh. She didn't buy the
'dieting into a suit' line one bit but his weight had been
mentioned too much already and she could tell it was starting to grate with him.

'And me,' said Courtney, tapping her cheek with
her finger.

'You don't make it easy for anyone, do you, Court,' he
said, kissing her, despite his annoyance.

'Please eat, Sunny. I might be starting to worry about
you. And ring me. And ring Mum.'

Shay gave her daughter daggers when Sunny had gone to
find his father to say goodbye.

'What?' Courtney answered the look.

'You, that's what.' She suspected Courtney was a little
jealous of Karoline too.

'Can you blame me? Karoline's still got a stick up her arse.'

'No she hasn't. You made that awkward for your brother.
You might as well have asked him to pick a side,' said Shay.

'I think that's what she's made him do already, Mum,'
Courtney answered her. 'Does he look like Sunny any more
to you? Because he looks like a drippy weed to me. He's
withering away to nothing. I can't get my head around the
dynamics of that relationship at all. He's changed so much
since he's been with her. It's as if she's sucked the essence of

him out like some parasite and I can't think why she'd do that. Why do people fall in love with you for what you are and then want to change you? Now, where's Dad, because all this bear-baiting has made me thirsty.'

'I hope you aren't driving home.'

Courtney huffed. 'No, of course not, I'm getting a lift from—' A beat. A horribly telling one. 'Someone.'

'Oh no, Courtney. Please don't tell me you mean Dingo.'

'I know what you're going to say, but hear me out. Completely fresh start. He's finally got his act together. He's going to be a competitive eater and set up his own YouTube channel and earn a fortune. And, he's now on an anger management course. Oh, and he's allowed to drive again. He's a new man, Mum. Really.'

And with that Courtney, the daughter who could apparently see her brother's relationship with a clarity that she couldn't apply to her own love life, was gone to hunt her father down.

Chapter 20

'Sure you don't want some of this?' asked Bruce. He'd flung two pasta packet mixes into a pan and added boiling water which was in line with his culinary expertise.

'No thanks,' said Shay, still in her black getup. Unlike him, she hadn't changed into something more comfortable, as if on some subconscious level, it kept her connected to the day, to her mother.

'You haven't eaten anything all day, have you?' Bruce stirred, channelling his inner Gordon Ramsay. 'Mind you, I'm surprised anyone got near the buffet with that greedy pillock around. His plate was piled up so high there was a bloody Sherpa perched on it. His first plate, anyway. God knows how many times he went back.'

As soon as the cling film had been removed from the buffet plates, Chris, true to form, had been in like Flynn. He would have given new competitive professional eater Dingo Shaw a run for his money.

'Yes, he likes his food, does old Chris,' agreed Shay.

'He likes his *free* food. Sponging arsehole, I can't abide him,' Bruce declared. 'I was standing outside and he arrived for a smoke, big fat Winston Churchill cigar. I knew he hadn't come to seek me out for witty repartee, so I let him do the small-talk lead-up to wherever he was heading and guess what? He wants me to invest in his fancy water filter business. I'm at my mother-in-law's funeral having a breather and he's rattling on about poncy taps and guaranteed returns on my capital while polluting my airspace.'

'You're not going to, are you?'

Bruce's jaw dropped and he pushed up his hair at the front. 'Shay, do I have dick written on my head? If business is so good for him why is he mortgaged up to the hilt with debts up to his nostrils?'

'You don't know that for sure, Bruce.'

'Yes, I do. I did my homework on Chris Houston the last time he asked me to jump in on one of his surefire deals.' He tapped his nose. 'I know people in the know.'

And Shay wanted to say then that he hadn't known people in the know when she'd wanted help with her mum's neighbours.

That thought came again, the one she couldn't pin down when she'd last asked him about the building work at her mum's house, dipping into her mind and straight back out again. Like it mattered now anyway, whatever it was.

Shay was tired, dog-tired. She'd barely slept the previous night, though adrenaline had kept her propped up for most of the day while she orchestrated the funeral as best she could, made sure it went as seamlessly as possible. But once people started drifting off home, it left her system with a whoosh and there was nothing to replenish it but weariness and worry: her indecipherable son, her unfathomable daughter, anxiety about meeting with Paula the next day and outshining everything with its nuclear brightness was the cold, hard certainty that she would never see her mum again. She was on her second large glass of red wine and it was doing nothing to cauterise her frayed, ragged nerves.

'Sunny looked slick in his suit today, I thought.' Bruce came over to the table carrying a bowl of pasta. He hadn't stirred it properly or added enough water because the sauce looked clotted. 'He'll be laughing when Karoline inherits all her parents' money. I bet Chris can't wait to sidle up to them at the wedding and dangle his worm for an investment, the slimy—'

'Money isn't everything, is it?' Shay interrupted him. 'And Sunny doesn't look like himself or act like himself at the moment. He's like a shadow of what he was when he lived here and—'

Bruce dropped his fork, by design or accident Shay wasn't sure.

'Oh, please don't start with that again. He's not a little smiley boy any more, colouring-in pictures. He's a grown man with responsibilities. If he's unhappy then that's for him to sort out. What he does is nothing to do with you.'

'What?' Shay shook her head as if to rattle all those words into a sentence that made sense.

'You're imagining things. Sunny's fine, how can he not be? Karoline's gorgeous, she's got her head screwed on and she's got a few bob to her name. Now she might not be your choice but she's his. And Courtney's . . . well, Courtney. You can't even try and sort her out because she'll do what she wants to.'

'So that's fine in your book, is it then?' said Shay, suddenly irritated. 'Because they're grown up, I have to cut myself off from worrying about them?'

'Well, yes,' said Bruce, as if that was obvious.

Shay reared internally.

'Bruce, I would be delighted to cut the apron strings. I would gladly stand on the doorstep and wave goodbye to my two chicks flying confidently off in the direction of the sun, so if you think I'm just fretting because I'm bored, trust me I am not. Neither have I any intention of clipping their wings just so they'll stick around us so I can keep a beady eye on them, but don't expect me to watch them falling out of the sky and stand by doing absolutely . . . fuck all, while they crash and burn.'

Bruce stopped chewing for a second as the shock of hearing his wife use the F-word disabled his jaw.

'What are you talking about – birds? They're not bloody birds. They're people and they don't need us any more, Shay, and the sooner you get that into your skull, the better it will be for everyone.'

'They're *young* people and of course they still need us. Don't you see what's going on with them, Bruce? Have you ever?'

'What's that supposed to mean?'

Somewhere in Shay an alarm bell went off, informing her that she was about to overstep a mark. She pressed on the snooze button to silence it and let rip.

'You've never put the effort into them. It's as if once my egg was fertilised, your job was done. When Courtney was playing up at school, who went to see her teachers? Who sat up with her all night when she'd taken that pill and was gurning like a lunatic and which one of us went to bed? When Sunny was being bullied, who went to talk to the parents? Who queued up hours to see Santa with them, who went to watch them in their school concerts, who was there in the audience when they were picking up their awards . . . and who wasn't?'

'I was bloody working,' replied Bruce, stabbing himself in the chest with an affronted finger.

'So was I,' yelled Shay. 'I was working *and* washing *and* cooking and raising *our* children *and* putting your drunken father to bed *and* looking after your mum, juggling, keeping all the balls in the air however bloody worn-out I was. Being a parent means a little bit more than slapping a wage down on the table every week and then putting your feet up because in your eyes, that's the whole father duty thing taken care of. You chose to hide behind your work and leave everything to me without a second thought. The only way you'd have ever noticed how much I did, Bruce, is if I stopped doing it and I wish I had, just for a week so you'd see. You don't know the half of it because you left your mum and moved straight into another house where another woman was expected to do everything except twist wires together and drive a van. What I do is just shove clothes in a washing machine and flick a duster at things and put new sheets on beds and faff about a bit on a laptop booking hotels. How have I the brass neck to get tired?'

'If you're tired then you've been doing too much, haven't you?' Bruce matched her for volume. 'Far more than you needed to because there's something inside you, Shay, that is terrified your kids will fall off the end of the earth if they make a mistake. Okay, you had a friend who topped himself and that's probably why you've hovered over your kids like a—'

Shay was straight on the word. '*Your?*'

'Okay, *our* then. You know what I meant.'

'Do not accuse me of being a helicopter parent, if that's

where this is heading. I'm just being an ordinary, caring parent. And if I did such a crap job of it, if you were any sort of father you'd have jumped in and done something a bit more constructive than stop your children's pocket money for a week.'

Bruce prepared for a full-on volley. 'Maybe that's why our marriage is the way it is, because being a parent is so much more important to you than being a wife.'

'And maybe if you'd pulled your weight as a parent and I didn't have to be both mother and father to our children. Maybe if you'd pulled your weight as a son and hadn't buried me under all the responsibilities you couldn't be bothered to carry. Maybe if you'd been more of a husband, I'd have had more time to be a wife.'

That stunned him, she knew, but she hadn't finished, not by a long chalk. 'You know, Bruce, everything good that's happened in this marriage is because of me. I decorated this house, I chose the furniture, I painted the walls. I picked the holidays, I bought the clothes, I packed the suitcases, I organised parties, outings, booked meals, weekends away, stuck the photos in the family albums. I put the Christmas decorations up, I wrote the cards, I bought all the children's presents, I wrapped them and then I stuck them under the tree that I'd put up by myself. And we both have allowed you to believe that it was all a joint effort.'

A combustible silence followed, waiting for a match, but Bruce, this time, had no rejoinder. He just stared at her for so long after her last word that she wondered if he was in fact anticipating an apology.

'Well, that's been sitting waiting inside you to come out, hasn't it?' he said eventually, more breath than voice.

She didn't answer, because she hadn't known she'd had

all those words inside her either. But she stood by them, every one of them.

Bruce dropped his eyes as if the sight of her burnt him. 'Well,' he said again. Shay imagined inside his head a legion of small soldiers battling back the absorption of her words before they could be digested and were converted into shame.

He got up, scraped his clotty meal into the bin and then without anything further being spoken, he went upstairs, his feet a slow, heavy rhythm of indignation.

Shay put her head in her hands and just breathed to steady herself. No tears came because she was dried out, she felt empty, hollow. She wished Tanya were here, with her wisdom and her softness. Les would have said, 'Just follow him upstairs, have a shag and it'll be forgotten by the morning', her standard mantra. Tanya would have made her some tea to wet her overworked throat and then forbade her from starting the self-recriminations, because it was all true and should have been let out long ago.

But was she over-protective, as Bruce had levelled at her? Didn't all parents want to gift their children the wisdom they'd built up, a guide to avoid mistakes they'd made and garnered experience from? The trouble was, those mistakes formed you, made you wise, you had to live them to learn. Maybe she had wanted more safety for Sunny and Courtney than some parents, she would admit that Bruce was probably right about that. Maybe her own neuroses had pressed Sunny flat and made Courtney rebel. Maybe she had generated the very things for them that she feared: a self-fulfilling prophecy. Then again, maybe all this was just natural; kids ignoring parents, isn't that why she'd scoffed at her mother at the church door, sure she knew better? It was the hardest part of raising children, standing back and letting them run their own show, play to their own script, ignoring the more cautious and sensible one you had written for them.

A wave of weariness claimed her. The day had been interminable and she needed to plug herself into the mains of oblivion. She turned the lights off and climbed the stairs. Their bed was still made from the morning; Bruce was back in the spare room, it seemed. Had she really expected anything less?

Chapter 21

Bruce was gone to work by the time Shay's eyes fluttered open. She didn't think she would sleep, but she had. She thought she would dream of her mother, but she didn't; there was nothing. Her sleep was a blanket of warm, deep black and she awoke with the feeling that she had slept for days, not hours.

Paula's Merc was already parked in Roberta's drive by the time she got there. It had a personalised reg with a black screw cap strategically placed between two '1's to make an H and it made Shay think about Courtney's observation in the limo. Was that really only yesterday? Time had warped.

Paula had come early to snoop around, Shay guessed. She could imagine her sister opening drawers, looking for her mum's jewellery, bundles of cash, like a grey-haired, greedy magpie. As soon as she stepped inside it, Shay felt the unaccustomed chill of the unheated house. Gone were all the familiar scents that usually rushed at her like an old friend whenever she walked in: sometimes fabric condi-tioner from clothes drying on an airer, at other times toast, or the oil in Roberta's rose reed diffuser that Dagmara had bought for her birthday. Its absence pierced her heart more than its dear presence would. She steeled herself against caving in to emotion, because she needed to be strong. In fact, she needed to be *very* strong today.

'In here,' said Paula, calling from the kitchen.

She was sitting at the table with the old will in front of her that she'd taken from the drawer and a notepad. 'Kettle's just boiled. Make yourself a drink if you want one but there's no milk.'

Shay made herself a black coffee, quite aware that this might end up over her face within five minutes. Good job she'd worn a black top.

She put the concertina file she'd brought with her on the work surface; it contained some jewellery she'd located behind the bath panel and the incendiary new will.

'No doubt we'll have to go through the probate process so we should really start that ball rolling. I've had a word with my solicitor and he'll sort that out for us. Oh and someone put a letter through the door, saying they want to buy the house. Andrew Balls. That'll save us putting it up with an estate agent and incurring fees.'

Shay stirred her coffee slowly.

'You think I'd sell Mum's house to those two next door?'

Paula made a small 'hmm' noise. 'Yes, I see what you mean, but does it really matter now who it's sold to? Plus that's for both of us to decide, not just you,' she said, pasting on a smile, albeit the sort of smile a boa constrictor might give a small animal before it coiled around its body and began to squeeze.

'Actually, Paula,' Shay began, stalled, swallowed. Oh God, she really was dreading this. 'Actually it is for me to decide. Mum made me her executor, and she wanted me to take sole charge of her estate.' She flipped open the file and pulled out the folded papers in the first pocket; The Last Will of Testament of Roberta May Corrigan, dated three years previously.

Paula snatched it out of her hands, read it silently. Shay watched her sister's eyes moving manically from side to side like the carriage of a typewriter as they swept up the words. The way she turned the pages illustrated perfectly the extent of her annoyance.

David Charles the solicitor and Roberta had crossed all the T's, dotted all the I's, made it watertight and bomb-proof. Roberta had appointed her younger daughter as sole executor unless she was unable or unwilling to be. Her duties consisted of orchestrating the funeral, organising the selling of her house, distributing gifts to family, friends and neighbours as listed, the disposal of her furnishings and possessions as she alone saw fit.

Paula threw the will down on the table and said in her best scoffing voice, 'Well if that isn't clear evidence of her dementia, what is?'

'She was totally compos mentis when she wrote it.'

Shay could see the muscle working in Paula's jaw; her brain must have been going ten to the dozen to work out how to negate this new will in favour of the old.

'Why would she write another will so obviously in your favour?' Paula looked at her sister through narrowed eyes. 'This is your doing, why she hasn't split everything down the middle, isn't it?'

Shay's mouth was bone dry. Paula could be as terrifying as a cobra when riled.

'Mum did split it down the middle. That's what the old will you have there stipulates, the one she wrote after her divorce. But then, in the following two years, you'll recall you had quite a lot of your inheritance up front, and Mum wrote another will taking that into account. If you add everything up, it's still a fifty-fifty split. She wrote a letter explaining it which she lodged with her solicitor, supported by her bank statements to prove it should you try to contest it.' She wet her lips with a mouthful of coffee. Roberta might have been slipping further away from them, but once she'd decided Paula had had her fair share, the bank transfers had ended; she hadn't fallen prey to any further requests or manipulation. Shay had checked all the historic statements her mother had kept, highlighted, scribbled on. Tens of thousands of pounds.

Shay noticed how mottled her sister's neck was beneath the hand stroking the skin there. She was undone, and rattled about it.

'She had the house in Millspring valued. That's why she left it, plus the forty-five thousand in her account, to me and why you have five to come. There's also a life insurance policy worth eight thousand which will be split between us when it's paid out. When this house is sold, then the monies will be split four ways: a quarter each to you, me, Sunny and Courtney.'

The mottling on Paula's neck was getting worse, spreading up her cheeks now. If it went any further, her head would look like a block of corned beef. Eventually she spoke, through gritted teeth.

'You've got your family well and truly looked after, haven't you, you sly little cow.'

Shay felt her hackles rising. 'You're actually calling me sly, Paula, when you were the one trying to bleed her dry?'

'They were loans.'

'They were your inheritance up front. Mum told me a couple of weeks before she died. I didn't know what she was leaving to whom until I was sent the will so I could organise her funeral as per her instructions. And she loved her grand-children. It was her money to do what she wanted with.'

'When was the last time they even saw her?' hissed Paula.

'They saw her more than you did,' Shay spat back. 'And they saw her because they wanted to, not because they were under duress or after money.'

Paula stood, her mood volcanic.

'So I'm just supposed to accept this, am I?'

Shay gave a dry chuckle. 'Well, yes. It's Mum's wishes, not mine.'

'I'm the elder daughter. This is MY job to sort.' Paula poked herself in the boob so hard she'd have a bruise there to remind her of this moment.

Shay knew she had to keep her cool; she had a duty to her mother to carry out her behests and she would have done, whatever they were.

'Mum wanted me to do it because she knew I'd be fair.'

Paula's turn for a hoot of laughter now.

'The inference being that I'm not?'

'Infer what you like, Paula.'

'Where's my mother's wedding ring?' yelled Paula in the manner of quite a dangerous child who would strike out if her demands weren't met.

'She left that to me.'

'Jesus Christ, is there anything you haven't got your greedy fucking mitts on?'

'If you'll just shut up a moment, she left you her engage-ment and eternity rings.'

The prospect of owning the one-carat diamond in the

former and the emeralds in the latter was far more attractive than the sentiment of the wedding ring. Paula was momentarily appeased.

Shay went on, 'Plus there are other pieces that—'

Paula held her hand out. 'Give them to me now, please.' Never had a please sounded less like a polite request. 'I want the diamond brooch as well.'

'She left that to Dagmara.' Shay opened up the file and took out a bag full of jewellery in their boxes, put it down on the table. 'She left you these. They're all itemised in her will.'

Paula folded her arms, tilted her head, stared at her younger sister with wry amusement.

'You power-struck bitch. You're enjoying this aren't you?' she said.

'No, Paula, I'm not *enjoying* any of this. I'm just doing what Mum asked me to do.'

'She pitted you against me.'

'No, she didn't.'

'I can see you now, drip-dripping poison into each other's ears about me,' said Paula with quiet, measured menace as she stood there, faint smile playing on her lips.

'That didn't happen,' replied Shay. 'Why would it? Mum loved us both and she wanted to be fair.'

'I have a right to half.' Paula screamed. But she wasn't facing a flimsy office junior now who would cower and sweat.

'And that's exactly what you have got,' Shay returned, calmer on the surface than she was below it.

Paula snatched up the jewellery and her handbag. 'Well you'd better get ready for when Dad dies. You'll see.'

Shay shook her head, 'Why would you even say that? Just stop, Paula.'

But Paula was on a roll now. 'Spoilt little brat daughter. There were never any arguments between them before you came along, did you know that?'

'You really can't be suggesting that's my fault.'

'Mum went away from home for six months. I bet you didn't know that either?'

'What?'

'Seven months after she came back, you were born. You were enormous for a *premature* baby. Everything changed when you arrived. Mum and Dad were never the same. And I was supposed to love you like that' – she clicked her fingers, a hard bitter sound. 'I hated you. They pushed me to one side for you, both of them, if that isn't ironic.'

There was glee on Paula's face now, as if she was sucking a sweet and had found the runny, flavour-rich centre.

'What are you getting at, Paula? If you have something to say then please just say it.'

'Oh, I will, don't you worry,' Paula went on. 'Dad wouldn't have started playing around if it wasn't for you. They wouldn't have had to pack up and leave a place they loved if it wasn't for you. Dad wouldn't have been lying there stressed into a coma if it wasn't—'

Shay had had enough now. 'How – really – can you blame me for any of this?'

Paula smiled then, a slow smile that spread across her face like black poison in a bloodstream. 'Don't you get it, Shay. HE'S. NOT. YOUR. DAD. I always wondered. You with your darker skin and your brown eyes. Italian throwback my arse. As if.'

She really was spoiling for a fight, thought Shay. Well she wasn't going to get one.

'Paula, stop, really. Mum wouldn't want this—'

'I don't give a fuck what Mum would want,' said Paula, spittle flying from her mouth. 'She's dead, gone and if she weren't living in this house she wouldn't have had problems with neighbours would she? She wouldn't have fallen over and died, so that's also your fault as well, isn't it? Everything had a knock-on effect. You destroyed the whole shebang.'

This was Paula all over, scattergunning spite when she didn't get her own way. She'd always been the same; but here, the day after their mother's funeral, it was too much. 'Don't you dare—'

'Oh, I dare.' Paula's face was screwed-up and ugly. 'I always knew there was something cuckoo's egg about you. Always. So a couple of months ago, I took some hair from your brush in the bedroom, and from Dad in the hospital. I had a DNA test done. Illegal I know, but I'll just say that I thought the hair was mine. It was more than worth the risk, especially seeing the look on your face right now. You're not a match, by the way. Who'd have guessed? All that shit about you looking like Auntie Stella, who was never off the sunbeds and the hair dye, which idiot would have fallen for that? Christ knows whose kid you are, but now Mum's gone, we have nothing in common except her money. I want everything totally accounted for or I'll take you to the fucking cleaners.'

Then Paula flounced out, wearing her best victory smile because detonating that blast had been almost as good as an inheritance.

Chapter 22

Shay didn't so much sit down as collapse into the chair which her sister had just vacated. Oddly, the plastic cushion was cold, as if her sister was incapable of giving out any warmth. A portion of her brain was working frantically to rationalise Paula's words, dismiss them as nonsense; they had been said to wound, bullets of pique. But Paula was thorough, she would have done her homework, on that there was no doubt. She wasn't the type to randomly fling mud; instead, she'd moulded her evidence into a grenade full of acid so it would blister and scald and cause as much damage as possible, to be hurled at the right time for maximum effect. Knowing her sister, that would most likely be when their father died, but then this delicious opportune moment had landed in her lap.

Her father.

She thought of Harry lying in the nursing home, of her fingers entwined with his. She thought of him bringing her a Mars bar at exam time and holding her tightly when she thought she was going to fall into an abyss. Never once had she felt that he wasn't her dad, he *was* her dad. She had his name, he was her children's grandfather. He'd taken them to the park to feed the ducks and play on the swings, he'd bought them little lawnmowers so they could follow him around the garden pretending to cut the grass.

The clock in the lounge sounded the hour with its customary bing-bongs that sounded too loud in the silence. This time yesterday, she was just putting on her black dress for the funeral. And now her mum was gone, and with her all the answers to the questions spinning around inside her.

She heard a knock on the front door, but ignored it. She didn't want to speak to anyone, she didn't want any well-meaning neighbour dropping off flowers or a cake or a 'sorry for your loss' verbal message or written card that they hadn't managed to deliver at the funeral. She was, at that moment, like a building, rocked from a seismic shock, hardly daring to breathe because she wasn't sure if she would still be standing if she did.

She heard the door creak open, her name being called, and then there in the kitchen doorway stood little Dagmara.

'Hello Shay,' she said. 'I don't want to disturb, but I saw Paula leave the house. She made a zoom off.'

'We had a row,' replied Shay. 'She didn't like what Mum's will said.'

'Of course,' Dagmara replied. 'I'm sorry it was left to you. Roberta should have told her.'

'You knew all about it.' It wasn't a question, but a statement.

'I know everything.'

Shay smiled at that. 'Oh, Dagmara, I wish you did.'

'Your mama and I were friends for many years. We have had a lot of time to talk. I know *everything*.' Dagmara said it again, like a piece of cheese trailed in front of a mouse. The mouse went for it.

'Did she tell you that my father wasn't my father, Dagmara? Because that's what Paula just did.'

Dagmara let loose a long outward breath.

'Yes, I knew this too,' she said. 'Ay, ay, ay. Shay, you need to come with me to my house. I have to show you something.'

Dagmara's bungalow had the same layout as her mum's, but there the similarities ended. This house had a surfeit of heavy dark wood furniture, tapestries on the walls, cheerful clutter, patterns on soft furnishings and curtains that should have jarred but somehow melded into homely, chalet-chic. There was a smell of spicy apple pot pourri, a faint air of Christmas inside at odds with midsummer and a raging sun outside.

'Sit, sit,' commanded Dagmara and Shay sank onto the oversized sofa. It was soft and squashy and received her as if it were grateful to be utilised.

Dagmara walked over to an ornately carved dresser and returned with a small glass full of dark liquid and a notebook.

'It's Latvian brandy,' she explained. 'It's for shock. It's for anything really, but today for shock.'

Shay picked up the glass and did something she had never done in her life: downed it in one. It was like drinking fire with nails in it. It burned and hurt the back of her throat and she coughed in response. She didn't feel any better for it, so whatever it was supposed to do didn't work. She'd need a lot more than one to numb her against the onslaught she'd just received.

Dagmara sat on the adjacent chair, the notebook balanced on her knees. It had been handled a lot, that was clear by the curled edges and the creased front.

'Shay,' began Dagmara, in earnest. 'Roberta was my friend, as you know, and we could – and did – talk about everything, and I . . . I always felt it was wrong that she kept some things from you but at the same time, I understood why. She thought you would never find out, so why would she risk hurting you, destroying everything you believed. She said that sometimes the value of truth is overrated, keep the past as the past, unless it ruins the present. Unless it ruins the present.' She repeated the phrase, her finger beating for emphasis. 'Then that skip arrived and it made all sorts of things come to the surface in her head: the past she had tried to keep in the past. She realised her mistakes so clearly, when her mind was at the same time so confused. I think she wanted to tell you in the end but it was too jumbled up. She chose her path, she thought it was the right one. She chose the way, with love for you.'

Dagmara placed the flat of her palm on the book. 'When she started to forget, we used to sit together and I would write her memories down with her. I told her it was an exercise to help her brain but I always feared today would come and this I did for you. So I ask you, dear Shay, do you want me to open this book or do you want to keep the past you have?'

'Open it,' said Shay; with no doubt in her voice. She didn't want lies, they had damaged her too much already.

Dagmara nodded, opened the first page.

'In the 1970s, there was a Cold War in the world between Russia and America and all their respective allies. The British government wanted Russian-speaking teachers for an accelerated learning programme. Your mother was asked to go, of course she was. It meant living away from her family for a year but it was important work and she wanted to do it, so she went. Harry and Stella between them looked after your sister.' Dagmara paused, swallowed. 'One of her pupils was an officer in Egyptian intelligence called Ammon Habib. She told me . . . everyone said he looked just like the film star Omar Sharif.'

Shay's breath snagged. Broken pieces of her mother's recollections began to drift together, fit in place.

'She said he was the most beautiful man she had ever seen,' Dagmara went on, smiling, eyes bright. 'From the first time she saw his face, she knew that what she had thought of as love before was a mere pale imitation. He was clever, intellectually very gifted, a talented artist too. Look what he drew.'

She turned to the back of the book and took out a piece of paper which had weakened badly along the places where it was folded. It was a pencil portrait of a young Roberta with her long wavy hair, almost photo-perfect, drawn with a skilled hand; even the light in the woman's eyes, just paper untouched by the pencil, was masterly; and in the bottom right corner, a signature, 'Ammon', and a date, June 1974 – eight months before Shay was born.

Shay's finger brushed along the faded name; this was the closest she would ever get to him.

'Is he my father?' But she knew the answer before Dagmara even said the word.

'Yes.'

Such a small word to have so great an effect on her. Her arms, legs, hands, feet, scalp began to prickle with shock. Had she been standing, she would have had to sit down. Her planet was jolted from its axis; her whole life had been built on a lie.

'Did they go to the seaside and eat chocolate ice cream?' asked Shay.

'Yes,' said Dagmara. 'I have written about it in here. They caught a train to Weston-Super-Mare and had ice cream and someone ran past and her face went into it like this.' Dagmara demonstrated a cornet ramming upwards. 'You were growing inside her then and it was the day she told him. They fell in love with each other and she knew it was wrong but she said she couldn't help it. She couldn't have stopped it and she didn't want to stop it.'

'I'm half Egyptian then.' A crazy thought, Shay couldn't absorb it.

'Yes, you are. His mama's name was Shay.'

Shay let out a small, dry laugh, remembering how she'd looked up the name of Omar Sharif's mother because there was something in Roberta's story that didn't quite rule out her claim being wholly ridiculous.

'What happened to him?'

'When she found out she was pregnant, she was going to leave the programme and go with Ammon to Egypt. It was impossible situation because it would mean leaving your sister; she knew Harry would never give her up. Then Ammon was recalled for urgent matter and the military plane he was in had to take detour in bad weather and was shot down. The Libyans blamed the Israelis, the Israelis blamed the Libyans. Whoever, he died and your mother was broken.'

Shay's hand came to her mouth, she felt her fingers trembling against her lips.

'Your mother went back to Harry. She was only five, six, maybe, weeks pregnant. She said she had no idea how she kept hold of you because her heart was in pieces.'

'Did Dad . . . Dad know?' *Dad*, how alien that word felt in her mouth now.

'Your mother said he always thought you were his. He never questioned it, it was never spoken about.' Dagmara shook her head slowly. 'I wonder, though. I think he loved your mama so much and he knew in his heart that she was changed when she came back and why that could be.'

Is that why he kept cheating on her, because he was punishing her, Shay wondered. How hurt he must have been if he had guessed she had fallen in love with someone more than she could ever have loved him.

'I don't know for sure, but can you hide a big truth like that and not expect it to push through the lie?'

Her mother's scrambled words thudded into her brain: *If only I hadn't gone, it would have been all right then. I wouldn't have known any different.* They hadn't made sense at the time; now their meaning couldn't have been clearer.

'Are there any photos of him?' asked Shay.

'No, I'm sorry,' said Dagmara.

'Mum would have destroyed them anyway, wouldn't she?' Her modus operandi for trying to bury the past, except a small part of her, the part that kept the drawing, couldn't quite let him go entirely.

Shay didn't realise she was crying until she felt the tickle of a tear weaving down her cheek.

'Don't hate her, Shay. Don't hate my friend.' Dagmara was visibly distressed.

'I couldn't hate my mum, Dagmara,' replied Shay.

'We all have secrets in our hearts,' said Dagmara. 'Our children see us as grown-ups and old people and never as silly, young things floundering, learning, believing the signs on the road that say *this is the way you need to go.* She tried to give you a stable home life, a family and she did because Harry loved you very much. But at the end, I think she realised that some things shouldn't be run from but confronted; because if they are not, they haunt you, they follow you.'

'Did Mum say anything about a letter that came for me from Millspring? I don't know when it could be: years ago.' Shay realised, as soon as she opened her mouth to ask, how much of a long shot it was.

But it wasn't. 'Yes, many years ago. A letter arrived for you from someone, but I don't recall the name, and Roberta was terrified that it would rake everything up for you. It was from a boy is all I can tell you.'

Jonah. It could only be him. She felt her heart bounce in response to the possibility.

'Did she tell you what it said, Dagmara?'

'Only that if you didn't reply, he would never bother you again. You were about to be married when it came. I think that is why she destroyed it.'

Shay closed her eyes and remembered the morning of her wedding, outside the church; her mother exacting from her that she wanted to marry Bruce and had no doubts. What a mess. And all in the name of love.

Shay's head was like a shaken snow-globe when she left Dagmara's house and she had to force herself hard to concentrate on driving home. Later she realised it was not a good idea, when stuck in a traffic jam, to vent some frustration, anger, confusion and rail at the cosmos, *What next? How much more do you think I can take? Why don't you chuck something else at me?* Because the cosmos wouldn't ignore such a brazen gauntlet thrown down.

She walked into the house to find, propped up against the salt pot on the kitchen table, a note from Bruce.

Dear Shay
　　I think that it might be best if I moved out for a little while to give us both some space. I do love you but we haven't been getting on well recently and I think a break is what we need to think about the future.
　　Bruce

Love. That word again. Was there anything it didn't try and excuse?

Chapter 23

'What sort of despicable tool leaves his wife the day after her mother's funeral?'

Shay conjured up Tanya, standing by her sink, face a mask of incredulity, hands thrown up in the air. What sort indeed. She didn't know this Bruce who would do this to her when her heart was in pieces. She rang his mobile repeatedly, hoping he'd hear her pain, her confusion, her anger in the insistent ringtone, but he didn't pick up. That note was the door closed on the matter and said everything he wanted to say with no desire or need for a response. She read it over and over, looking for variations of meaning, words between the lines. She'd questioned the lack of a kiss after his name, how long 'a little while' was supposed to mean, how he could say he loved her and yet walk out of her life now when she was so evidently floundering. Had this been a sudden decision? Had he gone out to work and then shot back for his belongings? If she hadn't been to Dagmara's would she have caught him *in flagrante* packing his Calvin Kleins and shaving kit?

She went upstairs to check what he had taken. The two

large cases they kept under the bed had gone, his underwear, at least three suits, the more expensive shirts, shoes
and trainers. She imagined him throwing the best of his
clothes into them quickly, carelessly until they were full. His
passport had gone from his bedside drawer; why? And why
would he pack his suits if he were only having a couple of
thinking nights in a Premier Inn? Did he imagine she was
going to do a Lady Graham-Moon and hack at them with
a pair of scissors? And if so, what reason would she have to
do that? It was, as her daughter would have put it, a fucking
head–fuck.

'I wish you were here, Tan,' said Shay, hoping against
hope that her dear friend would suddenly materialise, summoned through her angst. It wasn't beyond the realms of
possibility after all that had happened recently. She hadn't
just lost one parent this past fortnight, she'd lost two. Her
lovely dad wasn't her dad after all, and they'd never be able
to talk about it. Her father was a man from Egypt she would
never know and all she would ever have of him was a faded
name on a pencil drawing.

She dragged her phone over and rang Les. As expected,
it clicked onto voicemail and she poured herself into the
message she left. It was unashamedly needy and desperate
and tears rained down her face and snot from her nose as
she recorded it: *please ring me, Les, I don't know what to do.*
She had no one else she could talk to; she didn't know what
was happening to her, she didn't even know who she was
any more. Her life felt as if it had broken like an old biscuit
and the crumbs were falling through her fingers too fast to
stop them.

*

A full week passed. Shay hadn't heard from Bruce at all, nei-ther had she heard from Les but she didn't have brain space for her on top of everything else. She'd had too much time on her hands to think, to cry, to torture herself. She hadn't slept, she'd barely eaten. Her concentration levels were zilch, she hadn't done anything in the house other than wash a couple of plates, cups and spoons. Colin had sent her a lovely email saying that he hoped she was okay and when she felt able to come back to work, could she 'attack this list with vigour'. She didn't blame him for wanting her back on the work horse and she did what he'd asked and ended up being grateful for the push. Paperwork was a saving grace, giving her head something practical to do. The accounts part of her work was especially well received because figures didn't mess her about, they didn't lie – like the diamonds in Shirley Bassey's Bond theme; she was in total control of them and she felt in very little control of anything else.

Courtney rang to see if she was all right and did she want her to pop over. Shay plastered on her 'I'm perfectly fine' voice, an Oscar-winning performance of such conviction that Meryl Streep might have envied it. Then Courtney hit her for another two hundred pound loan, saying she felt really bad about having to ask. Shay paid up without a lecture, tears flooding as she was talking to her daughter but she attributed them to a cold, said she was just a bit run-down. It wasn't her job to elicit sympathy from her children, it was hers to administer it to them when it was needed. Neither of them knew that their father had walked out of the family home to an undisclosed location for as long as he saw fit. Neither of them knew that their grandfather wasn't related to them by blood but was a cuckold that their grandmother had lied to for forty-six years.

She picked up her mother's ashes from the funeral parlour. She fastened the urn into the front seat with a safety belt, leaning over to secure the clip as she so often had done with her mother whenever she drove her anywhere. She had to sit in the parking space for five minutes putting herself back together before she set off home.

'I wish you were still here, Mum,' she said aloud as she drove. 'I've got so many questions for you. I wish you'd told me about Dad. I wish you'd told me about the letter that came for me years ago. Was it Jonah who wrote? What did it say? I don't blame you, Mum. It's so hard being a parent, wanting to do the right thing for your children and doubting yourself all the way but you should have talked to me.'

She imagined her mum sitting there instead of the urn, looking out of the window, pointing at the housing estate that wasn't there the last time she'd been here, recounting her memory of the large Co-op's previous life as a wonderful Italian bistro. Shay didn't want to be disappointed in her, but she couldn't help it. Maybe she shouldn't have asked Dagmara to open up her notebook, put Paula's disclosure down to bitchery and left Pandora's box intact.

Her mum hadn't stipulated where she wanted her ashes to go, only that Shay put her somewhere 'appropriate', whatever that meant. Shay needed time to think where was best; for now, Roberta could sit on the shelf in the lounge. She'd always thought it was a cosy room, with the living flame gas fire and the big sofa, even though the springs had gone on one side thanks to Courtney's bouncing. Shay was just arranging a few family photos in frames around the urn, an attempt to give her mother some company, when her phone rang and Sunny's number flashed up on the screen.

'Hello, love.'

'Hi Mum, just ringing to see if you're okay.' Sunny's voice was croaky and hoarse.

'Good lord, you sound awful.' She cut off the mother stream of 'have you's queued up in her mouth. *Have you got some medicine for that? Have you taken some time off work? Have you been to the doctor?*

'It sounds worse than it is. I just wondered if you were free any time?'

'I'm coming into Leeds tomorrow actually, to see your gran's solicitor.'

'Can we meet for a quick drink maybe?'

'Yes, that would be lovely,' said Shay. Something to look forward to instead of trying to conjure up dead people to have conversations with and second-guessing what was going on in Bruce's head. 'Is . . . everything all right?'

'Yes, absolutely,' came the answer, a little too chirpily to be wholly convincing.

The White Swan pub was equidistant from Sunny's place of work and David Charles's office. It was a large new build meant to look old and quaint with beams, rough plaster-work and a myriad of cosy nooks and crannies. The hefty prices were reflective of the business quarter in which it was situated but didn't off put any of the young executives who filled the place after they had left their various offices for the evening.

'I got you a pint of diet cola in,' Shay said, standing to greet him. 'I wasn't sure if you wanted to drink alcohol in your lunch hour.'

'Thanks, that's perfect,' replied Sunny. He bent to kiss her cheek and she felt the scratch of stubble against her skin. She knew he would have shaved that morning, but it grew so fast and she wondered if that was because of Bruce's genes or Ammon Habib's.

'How are you, Mum? You look tired.'

'Thanks.' She smiled.

'Sorry,' said Sunny, wincing. 'I'm glad you're here. I wanted to make sure you were okay. I didn't see Gran as much as I should have this year and I don't ever want to let something like that happen again.'

Shay noticed that his shirt looked too big for his neck. He would have bought it to fit.

'Don't beat yourself up about that, Sunny. Who knows what's around the corner?'

'How's Dad?'

'He's fine,' replied Shay. No point in telling him that Bruce had gone off to a cave with all his best clothes and his passport; at least, not until she had to.

'Do you need any help doing paperwork or anything?' Sunny lifted up his glass and Shay noticed how bitten his fingernails were. Courtney had bought him a manicure set once because he always took pride in his nails, his hands. His tools. 'I suppose you'll be packing up all Gran's stuff at some point. Courtney and I will come and help you do that. You shouldn't do it alone.'

'I can't sell the house until probate has been granted and that'll take a couple of months at least, I think. I can't face dismantling anything at the moment anyway. I have to let go in stages.' She lifted her fresh orange juice and wished it had a double vodka in it.

'Is there a lot to do?'

She laughed a little, a dry, tired sound. 'Yes.'

'I'm guessing Auntie Paula isn't doing her fair share?'

'*Fair* and *share* aren't words in your Auntie Paula's vocabulary,' replied Shay. They didn't sit well with *destroy, annihilation, greed, illegal DNA tests.*

'Dad'll be too busy working, I expect.'

Shay didn't answer that.

Sunny raised his head and she looked at his eyes, so like her own, the colour of cocoa, thick black lashes, their shared Egyptian heritage. Should she tell Sunny about his real grandfather? By giving him a stranger, she would take away the man he'd always known in that place; Harry Corrigan, who played cards with him and bought him books, pens and pencils. *Is this why my mother didn't tell me? Is this what was running through her mind every time she thought I deserved to know?*

'So much seems to have happened in such a short time,' said Sunny, the cool drink not alleviating that painful-sounding rasp.

You don't know the half of it, thought Shay, but she answered, 'Yes, there's been a lot to get our heads around. But your gran wouldn't want us moping. She always said that people should grieve up to the funeral and then stop, otherwise it becomes maudlin. Although that's easier said than done in practice. How's Karoline? Is she still off work?'

'Yes,' said Sunny and the unprompted thought came to Shay that maybe that's why her son was out at work with a sore throat. It was an unkind fancy she was immediately ashamed of.

'I imagine she'll be using the time off to refine her wedding plans – six weeks now, isn't it?'

Shay saw the cloud that passed in front of her son's face at the mention of it, saw his expression droop.

'It was never supposed to be this big. I didn't want the fuss.'

'Well why didn't you put your foot down?'

'I'm not the type, am I? I'm a wimp.' He laughed a little, in the same self-deprecating way Denny used to and a shiver wriggled down her spine at the comparison.

'You're not a wimp, but you always were accommodating. You'd give way if it meant peace, but not every time.' On the occasions when her children squabbled, Courtney would win the argument, but nearly always because her brother let her.

'Accommodating . . .' Sunny smiled. 'I like that.'

'What made you want to get married so quickly? You were going out for hardly any time at all when you got engaged.'

Sunny shrugged. 'I can't remember. We went out with her friends, we all got blasted. She told me the next morning I'd proposed and it was full steam ahead from then on. It was a bit fast, I know.'

'And you can't remember?' Well, that wasn't dodgy at all.

'Nope. But I must have.'

'Oh, Sunny. It's not too late to put the brakes on.'

A little laugh of disbelief. 'It is. It really is.' He pinched the top of his nose and shook his head and made a noise of such utter despair that it scared her.

'Is this why you're losing weight and getting sore throats?'

'It'll be okay when it's all over and done with.'

Shay recalled the pressure of her own wedding: the reception venue cocking things up, the flower woman being poorly and having to find someone else at the eleventh hour. And she knew that deep down she had wanted a big, splashy wedding to try and obliterate the memories of what had happened five years before on the same date. That's what scared her, because sometimes weddings were just big fat smoke screens with canapés.

'We haven't really gotten to know her, have we?'

'She's not a great socialiser.'

'Love, you can stop the ride now and get off. Every day you leave it, it will be harder to—'

'No, Mum. Please. I can't and that's that.' His voice was hard, adamant, so she left it, though she didn't want to.

'Are you having Jamie as your best man?' she asked, taking the heat out of her voice.

Sunny and Jamie had been best pals from primary school, close as brothers all the way through their lives. Close as she and Denny Smith had once been.

'Of course.'

'Do you still see him? At rugby?'

'Yeah, but not much outside that. He's busy, I'm busy.'

Shay leaned forward, reached for her son's hand; his long fingers felt cold and his knuckles were cracked and dry. Stress was telling on him right to the ends of his extremities. She remembered when his hands were small, soft and always warm and often spotted with some paint he'd missed when washing them. She'd loved holding her children's hands as they walked to school, skipping, happy little souls. If only she'd known when it was the last time, because she would have savoured it like a treasure.

'Sunny, if you have anything you need to tell me, you can. Whatever it is. However difficult a scrape you're in. God knows your sister's never been frightened of holding back.' She paused, wet her lips with her tongue. 'I never told you this but I had a friend when I was young who killed himself. He wouldn't open up to me and—'

Sunny's response was immediate. 'There's nothing, Mum. Honestly. I'm okay, just a bit overworked. I'm fine, really.' He looked at her square in the eye, to convince her that what he was saying was the truth. The same way she had looked into her mother's eyes outside the church on the day of her wedding.

Chapter 24

The phone woke Shay the next morning at nine-thirty. It wasn't exactly a lie-in because she and sleep were presently enemies. She'd been watching crap TV until three, wondering what her son wasn't telling her and what her husband was doing. She didn't know whether to be upset more than angry, angry more than worried and so her mood rebounded between all three. Mental exhaustion was the only method of getting to sleep at the moment.

'Hello, Auntie Shay, I didn't get you up did I?' Little Mort's deep bass voice.

'Not at all, love,' she lied. 'Everything all right?'

A beat. A telling beat.

'Can Dad come and see you? I'm so sorry about your mum and I know the timing is well off, but he needs to talk to you.'

Shay sat up in bed. 'Is he okay?' Stupid question; Morton would be a wreck and his son was obviously worried about him.

'Not really.' The answer she expected. 'I wouldn't ask if it weren't important, Auntie Shay, but ... Please.' There was something in his voice that she didn't want to refuse, but she had nothing of herself to give at the moment.

'I don't know what I can tell him though, Mort. I haven't heard from your mum. She's not returning my calls or my texts or—'

'Auntie Shay, please let my dad come to see you.' That note of pleading had segued to urgency. 'He'll tell you about Mum.'

Her breath caught in her throat. 'Oh God, nothing's happened to her has it?' She knew she was wired to think worst-case scenarios; a legacy of the past.

'No, not like that. But he wants to talk to you face to face.'

Shay's nerves backed off from the ledge.

'What time does he finish work?'

'About half-five.'

'Tell him to come over then. We can talk over something to eat.'

Relief in his voice. 'Thank you.'

'Mort, are you okay, you don't sound it?'

'Yeah, I'm fine, sort of,' he replied, unconvincingly. 'I will just tell you that I wanted to come to the funeral with Courtney but she's back with Dingo Shaw again. Please, will *you* try and get it through her thick head that he has absolutely no redeeming features and never will have, because I'm done with her.'

Then he ended the call before Shay could even roll her eyes in despair.

Shay drove to a farm shop that afternoon to pick up something for tea because she had nothing in. She bought a pie – Morton was a pie sort of man – then she tidied up a bit because the surfaces hadn't seen a cloth or a duster for over a week. The house, in fact, looked like her state of mind; disorderly, untidy, needing a strong fettle.

His ancient jeep drew up outside at six on the dot. Shay saw him get out and walk down the path and she was mortified, because he was carrying a bunch of flowers and wearing a suit; a dreadful suit with pin-stripes and 1970s flappy lapels that not even Harry Styles could have pulled off. Under the jacket, rather than a shirt, was a white polo neck. It was a perfect wardrobe fusion of submarine commander meets Worzel Gummidge. Shay hoped to high heaven that 'come round and talk over a bit of tea' had not somehow been translated as 'this is a date night'.

She opened the door to Morton who smiled, but looked terrible. He had dark circles under his eyes and he'd lost so much weight that his cheeks were sunken in. In all the years she'd known him, she'd never seen as much as a hint of one of his cheekbones before.

'Hello, Shay love,' he said and threw one arm around her by way of greeting; her nostrils were filled with a pungent whiff of mothballs mixed with an overpowering aftershave which might have smelled nice had it not been applied quite so liberally.

'I brought you these,' said Morton and pushed the bouquet into her hands. 'I know birds like flowers, they're a cheer-up aren't they and fuck me, we both need cheering up at the moment.'

'Thank you, Morton, you didn't have to bring anything but that's kind of you.' They were from the supermarket, she could see by the sticker, but they were one of the pricier bunches with roses in. 'Can I get you a beer or a glass of wine? Have a seat.'

'Ta, I'll have a beer. I'm driving so I won't be getting

arseholed. I've been overdoing it a bit recently and it doesn't help, does it? You just get bad dreams, wet the bed and wake up with a thumping headache.'

Shay flipped the top off one of the beers she'd bought in the farm shop. He didn't want a glass; Morton said it tasted better from the lip.

'I was sorry to hear about your mum, Shay. Mort told me you'd been having hassle with her neighbours over the building work and then ... well ... what came after. The building laws are a shambles at the moment; the lunatics have taken over the asylums.'

She had that thought again, the one that kept chasing into her brain and out of it. But this time she caught it and held it fast. Why hadn't Bruce suggested she ask Morton about what Drew Balls was planning to build? He was their natural first port of call with his wealth of knowledge. She remembered Dave from next door popping round after Christmas for advice about a conservatory and Bruce had been straight on the blower to Morton. Not that it mattered any more now.

Shay turned the heat off underneath the pan of peas and then took the pie out of the oven and put it on the table.

'Mort was very helpful.'

'He's a good kid. I'm glad I've got him. He's a rock. Mind if I take my jacket off?'

'Of course, make yourself comfortable.'

'How are your kids doing?'

Shay cut a large slice of pie for Morton, put it on a plate and poured peas over it as she continued their conversation.

'Sunny's working for an insurance company in Leeds. Courtney's ... well, Courtney. She lives in a flat with her pal and has a boyfriend who thinks the world owes him a living.'

'Our young Mort doesn't like him, I know that,' said

Morton, picking up a fork. 'Says he's a wanker, and he's a good judge of character is my lad. He also says your lass could have a crack at making something of herself in the boxing world if she wanted to. Go pro.'

'Oh, please no to go pro,' replied Shay. 'There's enough violence in the world as it is.'

'She's good, I've watched her in the ring up at Tommy Tanner's gym. I wouldn't like to be on the other side of one of her uppercuts and she's got a cracking right hook. Some proper brute strength in them fists of hers.' Morton scooped up a slab of pie and shoved it into his mouth. 'Tommy seems to think a ring is her natural arena.'

Shay didn't doubt it, although she'd always hoped that a ballet school would be her daughter's natural arena. Fat chance after she was barred for battering one of her fellow pupils with her pointe shoes.

'It'll channel her aggression and she's got plenty to channel, by all accounts,' chuckled Morton.

'Great, that's all we need. A professional killing machine instead of an amateur one,' huffed Shay.

'Our young Mort's been in love with her for years, did you know?' Morton said, spitting out some mince as he spoke, which he poked back into his mouth with his finger.

'Yes, I think the only person who hasn't guessed that is my daughter,' replied Shay.

'She could do a lot worse.'

'Courtney couldn't spot a decent boy if he turned up with a written recommendation from God himself,' returned Shay.

'They're a worry, aren't they – kids?' said Morton. 'But I'd still have had loads of them if I could. It just never happened for us.'

Now was not the time to tell Morton that Lesley had been secretly on the pill through the whole of their marriage. She had let her husband think that the rubbers were their only form of contraception.

'I told our Mort you've got no chance with a lass that looks like Courtney Bastable, so he'd better forget that idea and I think he's finally realised it.'

'Oh?'

Morton nodded. 'He took a lass out to the pictures last week. He was supposed to go out with her again but he fell off a ladder at work and had to go to hospital because he thought he'd punctured a lung. Cut himself badly on something the way he landed.'

'Oh Morton, that's awful. He didn't sound right on the phone this morning.' That explained it then, thought Shay.

'He was only in a night and that was one night too many for him. He's off work for a bit but he doesn't like it, because he's a grafter, is my lad. He's been staying back at the farm for a bit, to keep me company. He doesn't half scrub up well, you know.'

'Maybe he's too good for Courtney, not the other way round.'

'You've got to know your limitations though,' Morton argued. 'Okay to have a bit more pie? This is the most I've eaten in two weeks, it's bloody lovely.'

'Of course, help yourself,' said Shay to that. 'And Mort is a credit to you. I wouldn't want him to sell himself short.'

'If I'd thought for a minute you weren't out of my league by a country mile, I'd have had a crack at you,' said Morton, pushing more pie onto his plate. 'I always fancied you.'

Shay felt herself colouring at that revelation. She'd never even suspected it.

'In fact when Les was cooling off me at the start, I told her that and suddenly she was back on me like a fly on shite.' He laughed as he plopped a dollop of peas on his pie and Shay couldn't think of a single thing to say except, 'Would you like another beer?' His first one had gone down in two gulps.

'Ta, I will if you don't mind.'

Shay went to the fridge, took one out.

'I bet you've cried a lot recently, haven't you?' said Morton.

'Yes, I have,' replied Shay, handing over the opened bottle. 'A hell of a lot.'

'I have an' all.' Morton had a break from eating. 'When Les first left, I thought I'd never stop and I only ever cried three times in my life before that: when two of our dogs died and when Mort was born. Roared like a bairn. And there was Les with her legs up in stirrups getting her clout stitched—' He laughed, then apologised. 'Sorry. I've been dragged up and I've never had a safety catch on my gob. God knows how our Mort turned out the way he did with me as his dad. Total opposites, me and Les, aren't we? Me coarse as a bear's bum-crack and her wanting to be lady of the manor. And now she is. But she doesn't know that I know that and I can't wait to tell her that I know.' Morton smiled gleefully and loaded his mouth with pie.

Shay stopped chewing though. She wasn't hungry anyway; she was just picking at it to be polite.

'I'm not with you, Morton. What do you mean?'

'Les. I'm on about Les,' Morton said, as if it was obvious.

'What's going on, because Mort said that you wanted to tell me about her. She hasn't been in touch with me since I met her six weeks ago. She didn't even ring me about my mum.'

'Well, she wouldn't, would she?' Morton speared some more pastry, delivered it to his mouth, chomped on it angrily, all the while looking at Shay, reading her expression, which was one of abject bewilderment.

He swallowed. 'Oh Shay, love, I've summat to tell you that you aren't going to like.'

Shay felt something cold slip down her spine, like an ice cube dropped down her collar. She braced herself for the impact, without a clue what form it was going to take.

'Les won the lottery,' Morton said. 'Twelve million quid. That's why she buggered off and tried to divorce me quick so I wouldn't find out about it. Then, I imagine, she'd pretend she won it after.'

This was a joke, surely. Shay waited for Morton to laugh, because he was good at leg-pulling, but he didn't, his face remained straight.

'Les?' asked Shay.

'Yes, Les. Which is why your husband is driving around in a brand new fucking Audi,' Morton added.

And that's when Shay's heart left its place in her chest and began to beat a loud tattoo behind her teeth.

Chapter 25

Something pinged in Shay's head as if every blood vessel in it suddenly burst; she felt herself falling sideways from her chair and would have hit the floor had Morton not jumped up and righted her.

'I'm sorry, love, I didn't know how to tell you.'

Shay uttered things that weren't words, awful sounds that a wounded animal might release. Inside her, an emergency system was triggered to deal with this enemy invasion of information as best as it could: adrenaline flooded her, blood vessels constricted to conserve energy for her vital organs. Her body turned into the SAS on a damage-limitation mission; one doomed to failure because it had no blueprint to follow.

'I feel bloody crap now, love. I'm sorry, I thought you might have an inkling they were shagging.' Morton had pulled his chair next to Shay's so he could put his arm around her. 'Mind you, I never guessed. I'd still be guessing now if I hadn't paid for a private dick who came up with the goods this week. He can get where water can't, that fella, best money I ever spent. I started to suspect she had someone else because Les needs rumpy on tap yet she'd gone right off it with me, but I never thought she'd nick her old mate's fella. Have you any brandy for shock?'

Shay must have pointed next door to the lounge, not that she could remember, but Morton went there and returned with a bottle and two glasses. Why did everyone presume brandy worked wonders? She had no idea, but she let him pour her a stupid measure and press a handkerchief from his trouser pocket into her palm.

'It's clean,' he said. It was snow-white and folded, corners lined up perfectly. Yet another example of world order being turned on its head: Morton's hankie should be a balled-up piece of cheap, scratchy material with suspect stains.

Morton poured himself a large one. 'Is it okay if I leave my car here and get a taxi? I'll come for it early in the morning, but I think I need a stiff drink myself.'

'Yes of course,' said Shay, stunned that she'd managed to speak some intelligible words. Everything seemed so heightened, every word or breath carried a strange weight and left the tail of an echo in its wake.

'I loved my wife, but I'll never forgive her for this. Not that she'll come looking for it anyway. Not now she's got her fancy man,' said Morton, wobbling his head a little as he alluded to Bruce. 'Let's see if he can keep up to her demands like I did. She never went short; I was always ready for duty in the bedroom department so it's a good job I've the stamina of a teenager. I'm surprised I've got any tongue left the amount of use it's had on her.'

Shay winced and reached for the brandy. If it could deaden anything, she hoped it would be the images he'd just put in her head.

'She looked down on me, said I had no class,' Morton

went on, 'but I have got a scrap of dignity left, whatever she might think. She makes a god of money, but it doesn't keep you warm at night and I think I know a different Lesley to you, Shay. She's not an easy woman to live with and if Bruce has any pride, that money will soon lose its attraction because she's not one for sharing, she'll use it to make him beg. He'll turn up with his worn-out tail between his legs so get ready, lass. But if I were you, I'd sooner be covered in honey with my tits stapled to a beehive than take him back after what he's done.'

Morton might not have graduated from a conservatoire of rhetorical excellence, but his words hit home and came from a site every bit as broken as the corresponding scene of devastation within herself.

'I should have read the signs, they've been there for years,' he said ruefully. 'Looking back, she was always saying things like, "Why can't you be more like Bruce with his nice clothes and knowledge of wines?"'

'Knowledge of wines,' repeated Shay drolly. If she could have conjured up a laugh, she would have let it loose. Bruce didn't know anything that wasn't on the label. He couldn't tell a blackberry note from a jammy finish. What he'd always had, though, was a hankering for the good life way beyond his means and if what Morton was saying was true, the bird of opportunity had flown right into his lap and laid a golden egg. *Monte Carlo here we come.*

'I think Les was jealous of you. In fact I know so,' Morton continued. 'She was never happier than when she was having a bit of a bitch about Tanya or you, but especially you. Whenever you were summoned up to school because of Courtney, she'd go on about how you wouldn't be able to be so Miss High and Mighty for a while.'

Shay was stunned. 'High and Mighty? Me?' Was that how she came across? To her own best friend?

'Don't be taking that as what you are,' Morton was quick to jump in, sensing her thoughts. 'I'm trying to tell you about her, not you. Tanya and you were stunners when you were young. You got all the boys and she'd say she wasn't bothered but of course she was. Any chance to get one up on you and she'd take it. That's why she had to have the best kitchen, the best fitted wardrobes, the hot tub, the steam room, the best this and that in the house.'

Shay was felled by this landslide of information. She thought of Les showing off her pergola and her wet room when Morton had built them for her, but she and Tan had never been resentful, nor jealous, just happy for her because it was lovely to see someone you liked have nice things.

'Are you sure she and Bruce . . . ?'

'You don't want to know how sure I am.'

'But he can't—' She broke off what she was about to say, faithful to the last.

'Can't what?'

'He's . . .' *just say it,* said a voice inside her, a voice that sounded very much like Tanya's. *Why should you protect him?* 'He's . . . having problems. Down there.'

Morton hooted. 'Guilt can do that to a man. Either that or he's lied to you, Shay, but trust me when I tell you that he's not impotent with my wife.'

Shay didn't ask how he knew that, but she didn't want to be presented with any photographic proof.

'Anyway, she won't get away with what she's trying to get away with. She thinks she'd hidden all her brass so she doesn't have to give me any. I don't even want it, but I might take it and put it in a bank for our young Mort. The nerve of her. She eventually sent me a text saying we were over and not to try and find her because she'd told no one where she was and if I played ball, she'd not force me to sell the farmhouse and pay her half, but I still thought she was having a huff about something and would turn up after she got bored. What did Bruce tell you? When did he bugger off?'

'Last Wednesday.'

'Only last Wednesday? I hate to tell you, but I think it's been going on since she started having all that work done on herself.'

'But that's months . . .' Shay's voice lost its volume. Her brain was doing a horrible calculation. It was months ago when she had felt Bruce drifting away from her, getting short with her, coming home later fresh and showered from the gym, when he had started turning from her in bed. A new wave of disbelief and hurt washed over her, cold enough to take her breath away.

'He left me the day after my mum's funeral. I came home to find a note saying he needed some space but he still loved me.'

'What a walking bollock, he's wedged the door open then?' Morton said with a disgusted snort. 'D'you know, I'd have crawled over hot coals for Les. I was that grateful she gave me a son and it wasn't all bad for her, I reckon. I never cheated on her, she could have had anything she wanted from me. It was always me on the begging end, I knew I loved her more than she loved me and I learned to live with it. But this . . .' His voice crumbled and Shay saw the tears stored in his eyes spill over, down his cheek. He wiped at them hurriedly, embarrassed by the show of emotion. 'I was never going to be the Prince Charming she wanted with the designer stubble. If I put on a Tom Ford suit, I still look a tramp, but I thought after all these years, we could have stuck it to the end.'

'Oh, Morton.' Shay felt so sorry for him.

'I'm okay, I'm okay,' Morton insisted, batting away the sympathy. 'I'll just have to get used to being by myself, won't I? And so will you.' He wiped his nose with the back of his hand, then wiped his hand on his trousers.

'Where is she . . . they living?' Shay asked.

'Monkcliffe. It's a hamlet near Hathersage. She's renting a big house on a hill. You can't miss it, it's got a blue roof and electric gates. His and her Audis parked in the drive, little red one for her, big black one for him.'

Courtney had said she'd seen her father in a brand new black Audi. Shay pictured how seamlessly Bruce had lied when she'd asked him about it, said Courtney was blind and mad.

'I went to the solicitor this morning with a file of evidence. She's got a right shock coming, I tell you. You'll laugh, but I had an idea about you and me getting together. That'd teach 'em, wouldn't it?'

He grinned, but he was looking at her intently as if it wasn't entirely a joke.

'We could pretend,' he went on. 'We could go out and have some nosebag and let 'em hear about us through the grapevine. We could even—'

'That's not a good idea.' Shay shut that nonsense down immediately. 'No games. My head's cabbaged, Morton. I've just lost Mum and—'

'Of course, sorry,' he came straight back at her. 'But if you want to go anywhere for a bit of company, I'll take you. I'll pay.'

'Can I get you a coffee?' she asked, hoping he didn't

think it was a euphemism, so she added quickly, 'before you go.'

'I'd like that,' he said, taking his phone out of his pocket. It was a huge thing with a cracked screen held in place by Sellotape. 'I'll ring a taxi while you put the kettle on.'

As it boiled and Morton finished off his pie, so many thoughts started swimming upstream into her brain like evil salmon. So Les had been sleeping with Bruce when they met for lunch. When she'd told Les about Bruce's impotence, boy she must have been laughing up her sleeve about that. Les had played her like a cat plays a mouse that afternoon. Of course Bruce wouldn't be having an affair, she'd said. Of course Shay should believe him and not pressurise him. Is that why she'd suggested meeting up? To check that 'her man' hadn't been unfaithful to her by bedding his wife on their anniversary? But this was Les, her best mate. The old Les and the new Les were two opposing magnets that would not sit together for processing however hard she pushed.

When Morton left, Shay had the urge to slide down the door she had just shut and dissolve into a pool on the floor, become a liquid that would sink through the carpet, the floorboards, seeking oblivion. Instead she topped up the half-drunk brandy until one more drop would have spilled it over the rim. She lifted it to her lips. *Let's see if this bad boy can numb the maelstrom in my head,'* she said to herself. It would be worth the hangover from hell in the morning if it did. Then her mobile rang. Courtney's name filled the top of the screen.

'Hellooo, Mummy,' said Courtney, sounding excitable.

'You okay, Court?'

'Yep. But I've got to tell you this. I found something out today. A friend of my manager came into the shop to talk to her. Guess where she works?' She left the smallest gap for her mother to jump in before answering the question herself. 'Or should I say guess *who* she works for? Only Karoline, Bride of Frankenstein.'

'Sunny's Karoline?'

'Yep, the one and only. And Karoline's off work because she's been . . . suspended.'

'No, she's off work with stress, Sunny told me,' Shay answered.

'Wrong, because she's the one causing all the stress. My manager's friend has had to take time off because of her and she's not the only one. Karoline's actually off pending an investigation about bullying in the work-place. Apparently she's vile to work for. Couldn't see that coming, could you?' She sniggered. 'What has our Sunny got himself into here? You need to be having words with him, Mum, because he wouldn't listen to me and Dad's not bothered. He'd roll out some "he's made his bed so he has to lie on it" trope.'

Yes, that's exactly what he would have done. She'd failed her children, enabling Bruce to sneak all his responsibilities onto her shoulders. And could that be true about Karoline? Is that why her mum's intuition had shouted so loudly about the woman and why she'd started having her own prickles of anxiety about this forthcoming wedding? Shay barely had room in her head for more, which was unlucky because Courtney had by no means finished.

'Mort's been in hospital,' Courtney carried on. 'I feel really bad about it as well because it was my fault.'

'Oh?'

'Yeah, well Fiona was away so I let Dingo stay in the flat, only Fi rings up and says she's coming back early and Dingo wouldn't leave so I rang Mort to help eject him as Fi would have gone ape.'

Shay felt her blood rising.

'So Mort comes up and there's a fight and Dingo picks up a knife and if I hadn't hit him over the head with a toaster, Mort would have been stabbed more than he was and—'

Shay gulped. 'Stabbed?'

'Well, the knife went in – only a bit though – and he had to get stitches and stay overnight. He told his dad he fell off the ladder at work so he wouldn't worry. Anyway, that really is it. I'm done with Dingo now. It scared me so much and I had to do a proper repair job on the flat before Fiona got back after I'd taken Mort to hospital. Luckily there wasn't much blood and it came out with some Vanish.'

That *right there* was the straw on her donkey's back. Courtney was now warbling on about her car and the insurance and her rubbish wage but it was just static noise in the background, secondary to Shay's own heartbeat booming in her ears.

'ENOUGH,' she said loudly, silencing her daughter. 'Courtney, are you actually listening to the words coming out of your mouth?'

'Yeah, I know Mum, but let me tell you this bit—'

'No. I thought when you moved out that you just might start to grow up. I didn't want to see you leave, it actually broke my heart, not that you even considered it might because you didn't even look behind you to see,' said Shay, marvelling at how calm she sounded considering how fast her pulse must be racing. 'That's fine, I try not to be needy. It was just part of the mother job like having to go into school and speak to teachers when you kicked off, go looking for you when you played truant, even sit up with you all night after you'd taken something in a club that made you believe – for some strange reason – that I was Mary Queen of Scots. I've watched money fall through your hands as if they had stigmata holes in them, I've watched you put deadbeats on pedestals while you use and alienate good friends and now you think it's fine to put them in real danger.'

She took in a breath and Courtney seized the beat to interject but Shay steamrollered her attempt at protest.

'Because of your self-centredness, because of your utter disregard for anyone outside your circle of "me", Mort could have died; do you understand that? He was *stabbed* by that . . . that specimen of dysfunctional crap that your tiny intellect refuses to give up. Well, I have no words. Actually, I do. To expect people who love you and care for you to keep pulling you out of messes of your own doing and patch you up only to watch you walk straight back into yet another disaster is now beyond tiresome and selfish, selfish, SELFISH. Did you know that even Mort has got fed up of trailing after you like a loyal rescued greyhound? Did you know that he'd started seeing a girl and it was probably the last thing he wanted to do to come running when you snapped your bloody entitled fingers?'

She heard the breath catch in her daughter's voice; clearly she didn't know that.

'You might think it's wonderful having two men fighting over you, but it's not. Especially not when you have to hit one over the head with a toaster to stop him killing the other. Everyone has to rescue you at their own inconvenience and, Courtney, we are all sick of it.'

There was silence at the end of the line. Then Courtney lit the touch paper to another stick of dynamite.

'So, is this what you really think of me?' she said icily. 'Does Dad share your opinion?'

Dad. Bruce. Twat.

'If you rang him and asked him maybe you'd find out, but you only ever ask *me* for support, money and advice – advice, I may add, that you totally and utterly ignore. Maybe you should ring people to ask how *they* are instead of telling them how *you* are or what you want. That way you might find out that actually I'm in hellish pain, not only because I will never see my mum again but because your father has left me. And you'd find out that Mort has not only been stabbed by Dingo sodding Shaw but that he's suffering too because his mother is shacked up with your dad in a mansion in Hathersage because Les won twelve million quid on the lottery.'

And breathe.

Well, that was an information dump to end all information dumps. Shay wondered how the boot felt on the other foot for her daughter.

'And I'm going away for a few days or a couple of weeks, or months or years, I haven't decided yet, and will be totally incommunicado, so please let me do that in peace. If you need anything do not ring Mort either, leave him alone. Ring your father for a change. But preferably take some responsibility for yourself, get your act together, stop being a pain and an emotional drain, Courtney, and finally grow up. I love you.'

Then Shay pressed the disconnect button on her phone, then the off switch. The full glass of brandy beckoned; she picked it up and tipped it down the sink. She needed a clear head to think. She'd told Courtney she was going away, which wasn't the worst idea actually. This house was full of the detritus of her marriage that upset her to be around, and she was too accessible to Morton, who just might make a pest of himself now that they had so much common ground. She couldn't decamp to her mum's house because there would be too many well-meaning neighbours bringing Tupperware boxes of macaroons and home-grown tomatoes, plus she was likely to murder Drew and Ann Balls. So where could she go?

It was high season so a nice twee little cottage in the Cotswolds was out of the question. There was always a soulless cheap hotel room, but that would be hard to live in for any length of time, she supposed. But there was Candlemas, the rental cottage in Millspring that her mother had willed to her; presently vacant, waiting. The thought of it filled her with fear though. She couldn't go back there. Or maybe now was the time when she should.

Chapter 26

Shay didn't sleep well that night, her brain would not power down, instead it tortured her with pictures of Bruce and Les, laughing at her. So that's why Bruce hadn't suggested she ring Morton when she wanted information about all the building work Drew Balls was having done – because he was screwing Morton's wife and didn't want to encourage him into their lives any more than he had to be. In the early hours of the day, Shay lay there, wide awake, picking over their anniversary weekend. How could Bruce have lied to her about his 'problem' – the one that Les said men never lied about, which was a genius bluff? The guilt must have pushed through on occasion, hence the gushing 'I love you' and 'You're beautiful' moments. Either that or he'd been listening to too much James Blunt. It was the manipulation of her by both of them that stung most of all; they'd played her like a spinning top. Her friend of twenty-eight years and her husband of twenty-four years, the father of her two children whom she'd cooked and cleaned for, slept and dreamed with, loved. It wasn't tears that kept her awake, it was cold, hard anger and she had nowhere to put it.

She got up at six, tired of tossing and turning and chasing sleep. It was an effort to take a shower, get dressed, open the curtains but she made herself put some make-up on, have a coffee, empty the dishwasher because moping around feeling sorry for herself wouldn't help one iota. Going away for a few days was an idea that hadn't left her so she decided to trot along to Merriment Close and double-check that it was fully secured. That would be one worry off her plate if she did skedaddle, leaving just the remaining three hundred thousand.

There was a lot of movement at the neck of the Close as she approached it but not of the type she had come to expect. There was only one builder's vehicle parked up but also a police car and a small van with *'Daily Trumpet'* signwritten on it. All the neighbours were gathered on the pavement and as Shay drove past the Balls's house, she could see where the interest lay. Lodged firmly in the troublesome extension was the large digger which had been in the middle of the grass circle the last time Shay saw it. Not only that but it had rammed further into the main house and was sitting at an admirable tilt on top of some kitchen units. Through the gaping aperture, currently being photographed by a *Daily Trumpet* reporter, what remained of the Balls's new party room and their lounge and most of their kitchen was a merry mess of rubble, roof, brick, smashed furniture, plaster and glass.

'Terrible, isn't it?' said Dagmara, moseying over to Shay when she had parked and got out of the car. 'Who would do such a thing when Mr and Mrs Balls have gone to Spain for week's holiday?'

Derrick from number five sauntered over.

'I've just told the police that none of us have any CCTV. No one heard a dicky bird either, because we're all deaf and old.'

'Very deaf,' echoed Dagmara, shaking her head sadly.

'It's a complete mystery,' said Derrick with a sigh. 'I mean, it would take someone with a knowledge of plant machinery to drive something like that, I would have thought.'

'Like Nagraj, you mean?' asked Shay, eyebrows raised.

'Oh he might have been able to many years ago, but he couldn't manage it now of course. Plus he'd have had to be able to start it up without a key, all of which would be highly illegal.' There was a smile playing on Derrick's mouth that Shay found she liked very much.

An infuriated builder was insisting to the police that he had not left any keys in the ignition. He was also saying that he had been expecting to wrap up this frigging job by the end of next week. He'd got a lovely extension cued for a couple who weren't a pair of bellends whom people hated for good reason.

'Poor builders, it's not their fault,' said Dagmara.

'But they'll be rubbing their hands soon,' Shay gave a brittle laugh. 'Balls will claim on his insurance and they'll get the job of rebuilding the house.'

'Maybe they don't have insurance.'

'They'll definitely have insurance, Dagmara,' replied Shay.

'Maybe the renewal documents came to number 1 instead of 1A by mistake. Maybe someone told the insurance company that they didn't want the renewal to go ahead this year, thank you, and cancelled the policy.' Dagmara's eyes were shining with mischief.

'Dagmara,' said Shay with a gasp.

'A present for your mum,' said Derrick. 'We were never

going to let them get away with it, love. Not while there's breath in our old bodies.'

'Come in and have some tea with me, Shay,' said Dagmara and wouldn't take no for an answer.

'You look tired, darling,' she said, when Shay was seated in her cosy apple-scented kitchen drinking tea. 'Can I help you?'

'I think you've done enough,' replied Shay, nudging her head in the direction of next door. 'Mum will be laughing her socks off in heaven, if there is one.'

'Of course there's a heaven, I know it. And maybe your mama has found Ammon there, after all these years. What is troubling you, dear?' She shifted in her seat and Shay didn't know if the resounding creak came from her or the chair.

Shay groaned. 'I wouldn't know where to start, Dagmara. My whole world is in a worse state than the Balls's bungalow. I don't know what to do. I need to go somewhere, get out of the way for a bit.' And then she told her all about Bruce and Les; it poured from her like a river bursting its banks. Dagmara listened silently until the end.

'Ay, ay, you've had a lot to get your head round in a short time,' said Dagmara. 'I think your mama will not be lying still until you find your peace.'

Shay picked up the delicate china cup: the tea in it was rose-scented and it brought to mind the little café on the high street in Millspring, run by the woman who thought she was in charge of the Ritz. There were roses painted on the windows, white ones because it was called the Yorkshire Rose Tea Room.

'I don't know where I'll find my peace. It's all been so wrong for so long. I wish we'd never left Millspring,

Dagmara. I wish Dad had won the case for staying put. It would have been hard, I know, and I understand what Mum wanted to save me from but by leaving, I didn't get the chance to stand up to what happened, people would have taken us going as an admission and so I've never . . . never got over it.' She saw it so clearly now, how the life that had been built on top of that time was destined to ultimately collapse because the foundations were weak, marred by lies. 'And now it's too late.'

'Is it?' asked Dagmara.

'Even if I did go back, how would I change anything? It's been twenty-nine years.'

'It has also been twenty-nine years for the woman who lied. Maybe she hasn't forgotten that either and it haunts her too.'

'I don't even know if she's still alive, Dagmara. And if she isn't, there's no one else who could do anything to help me. Even if she is, she'll hang on to the truth she's made for herself. Why wouldn't she?'

'But, as you know, those fake truths, they break free of their chains eventually. Maybe it's time you addressed the past, on your own terms.' Dagmara gave her hand a squeeze. 'Maybe, my darling girl, you need to go backwards in order to go forward.'

Rising

*The Phoenix has to burn to the ground
before she can rise from the ashes*

LINDA FLOWERS

Chapter 27

After packing a case and a couple of boxes of essentials, Shay dropped a spare key off and a forwarding address with her neighbours Dave and Sylvia who promised to keep an eye on the place while she was away, and send on any mail until further notice. They didn't ask any questions although they figured something was wrong, and Shay was touched by their concern that she take care of herself and to call them should she need anything and not to worry as they'd put the bins out for her. They'd been living there when she and Bruce moved in; Dave had often had a kickabout with baby Sunny in their garden – more than Bruce had ever done – and Sylvia had attempted to teach a young Courtney to knit. She'd made some bright green nunchucks and never another thing.

While she loaded up her car, Shay's thoughts tried to drive her into reverse thrust. *Why would you think of going back there after all this time? What if you're recognised? What if you rake everything up again?* She didn't have answers, all she knew was that she needed to at least try and straighten out her life and for that she had to go back to the beginning of when it all went wrong. Candlemas was empty and waiting like an open pair of arms to receive her. She had no idea what to do when she got there, but this was the first step and she'd suss out the next one when she was in situ.

As she was heading out of the door, she knocked over Bruce's stompy wellington boots in the hallway and righted them. They stood next to her jolly red ones, Courtney's pink ones with the flowers on them and the largest of them all, Sunny's plain, sensible blue Hunters. The sight of all four pairs lined up together in their family formation made her eyes sting and she shifted her gaze away from them quickly. She had to concentrate on herself, for once, and she couldn't do that while she was still the squashed flat middle of a sandwich. She was lost and she needed to find her place, anchor herself to where she belonged – if she could find it; she had to locate her future in her past.

She drove through Sheffield, avoided the motorway, took the scenic route. Millspring was just a hop away from Penistone where she picked up the key for the cottage from the estate agent. As she drove down the High Street, her eyes slid over the buildings and shop fronts she remembered and snagged on the new; a curious blend of recognisable and much changed, as if she'd been here before, only in a previous incarnation, which in a way she had.

Her mother had made a steady income, but not a massive profit, from the cottage rental because it was managed by the agent who was paid extra to oversee the deep clean upon vacation, look after the general maintenance and field any niggles from tenants, but the arrangement had worked well over many years. Candlemas was a dear little place, the end in a row of five cottages all of which her parents had owned at one time: 1, Milk Lane. When she parked up in front of it, it looked smaller than she remembered, the strip of front garden longer. Time warped some memories, but not others which stayed forever in perfect form and dimension. Some in her mind were as sharp as the day they were made, which the years had not managed to soften or smooth.

Shay hefted a case out of the car and down the path. She dropped the key when trying to open the door, realised her hand was shaking and wasn't sure if that was because she was nervous or had hardly eaten anything all day. Most likely it was a mixture of both. She had to push on the door with her shoulder because the wood had swollen in the jamb and if her dad had been with her, she knew he would be itching to get a plane to it. A rush of old cottage smell greeted her when it eventually gave and as she walked into her new temporary home she felt the years peel back to when she had been on course for a different future than the one she had ended up with.

She was a teenager the last time she'd been inside Candlemas, helping her mum to clean it in between tenants for extra pocket money. It never took very long. It only had two equal-sized downstairs rooms, the front one doubling up as both kitchen and lounge and the back one as a more formal sitting room with a desk under the window and a large leather Chesterfield sofa. There was a bijou toilet and handbasin under the steep staircase and a bathroom and two bedrooms on the first floor. She decided on the quieter back room with the views of the Pennines in the distance and closer, the edge of Millspring woods. It had a single bed in it which was better because anything larger felt terribly lonely at the moment, the space screaming that the husband who should be in it with her was sleeping with her best friend.

A silver kettle stood to attention on the kitchen worksur-face, polished to a shine by a meticulous hand. After she had brought all her stuff in from the car, she filled it up from the tap and switched it on, made herself a coffee. She settled on the fancy cabriole sofa that sat in front of a functional, but not pretty, gas fire. Her mother had bought the piece from an antique shop years ago for the Old Rectory and when they moved house, it hadn't come with them. She always wondered what happened to it because she'd liked it, but presumed it had been given away. The sofa wrapped around her like a welcome and she felt calm, cradling her mug, sitting there in the silence, as if her brain had given her a temporary ledge to rest on, in order to gather some strength.

She switched on her phone to find a string of texts and missed calls from Courtney, all on the same theme,

Mum, I'm sorry. Are you okay? xxxxxxxxx

She replied with a simple message. She might not have wanted to engage, but neither did she see any sense in worrying her loved ones stupid by totally ignoring them.

I'm okay, don't worry. I'm just taking some time out. I'll be in touch soon. Love you. Mum x

There were also a couple of missed calls and texts from Morton.

Hello r u in?
Calld to av a natter. Nieghbor says you av gone away. Hope you is allright. Al ring tomoz.

She sent him a quick text too, that she had gone away for a break. As much as she felt sorry for him, she would not be drawn into being a plaster for someone else's wound. She was overdue some 'me' time and she was going to spend it wisely, whichever way that might be.

She yawned, hoped that tonight she'd get some sleep, sleep that didn't involve too-real dreams that jerked her awake to an unsettling few moments where the lines between fantasy and reality were horribly blurred. She swilled her cup under the tap, it was still early but she would go to bed, wake up with no particular plan in mind; she just wanted life to carry her like a leaf downstream for a while. Tomorrow was another day, but tonight she wanted only space and nothingness.

Chapter 28

Shay slept until ten o'clock the next morning in the small, but cosy bed. It was softer than the one they had at home because Bruce had insisted on an orthopaedic mattress for his back. She wondered if he'd do that with Les and then dragged her thoughts from them. There was no sense in moving away and bringing them with her.

She had a shower which was very different from the one in their bathroom at home, a much weaker flow bordering on a dribble, but it did the trick, even if she didn't have any soap and made a mental note to add it to a shopping list. She had a coffee and a slice of toast from the loaf and tub of butter she'd brought with her, then thought she'd brave the supermarket on the High Street, if it was still there. The thought of venturing out, mingling with people she might recognise – who might recognise her – brought a ball of dread to her stomach, even though it had been twenty-nine years since she was last here. She fought the fear, picked up her handbag, put on her shoes, locked the door behind her.

The High Street was a mere left and immediate right turn away from Candlemas and for every change she spotted, there was a counterbalancing familiarity. The archetypal village post office had been extended into the buildings at either side and through the large windows, it was unrecognisable with its four counters. Back then, there had just been two hatches and behind them either the wizened Enid Leathem or her sister Maud. Both of them had fuelled gossip about her in this village, tipped petrol on the smallest spark, embroidered salacious stitches into the tapestry of the tale, whipped up hostility, twisted the lies until they were even bigger and more warped. She supposed they must have died by now and be franking letters in hell. The quaint old ironmongers had gone, replaced by a card shop; Olive's bridal boutique was now a newsagents, Mr Clegg's newsagents was now a Chinese takeaway. The Yorkshire Rose Tea Room was still there but now it was called Bees n Cheese and the roses painted on the plate glass window had been replaced by buzzing bees, honeycombs and hives. It looked busy; a young waitress in a black dress and white apron was delivering scones to a table of two. The menu stuck in the window featured a lot of cheese and honey: honey cakes, afternoon tea with honey, honey scones. Also apple pie baked with Yorkshire Crumble cheese, the same cheese featuring in a variety of toasted sandwiches. She'd passed this tea room too many times to count. She and Denny had gawped through the windows at the cakes in the glass case and vowed that when they were a bit older they'd come in every Saturday and sample every one of them in turn. There had never been a reason to think it wouldn't happen.

The supermarket was still in the same place but much bigger. She filled a small trolley with shopping and a local newspaper. She wouldn't have been surprised to see her photo splashed on the front page and the headline 'Local

Killer Returns'. As she walked up and down the narrow aisles, she felt her anxiety levels twitch up, as if she were waiting for a siren to begin wailing and everyone's attention to swing to her. She couldn't get out of there fast enough. It was too early to be brave, right now she was an animal who needed to curl up into a ball and lick her wounds, let herself adjust to the respite of not being beaten.

She made herself an omelette and read the *Pennine Times*, the Millspring edition, cover to cover, but there were no names she recognised. There was mention that plans had been approved to build a sixth-form wing onto St John's School. The name was enough to flood her with memories, whizz her back into her dark blue uniform, Jonah Wells strolling towards her in the corridor with the wall of lockers in it, feeling her heart rate begin to increase in response. He rocked that uniform. He rocked everything, especially her world. She wondered where he was now. He'd have gone on to uni and then probably on to some high-powered job abroad. He'd have a glamorous wife, a son and a daughter both set to follow in his footsteps and she'd flit across his mind once every ten years, if at all. She hoped she'd got that right for him. He'd done nothing wrong, only she'd been blamed. Only she'd been lied about.

For the next week, her routine was simple, regimented. She got up when her internal alarm clock went off, she had a coffee, walked up to the High Street supermarket to buy a newspaper and whatever else she might need. She checked her phone periodically in case her father's care home had rung. She'd had a text message from Sunny as Courtney had obviously been in touch with him, though how much she'd told him was anyone's guess.

Hope you're okay, mum. Giving you space but
ring if you need me x

To which she'd replied:

Thank you, I will. X

She set up a temporary office in the front lounge and did
whatever Colin sent her to do from there. She made work
for herself when her prescribed jobs ran out: updating
spreadsheets and learning her way around the new version of
Word, Excel, Powerpoint. She checked out what was happening with the company pages on social media and made
some suggestions for change. 'JoMint Media' who were
managing it for Colin weren't great and they were charging
an absolute fortune for their services; she knew that because
she processed their invoices.

Even she, with her limited knowledge, could do a better
job and she watched a few YouTube videos on how to do
what on Insta, but there was too much to learn. Courtney
was a wizard on it. She knew everything about engage-
ments and reaches and how/when/what to post. She knew
about hashtags and archiving, framing, layouts, geo-tags,
it was as if her brain was made specifically for showing off
to the world via a screen. Sunny had never been one for
giving up his every move to strangers though, and Bruce
didn't have the want or need for promoting himself or his
business online.

Shay found herself unable to resist looking up Les on
Facebook but couldn't find her any more, suggesting that
she'd probably been blocked. Pre-social media days were
so much kinder on dumpees, she thought. There were no

glossy loved-up photos to torment the rejected, no air-brushed new partners to smash an already damaged ego to pieces. Les had done her a lesser kindness by shutting her out, if that's what she'd done. A very lesser kindness.

She had been living in Millspring for a week and a half when she saw the postman wandering up the path with a large white envelope in his hand which, seconds later, landed on the doormat. Redirected from her home address by the neighbours, it had a franked sticker in the corner: 'Douglas, Fellowes and Tapp – solicitors'. Whatever she was expecting the envelope to contain it was not a divorce petition. Her eyes gobbled up the type, absorbing little but the odd word: *client; Bruce William Bastable; irretrievable breakdown; unreasonable behaviour.*

She gulped breaths like a goldfish deprived of his bowl, sat on the sofa, forced herself to concentrate. The grounds for divorce were laid out clearly and concisely. She was not supportive. She was concerned only with other people's business outside the marriage. She did not contribute enough financially to the marriage. Didn't undertake her fair share of tasks in the house. She had psychological problems which made living with her a strain. She was insensitive to the plaintiff's needs. She was emotionally distant. Boy, he was really scraping the bottom of the barrel trying to find something that stuck.

Shay read on, unable to recognise herself in this wife of 'the plaintiff'. Not supportive? She'd been the one who told him to take the leap and go self-employed. She'd sold her car to buy him his first van. As for being concerned only with other people's business outside the marriage – presumably their parents and children? They'd have been up a certain creek without a paddle if she'd had no time to spare for them, she'd had to be on hand for them all twenty-four-seven.

Psychological problems? Was that a dig at her being slightly concerned that their son was fast-tracking down the aisle with a woman he couldn't even remember proposing to, and for their wild daughter who battered people with toasters? How bloody cruel could someone be? He hadn't just stuck the boot in, he'd changed it halfway through for a bigger, harder, heavier boot. Her default position at the moment was a low-lying anger which worked to keep every other possible emotion at bay, but it had just revved up to max after reading this.

Plaintiff Bruce was, however, suggesting they split the costs. She laughed at that.

So, in a nutshell, she surmised aloud for herself, her husband of twenty-four years, who had just left her for her multi-millionaire best friend, was divorcing *her* for unreasonable behaviour?

She threw the papers down on the work surface, grabbed her handbag and keys and rammed her feet into her pumps. She needed some air and she needed it fast.

She slammed the door behind her, stomped down the lane and onto the High Street not really knowing which way to turn after that. She just needed to burn off some of the awful energy filling her limbs with bitter toxicity. *How dare he, how really really dare he?* She could feel her eyes begin to sting and then blur. What a mess, what a nasty, vile mess she was in the middle of. And what was she even doing in Millspring and why? She'd come here without any proper plan, expecting the past to roll out a red carpet and allow

her to shift around pieces that would somehow make everything all right again. What sort of fool was she? She'd just
transplanted all her sorrows from the city to a village, without anything changing for the better so far; in fact it had
just gotten worse.

She was marching like a sergeant-major toy stuffed
with fresh batteries until she spotted someone looking at
her in a strange way as she passed them. She slowed her
pace, took a breath and found herself level with the Bees n
Cheese tea room. Good idea. She'd take ten minutes out,
ram a piece of cake in her gob and an industrial-strength
camomile tea. She walked in, heard a tinkly bell above the
door announce her arrival and a young woman behind the
counter smiled a hello.

The air of the tea room was like a salve. String music at
low volume was being piped through speakers and there
was a gorgeous aroma of honey wafting from lit scented
candles. She took a seat in the back corner, picked up the
bee-covered menu. It didn't matter what she chose, she'd
be too angry and upset to taste it anyway.

A minute or two passed; the waitress gauged she'd left
enough time to take the order.

'Just a coffee, please,' Shay answered, changing her mind
about the tea.

'Americano?'

'Lovely, thank you. White.'

'Anything to eat?'

'A slice of banana drizzle, please. A very small one.'

She put down the menu, took in her surroundings.
Someone had taken real care over this place, evident in
the arty touches: the tiny bees painted on the lemon walls,
the sugar bowls on the table in the shape of honeypots, the

wedge-of-cheese graphics on the serviettes. She imagined herself and Denny walking past, glancing through the window at the 'old people' inside taking tea. He pale and lanky, anxious for the fine down on his face to turn into something more manly. His eyes grey-blue, bright, skin like cream – unravaged by teenage spots, unlike everyone else's at that age; his lips full, pink, unkissed. The thought that he had died unkissed had crippled her through the years. He had deserved to be kissed and loved and she wished she could have felt for him what she knew he felt for her. How much simpler life would be if we could turn on and off our feelings at will, she thought. Emotion was a double-edged sword.

Her cake arrived and if that was a small slice, she'd have hated to see a big one. It had fluffy cream cheese icing on the top and a sweet banana sauce drizzled over it. Her coffee came with two button-sized honey biscuits balanced on the saucer. The food and drink served no purpose other than something to swallow while she gathered her thoughts and tried to put them into some order, but it was delicious all the same.

How dare Bruce divorce her for unreasonable behaviour. There were a million and one reasons why she should divorce him. For a start, for not even telling her he was thinking about a divorce. The last she'd heard from him had been to say that he was basically doing them both a favour by initiating a temporary break. She seemed to remember he'd thrown in an 'I love you' as well. As for not doing her fair share of jobs around the house – he was right on that front; she'd been lumbered with a totally *unfair* share of them. Somehow they'd slipped into being characters in the Ladybird Book of Male and Female Stereotypes where he did the garden, i.e. mowing the lawn once a fortnight which took half an hour, with the occasional bit of weeding, and any heavy-duty DIY which involved a power tool. She did everything else which, according to what he must have told his solicitor, was to serve up Pot Noodles and wash some socks.

No, she didn't parade that she'd defrosted the fridge the way he shouted from the rooftops if he'd stopped a door squeaking. She didn't highlight every stain she'd got out of shirts and carpets, the pizzas she'd made from scratch, the windows she'd washed, the buttons she'd stitched on, the fancy dress costumes she'd stayed up until the wee small hours making, the homework she'd helped the kids with . . . How had she ended up being loaded with more baggage than a Buckaroo horse with a broken spring?

And if, in the early days, she'd been really proud to put a dinner down on the table in front of him when he came home from work, why hadn't he been equally proud to hang out the washing for her? As for 'being insensitive to his needs', what did that even mean? Accidentally treading on an eggshell by saying hello, when he had a face on him like an owl with haemorrhoids? Wanting to have sex with a husband who was trying to stay faithful to his mistress? How dare he, how DARE he?

She was vaguely aware of the waitress taking another order to a newly arrived couple in the window and a plump woman walking out of the back room behind the counter and heading in her direction, most likely to ask the standard 'Is everything all right for you?' question. But the woman didn't, she said a very tentative, 'Excuse me, are you Shay Corrigan?'

Shay felt a cold wash of dread fall over her as if it had

been tipped out of a bucket at height. She raised her eyes to the woman but she didn't recognise her. She opened her mouth to issue a denial but had left too long a pause. The brief silence had given the woman her answer. She pulled out the chair at the other side of the table and said with a smile: 'Shay Corrigan. I've been waiting twenty-nine years to see you again.'

Chapter 29

'You don't know me, do you?' the woman asked, nervous smile on her lips.

'No, I'm sorry,' Shay replied. There was something slightly familiar about her eyes but not enough to identify her outright. Shay's brain flicked through all the friends she'd known at school, searching for a match, but nothing came.

'I knew it was you. I saw you passing the window the other day and I nearly dropped my tray. By the time I'd got to the door I couldn't see you anywhere, but I *knew*.' The woman was grinning as much as if she'd just laid eyes on a film star.

Slightly awkward, thought Shay. 'I'm sorry, I—'

'If I tell you, promise you won't get up and walk out,' the woman went on, before dragging in a fortifying breath. 'Terri. Theresa, as I was back then. Briggs.' She held the flat of her palms out as if surrendering. 'Can I get you a fresh coffee? I'd love to talk to you for five minutes.'

Shay couldn't have moved if she'd wanted to. She would never have guessed this homely, plump woman with the neat blonde bob and the friendly face was the same lean, mean Theresa Briggs with her angry scowl and scrub of auburn hair.

'Chloe, can you bring us two honey coffees, please,' said Theresa – Terri, as she said she was now – calling behind her to the young waitress. She was wearing the widest smile her lips were able to stretch to when she turned back to Shay. 'You can't know how much I hoped I'd bump into you over the years. And here you are.' She reached over the table, grabbed Shay's hands and gave them a squeeze of excitement. 'Are you up here visiting?'

'I . . . I've just got a bit of business in the area.'

'Oh Shay, it is so lovely to see you. I've had an apology sitting in my heart for you so long it's taken root and grown a tree,' Terri said, smile still burning.

'Have you?'

'Oh yes, I really have,' replied Terri. 'All those rotten names I flung at you at school. I was a proper piece of work back then. I hope I'm not any more.' She laughed.

Shay shrugged. 'It's a long time ago. I can't really remember.'

'Well I do.' Terri stood up. 'Let me just give her a hand with these coffees. Please don't go anywhere. Have five minutes with me, that's all I ask.'

Terri went into the kitchen behind the counter and Shay sat there dumbfounded. Theresa Briggs – blimey. The one person, apart from Glynn 'flat nose' Duffy, that Shay never wanted to bump into again and here she was about to have a civilised cup of coffee with her, because there probably wasn't enough time to make a bolt for the door. She'd fancied Jonah and when it became obvious Jonah fancied Shay, her jealous resentment ramped up notches. How she must have loved it when skinny Shay got her come-uppance. So why the overdue friend act now? Made no sense. Another head-fuck to add to the already too-long list of them.

Terri reappeared with two large china mugs, still smiling as she put them down.

'Not gone then?' she asked. 'Can't say I'd blame you if you had.'

'No, I'm still here,' replied Shay.

Terri took a seat.

'I always hoped you'd do exactly what you've done, walk in here and let me say what's been on my mind for all this time.'

'You weren't that bad,' said Shay.

She really was though. And Terri agreed with her unsaid thoughts.

'Oh I was. Total cow. A screwed-up, miserable, horrible mess and I was so jealous of you.'

'Me?'

'Er, yeah. You were beautiful and clever and you had Jonah Wells in the palm of your hand. You do still remember him?'

'Yes, I remember him.' He was someone impossible to forget.

Terri's smile faded. 'I felt so bad for you after what happened because it wasn't right, everyone coming after you like that. It was nothing less than a witch hunt and you didn't deserve it. Jonah fought every rotten word said against you.'

Shay swallowed. Her throat suddenly felt too dry to speak.

'He and I own this place. I'm Terri Wells now. She's a long way from Theresa Briggs.'

Terri continued to talk, something about why they took it over but Shay's attention had stalled at her name: *Terri Wells.*

She'd married him. He had no brother, just an elder sister and surely she couldn't have married his dad.

'You've hardly changed at all,' said Terri. 'I knew you straightaway.' She chuckled and sipped at her coffee. 'Can I get you anything to eat? On the house.'

'No thank you. I've just had some cake,' replied Shay. 'It's a beautiful teashop.'

'Every time I walked past it I wished I owned it.' Terri looked around the room as if seeing it through a fresh visitor's eyes. 'Who'd have thought back then that one day I would. Well, a half of it anyway. I'm the bees.'

'Bees?'

'I'm the bees as in "bees n cheese". We have a bee farm. Me, eh? Theresa Briggs with a café and a bee farm – mad, isn't it? Jonah's the "cheese". His creamery's just up the road, five minutes away if you remember where Watson's cheese factory used to be. He's done exceptionally well for himself.'

Jonah. His name still had the ability to do strange things to her insides, churn them like butter. So he was here in Millspring and at that moment he was 'just up the road'. She felt as if she were standing near an electrical substation, feeling the power of its current tripping along her nerve endings.

'To be honest, the Wells family saved me,' Terri continued. 'My lot, as you know, kept the police busy. I'd have gone the same way had it not been for them.' She went on: 'But what happened to Denny Smith all those years ago changed a lot of things. I saw what it did to Jonah, it crucified him. And what hurt him hurt me. I had such a crush on him.'

Shay could guess the rest of the story. Terri gave him emotional support, he ended up falling for her and that was it. What else could it be? She was glad he'd found happiness, success, love. So why did she feel a pain as sharp as if she'd just been stabbed with a hat pin, thrust through a space in her ribs?

Shay made a pointed glance at her watch. She didn't want this trip down memory lane.

'I'd better go, I—'

'Oh please, just finish your coffee off,' Terri interrupted her. 'I've always wondered what I'd say to you if I saw you again. I've gone through every possible scenario of what might happen: you chucking a drink in my face as soon as you clocked me, me crying, me chasing you up the road to finish off what I had to say to you.' She twisted in her seat, looked round at the counter. When she turned back, her eyes were shining and she wafted at her face as if to shoo the emotion away from it.

'God, look at me,' she said, snatching up a serviette. 'I didn't think I'd fill up like this.'

'You don't need to get upset for me,' Shay shook her head slowly. 'As I said, it's all a long time ago.' She sipped her coffee; the sooner it was drunk, the sooner she had the excuse to go. It was very nice, a hint of honey in it, just enough.

'That's my daughter,' said Terri and thumbed behind her at Chloe. 'She's got all the Wells looks, which we thought would be better than my lot, thank God. And their temperament.'

Shay looked over at Chloe and saw now the likeness, the thick chocolate-dark hair, the large hazel eyes that carried a smile in them. *That's what our daughter might have looked like,* she thought. It was too much. It still hurt hearing about him, even all these years later. This hadn't been her best idea, coming to Millspring: what had she been thinking? She drained her cup as quickly as she could.

'Thank you, that was lovely. I'm here for a week or so. I'll call in again.' It was a lie of course. She stood up.

'Just a couple more minutes, Shay, please,' said Terri, looking behind her yet once more.

'I'd love to but—'

Shay froze. As much as the years had changed Theresa Briggs, they had only gently edited the man who appeared in the doorway of the kitchen. The man of the boy who was Jonah Wells.

Chapter 30

'Thank crikey,' said Terri, half under her breath. 'I thought he'd never get here.'

Shay couldn't move. And it appeared that Jonah Wells couldn't move either because he stood stock-still staring at Shay.

'You're in the way,' said Chloe, butting him with her hip. 'Shift.'

He must have teleported over to her side because when Shay thought about it all later, she couldn't remember him moving towards her, only that one minute he was at a distance and then next he had his arms tight around her, then he was holding her out in front of him, his hands warm cups on her shoulders.

'Shay Corrigan,' he said. 'I cannot tell you how good it is to see you.'

He had aged, of course, but in the best way. His hair no longer a thick youthful flop of dark brown, but shorter, pushed back, still dark but greying above his ears. There were sunray wrinkles at the corner of his eyes which were every bit as bright as they once were, the colour of autumn.

He was taller, stronger, his shoulders bigger, but his smile was still the smile of Jonah Wells, capable of knocking the beat of her heart from a steady to a syncopated rhythm.

'I thought you'd got lost,' said Terri, giving him a playful slap on the arm. She addressed Shay then. 'I had to let him know you were here. He would never have forgiven me otherwise.'

Jonah looked mesmerised by her. Shay didn't realise he was holding her hands until the grip became almost painful.

'Sorry,' he said, his voice deeper by degrees than she remembered it. She recalled laughing at the yodel he made sometimes as his young voice sought its adult tenor. 'Oh, Shay, it's so good to see you. How long are you here for? Are you staying in Millspring?' *Where, when, how, why.* Questions came missiling at her until Terri butted in.

'Give her some space to answer, Jonah.'

'I'm sorry,' he said.

'Excuse me ...' Terri's attention was pulled away by people sitting in the window table.

'See you soon, Shay. Promise you'll call back.'

'Thank you, Terri.' She didn't promise.

'I got here as fast as I could when Terri rang me. Are you around later today?'

'I'm staying for a while, yes.'

'Thank God. Look, I'm in the middle of something at work that needs me and I have to get straight back,' said Jonah in a rush of words.

A sigh of disappointment inside her, covered up with a smile. 'It's fine, it was nice to see you, nice to ... know you're doing okay and—'

'Oh, no, no, we're not leaving it there. Not after all these years,' said Jonah. 'That's absolutely not happening. Can we meet up later – tonight? I'll pick you up. We can have dinner and a chat and some wine. Are you here by yourself?'

'Yes, there's just me.'

Did she see an outward breath of relief or had she imagined it?

'Six o'clock? Tell me where.'

'Number one, Milk Lane, just at the back of—'

'I know it,' he said. 'I'll be there.' He leaned forward and planted a long kiss on her cheek. 'You really don't know how good it is to see you. I won't be late.' His smile had turned into a beam and there was a wash of tears in his eyes, she was sure of it. As there was in hers.

Well, that's knocked the arrival of the divorce papers into second place of importance, thought Shay as she left the café. She had wondered over the years what she would do if she ever saw him again and she couldn't call it. Exploding was a possibility, but she hadn't figured on this slow burn where finding herself with him was too big for her to take in all at once. Shock had temporarily numbed her, preserving her heart from bursting; it was only when she got out onto the pavement and began walking that she started to feel the full effect of being in the orbit of Jonah Wells once again: light-headed and shaky as if her blood had turned into champagne. He'd looked happy, content and she was glad for him. But, unreasonable, selfish and stupid as it was, she couldn't help the stray wish that he'd been on ice for twenty-nine years, waiting for her return.

She didn't turn down the street that would lead her back to Milk Lane but went straight on, following the route she had taken so many times before. Past the betting shop, past the butchers – both still trading. Past the small park where she and Denny used to spin each other on the spider's web. It wasn't there any more, probably removed by an over-zealous health and safety officer who didn't appreciate how much fun that whirling until you couldn't walk straight and wanted to vomit could bring. How they'd laughed in that park.

St John's School was closed for the summer holidays, the gates were locked up so she could only look through the railings at it. The last time she'd been in there was to sit her maths GCSE. She recalled walking out, the feeling of elation that all the exams were over and there was a long summer to look forward to before they went to the sixth form college in Penistone. Woven in with that joy had been a tinge of sadness too, for something had come to an end. She'd felt it, like a shiver, a portent. She remembered it vividly, a second at most, yet it had stayed with her all those years. She'd been happy here in this school. So happy. The door to the left led to the lockers, the door to the right, the PE block. The crumbly old science labs had been extended and she wondered if kids studying there today still used Bunsen burners plugged into gas taps on stodgy wooden work benches.

She took a right after the school, down to the end of the leafy Church Avenue. The Old Rectory was the last house, renamed now 'Malcoria House' which was dreadful. Malcolm and Gloria, presumably, should have left well alone. She wondered if another little girl slept in the pink attic room, and if the red Aga stove remained to warm up the huge kitchen. And if her wooden hedgehog house in the garden had lasted the course.

Did the owners eat their breakfast in the room at the back where the sun poured in through the windows in the morning? Were the cellars still damp and cold and scary? It was a beautiful house and compared to it the bungalow in Merriment Close had felt soulless. There was no history in its new bricks, no layers of emotion pressed into its air like an indelible watermark, no residue from families who had grown up in it, but then Roberta had been eager for a clean canvas to begin painting a fresh picture for them all.

Shay walked back along the avenue, crossed the road and stared down the twisty country lane in front of her. It led to what had really brought her here, which wasn't to revisit steps taken in school shoes or remember old Victorian houses which drowned in a sea of leaves in autumn. Up there was Starling Farm, Denny's home, where she had seen him alive for the last time and his words to her had been so untypically harsh. Whatever had forced him to take himself off into the woods, throw a rope over their tree and hang himself had been there in his mind when he was pushing her away. She would do everything she could to dig it out of the lies and hold it up to the light because she needed to see it, needed everyone who had ever judged her wrongly to see it too. And yet she wasn't ready to walk up the hill yet because she was frightened she'd find nothing. And what then?

Chapter 31

She'd brought no smart clothes with her for going out in because she hadn't expected she'd need any. She teamed up a pair of comfy black chinos with a flowery red shirt, hoping that was what one wore to have dinner with an ex-boyfriend and the school bully who was now his wife. She wondered what they'd talk about as they sat around the table. She'd prefer to listen than answer the fateful question, 'So what have you done in the past twenty-nine years, Shay?' A lot of water had flowed under their bridges in that time. It had all but carried her away.

She heard a car draw up at five to six and the cheerful pip of a horn. She slung her bag over her shoulder, picked up her keys from the worktop, dropped them, picked them up again, giving herself the hard word to calm down. She was stupidly nervous, wondering if this reunion *à trois* was a big mistake. Was it a good idea to go poking about in the past in the hope of dragging it into the future, she asked herself – before the sharp realisation hit her that this was her prime reason for being in Millspring.

There was a shiny black Jag sitting outside Candlemas,

with a cream leather interior, as she found out when she got inside.

'I set off slightly early,' said Jonah, smiling a hello. 'I've been driving around for ten minutes as it happens.'

She noted the polo player insignia on his dark blue shirt; Ralph Lauren. He still looked good in the colour.

'I'm sorry I don't have anything a bit more dressy to wear,' she apologised.

'It's just dinner with an old friend, nothing to dress up for,' he said to that, turning onto the High Street. 'Can you remember after the GCSEs, I got a job in Watson's cheese factory? Well I ended up running it and then buying it.'

'I do remember that, yes,' said Shay. 'At least I remember you telling . . . us you'd got the job.' *Us.* She and Denny. She was excited because she'd landed a position in the ice-cream parlour and Denny was going to spend the summer working for a landscape gardener and, as she recalled, Jonah wasn't that keen about the cheese factory, but the pay sounded good.

They headed up the hill where the factory was. Where once there was a small, hand-painted sign denoting the location of Watson's Cheese Factory now there was grander signage: Millspring Barn Creamery – Home of the Yorkshire Crumble Cheese. The Jag took the turning immediately after it, down a long crunchy gravel path, and parked in front of a long barn converted into a modern home.

'How lovely,' said Shay.

'It wasn't when I first bought it,' said Jonah. 'It was a proper labour of love that took forever. Come on, let's eat and talk.' He turned to her and the years melted away and it was Jonah the boy who was smiling at her again.

*

'At times I thought I should have just pulled the lot down and started to build a house from scratch,' said Jonah, locking his car with a zap. 'It was a total never-ending money pit, but I persevered. I should have gone into building rather than cheese, I'd have made more profit.'

She doubted that; this was the house of a man doing very well for himself.

There was a deep woof as Jonah went to unlock one half of an arched wooden door that wouldn't have looked out of place on a *Game of Thrones* castle.

'You okay with dogs? They're soft but big.'

'I'm fine with dogs,' said Shay, though she started a little when three giant animals spilled out in greeting, sniffing the newcomer before concentrating on giving their master their attention.

'They're all from the local rehoming centre and like the barn, have needed a bit of work,' explained Jonah and pointed to each dog in turn. 'That's Atlas, Moose and Buck. Between them they've got about forty different breeds covered. Moose is afraid of the dark, Buck won't let you touch the top of his head, Atlas doesn't like people with beards so Mrs Wardle wouldn't have got near him.'

Shay laughed. There was a blast from the past – Mrs Wardle the music teacher with the walrus hairs at the side of her lips and sprouting out from her chin.

'Come in,' Jonah said, ushering her inside. The barn was cavernous and open-plan, with an abundance of wood and rustic bumpy walls painted with cosy cream paint. There was a magnificent fireplace to the right serving three sofas and to the left a dining table with heavy baronial chairs and beyond, a *sang-de-boeuf* coloured kitchen. The mix was quaint, charming and very stylish.

'Excuse the décor. I was never that great at coordinating.'

'You're underselling yourself,' said Shay. There was a massive floor-to-ceiling window that afforded a view of a wild garden at the back and a small lake.

'Oh my, look, that's fantastic,' said Shay, her breath stolen.

'I always wanted one, so I had it dug out when I could afford it,' said Jonah. 'No point in hanging about. We both know how short life can be.'

She knew what he meant, knew what had driven him to reach for his own stars.

'Can I get you a drink? I have everything you could possibly want.'

'A glass of red's fine, thank you,' replied Shay.

'Shiraz, Tempranillo, Malbec, Pinot Noir . . . ?'

'Pinot Noir would be lovely.'

'Come and sit while I dish up.' He pulled out one of the chairs at the dining table which had been set only for two and then went into the kitchen, returning with a bottle of wine which he opened, poured and left on the table. The aromas of tomato and garlic drifted enticingly on the air.

'I never asked if you were vegetarian or had anything you couldn't eat so I hope this is okay,' said Jonah. 'It's just pasta.'

'I eat anything,' replied Shay, watching him open up the oven. He seemed to be taller than she remembered, but then he had at least two years growing room still in him at sixteen. His waist was thicker, his shoulders broader, but even from the back, she thought she would have recognised him somehow, despite life's tweaks.

'In all honesty, Shay, I'm not sure I could have cooked anything that wasn't simple tonight. I've been a bag of nerves.'

'You shouldn't have gone to any trouble, really.' She

watched him bring the dish of pasta over to the table, set it down.

'I like to cook, I'm not bad at it either. It relaxes me after a hard day's graft, which sounds daft I know because it's just more work.'

'Isn't Terri here?' Shay asked.

He spooned some pasta into a dish, his hand shaking slightly.

'Terri, no. She's at home.'

'You don't live together?'

Jonah flashed her a glance. 'God forbid.'

Shay was totally confused now. 'Isn't she your wife?'

Jonah chuckled. 'Is that what you thought? No, she's not my wife, she's my sister's wife. Remember Amanda? She was two years above us at school. Won all the awards for football.' He laughed anew. 'Wait until I tell her that, she'll think it's hilarious.'

'Chloe's not your daughter then?'

'Nooo. Terri didn't want to risk her family genes being passed on, so they decided that Amanda should carry the baby.'

'But she fancied you like mad at school,' Shay threw at him.

'I know, she told me. But I think she was confused from the get-go and thought she liked me more than she did. That was part of the bigger problem because the Briggs family weren't very accepting of that sort of thing. I don't think she saw it coming that she'd fall for my sister but she did, after a short and awful marriage to a man. Lots of things changed after Denny died, some for the better, some not so.' Jonah handed her the bowl, inviting her to help herself to more. He appeared to have made enough to feed a small emergent nation.

'You're not married to anyone then?' She couldn't help herself. He had no ring on his finger, but then Bruce had never worn one either.

'No. I was, years ago, but it didn't work out.'

He filled a bowl for himself, having a battle with some stringy mozzarella that seemed determined to stay united to the motherlode in the big dish. 'I met someone else about ten years ago I thought I could get serious about, lovely woman, but there was just something missing and that ended too. What about you? I see you're married.'

He nodded towards her left hand; she was still wearing her rings because taking them off felt like a massive deal, even though there could be no U-turn.

One of the dogs, the shaggy one, wandered over, came to lie at the side of Jonah and rested its head on its great paws.

'I'm separated,' said Shay, using the word for the first time. She thought of the divorce papers sitting in Candlemas waiting for her response. 'We've just started divorce proceedings.' She speared some penne with extra viciousness when she thought about some of those grounds Bruce had cited. She fluttered her left hand. 'These are still on my fingers out of habit but I should take them off really, they don't mean anything any more.'

'Been married long?'

'Twenty-four years. Two children, a boy and a girl, twenty-three and twenty-two.' She moved the subject on, not wanting to talk about them. 'Are Denny's mother and sister still around?' She lifted her glass and took a sip of wine which left a warm trail down her throat.

'Hmm,' said Jonah and she heard the bristling tone blow through the sound. 'They're still there. Still in that hovel, though they don't keep any animals any more apart from a few chickens. They go into Millspring together for their shopping. You wouldn't think that Rachel was only a woman of fifty and Ella was sixty-five. If they were odd before, they're *really* odd now. They pulled up the draw-bridge completely when Denny died, not that it was down much when he was alive. I'm surprised the place is still standing, it's falling down round their ears but they won't accept any help and they won't move and buy somewhere smaller and easier to manage. It makes no sense because the land is worth a fortune. I'm not sympathetic, I have nothing but contempt for them, mostly for Ella but Rachel had her part to play too, she's not as green as she's painted. I told Ella once, I couldn't stop myself. I told her that I knew she'd lied about you and the truth will come out one day because it always does. I scared her a little bit more than I expected to, but I didn't really care.'

Jonah lifted his eyes from the plate to Shay and smiled warmly at her.

'Tell me more about you, because you have no idea how many times I've wondered how you are. You had it so bad.'

'Not that much to tell, really,' said Shay. 'We moved to Sheffield; I had a year which is best forgotten. Then some-how I felt patched up enough to go to sixth form, met new friends. I worked in offices then became a virtual assistant based at home so I could fit my job around my family. And that's all.' Her résumé ended with a yawn as well as a full-stop.

'There must be more than that.'

'Not really. I'm very ordinary.'

'You were never ordinary, Shay.' He looked at her with an intensity that brought the heat to her cheeks.

'You were going to run ICI as I remember,' he went on.

'And you' – she pointed her fork at him – 'were going to play rugby for England.'

'I played for Penistone first team and that was enough,' replied Jonah. 'My nose survived but not my ears, look at them.'

He tilted his head from side to side so she could see his cauliflower ears.

'They're beauties. My son plays,' replied Shay. 'I dread him getting his lovely face damaged.'

Then Jonah blurted out, 'I cut it down – the tree. I borrowed my dad's saw and it took me days but I cut it down by myself. Dad went mental. Not only because I broke his saw but because I could have been crushed; but I couldn't stand that it was still there.' He took a moment, steeled himself. 'What really made Denny do that, Shay? Do you wonder if there was something wrong that we couldn't have known about?'

'I'm sure there was. And that's why I came back,' she answered.

They ate as they talked, reminisced. Jonah filled her in on where some of the people they knew as kids were now. Their sleazy art teacher Mr Button ran off to France with a fifth-former on her sixteenth birthday; Hannah Coles in their class had had four surrogate pregnancies for people. Little Paul Midgeley who had a permanently snotty nose went into the army and rose to the rank of Lieutenant Colonel, Jess Lyons had eight children to a man she'd married at eighteen who was thirty-five years older than her – and they were still happily together. James 'Brainbox' Boxworth, on course to become a doctor, instead became a priest. Big Maria Morrison, who was a martial arts champ, won a gold in the Olympics. Extraordinary lives within the parameters of ordinary ones.

'I feel so boring,' said Shay. 'All I've done is ferry parents to hospitals, put meals on tables, do shopping, mend school trousers. Stuff like that.'

'Never underestimate "stuff like that",' replied Jonah. 'I've taken on kids at the creamery who were written off as teenagers and I know that their lives would have been so different for a bit of discipline and guidance at home; buttons sewn on their shirts, a breakfast before school, a kiss at bedtime, some kindness. I saw it with Terri, how she changed when she became part of us. Nothing spectacular about our family, but even a little love is very powerful. You know, I asked my mum once if she'd adopt Denny and she told me not to be daft because he already had a family. Then, when she went to his funeral, she cried and said she wished she'd asked his mother if he could come and live with us.'

'What happened to Denny's grandfather?' asked Shay. 'Did he ever come back?'

'Never. Disappeared into thin air. Some people said that Denny was so upset about him going that's why he killed himself. As if there wasn't enough rubbish said.'

'I'd like to go to his grave while I'm here,' said Shay.

'I'll take you,' replied Jonah.

Jonah drove her home. He'd just had the one glass of wine. Eating and drinking had not been the main focus of their evening. Everyone and everything outside their little patch of Millspring seemed a million miles away. She wondered if he'd try to kiss her when they pulled up outside Candlemas, and what she'd do if he did.

'I'll see you on Saturday morning then, shall I?' he said,

smiling. He turned to her, as unsure as she what might happen next.

'Thank you for a lovely evening. And meal.'

'You hardly ate.'

'Neither did you, we were too busy walking down memory lane together.'

His smile closed then and he looked suddenly serious.

'I can't tell you how glad I am to see you, Shay Corrigan.' His hand came out, cupped her cheek and she felt her head instinctively press into it. He leaned towards her, she felt the soft click of his kiss on the corner of her mouth and inhaled his scent, a mix of his aftershave and some indefinable other that her brain remembered from long, long ago.

She needed a stiff drink when she got in. And another.

Chapter 32

She crashed to sleep after too much wine and awoke at seven o'clock flat out on the sofa. The divorce papers were on the floor; she'd drawn an enormous cock and balls on them, complete with semen droplets spurting from the top. How old was she − thirteen?

What now? She'd planned on being so mature about all this. However much she was hurting inside, she was determined to keep her dignity. Kicking up a fuss would only be counterproductive. And she wasn't Cheryl Cole fight-fight-fighting for this love, especially after the way Bruce had dumped her, the day after her mother's funeral, which was something she couldn't excuse. She'd have respected him more if he'd faced her head on and told her what he'd done, rather than presume the word would eventually get back to her via a third party. It was callous and cruel and, even after all their years together and two children, he'd crossed a line that couldn't be uncrossed. Or could it?

She had once told him that she would never want to repair their marriage if he was unfaithful. She'd seen what it had done to her own parents' relationship and she knew she could never forgive the deception and the lies, the lack of trust. But would she have felt the same if the kids were little? Would she have left the door open then as her mother had for her father, to keep the family unit functioning? Roberta had said to her that she 'forgave him the first time, it was only fair I let it go' and Shay hadn't understood what she meant by that, but she did now. Tit for tat. Except it evened up nothing. It was much easier to think about it objectively than to be living it subjectively, that was for sure. But Bruce was the father of her children and, even though they were grown up, the family would still be fractured and that scared her, made her sad that they had failed. She could understand why her mother had desperately tried to keep holding on to what was slipping through her fingers, knowing it was she who had set that ball rolling in the first place.

She wondered how it had come about between Les and her husband; who had made the first move. Maybe it had started off as an opportunist fling, a 'bit of strange', then Les landed the big lottery fish and had woven Disneyland into their affair. They'd always had a laugh together; Les on top form was hilarious, great company. Or maybe it was sex on tap, although Bruce had never really expressed any interest in the sort of adventurous organ-grinding that Les had bragged about having with Morton. She liked sex against trees and in the backs of cars, she had more toys than an X-rated Santa. She'd asked Morton to spank her with a paddle that left the imprint 'SLUT' on her bum cheek; she'd made him dress up as Robin Hood and chase her – as Maid Marian – through their field. Shay and Tan had been in stitches at tales of her escapades. Somehow it wasn't as funny imagining your own husband fastening your best mate to the bed in furry handcuffs, though.

She looked up on the internet what to do when someone had drawn a phallus on divorce papers and, not surprisingly, couldn't find any guidance. She needed her own solicitor, she decided when she was having a cool shower to try and shift a niggle of a hangover. Yes, Bruce could have his divorce, but not all on his own terms. It would wait, she had other things occupying her mind. But she made her first decisive step towards their dissolution and removed her wedding and engagement rings.

She was just firing off an email to JoMint the social media people asking for a breakdown of the exorbitant invoice they had sent over, when there was a knock on the door. She opened it to find Jonah there on the step.

'I'm sorry to call unannounced but I don't have your number and . . .' He stalled, scratched his head. 'This is going to sound really stupid but I wanted to make sure you were still here, because if you took off, I wouldn't have any way of finding you again.' He made a face of pain and took a step back. 'I'll go. I'm coming across as a nutter.'

Shay laughed. 'Have you time for a coffee?'

'Maybe a quick one.'

'Come on in.' She stood aside and let him enter. He looked around.

'This is sweet.'

'My mum owns . . . owned it. It's mine now, but I'm not sure if I'll sell it or not. I'm just in the process of dealing with all that. Have a seat. Tea or coffee?'

'Coffee please. Black.'

'It's just crappy instant.'

'I'm not fussy. When did you lose your mum?'

'Five weeks ago.' Shay switched on the kettle and took a

couple of mugs out of the cupboard. Past tenants must have left them because there was quite a motley collection.

'I'm sorry to hear that. Must be hard, I can't imagine.'

'I'm trying to keep busy,' replied Shay, 'and not give myself the space to think about it.'

'Is your dad still around?'

'Yes, but he's in hospital. He had a stroke and can't recover from it. Sorry, I sound all doom and gloom. I hope yours are okay.' Jonah's parents were lovely people, kind, welcoming.

'Niggles, you know, but they're all right – touch wood. I enjoyed myself so much yesterday, Shay.' He smiled at her and she couldn't believe so many years had passed since he had been her boyfriend. 'Terri rang me this morning to see how we'd got on and you should have heard her laugh when I told her you thought we were a married couple. She thought she'd told you about Amanda but I guess she was just all over the place to see you.'

'You get on well, don't you?'

'Yeah, she's a good lass,' said Jonah, standing to take the mug of coffee from her. 'You'll have to come up to the creamery and I'll give you a guided tour.'

'I will.'

'Some of the locals call me Mr Cheese and I'm not sure I like that.' His smile widened to a grin which mirrored her own.

He noticed the paperwork on the table.

'Have I disturbed you working?'

'No, I've got more than enough time to do what I need to.' She sat down opposite him. 'To tell you the truth, Jonah, I'm building myself up to calling in on Denny's mum. I don't know how much of a wild goose chase I'll be on, but I have to try and talk to her.'

'I'm not sure how much sense you'll get out of her but if you want me to come with you, I will.' He took a sip of coffee. 'Why now, after all these years?'

'Oh, it's a long story, starting with a big orange skip. The short answer is that I realised I've never been able to put what happened here behind me. I wish we'd never left Millspring.'

'I wish that too,' said Jonah.

Shay's focus fell on his hands, large and square and she remembered how gentle they were when they touched her.

'I was a bit of a mess as well,' he carried on. 'I tried to come and see you but your mum wouldn't let me. I know she was just being protective but I was desperate to talk to you. I wrote notes for you that she said she'd pass on?' It was a question, not a statement. He was asking if she'd got them. Shay shook her head slowly. More buried secrets winkled out.

'I was heartbroken when you left. One minute you were living here, the next minute the house was empty and no one knew where you'd gone. And I mean heartbroken. You hadn't done anything wrong and I told everyone that, even though calling a dead boy's mother a liar didn't go down well in certain quarters. Not that I cared.'

'I didn't lie, Jonah. I never said any of the things to Denny that Ella Smith accused me of. He was upset and it wasn't because you and I were together, I know it wasn't.'

'I found your mum and dad on the internet years ago; the electoral roll. I wrote you a letter saying how much I was still missing you and please get in touch with me. If you didn't reply, I'd take that as your answer that you really didn't want to talk to me and I'd leave well alone.'

The letter that her mum said she'd received. It was from

Jonah then. A letter that fate had timed to arrive just before her wedding. She wouldn't have ignored it – and everything would have changed. *Oh, Mum.* She'd tried too hard to protect her daughter.

'I didn't get that either,' said Shay.

Jonah drained his cup and stood to go.

'Well, whatever finally led you back here did so for a reason,' he said.

Shay only hoped that was true.

Chapter 33

On Saturday morning, Shay went up to the florist on the High Street and bought a bunch of the brightest flowers they had and a pot vase. While she waited for Jonah to arrive, she cut and arranged them and filled up a bottle of water to take with her.

He was on time; she was aware how quickly her feet closed the distance between her cottage and his car.

'They're lovely,' he said, as she got in; he held the vase for her while she clipped herself in.

'I didn't want to go empty-handed.'

'Me neither.' Jonah nudged his head towards the back seat. 'I always take my tools and tidy things up for him.'

Shay was touched by that. 'Do you go there often?'

'About every six weeks from spring to autumn. I sometimes find flowers put there but no one does any maintenance.'

Except you. It was kind of him to do that, testament to the deep and caring friendship they'd shared.

They headed up the hill that led to the church and its pretty graveyard and also to Millspring Wood.

'Jonah, can I see where the tree was first?' she asked him.

'Yes of course,' he said and indicated right.

They parked up at the bottom of the small dirt road where late-night snoggers used to go for privacy in the dark. It was an odd feeling seeing the woods again, through the eyes of adults who saw only trees and not adventure.

'You okay there?' asked Jonah, reaching to steady her as she stumbled over a knobbly root sticking out from the ground.

'We must have been as sure-footed as goats in our youth,' laughed Shay, picking her way carefully across the forest floor.

'We just knew it so well, didn't we,' said Jonah. 'Give me your hand.'

His fingers folded around hers and the warmth of them travelled all the way to the centre of her. She had a flashback to the first time he had held her hand, lying on top of their sleeping bags in the wood, looking at the stars through the dark lacework of branches. She thought she was going to spontaneously combust from joy.

It had been many years and yet she still knew the way. Her feet remembered to side-step this tree and turn right at that one. Then they were at the clearing and the hewn stump of their tree that was all that remained of it.

'Someone, I presume the council, moved the trunk away,' Jonah remarked.

Shay let go of his hand and walked slowly around the place that had been so dear to them. They always pitched their tents in the same formation, Denny's here where her feet were. He'd bought it from a car boot sale for twenty pence and Jonah teased him that he'd paid twenty pence too much.

It was functional though – after they stuck electrician's tape over the holes, anyway. Jonah had given him his sister's old green sleeping bag and he'd been over the moon with it. Over there was where they'd stored the barbecue grill in a plastic sack, covering it with foliage so it wouldn't be found and nicked. She looked up to the sky as if she were her young self staring at the stars again, tracing the shoulders of Orion upwards from his belt, hardly daring to breathe because she was here with Jonah Wells, the two of them alone together, and there was expectancy in the air, thick and sweet as molasses. There had been so much laughter and fun and affection in this place before Denny had wiped it away with his final actions; they could never have come back again.

A cool breeze shivered through the trees and made her spine tingle.

'One of the policemen called me a prick-tease. The others were kinder but it's only him I remember. He made me believe for a while that's what Denny thought of me.'

'You weren't. And you didn't lead Denny on at all,' Jonah was quick to refute that. 'You were lovely to him. Can't you remember standing up to Glynn Duffy for him? He even terrified me. I'm just glad I had half the rugby squad with me that night.'

'Oh God, he really was a beast, wasn't he?'

'He's been dead about twenty years, which might come as no surprise. Tried to be a gangster in Manchester but there's far harder than him over there.' Jonah dropped a sigh. 'I have to say, the police were really good to me when I was interviewed, Shay. I told them it wasn't your fault, I told them to believe your version of events before Ella's.'

'I can't bear that he did it in this lonely place. He must have meant that we'd find him before anyone else.'

'Denny's grandad was always bragging that he had a woman and he was going to run off with her and "dump his useless baggage". I think he did exactly that and the responsibility fell on Denny to look after his mother and Rachel and it was all too much for him. I can't think of any other reason and trust me, I've tried.' Jonah shook his head. 'But then again, Bradley Smith wouldn't have just left them to sit on the money the land would have fetched. He'd have sold up, surely? Unless he'd won the lottery and could afford to.' He made a little laugh and so did Shay, though it was a very different sort of little laugh to his.

Denny's grave was in a quiet corner, tucked out of the way as he had been tucked out of the way in life. His stone was small and plain, the words on it simple and few.

DENNY SMITH

14.3.75 – 20.6.91

DEAREST SON AND BROTHER

BELOVED FRIEND

'THINK OF ME IN GOD'S GARDEN'

It was hard seeing his name chiselled into the stone. It was the name of a long-dead person, not a boy with all his life in front of him. Not a boy who should be a man now, with children and a job working in the open air and a house and a dog and a garden full of trees and flowers.

The graveyard was beautiful, serene, a place to be at peace. She had always imagined if she came here that she would feel his presence in the air, a benign warmth wrapping around her, but there was nothing.

'There was a collection for the stone,' said Jonah. 'I'm not sure Ella was going to bother, though I don't think she would even have known how to get one. She was never the brightest bulb in the hardware shop.'

'What are they living on?' asked Shay.

'They sell eggs and I imagine they're getting some sort of benefits for Rachel but other than that, no idea.'

'I wanted to go to the funeral but Mum said I shouldn't. I'd have been damned either way, wouldn't I?'

Jonah gave a small unconscious nod; that's exactly what had happened. The village gossips, like those two bitch sisters at the post office, had had a field day when none of the Corrigans turned up. Jonah's mother had given them a very public piece of her mind about the malice they were spreading.

'You had more friends here than you might have thought you did,' said Jonah.

She hadn't realised that, imagined herself judged as a blanket pariah. She reached in her handbag for a tissue, saturating it almost immediately. Jonah pulled her towards him, his hold tight and kind. It felt wrong and right at the same time.

'I hate his family,' she said. 'I know it's wrong of me, but—'

'It isn't wrong of you, Shay. They destroyed us. They twisted our friendship out of shape and made it into something it wasn't. Neither of us would ever have hurt Denny. Can't you remember how happy he was for us when we told him?'

'Or was it an act, Jonah? Was he saying what he thought we wanted to hear?'

'He wasn't that great an actor or a liar,' said Jonah, taking the tools from his bag. 'He was happy for us, I know he was.'

Chapter 34

Instead of driving her home, Jonah pulled into the car park of the Black Sheep. There was no more apt name for a pub than this one, thought Shay with a wry smile to herself. It had been the Shoulder of Mutton back in the day, very much a man's sanctuary. Women didn't go in on weeknights, they'd have choked on the testosterone, pipe smoke and barely veiled hostility. Only the most brazen crossed the threshold on Sundays. No one wanted 'pudding burners' in their midst.

Now it was a totally different story, it was family-friendly and an indoor play park had been built on at the back. There was, as Shay discovered, even pot pourri in the ladies; a sure sign of the sea change that had occurred.

She had nothing to rush home for so yes, she said, a spot of lunch would be nice. She noticed how Jonah put the drinks down on the table, how he carefully pulled back his chair to sit down, and she unconsciously compared it to how Bruce jerked and dragged, banged and slammed everything. It was as if every action he made had to have a soundtrack: throwing cutlery into the sink, ramming plates in the dishwasher. She remembered that Jonah, young as he was, had treated objects with as much care as he did people. The same could also be said for Bruce.

They gave their order to the waitress and then sat in a contemplative silence for a while until Jonah asked her if she was all right.

'Just a bit of memory lane overload,' she replied. 'Graves freak me out a bit, to be honest. I'd rather imagine Denny's ashes being carried by the air, travelling all over the world to beautiful places than him lying there still for eternity.'

'He's not there, Shay,' replied Jonah with a soft smile. 'He couldn't sit still for five minutes if you remember. I'm sure he'll be up a tree somewhere looking at birds' nests, recording his data.'

Shay smiled back. Denny had a small book that he carried with him everywhere, recording the birds he'd spotted, the nests he'd found – not that he ever interfered with them. Then he'd go home and write everything up neatly in a large desk diary. She bought him one for Christmas once and he'd liked it so much, she'd given him one every year from then on. Putting his thoughts to paper was probably what kept him sane living in that madhouse, she'd come to think. Had he been around today, he would have had hundreds of photos on his phone of flora and fauna; a total nature nerd.

'Tell me,' asked Jonah, as their food arrived. 'You mentioned that why you came back had something to do with a skip.'

Shay rolled her eyes. 'Mum's memory had been slipping for a couple of years and her neighbours were having some building work done and had a skip delivered with the name Sharif on the side. It acted like a key in her mind to a very dusty room, churned all sorts of things up that she'd tried to forget and plaster over, pretend they didn't happen.'

'Like the notes and the letter I sent.'

'Yes. But you can't overwrite unfinished business so easily, I learned that for myself. I got married on the date when Denny died, hoping I'd have something else to think about whenever it came round.'

'Did it work?'

'Maybe a little, but it was always there, in the background. What happened to us bled into my whole life, my choices.' She took a sip of orange juice, wet her throat. 'I could have gone to university, but I told my parents I didn't want to. The truth was it didn't feel right to go when Denny didn't have the chance.'

Jonah listened patiently, his food untouched.

'I couldn't feel anything for a long time. I was a proper nutjob. Then I ended up meeting someone who got past my barrier and I was very grateful for that because it made me feel normal.' She both said it and realised it at the same time. Yes, grateful, that was what she had felt most of all.

'The man you married?'

'And the man I'm about to divorce.'

'Why did you split up?'

'He had an affair with my best friend who'd just won twelve million pounds on the lottery. He blames me for driving him into her arms.' She laughed at the absurdity of it and it coaxed out a laugh from Jonah too, for which he apologised.

'Part of his accusation must be true. It's never all one and not the other,' Shay said. 'I think we just lost each other along the way; habit slid into the place where love once was.' She cringed then, preparing to admit her misdemeanour. 'On a subconscious level though, I'm obviously not as willing to accept blame, as I appear to have drawn a rather large knob on my divorce papers under the influence of Coop Chenin Blanc. I'm quite ashamed that I can't remember doing it, either.'

Jonah threw back his head and laughed.

'Shay Corrigan, you're as much of a tonic as you ever were,' he said.

'Tell me about your children while I eat my burger.' He squashed it down with his palm before picking it up from the plate. 'My daughter is ... is spirited, bonkers, a little lost I think. A mass of contradictions. Very bright, leggy and beautiful, terrible choice in boys. I wish she'd find out where she belonged.'

'She will, I'm sure,' said Jonah. 'What about your son?'

'Gentle, quiet, very artistic. I worry about him most of all because I can't see into his head and I worry about my daughter because I *can* see into her head.'

'I felt like that with Chloe – my niece. There was always a part of me that worried she wasn't as happy as she appeared and I felt anxious for her. That's a legacy we've both inherited, I think,' said Jonah. He understood in a way that Bruce never could.

'Do your kids look like you, with your Italian ancestry?' A teasing smile.

Shay cleared her mouth of a giant lump of scampi before responding to that one.

'Turns out the Italian ancestry story is exactly that – a story. I recently found out that Harry Corrigan isn't my dad. My mother met my real father when she was teaching Russian in the 1970s. He was an officer in the Egyptian army intelligence corps and they had an affair. He died when she was pregnant with me.' Condensed to a few sentences, the truth about her heritage sounded more of a lie than the lie was. *Lies beget lies beget lies,* she thought to herself as she saw Jonah's expression of disbelief.

'In the past couple of months I have lost my husband, my best friend, my mother, lost my father and found a new one that I'll never know,' Shay went on. The nearest she could ever get to him was through the scraps of notes in the book Dagmara had given her and the drawing he had done of Roberta.

'That's a lot to contend with,' said Jonah, reiterating, 'A lot.'

'I needed to get away and give my head some breathing space.'

'On the plus side, you found me again.'

'Yes,' Shay smiled. It felt like a very big plus, sitting here with someone her heart had never forgotten. But she was battered, wounded, vulnerable and knew she should be careful.

Jonah put down his burger, picked up his serviette and wiped his mouth. He looked thoughtful, as if in two minds to say what he was about to.

'When you didn't reply to my letter, I knew I had to try and forget you once and for all. But I couldn't. Then I met Alice, we got engaged, had the big wedding and I tried to convince myself that she was enough, but I didn't feel for her what I felt—'

He broke off, speared a chip, shook his head. 'Sorry, this is probably not what you want to hear right now.'

It wasn't. It was. She looked at him, waiting for his next words.

He blew out his cheeks. 'Okay, I'll say it. No one ever came close to you, Shay.'

She felt her heart beating in her throat.

'I've been waiting all my life to find someone I loved as much as you and I never have. I don't expect you to do anything with that information, because ... I don't even have a clue what I can do about it. We've not been in touch for twenty-nine years and I've known you again for three days and I feel pretty stupid now. I'm sorry, I shouldn't have said it.'

She leaned across the table and squeezed his arm. It was a touch that said, *I feel the same*. And she hadn't a clue what to do about it either.

Over coffee Jonah asked her more about the father revelation.

'I don't feel any different. I thought I might but I didn't want to because I love my dad very much,' said Shay. 'I'm not even sure if he knew I wasn't his real daughter, I certainly never felt that from him. I was going to tell my son but I couldn't and it made me see a little into my mother's soul because I didn't want to rip him away from my children, they love him very much.'

'Blood isn't a guarantee of love and vice versa.'

'Tell me about it.' A picture of Paula loomed in Shay's head. 'I'll never be able to find anything out about my real father. He's just a name to me. But I have a different heritage now and it hasn't really sunk in what it means.'

'Some people just don't get to fill in all the blanks, Shay. So they find their own closure and decide their own identity,' said Jonah.

'Lord knows what my children will say. Actually, my daughter will sign up to a family tree site in the hope of linking herself to Cleopatra. I wouldn't be at all surprised if she succeeded.'

Jonah smiled, then he got up to pay the bill and wouldn't take no for an answer. Then he drove her home.

'I'm sorry if I said too much, Shay,' he said when they reached Candlemas. 'I didn't mean to put you on the spot and scare you off.'

'You didn't. You really didn't.'

'It's all a bit mad, isn't it?'

'Yes, mad just about covers it.'

He leaned forward, she felt his hand in her hair, his lips, a light press against hers and it was enough to make the whole of her body respond in a way that no one else had ever made happen. She felt like a girl again.

'Promise me you won't run scared and disappear in the night,' he said.

'I promise.'

There had been a couple of missed calls from Courtney and a rather sad voicemail left which was stripped of dramatics and sounded genuine in its concern. Shay rang her and it was picked up immediately.

'Hello Mum, are you all right? I've been ever so worried about you. Where are you?'

'I'm all right. I'm just taking some time out,' Shay answered.

Courtney sniffed. 'Can I do anything, Mum? You've been through so much and Dad's an absolute gonad. I hate him.'

'Don't hate him, he's your father.'

'You're too nice.'

'Trust me, I'm not.' One day she'd tell Courtney about the genitalia she'd drawn on the divorce papers.

'Are you getting a divorce then?'

A pause, a breath. 'Yes.'

She imagined Courtney would start wailing at this point that she was officially from a broken home, but she didn't.

'That's very sad,' she said instead. 'Morton's on Tinder but he's not had a lot of success yet.'

'Good for him. How's Little Mort?'

'He's okay, Mum. We're friends again.' She could hear the smile in her daughter's voice.

'And have you heard from Sunny?'

A growl. 'No, but Bridezilla la Twat was on Insta showing off at a dress fitting and she *is* having grown-up bridesmaids. Six dog-ugly heifers with no necks, a page boy, a flower girl and two baby bridesmaids.'

Shay felt for Courtney. But what could she do? The sooner this wedding was over and done with the better. It was making her son stressed, her daughter was now hurt and there was the horrible possibility that Bruce would bring Les along to it. She couldn't drum up the slightest enthusiasm for it, only dread, because it was wrong on so many levels.

'Come home soon, Mum. I love you,' Courtney said, without any attempt to then butter her up for a loan.

'I will and I love you too,' said her mum.

Chapter 35

Shay had only been to Denny's home – Starling Farm – a handful of times and never inside. Denny, though he never said so, was ashamed of it. They would meet at the outside gate but sometimes when Shay was early, she'd walk down to the farmhouse and Denny would scoot out in a panic.

'He doesn't like strangers, he's really rude,' he'd say about his grandfather. 'Please promise me you'll wait for me at the end.'

And she promised, but she reneged on it because she thought it was amusing to hurry him along. Then she'd witnessed Bradley Smith with his hands on Denny because of her and she waited at the end for him after that, until one fateful day when she'd been forced to use the leverage of his fear.

The next morning was Sunday, late August. The air was drowsy and heavy after a week of relentless sunshine and wisps of cloud began to join up in the sky; a storm was on a slow build. Shay walked up to the shop for a newspaper as usual but then stopped in her tracks when she saw the women across the street. Arm in arm, the bloated, taller woman with a carrier bag in her free hand, the smaller woman spindly, with a pronounced bend to her spine reducing her height. They were much aged and looked more like old sisters than mother and daughter; both with dark grey hair, peppered with white, pulled into an untidy ponytail, both in thick coats, despite the heat, lace-up pumps and woolly socks which had slid and pooled around their ankles. Denny's mother and sister.

Shay felt a rush of adrenaline blast through her veins. As pathetic and withered as Ella looked, Shay's hands twitched at her sides, itching to sink into that hair and shake her head until the truth was rattled out of her. The ferocity of that emotion scared her, anchored her to the spot as a security measure.

The two women headed towards the bus stop, stood there waiting. Shay watched them, unblinking, hardly daring to move, knowing she was unrehearsed for this moment and unable to predict what she might do if her instincts took over. Shay's eyes bored into them, willing them to turn to her, find her, see the woman they had made from the girl they had damaged. She heard the bus's engine round the corner and just before it drew up in front of the stop, Ella's head swung round. The look on her face was an unmistakable one of recognition. Then the bus pulled away and they were gone.

Shay knew she couldn't put it off anymore. This was why she was here. She had to face them soon, stop procrastinating. She couldn't sit in Candlemas for much longer in some odd limbo, pretending she was too busy working, faffing about with the intricacies of how social media functioned – hiding. She needed traction, she hadn't come here to idle on the spot, but to move forward. She wondered if Ella really had seen her and if so, what cogs would be grinding in her brain. She wondered if old boxes in her mind would now be springing their rusty locks and if she would feel fear that the day she had dreaded was heading her way, that her reckoning was close. She wondered if Ella looked up at the sky and saw that the clouds were gathering, a warning of the storm to come.

Starling Farm was a couple of bus stops away, but easily walkable. Shay followed the route of the bus on foot, up Starling Hill. She remembered going to Penistone library with Denny and searching in the local history section to find if the lane was named after the farm or vice versa, though she couldn't recall the answer.

The farm was just before the bus stop. The gradient seemed to have increased, she'd barely felt the pull on her calves when she was young and lighter. The hand-painted wooden sign for the farm was no longer there, rotted and buried under years of sticky-climbing weeds and feathery long grass no doubt. The five-bar gate where she used to wait for Denny had gone too and where there was a rough drive, wide enough for vehicles, now there was only a path which walking feet had trodden.

The landscape had changed. Once there was nothing but fields on three sides but the village of Millspring had spread and a housing estate now butted against their boundary. Starling Farm would be bulldozed in a shot when the Smiths sold it because it was prime building land. Such was the way of progress.

Shay unconsciously took in a breath that filled the capacity of both lungs before her feet began to walk down the forbidden route. She remembered it as being much shorter or maybe the farm, over the years, had retreated further back from the road like a frightened animal. Her mind flagged up what had been there before: the large square concrete yard and ramshackle barn, the farmhouse to the right and a massive greenhouse. All the components were still there but buckled and battered by time. The barn had all but collapsed, the roof fallen in; it would be unusable for its original purpose. The concrete yard had gaping holes in it and weeds growing through the many cracks. Part of the skeletal frame of the greenhouse remained, the glass long gone. Shay stood in front of the farmhouse, her eyes tracing up and across to where Denny's bedroom had been. She remembered that a triangle of glass had been missing from the bottom left corner pane, something stuffed in it to keep out the draught, and it still was. She willed him to appear there, a flash of a ghost image, a microsecond of his dear smiling face, but there was just a black soulless void.

The farmhouse was built from thick blocks of solid stone three hundred years ago. It would last longer, but it was tired and too old to withstand the ravages of damp. There were too many faults and gaps for the weather to find. Slates were missing from the roof, moss had found a home in every dip and crevice; the rotted wood of the window frames held fast single-width panes of glass; it must have been freezing in winter. Shay could remember the door swinging open and Denny racing out, his pale cheeks flushing and she'd laughed at him, not comprehending then the depth of his embarrassment because she wasn't mature enough to see it. She had not yet been refined and seasoned by age and experience and empathy.

She pictured Denny's grandfather loping out of the barn

in huge mud-encrusted wellies and rolled-up tatty trousers with braces. He must have only been in his fifties then, but looked ancient with grizzly grey stubble and a coarse, red, complexion. He was massive, powerfully built with arms that had been designed too long for his body, scruffy in an unkempt way rather than in a hard-working in the outdoors way.

'What do you want?' he'd barked at her once and his eyes had raked down to her shoes and back up again. She remembered crossing her arms, wearing them in front of her like an extra layer of clothing.

'I've come for Denny.'

He turned, bawled Denny's name up at his window. Then he'd gone into the house and when Denny came out, he was ejected with a violent push that landed him on the ground, and she'd felt terrible. But the last time she'd turned up at the farmhouse, she was prepared to take on ten of his grandfathers.

Shay closed her eyes, tried to soak in the air of this depressing space, picture it all as it was on that final full day of Denny's life. She'd been so cross. He'd made her break her promise not to come to the farmhouse but he hadn't turned up again, and this was the last time they could go camping in the woods before they started the summer jobs. What was wrong with him?

The chickens had scattered when she neared them, she'd heard the cockerel crowing from near the barn. She remembered knocking so hard she had to shake the pain out of her knuckles afterwards. She'd seen the tatty lace curtain at the downstairs window shift a little, knew there was someone behind it but no one came to the door. She stood back, called Denny's name up at his window. Twice, three times.

She opened her mouth for the fourth and then the door gave and there he was.

She'd asked him, 'What's up?' because he didn't look himself.

'Nowt,' he said.

'You've been crying.' His eyes were swollen and pink.

'I haven't.'

'Are you all right?' She stepped forward, he stepped back.

'You shouldn't be here.'

'Well I am. And you should be on your way to the camp with me so we're both in the wrong spot then, aren't we?'

'I'm not coming.'

'Why?' Wheedling disappointment.

'I'm just not. It's . . . not right any more.'

'What isn't?'

'The three of us. It's you two and me now, it's not the same.'

She remembered feeling the sting of that. She and Jonah didn't roll around snogging in front of him. When the three of them were together, they were the mates they'd always been.

'It is the same, Denny, don't be such a dick. But it won't be the same if you don't come. I've brought far too many burgers for just two people.' She tried another tack and added, 'Birds Eye – your favourite.'

She saw him pause, think, scratch his neck, he wanted to come, she could tell. She knew him inside out.

'No. I can't. I'm busy.'

'Doing what?' a cross note in her voice.

'It's none of your business.'

'I'm not leaving without you.'

'You'll have to, because I'm not coming, I've just said, haven't I?'

Her hands on her hips. 'Why are you talking to me like that?'

That twitch of the curtain again. It annoyed her for some reason. He lived with oddballs and she didn't want him to become one as well. She would not let that happen.

'Get your tent and stop being weird. Whatever's up, we can talk about it around a fire with some grub.' She picked the 'weird' word deliberately, knowing it would needle him, snap him to his senses.

'No, just get lost.' Tears dropping down his face. She hadn't meant to upset him.

'Den—'

'Are you DEAF?'

'No I'm not deaf, actually. And I'm not moving either. I'll stay here until your grandad turns up then, shall I?'

He strode towards her, pushed her back hard.

'Denny!'

'Shay . . . just . . . fuck off, will you.'

Her jaw falling. Even Denny looked shocked by the sound of the F-word coming out of him. She'd never heard him use it before.

'That what you really want – for me to go?'

'Yes, for God's sake. YES.'

She picked up her tent bag. 'Okay. But I'll be calling round tomorrow to see how you are because something's up and if you can't tell me what, then something's really up.'

'Don't.'

'I said I'll see you tomorrow, and I'll keep coming until you talk to me proper. And if you change your mind about spoiling our night then you know where we'll be.'

She remembered Denny standing there stiff, his fists still curled, his head down as if studying a patch on the ground. She remembered thinking that she'd be alone with Jonah – an unexpected bonus. But it wouldn't be, because they'd talk about Denny and they'd worry enough for it to dominate and sour what they didn't know would be their last evening together. And a short time after them packing up and going the next morning, Denny would arrive and put up his tent, with his sleeping bag inside, take the barbecue from the hiding spot and set it up. Then he would throw a rope over the thickest branch of their tree and end his young life.

Shay opened her eyes, just in time to see the net curtain in one of the bottom windows nudge. They were the same nets, she was sure, grey and old with a tattered, scalloped edge. She was in there, the woman who had changed the course of her life, sitting pretty without a care in the world. Without thinking, she took the three steps needed to reach the front door. She knocked hard on it. No response. She slammed her flattened palm on the wood.

'I know you're in there and you know who I am.'

Still nothing, but she didn't want to see them today. She just wanted them to see her. She wanted to be the worm in their brain that they had been in hers for too many years.

She heard a key turn slowly in the lock. They'd heard her then.

'I'll come back here every day until you talk to me, however long it takes,' Shay said, giving the door one final thump. She'd said similar to Denny and she hadn't got her answers, but she wouldn't fail with his mother and sister.

*

When she got back to Milk Lane, Jonah's black Jag was parked outside. He got out on seeing her.

'I was just about to drive off,' he said, beaming, as if the sight of her had caused that effect. 'I was passing and—'

'Liar,' she said and smiled. Milk Lane was a no-through road.

'I don't want to make a pest of myself. Tell me if I am.'

'You're not. Are you coming in?'

'I won't outstay my welcome.'

She opened the door of Candlemas and he followed her inside.

'It's odd having you here again, Shay. I feel a bit like a moth being drawn to a flame,' said Jonah, taking two mugs out of the cupboard while she filled up the kettle.

'I might burn your wings,' she said.

'I can think of no one who I'd rather be burnt by.'

She left it until they were sitting at the table with a coffee each before she told him where she'd been.

'They didn't open the door, obviously, but that's fine. I want to give them time to think about me. I want to bore into their heads.' She screwed her finger into her temple and realised how ugly and bitter she must look and felt a little ashamed. But Jonah only said, 'I don't blame you.'

'It was odd how much I remembered, being back there in the yard.'

'Like what?'

'Like what a bitch I was knocking on the door for Denny when he told me to wait for him at the end.'

Jonah's head tilted and he gave her a hard look.

'Do you ever stop beating yourself up?'

'Denny wasn't shouting at me because he was angry with us. He was pushing me away for some other reason, and it was bigger than just his grandad getting annoyed. He didn't want me at the farm and he was panicking because I was there, that's why he swore at me. He wanted to make me cross enough to flounce off, I knew his game. And that's why I kept my cool. And someone was watching through the window.' She remembered the single-width glass. 'They'll have heard every word.'

Jonah reached over the table, took her hand. His enveloped hers, it was so much larger than Bruce's.

'I don't want to play devil's advocate, Shay, but what will you do if you don't get what you want from them?' he asked.

Shay thought for a few moments. It was more than likely she wouldn't.

'Then at least I can go home knowing that you believed me. I've felt very alone in the truth, as if I was the only one swimming in it.'

'I never doubted you,' said Jonah.

'My mum did. But who can blame her? I was sixteen and it was my word against two adults. My dad said he believed me, but even he must have had some reservations.'

Jonah lifted his hand from hers and picked up his coffee. 'Will you stay in Sheffield after your divorce?'

She hadn't even thought that far ahead and said frankly that she hadn't a clue. The question hung around in her head though, long after he'd left. Where would she live? The dream villa in the sun was now long gone – if it had ever been anything other than a pipe dream anyway. The family home was now devoid of family and would be far too big for her to rattle around in alone, plus Bruce would want his half of the equity. She'd have to sell up but still remain fairly local because she needed to be near her dad's care home, until she didn't any more. And she couldn't go anywhere until she'd got rid of a lot of furniture in her own house and also the stuff in her mum's. She'd have to hire a skip. The irony wasn't lost on her that this would end where it all began.

Chapter 36

The following afternoon Shay took the car up to Starling Farm because heavy rain was threatening. The air had been almost too thick to breathe in the night and she'd been woken up by the rumble of thunder and flashes of lightning cleaving the sky. She hadn't slept well; she knew she couldn't put off any longer what she had come here to do and it was time to ramp up the pressure. She had been stuck in this limbo for too long and it had to end.

She parked on the road next to the entrance to the farm and felt a boulder of unease in her stomach at the thought of being here again in this depressing place. In the cold light of day, it didn't feel right, torturing an old woman; but she'd do what she had to. She marched down the path with intent, she knocked hard on the door, she squinted through the windows, trying to see beyond the nets. She knew there was someone there because she saw the shift of shadows. She spoke through the glass.

'Open the door, Ella. Talk to me and then I'll go away and you'll never see me again.'

She imagined the two women huddled together in a dark

corner, terrified. Then she remembered being sixteen and terrified because the horrible policeman had said she might as well have put that rope around her so-called friend's neck herself. She had been scared of everything for a long time afterwards; scared of staying awake and the thoughts and pictures that were seared on her brain, scared of sleeping and the nightmares about her forcing Denny's neck into the noose and pushing him off the fold-up chair he'd taken to stand on.

There was a disapproving grumble from the sky, then the rain started, large warm drops that laughed at shower-proof coats. It took a mere couple of minutes for her clothes to be plastered to her skin, but Shay stood her ground, banging on the door, watching it shudder in the jamb, her hair rain-clogged and straggly, water dripping in her eyes.

There was no answer, so she pressed her soaked face close to the glass window and said, 'I'll see you tomorrow. Or maybe I'll come back tonight.' It was a cheap shot, it wasn't her scaring people in their own homes. Or maybe it was; she wasn't quite sure who 'her' was any more.

She'd been back at Candlemas for an hour, fully dried out and taking her mind off things by processing some of Colin's expenses, when there was a knock on the door. She saw the black car outside the window as she got up from the table and tried to suppress the grin that the sight of it brought to her lips.

'Hi. Again.' Jonah stood there on the doorstep. 'Just a thought – want to come and see my Creamery? Which is not a variation on a theme of "want to see my etchings?"'

She laughed. 'Oh. I'd love to. When?'

'Now? Or later if you aren't free.'

'I'm free,' she said, a bit too keenly.

'Great.' He clapped his hands together.

She put her phone in her bag and followed him out into the sunshine. The weather had totally flipped again.

'I thought you might be at a loose end,' Jonah said in the car. 'I didn't expect you to drop everything if you were busy.'

'No, I've had a pretty steady day. And I can pick my own hours to suit,' she replied.

'What have you been up to today?'

'Expense sheets,' she said. 'Riveting.' *After haunting an old woman through her front window,* she added to herself. He didn't need to know that.

'Great having your own business, isn't it?' Jonah smiled. 'Mine ticks over pretty well unless there's an emergency, like there was on the day when I saw you at Terri's. One of the machines decided to play up and I had to get my engineering head on. You have to know how to do it all in this game. I was lucky though, Mr Watson was a great teacher.'

When they pulled fully into the creamery car park, Shay couldn't believe how big the site was. It didn't look a quarter of that size from the road.

'Ever been to Wensleydale or Birtwell?' Jonah asked.

Shay shook her head. She didn't want to bring Birtwell into the conversation.

'Ah, well, we're just building a visitor's centre like they've got. It'll perk up the local economy I hope, that's what I've promised a load of councillors, anyway.' He raised two sets of crossed fingers.

'It's huge,' said Shay. 'It was just a tiny place when you got the summer job, wasn't it?'

'You remember?' He seemed nicely surprised by that.

'Of course I do. And Denny was going to work with Mr Roseberry the landscape gardener.'

'And you at the ice-cream parlour. We were both looking forward to the freebies.' Jonah smiled, but it closed up quickly. 'I thought I'd got the worst deal out of the three of us, but Mr Watson was such a lovely man. Working here kept me going, to be frank. He held the job open for me until I was ready and then gave me a weekend job when I went to college. After my A-levels, he asked me if I wanted a full-time position here.' They walked across to the largest building on the site and he opened the door for her, ushered her in. 'He said he'd train me up to run the place and so I said yes. It was the best decision I ever made. I was the son he never had, I think. He taught me everything he knew and he knew a lot. And then when he retired, he asked me if I wanted to buy the factory for a ridiculously cheap price that I couldn't afford to pass up. Mum and Dad helped me finance it. They also helped Amanda and Terri set up the bee farm. You'll probably get an invite soon to go and see that. She's been asking me when you're going to pop into the café.'

'How did they get into the bees?' asked Shay.

'Amanda became a research student studying them after uni. One thing led to another, it's as simple as that. I thought she was mad, if I'm honest; she took a hell of a wage drop for a lot of years but money doesn't necessarily make you happiest,' replied Jonah and Shay wondered if it was making her husband happy.

Jonah chuckled. 'I remember them producing their first jar of honey and bringing it round to my parents' house, putting it down in the middle of the table as if it was an Oscar. Fast-forward a decade and the Wells family somehow ended up being Bees n Cheese. Can you get a more cheesy name than that, excuse the pun?'

'I don't think you can,' Shay said with a smile.

'Then the tea room came up for rent and Terri leapt in. She's training Chloe to run that.'

They walked along a corridor with glass windows.

'So the milk comes in from local farms and it's pasteurised in there,' explained Jonah, pointing to some giant silver tanks in the factory beyond the glass. They moved on until they were looking at another part of the process. 'Then it's cooled and poured into these milk vats. One of those will make half a ton of cheese. We add bacteria, sour the milk, stir it, add rennet which is a sort of fungus—'

'I think I'm going off cheese,' said Shay with a little laugh and a pretend gag.

'Ha. Sometimes it's best not to know too much. It starts to turn to a sort of jelly that we call junket. Then the solids get separated from the liquids – the curds and the whey – and all the liquid gets drained away.' He shook his head regretfully. 'How did I think you'd find this interesting?'

'It is,' she affirmed heartily.

'Wait till I show you the cheese mill then, it'll blow your mind.'

'Can't wait,' said Shay and followed Jonah onwards to the mill where the cheese was chopped into small pieces before being pushed by hand into round moulds of varying sizes.

'It's as if they're making sandcastles,' Shay observed.

'You aren't the first to say that,' Jonah replied. 'Then all these rounds are pressed to remove any moisture that's been hiding. That takes about three days. Then we come to the grand finale. Drum roll, please.'

At the end of the factory, workers were taking the cheese

out of the moulds, wrapping it in muslin bandages and then transferring it to the storage area to mature.

'The good thing, the *really* good thing about our cheese is that it's safe to freeze and it freezes better than any other cheese around which makes it ideal for export. And we do flavoured cheeses as well. We're just about to launch chocolate and coconut cheeses as a trial. It shouldn't work, but it does.'

'That sounds . . . interesting.'

'I'll drop some off for you to try if you like.'

'What happened to Mr Watson?' Shay asked.

'Couldn't keep him away from the damned place,' said Jonah with a fond shake of the head. 'He was here more after than before he retired. I ended up asking him if *he* wanted a job. Then he discovered the joys of cruising. Went on a ship, met a young lady of eighty and they live in wedded bliss in Sandbanks. We talk every couple of weeks on the phone, he's still as sharp as a cheese knife.'

'That's a nice happy story,' said Shay. She'd forgotten what they were.

They walked out of the door at the end. There was digging work going on in the near distance.

'That's the birth of the visitor's centre. There'll be a café and a shop and a bee section for Amanda and Terri to flaunt their wares. We'll have to get on top of all the internet stuff of course, which is the next step, so my niece tells me. That age group know so much more about it than us dinosaurs.'

'Yes, it's an essential these days. My daughter can't blow her nose without it appearing on Instagram. What she doesn't know about social media isn't worth talking about.'

'Does she need a job?' Jonah reached into his pocket, pulled out a business card from his wallet and handed it to

Shay. 'She any good at design? Seriously. Everything needs revamping, the stationery, the letterheads – these awful business cards.'

'Oh yes they do, don't they?' said Shay, giving it the once-over. 'Now my son's your man for this sort of thing. He's a fabulous artist. He got a first at uni. It breaks my heart that they don't capitalise on their talents. I don't want them to be less than they could be.'

'They'll find their way in life, we all do eventually.'

'I'm not sure I did,' parried Shay.

'You've still got time,' Jonah countered. 'You were never meant to fly under the radar, Shay.'

Chapter 37

She asked Jonah to drop her off on the High Street so she could go in and see Terri, even if she did think that was weird – calling in on a girl she once hated more than anyone else on the planet.

'Well hello, stranger,' Terri greeted her warmly and pulled out a chair at the table next to the counter. 'Sit here,' she commanded. 'Was that Jonah's car you just got out of?'

'Yes, he took me to see his creamery.'

'Oh, is that what he's calling it these days,' said Terri, deadpan.

'Muum, don't be so mucky,' said a disgusted Chloe.

'If you ever want to be really thrilled, come and visit the bee farm,' said Terri, ignoring her. 'Isn't that more interesting than your Uncle Jonah's factory, Chlo?'

'Oh it's amaaazing,' replied Chloe, suddenly finding her fingernails interesting.

'Sarky little sod.' Terri laughed. 'You okay if I take a break, love, and have a coffee with an old friend?'

'No worries. What you having, I'll bring it over?'

Terri slid a menu in front of Shay. 'Order anything you

like. I'm having a toastie. Cheese, tomato and onion caramelised in honey. Sounds weird but trust me, we've got the
recipe spot on.'

Shay had only planned a quick polite coffee but what
had she to rush back to Candlemas for other than more
work on Colin's expenses? 'Okay then, I'll try one. I'll pay
though for—'

'You bloody won't and that's final. Did you get that, Chlo?'

'I heard. You are just a foot away from me with a voice
like a foghorn.'

Chloe reminded Shay of a young Courtney, all baby-deer
legs and attitude, confidence and cheek oozing out of her
every pore. She wished life wouldn't take a swing at girls
like them and batter the chutzpah out of them with one
lucky strike, because it happened sometimes.

While Chloe was preparing the toasties, Terri took
a couple of orders and Shay watched her, barely able to
imagine this was the same girl at school who'd been such a
needle in her side. As if Terri was listening to her thoughts,
when she brought the food over to the table and sat down
with Shay, she said, 'I bet you're thinking how weird this is
that we're together here. Because I know I am.'

'Yes I was, actually.' No point in lying about it. Shay
picked up a knife and cut her toastie into four.

'You look exactly the same. I'd have known you
anywhere.'

'Do I?' Shay never looked at photographs of her as a teenager. She didn't even know if any still existed because her
mum had had a purge. She'd changed so much inside, she
imagined that change had worked its way outwards.

'Jonah's glad you're back.' Terri grinned. 'And I mean
really glad.'

Shay felt her cheeks warming as quickly as if there was a halogen ring hidden under her skin.

'It's good to see him again.'

She bit down on a toasted triangle. Terri was right, the flavours really did work together.

'He told me why you were here.' Then Terri added quickly, 'He wasn't gossiping.'

Shay didn't mind her knowing.

'Not sure I'll get what I came for.'

'Well maybe, if you don't, you'll take something else away instead,' said Terri. 'You know, you had more people in your corner than you might have thought. If you hadn't left the village, your family would have realised that. Ella Smith changed her story so many times it was obvious she was lying her arse off about something, and it was common knowledge that Denny had a shit life up there.' She nodded in the direction of Starling Hill. 'These days social services would have been down on them like a ton of bricks. And me. I might have ended up in a lovely foster home.'

'What happened to your family?' asked Shay, chewing on some pea shoots from the side salad as she listened.

'Drink killed my dad, drugs killed my two brothers and the other is on a whole life tariff in Durham prison. Plus you'll have heard about my cousin, I'm sure – remember Glynn Duffy?'

'He was your cousin?' Shay didn't know that.

'People coming from families like mine can follow the leader or change the pattern. I didn't like how people tarred me with the same brush, you know how gossipy villages can be, especially those two in the post office, that pair of witches. They once put a poster on the door with my photo on it barring me from going in in case I shoplifted – *in case*, just because I was a Briggs. I was so embarrassed, I can't tell you. When I saw it, my first thought was to throw a brick through their window. Then I thought, no, I'm going to show them that I'm not a typical Briggs so I suppose they did me a favour really.' She smiled. 'Sadly they both died and went to hell before they could see the full effect of how lovely I became.'

'Give me strength,' Chloe said, bringing two coffees to the table.

'I was married – to a man – before I jumped on the other bus,' Terri disclosed.

'Who even says "jumped on the other bus"?'

'Chloe, will you please keep your neb out of our conversation,' her mum said, giving her a pointed glance over her shoulder. 'She's got ears like a bat. Amanda's the same. As I was saying, it didn't last very long. I was a mixed-up young kid and he was . . . well, the sort of man Theresa Briggs was destined for.'

'Marry in haste, eh?' said Shay and a picture of Sunny loomed in her head.

'Well, I got out as quick as I got in, to tell you the truth. Luckily. Maybe if I'd had mates to guide me, but I never had any real friends at school, just girls who were a bit scared of me and wanted to keep on my right side. I used to envy how you interacted with girls, it all seemed so easy to you.'

'They didn't stick around though when I needed them, did they?' said Shay, stirring the foam into her coffee. 'They all dropped me like a hot potato.'

'They're called fairweather friends,' Chloe called over. 'You're better off without that sort, anyway.'

'Are you still earwigging, Chloe Wells? Is your daughter as mouthy as mine, Shay?' asked Terri.

'Oh lord, don't even get me started,' replied Shay.

'Jonah and I became good friends after you'd gone,' said Terri. 'Just friends. He was so cut up about you. His family gave me a place to stay when I ran away from my marriage and well . . . I started to live a much better life than I ever thought I'd have.' Shay thought that Terri Wells looked like a very contented woman and she envied her that.

After the toastie, Shay found herself saying yes to a slice of cake. It was so good talking to a woman again, the way she used to talk to Tan, the sort of conversations that could flow on for hours and yet later, you had no idea how you filled up so much time. They reminisced about school and people in the village. Then they chewed the fat over children, the fear of letting them loose in a world that seemed more hostile and unstable with every day that passed, about families and siblings from different planets and also about drawing knobs on divorce petitions. It was closing time before they knew it. Chloe dropped the latch on the front door but Terri forced Shay to have another coffee before she left.

'Blimey, I thought I could do competitive talking, but you two should join the Olympic squad,' said Chloe, as she cashed up the till. She made Shay laugh. She could imagine she'd get on very well with Courtney if they ever met.

'How long are you staying around for?' asked Terri at the door.

'I have my son's wedding in three weeks and I'll have to go back for that. And I've got the job of dismantling my mum's house and wading through my own divorce. The sooner I get it all done, the sooner I can get on with the rest of my life,' Shay answered, though the landscape of that rest of her life stretched before her like a barren, rather than a fallow, field.

'Jonah's a lovely man,' said Terri. 'I don't think he ever stopped holding a candle for you, Shay. I'll just park that one right there with you.'

Shay smiled. Both women reached towards each other at the same time and embraced. It was a hug every bit as sweet as the honey in the toasted sandwiches.

Chapter 38

Shay went to the Smiths' farm for the third time the next morning and once again she slammed the door with her hand until it throbbed, and once again there was no response. She was starting to imagine that both mother and daughter were now sitting in the cottage and laughing at her, even pulling up their chairs to watch the floorshow through the window nets. It was all beginning to feel a bit hopeless but she couldn't stop now, even if she'd wanted to, because there was no plan B.

The following day she headed there yet again. The blue August sky of yesterday had been gobbled up by lumpy clouds and the weather perfectly reflected her mood as she walked down the path to the farm. As she approached, she saw the curtain draw back and fall as if someone inside had been on sentry duty.

The farmhouse looked even more mouldered in the overcast dullness, but then not even the brightest of hazy summer days could prettify or add a hint of the quaint to it. It would do the area a favour to have this place pulled like a rotten tooth and excise the decayed depression that hung around it like a fug.

She banged hard on the door.

'Ella. It's Shay Corrigan. I'm here again and you know why,' she called, mouth close to the wood. She heard a key turn. She presumed she had just been locked out but then she saw the handle depress. The door opened slowly and Ella Smith appeared, squinting as if this were her first view of light after a long winter.

'You'd better come in,' she said.

It took a few moments for Shay to register the invite. She walked inside with a little trepidation. Rachel was standing nervously by the fireplace, arms wrapped round herself, long, loose hair half-hiding her curiously blank face. People had never known if Rachel was truly mentally incapacitated, or manipulative, sly. Shay thought it would suit her to be disingenuous.

'Get to your room,' her mother barked at her and Rachel scooted away. Shay charted her footsteps up the stairs, along the floor above them, until they stopped and she had the feeling Rachel had parked herself somewhere to listen.

Ella stood there, like a shrivelled old fruit, viewing Shay with eyes that were sharp and shrewd, her jaw twitching as if her back teeth were grinding, though Shay doubted she had any left. She'd only had a few, widely spaced-out, when Denny was alive.

Shay overcame the temptation to speak first, she let the silence build between them until it was uncomfortable, full of the unknown; she let it linger there with a million dust motes swirling in it.

'My daughter thinks you're a ghost,' Ella said eventually.

'Maybe I am,' returned Shay. 'I reckon I've been haunting your mind for a long time.'

Ella dropped a dry humourless note of laughter and followed it up with, 'My dad always said the dead can't hurt you, it's the living that do that.'

'I beg to differ, don't you?'

'Sit down if you want.' Ella gestured towards the kitchen table, a massive, scrubbed pine piece of furniture which had served generations. Shay sat at the end they obviously didn't use, covered in a furry film of collected dust. She noticed, in the middle of the table, sitting in the centre of a crocheted round, there was a black leather-bound book with a faded golden cross on the front. A bible, which was rich she thought.

Ella's eyes traced hers to it.

'Do you believe in God, Shay Corrigan?'

'Yes.' It was an honest answer.

'I never used to. Why would I believe in a god that gave me this life? But the closer you get to the end, the closer you seem to get to him. I've read that book cover to cover and back again while I was waiting.'

Shay didn't ask what she was waiting for. She wanted Ella to tell her.

'I've got a heart condition,' said Ella. 'I've had it for years. Although I never knew until they diagnosed it. My dad had the same, according to his medical notes. She's got it an' all.' Her eyes flicked upwards before returning to Shay. 'You nearly finished me off when I saw you across the street.'

Shay didn't respond with anything other than the involuntary blinks of her eyes.

'I should have died years ago, they said. They don't know what's keeping me alive. I'm a walking miracle.' If it was a joke, she didn't laugh.

'Maybe I've been kept alive for a reason, eh?' Ella's voice began to rise. 'What do you think? You've been here shouting for days and you're not saying a word now. What're you here for then?'

'You know what I'm here for, Ella.' Shay kept her voice controlled, self-assured, belying the chaos happening inside her: nerves ringing like bells, thundering adrenaline, the pronounced pulse in her throat. She was so close to getting what she came for, she could almost taste it on her tongue, an energy like burning metal.

Ella pulled out a chair and threw herself on it wearily.

'None of it is Rachel's fault, you know. She's not right up here.' Ella tapped the front of her head.

Shay let it unroll, unsolicited.

'I'm not a bad person, whatever you might think. I didn't intend for things to turn out the way they did. You got kids?'

'Two.'

'Hmm.' Ella licked some moisture into her dry lips. It was cold in this house and, despite the surfeit of windows, dark and dull. 'I can barely walk and I've less breath every day. Rachel will have to go into a home because she can't look after herself. The money from this place will make sure she gets somewhere nice to live at last.'

'You should have found somewhere easier to manage a long time ago,' said Shay.

Ella seemed amused by that. 'Don't think I haven't been punished for what I did, Shay Corrigan, because this house has been my penance.'

'And what did you do, Ella?' Shay wanted to clear the distance between them, stick her hand down the woman's throat and pull the words out of her.

'I protected my children, that's what I did. You're a mother, you know what you'd do for them.'

'I would never throw an innocent child under a bus for them,' Shay yelled, she couldn't help it, and Ella winced. Her head dropped into a hand that stroked it to soothe it. Then, in a volume barely above a breath, she said:

'I'm sorry.'

Shay felt her whole body empty of air. That apology – tantamount to a confession. She had waited so long for it, her brain could barely process it, repelling it in case it were a Trojan Horse. She needed to hear it again.

'What did you say?'

'I said I'm sorry.' The words begrudged this time.

'Why did you lie, Ella? Why did you tell people, the police, that we'd argued, that I'd sworn at Denny, taunted him, told him I never wanted to see him again when you know I didn't do any of that and I never would have because I loved your son.'

'And I loved him as well,' Ella screamed at her and stabbed her finger upwards. 'And I love her. And what I did, I did for them. To keep my girl with me and to protect my boy's memory.'

Ella reached for the bible in the middle of the table and slid it across to Shay through the dust.

'If you swore on that holy book would you break your word?'

'No, I wouldn't.'

'Huh, you would say that.'

'I would say that, because it's true. I'm not a liar, Ella.' Shay picked it up. 'What do you want me to swear to?'

Ella's beady eyes fixed her.

'I want you to swear that you won't do anything until

I'm gone. It won't be long, I can assure you; I'm officially on the way out now. Then you can do what you like.' She sighed heavily, as if the sound was scraped from the bottom of her soul. 'I can't carry it any more. I'm not a bad person. So you swear on that book that you'll wait until I'm gone or I'll say no more.'

Shay picked up the bible, because they'd get no further until she swore.

'I swear on this bible that I will take no action . . .' she kept looking at Ella for agreement that she was saying all the right words '. . . until you are passed.'

'Swear it on your children's lives,' said Ella.

'I swear it on the lives of everyone I hold dear,' said Shay. 'I promise you, and I give you my word.' She squeezed the bible as if pressing her vow into the pages. Ella nodded, satisfied, continued to stare at Shay before she eventually spoke again.

'You'll have heard the stories about us, don't lie and say you haven't.'

'I wasn't going to.'

'People always say, why don't they leave if things are so bad. It's not so easy when you've nowhere to go. And when you've been so twisted to see things as normal that aren't. It has to take a lot for you to snap.'

Shay felt a knot forming in her stomach.

Ella chewed on the insides of her mouth, building up to letting out the words which had sat stagnating inside her. She had been both the guardian of them and their prisoner.

'My son did what he did to protect us. And I did what I did because it was the only way I could pay him back, to keep his memory from being ripped apart by people sitting in judgement.'

Shay felt a draught from the window, it seemed to sink all the way to her bones.

'What did Denny do, Ella?' asked Shay.

'My boy killed my father,' said Ella. 'That's what he did.'

The shock was seismic, Shay felt the rumble within her; whatever she'd expected, it wasn't this. Dear, gentle Denny, there was nothing she could imagine that would have made him do such a thing. It was too big a revelation for her to comprehend and it made no sense. Her mind birthed a hundred questions, they burst in her head like snakes from eggs. Her mouth opened to ask the first of them but Ella pushed herself to her feet and shuffled over to a dresser, messy with detritus on its many shelves. She opened one of the cupboards in the base and pulled out a carrier bag.

'They're all in there,' she said, swinging it onto the table. 'They'll tell you everything you need to know. I could have burnt them. I would have, if I'd been a bad person. But I kept them . . . for you.'

'What are they?' asked Shay.

'Denny's diaries,' said Ella.

*

Shay couldn't get back to Candlemas fast enough. The books were parcelled in brown paper, written on them in thick black pen:

On my death, to be given unopened to Shay Corrigan, address unknown

Shay cut the string, unwrapped them as if they were treasured artifacts, arranged them in date order. She had bought all these hardback diaries for Denny, one every Christmas and he would buy her a *Guinness Book of Records* in return. She opened the first, saw her own schoolgirl handwriting in her practised italic pen.

> *To Denny, love Shay. Happy Christmas.*
> *This book is for you to write down all*
> *your thoughts and dreams*
> *Loads and loads of love xxx*

The child inside her swelled with a mix of nostalgia, sadness and affection. She remembered writing these words, how she drew spaced-out pencil lines, that she'd later rub out, to get all the lettering perfect. She turned the page, saw Denny's boyish scrawl, the long, thin joined-up font that started off neat but then hurried to keep pace with the thoughts pouring out of him.

Jan 1st.

This is the diary of Denny Smith aged 10. It's a present from my best friend Shay Corrigan and I'm going to write everything that happens down in it.

There was barely any white space left in the book, he'd scribbled and doodled and written in every available part of it. She closed it and picked up the last book, the diary of Denny Smith aged 16. The second half of the book was heartbreakingly empty of entries, the untouched pages glared too brightly. Her birthday was marked in February, next to a doodle of a flower. Jonah's on Christmas Eve, a small brown rugby ball drawn by his name.

She noticed her fingers had a slight tremble as she turned to June and she read what had led to their worlds being smashed apart. And then she cried and cried and cried.

Chapter 39

Later she drove up to Jonah's house and waited for him. It was after six and she thought he might be home; she should have rung first but she wasn't thinking straight. Shay was hunting in her bag for his business card when his Jag nosed into sight. She could see him smiling through the windscreen.

'Hello,' he said in warm greeting as he got out of the car. 'I've just driven round to your house and here you are instead. What a lovely—' He broke off on seeing her face. 'Jesus, what's happened?'

She looked terrible, she must do, though she hadn't checked her reflection in the mirror before driving here. Her eyes must be swollen, her cheeks red raw from salt burn.

'I went to see Ella. She told me what happened,' she replied. 'And she gave me all Denny's diaries.'

Jonah's eyes dropped to the bag she was carrying.

'Let's get you inside,' he said.

He opened up the door and the dogs greeted them in a friendly rush. He fussed them quickly then guided her into his dining area, pulled a chair out for her, pressed lightly on her shoulders to seat her because she was bewildered, her thoughts scattered.

'Let me get you a drink.' He lifted the jug of coffee from his filter machine and filled two mugs. 'It's been stood a while, so it might be a bit strong.'

'It doesn't matter.'

'Tell me what happened,' said Jonah.

'She opened the door and let me in. I had to swear on a bible that I wouldn't do anything with the information until she . . . wasn't here any more.' Shay shook her head to settle tears rising up inside her even though she didn't think she had any left. 'None of it should have happened, Jonah. He didn't have to do it.' Emotion had claimed her throat, she could barely speak.

Jonah put a coffee in front of her, sat down next to her. 'So you know?'

When she nodded, he felt suddenly winded.

Shay reached for the last diary, opened it to mid-June, passed it to Jonah to read.

Everyone has a different idea of normal I think. My normal is very different to Shay's and Jonah's. It's just something you live with, day in and day out and your brain adjusts to it so stuff doesn't become a shock all the time. I don't like my normal. I don't have any happy memories of anything in this house because even the best of them are spoiled. Everything nice gets broken in this house, he spoils everything. He says everything in this house is his and he can do what he likes with it. That's why he's started on Rachel.

'Started on Rachel?' Jonah asked, but there was no other way to interpret it.

He read on.

He keeps saying he's going to leave us as if it's a threat. He says he's got a woman but it's a lie, though I wish it weren't.

Jonah lifted his head. Shay nodded at him to continue.

. . . Mum screaming at him to leave Rachel alone . . . asking me to help her.

'Jesus Christ. He was a bloody animal.'

I feel so calm writing this, diary. I know it won't last because what I've done is so big and my brain is only letting me take in bits at a time, as if it's feeding me so I can swallow it properly. I didn't mean to kill him, I just wanted him to get off her . . .

Jonah lowered the book. 'Denny killed his grandfather? Oh my god, Shay, I can't read this.' He put it down on the table, pushed it away from him as if by doing so he would be pushing away the truth.

'Denny hit him with a brick that Rachel used as a doorstop. And something must have snapped in him because he kept hitting him. They cleaned up and Ella said they should bury him in the scrub down by their stream. It must have been a nightmare for him.'

'Why didn't they just ring the police?' asked Jonah, with a groan.

'They panicked. They didn't know what to do and Ella just wanted to shield them so she tried to make the problem go away, except it didn't. If you read on, Denny started to process it all and he wanted to ring the police, but they'd made it so much worse by burying him with his things to make it look as if he'd left, how could they explain that? If they confessed, Ella was frightened she'd be taken away from Rachel and that Denny would be locked up. And they'd have to say why they killed him and Ella couldn't bear the shame of people realising all the rumours about them were true, and so their only course of action was to brazen it out, pretend the old bastard had run off as he'd told so many people he was going to, and they'd just have to live with what they'd done.'

'Oh God, no, no.' Jonah rubbed his head as if to wipe away the images inside it.

'Every awful detail is in there. Denny killed his grand-father and when the enormity of it hit him, he couldn't live with himself. He knew people would say that they always thought he was weird, and he didn't feel he had anywhere to turn. Nothing would be able to erase the fact he'd killed someone.'

Jonah tilted his head back and squeezed his eyes shut as he tried to take it in.

'Why didn't he tell us?'

'Ella made him swear not to say anything to anyone, she's good at that.' A small dry laugh. 'She told him he'd have to forget it and carry on as normal and it would all go away but only if he never told a soul. She was probably right in that, because we'd have made him go to the police, wouldn't we? We couldn't have just said nothing.'

Jonah got up from his chair, walked around to expend the nervous energy which was building inside him.

'We would have been there for him,' he said.

'I know. And maybe if things had settled in his brain he would have realised that, but all this must have gone off like a bomb in his head and he didn't think he could ever put the pieces back together.' She picked up the diary and read one particular paragraph to him aloud:

'I feel as if I am in a nightmare. I have killed someone and I want to go to the police. I have begged mum to let me. I want to run away but there's no place to go. I can't breathe. I can't undo what I've done and I can't tell anyone because I swore. Even if I broke my promise, if I told Shay or Jonah I will be passing them the weight of this to carry too and I can't do that. They will never see me as I am again. I am changed forever.'

'That's why he was nasty to me when I went up to the farmhouse, he just wanted to keep me out of the mess.'

'Oh Denny, you bloody, silly boy.' Jonah smudged the tears out of his eyes.

'And the reason why he chose our tree to end his life was because he was happiest there.' Shay hiccuped a laugh, an ironic, mirthless laugh. 'It was his way of telling us how much he loved us, not how much he resented us. He set it all up as if we were camping together – our place, the three of us – the best memory he had to go with him, that's what he planned. Why didn't we even think of that before?'

Jonah slumped back down on the chair. 'And Ella knew all this?'

'Yes. Denny wrote his confession in the diary, he took full responsibility, and Ella kept it in case she ever needed it. Read it and you'll see that he was trying to protect his mother more than she ever tried to protect him. Of course, I'd played into her hands when I went up to the farm the day before he died. If people thought Denny was upset because of us, maybe they wouldn't go poking around for any other explanation. She said she didn't foresee it would cause so much damage. She kept the diaries for me, hoping to make amends somehow. She said she wished she hadn't lived so long.'

'Her and me both,' said Jonah with a grimace. 'The old bitch.'

He took her hand, rubbed warmth into it.

'What are you going to do with them, Shay?'

She shrugged her shoulders. 'Nothing yet. I'll keep my promise. But there's more to tell, Jonah.'

She pulled her hand from his, picked up another diary where she'd left a marker. 'There are some lovely memories in here as well as awful ones; listen.

'I love Shay Corrigan with all my heart. Tonight we were coming home from the cinema and we bumped into Glynn Duffy, Antony Shepherd and Kye McHugh. I thought we were goners. Shay pushed in between us and said to GD, 'GET LOST, NOSE'. He went ballistic. She just stood there while he was shouting at her, spit flying everywhere, and then the rugby boys came round the corner like an army. It was fantastic. Jonah Wells smiled at them and said 'HELLO LADIES'. I wanted to laugh, cry and throw my arms around him at the same time. He's fab.'

She picked up another diary.

'Camping tonight. Jonah's given me his sister's old sleeping bag which is better than sheets. We had Birds Eye burgers and hot dogs on the barbecue and some of Jonah's mum's homemade cake. Jonah asked me if I wanted to join the rugby lot. I said I'd think about it . . .'

She turned to another passage.

'Jonah said hello to me by the lockers today and everyone was looking at us. I feel really proud that he's my friend. I don't know why he is, but I don't care cos he really is . . .'

And another.

'Jonah and I helped each other with our exam revision tonight. He's got such a cool bedroom. It was magic just being the two of us. It was a brilliant night and I can now understand CALCULUS!!! . . .'

Finally, she read:

'It's stupid, I know we won't but I wish that when we grow up, us three would get a house together and live in it. I love Shay . . .
. . . but I'm in love with Jonah.'

'Mentions of me get less and mentions of you get more in the last two diaries.' Shay smiled.

'I never guessed,' said Jonah.

'He didn't want you to know. He didn't mind that you'd never feel the same, it was enough for him to be your friend.' Shay gave a little laugh. 'He was so made up when you and I got together. He said that the two people he loved most in the world loved each other and yet he never felt in the slightest cut out. He said the three of us made a perfect circle.' Shay closed the diary and pressed it to her heart. 'Poor, darling Denny.'

'I can't believe it,' said Jonah. 'I don't know what I expected to hear but it wasn't this.'

'I think Ella has been waiting for me to turn up at her door ever since it all happened,' replied Shay. 'She said once she put them on a pile to burn and the match wouldn't strike. She took it as a sign from God that she had to keep them safe.'

Jonah's expression said exactly what he thought about that.

'She kept those diaries for her, not you. She's fooling herself.'

'Well, whatever the reality, I have them. I have the truth.'

Jonah gave his head a shake of disbelief. 'It's all so . . . warped.'

'That's why she never sold up. They'd have unearthed her father's bones and possessions in his grave. So she stayed put and became their custodian and served her own twenty-nine-year jail sentence.' Ella's logic was undeniably firm and flawed in equal measure.

'They were no more free of him than when he was alive,' said Jonah. 'What a total waste.'

None of it should have happened, but it did. And now Shay could, at last, begin to mend. Now she could move forward.

They opened a bottle of wine and raised their glasses to their friend and wished he was there with them with his gawky, awkward smile and his mad hair and kind, bright eyes and the way he could get so excited over finding a beefsteak fungus or a kestrel's nest. And Shay wondered if there was any truth in the passage of his diary that read:

When anyone asks me what I want to be when I leave school I say, working for the Forestry Commission, but I can't ever imagine me as an adult. I can see Shay married and having a baby and I can see Jonah with a beard and a car, but me . . . I have the feeling, I'll never have those things. I don't think I'm meant to grow up.

Chapter 40

She'd had too much wine to drive home and he'd had too much wine to drive her home. Shay stayed over in his spare room and when Jonah had asked her if she'd be okay alone, she'd replied yes, though she hadn't wanted to. Taking off her rings had been the first step to singledom, but she wasn't ready to rush anything; not even with this lovely man who had carved a shape out of her heart so long ago that only he could fill.

She was woken by birdsong chirruping, sounds from the floor below and then the aroma of fresh coffee drifted into her nostrils. She sat up quickly in bed, momentarily disorientated; she couldn't remember sleeping as soundly as she had for a long time. She felt inexplicably light, as if a weight she had been carrying around her neck, like Jacob Marley's chain, had lifted.

'I was just about to call you,' said Jonah, when she came down the stairs. He was in the kitchen frying something in a pan. The three dogs were loitering hopefully nearby.

'Bacon, eggs, toast, pancakes and maple syrup. Anything

there you fancy?' He smiled at her and again she saw the beautiful boy who had loved her.

'All of it,' she said.

'Then please, take a seat, m'lady and dig in. Did you sleep well?'

'Better than I have for a long time.'

'It's the mattress, it's very good.'

'No, it wasn't the mattress.'

Jonah put a plate of pancakes down on the table. Put, not dropped as was Bruce's style. She'd barely thought about her life back in Sheffield these past days, but it was nibbling at her now there was space in her head for it. Sunny's wedding was looming; and, though she'd rung the care home to check her father was stable, this was the longest time she'd been apart from him. She didn't know if she'd feel differently about him, feel a fraud, she was a little afraid of the emotions that might rush to the surface when she was in his presence again. She had also to sort out her mum's house and belongings, lay her ashes somewhere fitting and lovely; she wouldn't ask Paula for her opinion about where that might be. Even now, she was still very much in the middle of the family sandwich and felt duties begin to press against her sides. But, there was a difference between duty and servitude. She'd learn to step back from Courtney and Sunny, because it was a skill to be acquired. She did not want to breathe into their sails and divert their ships onto courses they were not destined for. And she had to concentrate on finding her own place in life now; it was her turn for the light.

As if Jonah's thoughts were in tune with hers, he asked, 'You're going back soon aren't you, now that you've got what you need?'

'Yes,' she replied. 'I have to.' She'd decided to go today,

meet her duties head on, get them out of the way, the sooner the better.

'Is there any chance that your divorce won't happen?' He poured her an orange juice from a giant jug.

'Not a chance.'

Jonah's head jerked.

'I mean not a chance that it won't happen. I'll try very hard not to do rude drawings on the next set of papers I'm sent so it doesn't hold anything up.'

Jonah laughed then, made a pretence of wiping his brow. Then he nodded his head towards the carrier bag on the counter.

'I stayed up and read all of Denny's diaries. I'm glad we made him happy, Shay. It made me think, especially what he said about us being a circle. I'd like to start some sort of charity for teenage kids in his position, who need help but don't know where to get it from. What do you think?'

Shay smiled. 'I think that's a wonderful idea.'

'I'd call it Denny's Circle. Or is that too corny?'

Shay picked up her juice and sipped it. It tasted of new morning.

'No, it's not corny at all; it's perfect.'

'I wouldn't know where to start, though.' Jonah coughed. 'So if you fancy helping me . . . sort of, do it together. I know you work remotely. We can Zoom.'

Shay's turn to laugh. 'I'd love to help you.'

'Please stay in touch,' he said then, suddenly serious. 'You have mended parts of me that I'd forgotten were broken. I don't know what this is between us, or where it might go, but I do know that I don't want to lose you from my life again.'

He'd just said the words that were in her heart.

*

When she reached Candlemas, she packed her case, locked everything up and got in her car. Her lips still carried Jonah's goodbye kiss, full of affection, warmth, flavoured with times past and hope. They had made each other no promises, but they would stay in touch, work on Denny's Circle together and see where it led them. There were almost thirty years between the young people they were then and who they were now and they were both much changed. Time would tell if they had grown apart too much to come together again.

*

Shay drove straight to the care home and saw that Barbara had signed in twenty minutes before. She entered Harry's room to find her there, sitting by his side holding his hand, talking softly to him.

'Hello, love,' she said to Shay.

'Hello, Barbara.' Shay leaned over, gave her dad a kiss. She waited for something to slam into her from left field but nothing did; she just felt the same constant love for this man, her daddy.

'We were just reminiscing, about when we met.' Barbara lifted Harry's hand to her lips and kissed it. 'I never smashed up their marriage, Shay. It'd been broke for a long time.'

'I know,' Shay replied. There were so many pieces in the puzzle put together now; the picture was much clearer. Her father had really fallen hard for this woman, as much as he had for Roberta in the beginning. But, with Barbara, there had been true parity. He'd been loved as much as he loved and Shay was happy he'd found someone, even if they'd been properly together for too short a time. If ever there was a lesson to seize the day, it was here in this room.

'We used to laugh so much, me and your dad. We crammed so many memories into our years. I could never have had enough with him,' said Barbara. 'I know your dad felt guilty about leaving your mum alone and I thought my husband wouldn't have been able to cope by himself, but we couldn't give each other up and one mad day we decided to take our chance before it was too late and I don't regret it. I love him so much, but I've told him it's okay to let go, I'll be all right. I don't want him to suffer any longer.' She smiled away the wash of tears in her eyes, touched Harry's cheek, smoothed her fingers over his pale, smooth skin, a gesture indicative of the tenderness they must have shared; she'd given him what he wanted to find in Roberta, to be first-best.

'I found out recently that he's not my dad,' said Shay, saying it without any filter stopping her. 'I don't know if he ever knew that.' She pulled a tissue out of the box on the storage cabinet at her side. 'I wanted to tell him that it doesn't make any difference to how I feel about him.'

'Oh, love, he knew,' said Barbara, as if it had been a weight inside her given up. 'He always knew. And it didn't make a jot of difference to him either.'

Shay's head swivelled to her father's new wife. 'He did?' she asked.

'He told me. He and your mum never talked about it, but he must have guessed as soon as she came back from that place where she was teaching. He said that he wasn't really sure what he'd feel until you were born and when you were ... well, it was all there – you were his.'

A long sigh escaped from Shay's chest. He was to her what she was to him and that's all that mattered. Nothing had changed; that was all she wanted to happen, to carry on being Harry Corrigan's daughter.

'Thank you for telling me that, Barbara.'

'I'm glad you know the truth. It's a much better life when you don't have to pretend.'

'Are you all right, yourself? I know how hard this must be on you.'

Barbara nodded. 'As well as can be. I haven't been able to get to see Harry as much as I'd have liked to recently. My mum's not well; she's ninety-six now and fading a bit, and my daughter's having some problems. And I've not been top bill of health myself.'

Shay noted how she put herself last on the list.

'I bet you feel like you're in the middle of a sand-wich,' she said.

'Aye, one pressed so flat there's no flavour left. Do you know what I mean, Shay?'

Shay gave a slow nod. 'Yes, I know,' she replied.

Chapter 41

When she opened the door and walked in, the house looked exactly as before but somehow it felt a different fit. Or maybe it was her that had changed shape, left the round hole as a round peg and changed to a square one over the past two and a half weeks.

Shay texted both her children and told them she was home. Courtney rang her immediately and asked if she could come over after work – she'd bring fish and chips. She had some things she wanted to tell her – nice things, she stressed immediately. No need to worry one bit.

Shay told her that would be lovely and she'd be delighted to see her. But she was prepared to tell her daughter it was time to woman-up, if needed. Her days of being permanently erected scaffolding for others were done.

Courtney arrived at six with fish, chips, peas, curry sauce, breadcakes and two battered sausages. She put them down on the table and then threw her arms around her mother, kissing her cheek madly, as she used to do when she was a little girl. Her big daughter felt as good in her arms as her little one had.

'Are we expecting some extra company?' asked Shay, unfolding all the paper parcels.

'I had a bonus at work,' Courtney explained. 'I thought I'd spend some of it on you. Flowers are overrated, I reckon. They can't hit the spot a battered sausage can.'

Shay laughed. Yes, that was totally within her daughter's thought processes.

'Where did you go, Mum?'

I went back in time, love. 'I went back to where I was brought up.'

'You see old friends?'

'Yes, I did.' And old enemies who are new friends and old enemies who will stay enemies, she didn't add.

'You'll have to take me one day and show me the sights.'

'I will,' Shay promised.

'Must have been nice living in a village. You never talked about it.'

No, she never had. She'd dodged all the questions, side-stepped giving answers, cherry-picked the more benign details. Now, she could – and would – talk about it more because she was finally free of that sodden, dark cloud which had mired the sunshine in her sky.

'One of my friends owns a cheese factory now,' Shay told her.

'That sounds sexy,' replied Courtney, with a salacious smirk.

'He was telling me how he needs to get on top of social media and advertising. Made me think of you as I was driving back. You're so good at that stuff, I wondered why you haven't ever thought of getting paid for your services.'

'That makes me sound like a prossy.'

'Oh Courtney, be sensible for once.'

'I'm going to have to do something else soon.' Courtney cut a chunk from her fish. 'I'm bored working in a shop. It was fun at first, but my brain feels like it only gets one trip out per year.' She tilted her head to one side in thought. 'That's a good idea though, Mum. I'll mull it over.'

'Don't be like me and fly under the radar.' Had she led her children to be like her by example? To be a doormat? To live a little life?

Courtney hooted, pointing at her mother with a chip. 'Me? Are you mixing me up with someone else?'

'I don't want you to scrabble around on the ground.'

'I really missed you,' said Courtney. 'And your words of incomprehensible wisdom.'

'You hardly saw me after you moved out,' Shay countered.

'Yeah, but I always knew you were there if I needed you. These past couple of weeks I've felt as if you'd ripped off my armbands and pushed me off the side into the deep end.'

'You can swim,' said Shay, 'just stay away from the shark-infested waters.' Which brought someone immediately to mind. 'How's Dingo?' She braced herself for the answer that he'd been thrown off his anger management course for twatting someone with a teapot, or he'd got into the *Guinness Book of Records* for most Cornish pasties eaten in a minute and he'd proposed to her daughter in the historic, euphoric moment.

'Dunno. He's gone for good,' said Courtney and wafted her hand as if swatting an invisible mosquito. 'I've moved on.' She grinned and Shay's heart lurched in her chest. Who now? Whammo, Gizmo, Tommo, Bummo? A cage fighter – or a bloke in a Texas prison currently on death row? Whoever it was, she'd have to let her get on with it. There was a difference between lending a drowning man a hand and pandering to a child having a meltdown in a paddling pool.

'Do I want to know?'

'Mort,' said Courtney, shoving a gigantic chip in her gob and chewing gleefully.

Shay's heart sank a little and it must have showed on her face because Courtney quickly cleared her mouth in order to speak. 'I know what you're going to say, Don't hurt him, don't use him—'

'I thought he was seeing someone?'

'He went out on a couple of dates with her but it only reinforced the feelings he had for me, so he said.' Courtney smiled – a sweet gentle smile that rather suited her lips. 'That was a shocker. I never knew he fancied me until he came right out with it last week.'

Shay nearly choked on a chunk of batter.

'You must be the only person on the planet who didn't.'

'I've always liked him too. But I thought he was too good for me.'

'Why would you think that?' Shay asked her.

'Because I'm anarchy personified and he's always been steady, gentle, caring, lovely and so surely he deserves better than me.'

'Who are you, strange creature, to diss my daughter,' said Shay.

'He turned up at the flat with a massive bunch of flowers and said he was putting his cards on the table.' Courtney gave a little sigh, like a gothic Disney princess. '*Oh my god*, I thought. *He's gone insane*. But if he wants to take the risk, then who am I to deny him his dream?'

Shay wondered if aliens had grown a replica of her daughter in a pod and replaced her.

'He's lovely, Mum.'

'He is.'

'I can't believe I've seen him for all these years but not *seen* him, do you know what I mean? We're going to an opera in Leeds at the weekend.'

Her daughter really had been replaced by an alien.

'And wouldn't Courtney Jagger be the most rock and roll name ever to have?'

'Court—'

'Chillax, Mater. Everyone thinks Mort's a bit thick because he's big and galumpy, but he so isn't. We're going to have a wander around Amsterdam as well, see the Van Gogh museum and eat lots of cheese.'

Shay smiled at the cheese word. She wondered if she'd always have that reaction now going forward, like a variation of Pavlov's dogs but with a smile instead of salivation.

'Have you seen your father?' asked Shay, looking at the Alp of food on the table. It seemed to be getting bigger, not smaller.

'He rang me to "fill me in with his side of the story".' The corner of Courtney's lip rose like Elvis having a bad day. 'He tried to say that you weren't giving him attention and that's why he started shagging Auntie Les. I told him he was a wanker and to grow up.'

'Courtney,' Shay admonished her, 'you shouldn't call your father a wanker.'

'You know, Mum, he didn't sound full of the joys of spring to tell you the truth. It's her money, not his. Mort reckons she'll make him dance for it.'

Well, that's his problem, thought Shay.

'Is Mort okay?'

'Yeah. He batters punchbags in Tommy Tanner's gym when things with his mum and dad get too much. It's all got really nasty now that Morton's found out about everything and he's on the rampage. So it's a good job he's got me to calm him down.'

'That's what I'm worried about.' Shay rolled her eyes and Courtney hooted.

'It's good to have you home, Mum. You not being here made me think a lot about things. And what you said to me before kind of turned the mirror around onto myself.' Courtney reached over, rubbed her mum's arm. Just a small gesture but it said a lot. 'You've always been there for me and I've taken it for granted. I haven't thought what I've done has affected the people around me. You made me think what I'd feel like if I had a daughter who was always getting herself into trouble. And how kind Fiona is because I'd have chucked me out of the flat ages ago. Might have to find somewhere else to live soon anyway. Things are hotting up with her and her man and I think I should move out to let him move in. She's too nice to say it, of course. So I will.'

Shay liked this new daughter of hers, hoped she'd stick around. She didn't mind the shocking pink hair and the gothy make-up, or the weird clothes with all the straps, tears and buckles, they looked great on her. She would never be a twinset and pearls girl, not even in her dotage. She reckoned she and Mort would meet somewhere in the middle if it lasted the course. They'd be good for each other. He needed someone to care for and she'd keep everything far from boring.

'You can always move back in here if you like,' Shay offered. 'Wherever I am, there's a home for you.'

'Thanks, Mum,' said Courtney. 'You won't regret it. Promise.'

'I already am,' Shay grinned.

Chapter 42

Shay spent the next few days attacking her to-do pile. She went to see David Charles, her mother's faithful solicitor, and asked if he'd help her negotiate her divorce. He said of course he would and laughed when she told him about defacing the papers. He took down some notes and responded to the petition. She agreed to a fifty-fifty split on the house. She'd keep Candlemas and wouldn't touch Bruce's savings or pension pot. A clean, fair, full and final settlement and they could both go on their merry way.

She met Sunny in the White Swan afterwards. There was only a fortnight and a half left to the wedding now and she wanted to have the talk with him that her mother had had with her outside the church. That had been a bit too last-minute.

'You okay, Mum?' he said. 'I've been worried about you. It's so good to see you.'

'I'm fine,' she replied, determined not to mention that he really didn't look like a man eager to meet a bride at the end of an aisle.

Over Chicken Kievs they indulged in small talk. Shay

told him she'd been staying in Millspring reconnecting with people from her past and he told her that Bruce had been in touch to tell him his version of why he'd left her. It tallied with what he'd told Courtney, though Sunny hadn't called his dad a wanker, just told him that he was a thoughtless clot and hoped that he wasn't making the biggest mistake of his life. Shay circumvented the elephant wearing the wedding dress in the room until she could avoid it no longer.

'Sunny, when I was about to get married, your gran was waiting for me outside the church door. She said that if I had cold feet, to never mind about the cost, the expense, any embarrassment, all I had to do was get back in the car and my dad would tell the guests it was off and that would be it, no further action needed on my part.' She lifted her head and held his eyes. They were just like hers, just like she imagined Ammon Habib's must have been. 'She had a feeling she couldn't shake off that I was doing the wrong thing, she said. And . . . though I wouldn't have missed having you and Courtney for anything . . . if I'm being honest, I think she was right.'

There, she'd admitted it aloud. She liked Bruce, she fancied him, she enjoyed being with him, she was grateful to him for making her feel normal again, but she hadn't loved him to her full capacity. She'd grown to love him, over the years, the risk had paid off, but it had been nothing like what she had felt for Jonah Wells.

'Mum, Karoline's pregnant,' Sunny blurted out. 'I couldn't leave her even if I wanted to.'

Shay felt a lump of lead land with a thud in her stomach.

'When did you find this out?'

'Friday night. But we're waiting until she's twelve weeks

on before going public. Angela and Simon don't even know yet.'

Shay noted her son's downturned mouth, the lack of light in his eyes, the aura of sadness hanging around him like a grey fog.

'Sunny, darling, you don't look a quarter as happy about delivering that news to me as you should,' said Shay. She reached for his shoulder, squeezed it and she registered how he winced, how he jerked from the contact as surely as if she had just delivered an electric shock. 'It's really not too late to stop this ride and get off. Whatever the circumst—'

He leaned over, kissed her cheek and then stood up.

'I can't have this conversation with you, Mum. I'll see you at my wedding. Please, please just . . . let it happen.'

She stood also, and he pushed at the air between them to keep her away.

'Please, Mum. It's what I want. Really.'

She wasn't sure if he was trying to convince her or himself.

*

Shay, Courtney and Mort went over to Merriment Close to pack up Roberta's house. Builders were back at the Balls's house, undoing the damage the hooligans with the digger had made, although there was no sign of the dastardly duo themselves. Dagmara wandered over with a box of butterfly buns, some apple tea and her best gossip. One of the builders had told Derrick that Balls had instructed them to do only what they had to in order to make the property safe as he was thinking of selling up and shipping out. She told them that Derrick's son was still interested in Roberta's bungalow. Errol was as decent and amiable as his father. He wanted a quiet backwater dwelling for him and his wife and, as head of his own security firm, was definitely not the sort of person you'd want to get on the wrong side of. Shay told Dagmara to tell Derrick she was ready to talk to him about it and to give him her number.

Courtney was looking lovely, thought Shay. She was wearing jeans, a Varsity sweater and sneakers and thought that if this was a new American student phase of hers, then it suited her very well. She knew that Mort wouldn't be the sort to try and change her daughter, he'd loved her through every hair colour of the spectrum and every wardrobe variation. It was early days, but there was a change about Courtney that she liked. As if she'd grown up years in weeks. And Mort was his same happy-go-lucky self but with extra grins. Reciprocated love really was the stuff that made the world go round.

Shay folded up her mother's clothes carefully, helped by Dagmara. It was hard, so hard, to take them out of the wardrobe knowing they would never be put back in there again.

'You aren't throwing your mama away, you know,' said Dagmara, patting her chest. 'She's in here always, in your heart and your memories and your blood of course. You don't need dresses and cardigans to remember her by.'

She was right of course. And the clothes were too lovely and bright not to be worn by other old ladies who'd be grateful for a cheery bargain; who'd go out just to show off their new apple-green mac or a pink and cream swirly-patterned suit, feeling like the bees knees in it.

Shay had sent Paula a text asking if there was anything she wanted from the house. She'd received a curt reply that she wanted her mother's collection of Royal Doulton figurines, her Mont Blanc pen, the silver paperweight . . . a list of sellable valuables. She wasn't prepared to come and do any of this hard graft, but she'd take the spoils, thank you. If she turned up to Sunny's wedding, as invited, Shay thought that might be the last she ever saw of her sister. The presumption did nothing to upset her.

There were so many of her mother's possessions which would be unwanted by anyone else, but were her treasures. Only Roberta knew why she had never thrown away the broken jewellery box with the torn satin lining and the ballerina who didn't turn any more. Only she knew the significance of the saved postcards sent to her from people whose names Shay didn't recognise, or the curl of dark brown hair in a matchbox.

In Mort's car on the way home, Shay told Courtney about her meeting with Sunny. Her verdict was concise, detached and strangely wise.

'Maybe he's just happy being miserable with the horrible cow,' she said, stuffing the last of the butterfly buns in her mouth. 'And no point in getting close to the sprog because we'll never see it. How much do you reckon hitmen are to hire?'

Standing back was an acquired art all right; no wonder Roberta had had difficulty with it.

Chapter 43

Shay stood in front of the mirror and checked herself from all angles. Her pale green suit was the most expensive outfit she'd ever bought in her life but she wanted to look better than her best for her son's wedding. She looked Italian today, very Sophia Loren, if that wasn't ironic. The mobile make-up lady had pinned her long dark hair into a chic French pleat, just like her mum used to wear hers. She'd gone for smoky eyes and dark rose lips, silver jewellery. Funny but she couldn't get used to her wedding ring finger being bare; the imprint of the rings had taken days to disappear.

She felt sick, not at all excited in the way she would be if she were gearing up to see Courtney marry Mort and she now understood the full extent of what her mum must have been going through on the day of her wedding, contending with instincts too strong to deny, refusing to be rationalised away yet having to finally accept that her daughter knew best because she'd said as much. She'd tried to ring Sunny on a few occasions since she'd seen him a fortnight ago, but he hadn't picked up, just replied by text that he was perfectly fine and she wasn't to worry. Last night she'd sent

him a text wishing him luck and love and received only a
'Thanks Mum x' by way of reply. She had read all sorts into
those two words.

She wondered what she'd feel like seeing Bruce again,
and if he'd bring Les to the wedding, though that would
take some brass neck, flaunting their debut outing with the
family today of all days. He wouldn't, surely, but then she
didn't know this version of him and so he just might. She'd
bite her tongue till it bled if necessary and be a bastion
of dignity and civility, however much she might feel like
pushing him into the cake and battering Les with her stil-
etto. Jonah had offered to come with her for moral support.
He'd sit at the back of the church and just be there, he said,
and she'd thanked him, but declined. They spoke regularly
and she looked forward to seeing his name flash up on her
mobile when he rang. They talked about nothing in particular, touched base, answered the 'how are you' questions, like
friends. She missed him, like she had before when they'd
been separated, and she was scared of that.

She'd already started clearing out her own house, after
finishing with Roberta's. It was cathartic – decluttering.
People gathered so much stuff to themselves, like armour,
validations of love, symbols of self-worth. They kept old
love letters and cards, freezing themselves in the moment
of being desired. She'd squirrelled away all Bruce's cards for
birthdays and anniversaries since the beginning. When she'd
looked through them, she'd noted how the messages written
inside became shorter, lost degrees of warmth with passing
time. 'All my love, to my darling Shay xxxxxxx' from fifteen years ago had become 'Love Bruce x' last year. They'd
limped on past their natural end which had been disguised
by habit, by family, maybe even by the inertia that stopped

them doing anything about it, or the fear of loneliness. But she would never have disrespected him the way he had her by how he'd drawn a final line in the sand of their marriage.

Karoline's parents had booked Crastley Manor, which charged seventeen pounds fifty per head to use the toilet so lord knows what they'd charge for chuffing nosebag, so said Bruce when he'd heard Angela Stannop's venue plans at the engagement party.

Shay hadn't pictured her son's nuptials being this way. She would have loved to help arrange the day, be on hand to advise about the food courses and who to invite, without treading on even the smallest toes of the two whom the big day belonged to. She had wanted to pop open a bottle of champagne the night before, have a little weep on his shoulder on his last day as a single man, enfold her soon-to-be daughter-in-law in her arms and tell her to have the best wedding day ever. And she wanted to whoop that a little baby was on its way, a fresh plump new life, another generation of her family. Instead she had been left in a cold hinterland, admitted to join in the celebrations for a mere hour or two before the doors would be shut on her again. And when the baby came along, to be grateful for the merest crumbs on the table.

She sniffed, tilted her head back because crying was not an option, not with this expensive foundation dabbed on. She imagined Tanya at the side of her, telling her she'd been watching too many happy-ever-after films with Hugh Grant in them. She'd remind her that wedding days rarely fitted an ideal template and were more often than not powder kegs of stress, expense, family fuck-ups that not even Kofi Annan with his diplomatic skills and Nobel Peace prize would be able to diffuse. Then she'd reel off some of the weddings they'd been to like their old friend Sharon's where her maid of honour threw up in the church over the bride's train, and Les's wedding where Morton's dad goosed anything on the dancefloor in a skirt.

A cheery pip outside broke her reverie. Her taxi had arrived. She picked up her handbag, took a deep breath and sent up a prayer that when she got to the church she'd see her son smiling happily at the altar and all would be well.

The church had more flowers in it than Kew Gardens. Frothy pink and white arrangements with ribbon tails were pinned on the end of every pew and blowsy displays spewed from ornate stands on the altar. Bruce would already be totting up the cost of them alone and be sending up his own silent prayer that they hadn't been asked for any financial contribution. Shay could see the back of his head in the third row as she wended her way very slowly down the aisle. He was sitting alone, no Les beside him head to foot in Prada, for which she breathed a sigh of relief. Bells were ringing from the tower and, in front of an impressive backdrop of pipes, an organist was playing the traditional muzak one associates with the preamble to a wedding main event. Unlike the organist at her own wedding, a decrepit member of the regular congregation who couldn't hit the right notes with a heat-seeking missile, this woman was on a par with Elton John.

She'd thought that Sunny might have had his pals as ushers, but no, distributing expensively printed orders of service and hymn books were middle-aged men in grey morning suits, corporate looking, as if they'd just come out of a meeting at the bank. The bride's side of the church was full and had spilled out into the groom's side presumably, because Shay could recognise hardly anyone filling their assignment of seats. Markedly, none of Sunny's old pals were present: the two Marks, Daz, Pete and the rest. Mort Jagger was in the row behind Bruce, looking like a fridge in a dark grey jacket and beside him, Courtney, hair in peacock-feather colours, and a fascinator with an actual peacock feather standing proud from the top like a lightning conductor. In the pew behind her daughter was Paula, in that same black spaceship hat she'd worn to their mother's funeral. The lumpy, sweaty frame of Chris her husband beside her, no doubt poised and ready to sweep up some money from the collection plate when it was passed to him. Then Shay's eye was drawn to the front right, when her son stood up to do something strategic to his trousers. He didn't turn but sat immediately down again, facing forward, staring ahead at the altar as if it were a slaughter table and he were a lamb. He looked so alone; lost, even. Where the hell was his best man? Considering it was such a massive church with a high-vaulted roof and cross-shaped construction, Shay felt almost claustrophic.

Karoline's mother Angela Stannop was talking to the vicar, giving him orders by the look of it. She had a bright yellow suit on with pink shoes and a pink hat and looked not unlike an oversized Mr Kipling's Battenberg.

'Mrs Bastable.'

A light hand on her back as Jamie, Sunny's best man surprised her out of her musings.

'Hello, love,' she said, pleased to see his perma-jolly face, except today his smile of greeting looked strained. Shay drew the obvious conclusion. 'Nervous?' she asked. 'Hard job being the best man, keeping the rings, doing the speech, I think—'

He cut her off. 'Can I have a quick word with you? Outside?'

'Yes.' She felt a low rumble of foreboding in her centre that she didn't want at all.

Shay followed Jamie down the aisle, out into the blazing, cheerful September sunshine that was at odds with his expression. He walked around the side of the church, asked her if she minded if he smoked. She didn't. He lit up and sucked the cigarette as if it was supplying him with the oxygen to breathe.

'I haven't had a cig in a year and a half,' he said, wafting the smoke away from Shay. 'I bought my first packet yesterday and this is the last one.'

'What on earth's the matter, Jamie? Are you all right?' asked Shay.

'No, I'm not,' came the reply. 'I'm at my wits' end to be honest.'

The hand not holding the cigarette rose to rake through his thick brown hair. 'I don't know what to do, Mrs B.'

'Jamie, calm down,' said Shay in her best no-nonsense mum voice. 'What's wrong?'

'I shouldn't be telling you this but I have to.'

Shay felt all the muscles in her back tense. 'What?' That inner rumble was mounting.

'I wish those bleeding bells would shut up.' Jamie puffed on the cigarette, forcing the nicotine into his lungs. He looked at his watch, muttered an expletive. 'I haven't seen Sunny for ages, right. I'm busy, new woman, jobs, you know the stuff. We used to see each other at rugby but . . .' Another deep puff.

'You've stopped?' she guessed.

'No, I haven't, he has.'

'Sunny doesn't go to rugby any more?'

'He hasn't been to rugby for over a year.'

Sunny had lied to her then. Why had her boy lied?

'So . . . the two things that were always going to happen were that I'm best man today, yeah . . . and the stag do.'

'Okay.' Shay nodded that she was still with him because Jamie looked at her as if he wanted to be assured of that.

'I rang him. He said he wasn't going to have a stag do because Karoline didn't want him to be tied to a lamppost naked or stuck on a ferry to Rotterdam, as if we'd have done that. I pushed it a bit and he went to ground, wouldn't answer his phone. So on Thursday night, we kidnapped him from work.'

'Kidnapped?'

'Yeah, we had a van waiting outside his office: Phil was driving, Jon, Pete, Daz Waterhouse, Mark Harrod, Mark Collier, you know, the usual gang. We loaded him in the back of the van, we weren't going to do anything stupid. He really kicked up a stink. We were just going to dress him in a T-shirt with a picture of a stag on the front that we'd had printed, a hat with antlers, we'd all got 'em on, just daft. We knew how Karoline felt so we weren't going to push it, only have a couple of beers and we'd booked a Chinese banquet; he'd have been home for nine but we couldn't let him get married without . . . something.'

Shay had no idea where this was going.

'Mrs B . . . oh shit . . . when we got Sunny's shirt off, he was covered in bruises, scratches, bite marks . . . I've never seen owt like it.'

Shay went cold as Jamie paced up and down in front of her.

'Phil pulled up in a car park. Sunny just broke down. He said every time he was going to walk out, she'd promise to stop, and it was okay for a while, then it would start all over again. She'd go mad if he didn't pick up his phone, she put a tracker on his car, she was convinced he was seeing someone else and once she hit him so hard she fractured his eye socket and he had to lie and say he'd done it playing rugby, which was a bit of a wake-up call. He was ready to leave but then she said she'd kill herself and he called her bluff and she took some pills.'

Shay's blood started to heat up then. She could feel it begin to bubble and boil in her veins.

'She said she was sorry, begged him for another chance, promised to get some help and he fell for it because he's too bloody nice; cue bust lip. Psycho cycle: lovely, loving, this could work, Mr Hyde comes out again . . . Last month, he realised he couldn't take it any more, tries to end it with her, and she drops the bombshell that she's up the duff. She even did a test in front of him to prove it. Oh, and if he left her she'd have an abortion. He thought his only option was to go through with the wedding, stick around until the baby was born safely and then take it from there. Then Thursday morning – the day we saw him – he was looking in a cupboard and found a pack of joke pregnancy tests that would all read positive. In other words, she's as pregnant as I am. She's fucking evil, Mrs B – excuse my French.

'Needless to say, we didn't have hoisin duck pancakes. We sat in the back of the van and tried to talk him out of this shit show. I begged him, Mrs B. I said he could stay at ours. He's ashamed, he's scared, he doesn't know what to believe any more, he doesn't know where he is. The other lads haven't turned up because they can't face watching him do it. She's made him believe that if he called the wedding off her father would sue him, have his legs broken, have your legs broken, crucify Bruce's business on social media . . . you name it, she threatened it. And that's supposed to be love. I don't know what to do. I haven't slept for two nights. He said the only thing he could do was let her have her day and then get out after. She *really* wants this wedding. I reckon her plans were made for it before she even fucking met him. He made us promise not to tell you, said he knew what he had to do, but I saw you and I . . . can't . . . lie.'

Jamie was shaking. Shay put her hand on his arm and had to check that he wasn't standing on a vibrating plate.

Mother's intuition, eh? she thought. Something you really shouldn't ignore when it knocked on the door.

Jamie was now smoking the butt of the cigarette. He'd end up smoking his fingers in a minute.

'I want to stand up and say I object but I'm not sure I dare. Sunny made me swear I wouldn't do anything stupid. Am I letting him down by not doing anything, more than I would be by doing something? My head's as cabbaged as his is. I don't—'

'Shhh. Jamie, go into the church, take your seat and leave everything to me,' said Shay. Her blood was now the equivalent of magma but she felt strangely controlled because she *did* know what to do, without a doubt.

'I'm sorry I've had to dump this on you,' said Jamie, leaning over to kiss her cheek in relief and gratitude.

'I'm not.'

Shay thought, *Hell will freeze over before that bitch marries my son.*

She stood alone for a few seconds, closed her eyes, willed some strength into her bones. She felt her mother inside her, filling her limbs, straightening her spine. Her gorgeous, wonderful, selfless mother who had loved her more than life itself. There was no official guidebook on any of this parent stuff: when to rush in, when to keep in the wings, when to shout up and when to pipe down; you just had to go with your heart. And at that moment, her heart couldn't have been banging a bigger drum.

Shay went back inside the church. She walked down the aisle, feeling eyes from the bride's side of the family on her, appraising, evaluating, gossiping. She took a seat next to her daughter after Mort had shuftied up. She noticed they were holding hands, Courtney's looked tiny and lost in his big shovel of a mitt.

'Mum, you look gorgeous.' Shay could now see that Courtney was wearing a navy suit. From the neck down, she looked very glam and traditional. She probably had some rebellious underwear on but Shay would take her slightly nuts daughter over the 'normal' of her sister Paula or the Barbie Dollesque Karoline any day.

Bruce, on the row in front, swivelled around and caught Shay's eye.

'All right,' he greeted her perfunctorily, then turned quickly back. From behind she could see his neck start to blotch; he was imagining her eyeballs boring into his skull, she thought. He was safe today, she had bigger fish to fry.

Paula leaned forward and whispered in her ear.

'Thank you for the parcel of things you sent but I appear to be missing a couple from my list.'

Shay twisted in her seat.

'No idea what you're talking about,' she whispered back. 'Shame you didn't come and help us though. We found hundreds of fifty-pound notes in a suitcase under Mum's bed. They weren't on your list though, so I didn't send you any.'

Shay heard the gurgle of distress in her sister's voice. She'd presume the lie was the truth, because Shay had too much of a past history of being honourable, a good girl who flew under the radar so she wouldn't upset any more applecarts, who stood in the shadows propping up those who wanted to stand in the sun.

But Mrs Nice Guy was having a day off today.

Chapter 44

The organist severed her tune, a beat, then she started the opening salvo of the Bridal Chorus. She had arrived: Princess Karoline and her pink entourage. The whole church rose to their feet. Mrs Battenberg across the way beamed, pride pulsing from her like microwaves. Shay turned to see a dress taking up the width of the church aisle, a giant puff of satin, tulle, lace, and in the midst of all that white froth was the Jabberwocky bride with her jaws that bite and her claws that catch. Her son stood, looking blank and condemned, next to his best man whose forehead was as furrowed as a ploughed field. All that was missing from the scene was a black square of silk sitting on top of the vicar's bonce.

Karoline's father was obscured by the voluminous frock, squashed against the pews as he walked in pin-steps in sync with his daughter's pace, but his obligation was not to shine, just to fork out the dosh and speak when spoken to. Shay could see the red slash of a smile beneath Karoline's cathedral-length veil. She had wanted this wedding more than she wanted the groom. She would have stored her dress in a protective cover, the veil in tissue, her sparkling tiara in a satin-lined box, but the groom she had kicked and battered until he had to be patched up in the casualty department of the local hospital, pretending he'd been injured in a rugby game.

In front of Karoline, scattering rose petals over the red aisle carpet for her to tread on was a tiny girl, and a page boy dressed up to the nines, carrying a box on a cushion as carefully as if it were a UXB. At least they'd have had their moment of glory, thought Shay. Two child bridesmaids in pink flowery frocks followed Karoline, six grown-up ones in pink satin behind them, possibly relations because they all shared a similar look: short, busty, blonde, condescending, no discernible neck. Courtney would have stood out like a sore thumb among them but she still should have been there, rocking pink at her only sibling's wedding; instead she'd been rejected and that had been sitting on a slow burn within Shay as well.

No expense had been spared for this spectacle, that was clear. Two hundred and fifty people would be sitting down to a meal at Crastley Manor after posing for the family album. They'd be greeted at the door with waiters bearing silver trays of champagne and caviar blinis, then they'd be led through to a pink-themed room to dine on foie gras, suckling pig, fried baby squid and other courses, no doubt as fittingly cruel: vivisected slices of peach tart and gouged eyeballs of cheese and the like. Shay reckoned that 'Mrs Fattenberg' and her dopey tool of a husband couldn't have had change from sixty thousand pounds for this day. Shame.

Shay's heart was thumping so hard she was sure people could hear it over the organ music; even more so when the tune ended and the vicar asked everyone to be seated. Jamie, at the front, sweat clearly visible on his brow, flashed Shay a look of sheer desperation. It said, *please, Mrs B, PLEASE.* He needn't worry, she'd got it.

'Dearly beloved, we are gathered here today in the sight of God to join this man—'

My precious son, thought Shay.

'—and this woman—'

That obnoxious cow.

'—in holy matrimony . . .'

She felt a hand reach for hers – Courtney's. But when she looked to her right, the oddest thing happened because, for the slightest moment, she saw her mum in violent violet sitting there instead.

'If any person here can show just cause why these two people should not be joined in holy matrimony, speak now or forever hold your peace.'

Someone coughed, earning a look of disapproval from Angela. In fact, her head spun so fast on her neck, it was like watching a Richard Curtis version of *The Exorcist.*

The vicar opened up his mouth to carry on with the ceremony but Shay's voice rang out, beating the main pro-tagonists of this farce to say, 'I do.'

She levered herself to her feet. Her legs were shaking, her inner magma had turned to water but she'd done it. She was up, and there could be no retraction. The moment seemed to stretch, enough to take in that over three hun-dred pairs of eyes must be on her, not including those of all the monks, knights, saints and St George's dragon in the stained glass windows. Sunny's jaw was hanging loose, Jamie was blowing out his cheeks, Bruce in front had bowed his head and was saying, 'Jesus Christ' in a non-religious way.

Someone laughed nervously; Angela's jowls were juddering. Karoline's expression was pure 'Carrie White' just before she started going bonkers at her prom.

The vicar was twittering in a confused way, his nose wrinkling like a mouse in the orbit of Stinking Bishop.

'Sorry, folks, there will be no wedding today,' announced Shay. She stared at her boy, her thin, pale beautiful boy. 'I know what she's done to you, Sunny. You come home to your family.'

Angela rose from her pew. 'Sit down' she bellowed at Shay, as if she were a disobedient poodle.

'Go swivel,' replied Shay, the church-friendly version of the words on her tongue.

A mumble Mexican-waved around the church. To her blessed relief, Sunny took a step towards her, before Karoline grabbed his arm.

'Where the fuck do you think you're going?' she said, dropping her sweet, smiley façade for a choice moment.

'Touch my son again, bitch, and I'll drop you where you stand,' said Shay.

'Ushers!' called Angela, as if she were summoning the Household Cavalry.

Karoline hadn't let go; Shay saw her enormous pink bridal talons digging into his arm.

'Get your hands off my boy or I'll tell everyone in this church what a vile, nasty, violent, twisted, manipulative, abusive piece of shit you are,' threatened Shay, telling everyone in the church what a vile, nasty, violent, twisted, manipulative, abusive piece of shit Karoline was.

Sunny wrenched his sleeve away from Karoline's grip. Together he and his mother started to head towards the church door when Karoline, with a cry worthy of the

Incredible Hulk, launched herself at Shay, pushing her so hard in the back, she tumbled to the floor.

'You wait and see what happens next,' Karoline screamed, stabbing at them with her finger. 'You're dead, the lot of you.'

Then Courtney, who had been itching for such a moment, hit the red carpet.

'No one messes with my family,' she said, as she pulled back her fist and floored the bride with a right hook that informed anyone who knew anything about boxing, that Tommy Tanner's gym really did churn out some talent.

Chapter 45

They'd spilled out into the brilliant sunshine, thrown themselves into the back of Mort's van, and he'd driven them
home while they sat on bags of cement and let their nerves
climb down off the ceiling. It had to be right up there with
Shay's favourite taxi rides ever. She was shaking and adrenaline was masking the pain of a skinned knee and her stupidly
expensive skirt had ripped irreparably, so had her ten quid
tights, but it was a very small price to pay. More slugs and
snails than sugar and spice, thought Shay of Karoline. Her
mother's intuition had been right on the money.

'Someone want to tell me what all that was about?'
Courtney was nursing her knuckles. 'Bloody hell, Karoline's
face is harder than it looks. She made of granite? Don't
answer that.'

'You'll probably get arrested,' Mort said over his shoulder.

'Bring it on,' replied Courtney. 'A million witnesses,
including a vicar, will testify she made the first move, pushing an elderly woman to the floor. I had to lamp her, I had
no choice.'

'Elderly woman? I beg your pardon,' replied Shay and

despite this awful situation, she laughed, even though she didn't know where it had been dredged from. She still had laughter in her, she'd take that as a good sign.

Shay kept tight hold of her son's hand; he looked shell-shocked. Karoline had moved the goalposts of his life to a new, abusive normal, just as Denny had learned to accept that what happened to him was standard. She'd been too young to save him, but she'd saved her son.

'I wonder if they'll still have the reception?' Courtney mused then gasped with a sudden thought. 'It was being videoed, wasn't it? Oh my god, I have to get hold of a copy. That's going to get my followers up to a million on TikTok.'

'It was an amazing right hook, I have to say,' said Mort. 'Your best yet. I'm proud of you, love.'

'Please don't encourage her, Mort,' Shay implored him, but she didn't put much effort into the rebuke.

'Never mind about me; Mum, you were absolutely magnificent in there. That took some proper guts.' Courtney grinned and gave Shay's unharmed leg an affectionate tap with her fist. 'You know, at this moment, I can't tell you how honoured I am to be your daughter. I always wondered where I got it from.'

Shay didn't ask what 'it' was, because she knew. But once you'd stood up to Glynn Duffy, everyone else was a piece of cake. Sometimes you just had to follow your heart, and sometimes you got it wrong and sometimes you got it right.

'She is so going to cut the crotches out of your trousers, Sunny,' said Courtney with a chuckle, grabbing his knee and giving it a sisterly squeeze.

'Better a few trashed belongings than a trashed life,' said Mort to that, sounding wise beyond his years. Shay hoped the insane pairing of her anarchic daughter and this kind, solid boy worked out, but she wouldn't be hovering like a worried helicopter, she'd leave them to it, let it take its course.

*

So far so good, because two months later, Mort and Courtney were going from strength to strength and their influences were rubbing off on each other, cross-pollinating like benign bees. His clothing had been updated and she was no longer the equivalent of a mad metronome but more measured in her temperament; they were shaping each other for the better.

Sunny had crumbled after the wedding that never was. He felt humiliated to have been abused by a woman, weak and embarrassed and it took the full might of his mum, his sister, a psychotherapist and the rallying of his pals to set him on the road to recovery, but his feet were firmly on it now. The old Sunny was once again visible through the clouds and they were all grateful for that.

They'd been prepared for Courtney to be arrested but she never was. No one's legs were broken, Bruce's business didn't suffer any public trashing, no one was sued.

Courtney volunteered to get Sunny's stuff for him from the house. Karoline threatened to ring the police if she turned up and Courtney told her she'd bring the police with her to ensure safe passage after Karoline had threatened, in front of hundreds of witnesses, to end their lives. Funnily enough, she'd backed down then. Also not surprisingly, Karoline didn't give Courtney and Mort any trouble on the day, but then, she was a typical bully, picking on weaker souls and there was nothing weak about either of them.

Courtney left her with a threat of her own: that if she ever came near any of them again, her head would end up in her bumhole.

Karoline hadn't exactly folded Sunny's clothes before she put them in bags, or packaged his iMac in bubble wrap, but it was all intact, not a cut-out crotch or a crushed keyboard to be found. Courtney, pursuing another change of career, did consider then being an enforcer for a debt collecting agency; she had rather relished the menace.

But another seed had taken root in her fertile brain. Something her mother had said about exploiting her love of and talent for social media. But she couldn't do it alone. She needed a graphic artist to come on board, do all the 'wanky drawing bits' as she put it, while she pushed on the marketing side and dragged in business with her sparkling wit and expert people skills. Who better than her big brother? Karoline might have managed to convince him he was stupid for thinking he could make a career out of what was really a mere hobby, but Courtney managed to reconvince him that he was fucking fantastic, the best she knew and her idea was a big goer, they could do it together.

And here they were, Shay's chicks back in the nest, though just for a little while, because the family home was under offer. Shay was giving some of the equity to her children. They were soon to move into a rented apartment in a converted mill which would be their home and work headquarters for their new infant joint venture. They'd probably end up killing each other along the way but she rather hoped their love for each other would prevail. They were already up and running, doing a few free creative bits for Colin in the hope that they'd convince him to jump from the useless JoMint and from what they'd showed him so far, it was looking promising. But what they lacked was a company name; they couldn't agree on one and they needed to pin it down now that they were garnering interest.

'What about Sunny Court?' asked Courtney, as they brainstormed over lasagne.

Sunny shook his head. 'Sounds like an old people's home. What about Courting the Sun?'

'Sounds like an incest dating site.'

'Courtney.' Shay tutted at her.

'We could cash in on our Egyptian heritage,' suggested Courtney, making a lasagne sandwich with two pieces of garlic bread, much to the disgust of her brother. 'Cleopatra Concepts? Nile by Mouth Media? Hire-o-Graphics? What about something Pyramid?'

Courtney hadn't been half as blown away with the story about the Egyptian officer who stole her granny's heart as Shay had expected. 'I love the grandad I've got,' she'd said. 'I mean, it's all very romantic, but he means nothing to me.' Although she was very grateful to him for her beautiful skin-tone and the brown eyes that brought her so many compliments. Sunny had never felt anything other than a Yorkshireman. He hadn't even felt any leanings towards Italy, despite the throwback story, and by the same token he didn't feel in the slightest bit Egyptian. It was his granny's story, not his.

'. . . Ptolemy, Nefer-tweety, Pair of Ankh-ers?'

'Stop, enough.' Sunny covered his ears and Shay thought how good it was to see him with a smile on his face. And to see some flesh covering his cheekbones. She still shuddered when she thought about what might have happened had she not stood up in church. Roberta had been with her, she knew that without any doubt, but it sounded nuts so she'd kept that particular nugget to herself.

'I like the idea of having a one-word impact,' said Sunny then. 'Like: Ice, Fire, Gold, Fruit, Cream ...'

'Turd, Balls,' snorted Courtney.

'Ugh. Anything but that name.' Shay made a face. Drew Balls had put his house up for sale in the end and Derrick's son, who had just moved in to Roberta's old bungalow, had bought that as well. When Shay had last been to visit Dagmara, she'd told her some gossip that apparently Errol had 'made Drew Balls an offer he couldn't refuse' and she'd giggled like a schoolgirl.

'You are totally gross, Court,' said Sunny, watching as the sauce and mince escaped the bread and slopped down her top. 'Who makes a sandwich out of lasagne?'

Lightbulb.

'What about Sandwich?' Shay suggested. 'A perfect marriage between components. Everyone loves a sandwich.'

'Not that sort of sandwich they don't,' said Sunny, flicking his finger over at his sister's gastronomic disaster.

But Courtney wasn't listening, she was caught up in her own thoughts, rolling the word around in her mouth, letting her brain taste it, savour it.

'Sandwich. I really like it,' said Shay. 'It's out there and—'

'Please, Mum, don't do that thing middle-aged people do like saying "down with da kids", slam dunk, WTF, bantz, peng ...'

'Mum, I think you might have nailed it,' said Sunny, nodding.

Courtney was beaming. 'Sandwich, yep, I'm already seeing the graphics, hearing the taglines about us complementing clients, showing them off to their best, holding it together between us, ideal combos ...'

'High five,' said Shay and flashed the two palms of her hands.

Her children sighed but pressed their palms to hers because it would have been rude to leave her hanging, but more so because they loved her very much.

Chapter 46

The week after Sandwich was officially born, a call came through from the Whispering Pines care home to say that Harry's breathing had changed and these were very likely to be his last hours. Shay, Courtney and Sunny drove quickly over there. Barbara was sitting by his side, holding his hand, strangely calm though tears were rolling down her cheeks and the darkened patch of the bedsheet below indicated they had been dropping for some time.

Harry Corrigan passed away peacefully in his sleep within the half-hour, surrounded by those he had loved the most and who, in turn, couldn't have loved him more: his family.

There was no funeral for Harry, not yet. He had willed his body to medical science, always convinced that he would die of something that might be of scientific interest to investigate. He'd admired people who donated their organs and though he'd carried a donor card in his wallet, he knew that as he grew older, his organs became less and less valuable. He'd given blood for thirty years, his bog-standard O positive, as he referred to it, never thinking about how many lives he'd saved, or prolonged. He hadn't been a flawless man, but he'd been much more special than he realised.

Shay hadn't known where to scatter her mother's ashes and didn't want to let them go until she was sure she'd found the perfect place. It was Dagmara who suggested she take them down to Weston-super-Mare and sprinkle them in the sea next to the promenade, where Roberta had strolled eating chocolate ice cream with a handsome Egyptian officer as their baby grew inside her. They went together, like a Yorkshire/Latvian version of Thelma and Louise on a bright, sharp mid-November day. Shay let an eager breeze take her mum, stir her into the air where so many happy memories of ice creams and sandcastles, sunshine and the songs of seagulls, were cold-pressed in the layers of time.

Chapter 47

Shay was strangely nervous as she waited for her date to pick her up and she realised this was probably a favour too far. But here she was, in her heels and her favourite black velvet dress, the one she'd worn when she'd gone for her anniversary meal with Bruce. How long ago that all seemed.

She hadn't seen him since Sunny's aborted wedding. She'd tried to speak to him about the sale of their house because she'd needed to know if he wanted any furniture and if they should accept the offer that had been made on the place, because it was just a little less than the asking price but it involved no chain. She'd left voicemails for him and he'd texted his replies and that was how they communicated as and when they needed to.

He had rung Sunny after the wedding to ask what the bloody hell all that had been about, and also to ask him, 'What planet is your mother on?' And then when he found out what had been going on, 'How can a woman do that to you unless you let her?' Sunny had put the phone down and they hadn't been in touch since. Bruce had failed his son when he really needed him, unlike Harry Corrigan who

had stepped up for his child and made up for any of his previous shortfalls. Shay didn't recognise Bruce any more. That
made it so much easier to let him go. She didn't draw any
more genitalia on forms she was presented with pertaining
to the divorce; she didn't want anything slowing down their
journey to its end.

A car sounded its horn outside and she braced herself
for the evening. She locked up the door and waved at the
driver of the Range Rover. He'd traded in his old Jeep
for something he'd long fancied. Part of the new him,
he'd said.

Morton Jagger wolf-whistled as he got out of the car to
open the door for her. He'd overdressed by far, looking
more as if he was going to a society wedding in his suit and
waistcoat and carnation in the buttonhole. Young Mort had
gone through his wardrobe with him; out went the 1970s-
style suits and crap shirts, in came some top clobber. He
could afford it, it was just that he'd always spent his money
on Les and his son, on tools and materials and never on
himself, something young Mort said would have to change.
But he looked good. He'd had a haircut, too, short back and
sides and he smelt of something foresty, albeit with a faint
tang of sawdust, which suited him.

'By 'eck you look nice, lass.'

'So do you, Morton. You scrub up very well.'

He beamed and Shay thought he must have gone through
most of his life having barely a compliment paid to him.

'I've booked us in at the Walled Garden,' said Morton.
'That okay?'

Shay raised an impressed brace of eyebrows. 'That's
pricey. A nice Italian would have been fine. You'll be bankrupt if you pick places like that for every date you go on.'

'Well, I reckon if I can pass muster there, I can pass muster anywhere,' he said.

The restaurant was in the countryside on the outskirts of the city, perched on a hill with beautiful views. It was one of *the* places to eat in the area; moneyed folks went there a lot and enjoyed the status of being 'a regular', but it was definitely the top choice to go and blow a budget for a special celebration. Many proposals of marriage had been made in its beautiful walled garden, from which the place took its name. Shay was hoping there wouldn't be another one tonight, though.

The waiter led them to a table in the window and lit a candle that sat between them.

'That's romantic,' said Morton, with a wink.

'Don't get any ideas,' replied Shay. 'This is a dummy run.'

'Thank you for this, Shay. Because getting into this dating game again is a proper ball-ache. Well, I say "getting into it again", I've never been in it. Les was my first girlfriend . . . and my last.'

'Well, just make sure that they're not more interested in your money than they are in you. Take your time to find someone nice and not someone "who'll do".'

Morton picked up the wine menu. 'I know bugger all about these,' he said with a grumble. 'Not like your Bruce, able to tell the difference between his grapes.'

'I'll let you into a secret, shall I? Bruce knew as much about wines as I know about quantity surveying. Just read the labels, read the descriptions. And if you find one you like, stick to it. Would you prefer dry or something sweeter? Red or white?'

'I prefer a pint of Boddy's if I'm honest.'

'Then you must have a pint,' replied Shay. 'This is about you being you, Morton. You want someone to fall for *you*, not a false version of yourself.'

'Not very impressive sitting here with a pint though, is it?'

'Did you know that Prince Philip prefers real ales to wine? In particular Boddingtons, as it happens. So you're in right royal company.'

'Bugger off.'

Shay laughed. 'True, look it up. Now, I think I'll have a Pinot Noir.'

'You can have champagne if you like,' said Morton. 'It's all on me.'

'Morton, if I said I wanted champagne on a first date, I'd ask you to get rid of me. But I will have a fillet steak.'

'Ooh, me as well. What a treat.' He grinned at her. 'Boddy's and beef and a big, fat pudding to follow. What a cracking night.'

When Morton wasn't clowning around trying to cover up an inferiority complex, he was surprisingly good company. Shay realised he must have been trying to compete with Bruce's smoothness every time they were in each other's proximity, especially if his wife was forever comparing them, and he'd been coming off worse. What was clear, as they talked, was how much he loved his son and how hurt he'd been by Les's betrayal, but he still couldn't bring himself to rubbish her.

'I thought I'd take her back, you know, if she wanted. Right up till recently. I missed her so much. Then you start to question what it is you actually miss. It wasn't the company because she didn't talk to me that much, and I was on edge if we went out anywhere because she didn't want me to embarrass her by doing anything like ... breathe. I just want someone to take care of, Shay. And to have sex with obviously, I miss that.'

'Don't say that on a first date, though,' said Shay. 'Or swear profusely or try and impress anyone with how many seconds you can draw out a burp. And no references to farting, however funny your story might be. Save that for when you're on more familiar terms.'

'I need to change, don't I?' Morton sighed.

'No, you don't. You just need to let your personality shine through.'

'Do I even have one?' asked Morton.

'You absolutely do and I wish you the best of luck in your dating adventure.' Shay raised her wine glass and Morton raised his pint glass and they chinked. And at that very moment, into Shay's eyeline drifted two people being shown to their table. She, hair down to her waist, her once 32A chest now right at the other end of the alphabet, expensive dress, expensive shoes, expensive bag, trout pout – Les. In her wake, trailing like the hired hand, Bruce.

'Fuck,' said Shay.

'I thought you weren't supposed to swear on a first date,' said Morton with a hoot.

'Les and Bruce have just walked in,' she whispered quietly.

Morton looked to his side; the newcomers were staring at them, trying to work out what possible reason her ex and his ex might have to be here together in *their* restaurant. Les's expression was as thunderous as the Botox would allow her to assume; Bruce looked flummoxed. To Shay's surprise, Morton nodded courteously at them in greeting, before turning back to her.

'I reckoned that's what Prince Philip would do,' he said,

putting the last mange-tout in his mouth and dabbing at the edges of his lips with his best linen serviette.

'Thank you for this,' Morton said again while they were drinking their coffees, his smile both wide and generous. 'I don't want to be on my own for the rest of my life, so thank you for getting me into the swing again of taking a nice lady out. I've really enjoyed it. I can't remember feeling at ease like this going out ever.'

'It's a pleasure,' said Shay.

'I reckon Les will be fancying me again in this get-up, I'd better be on me guard.' He grinned. 'She's a bugger for wanting what she can't have.'

Shay nodded. 'You be careful, Morton Jagger.'

'It's shook you hasn't it, *him* being over there.'

'Yes,' replied Shay. 'More than I expected.'

Bruce looked very handsome in the suit he was wearing, which blew Morton's out of the water. He'd obviously settled well into a life of luxury; this place was probably his regular haunt now. She imagined he and Les would be snickering at the interlopers nearby, Shay in her old dress and Morton's effort to impress with his carnation. Oh, how he must have struggled over the menu with all the fancy terms: the veloutés and pithiviers – *chortle, chortle.*

Shay stole a glance across to find Bruce's eyes in her direction and the moment crystallised as beyond weird that her husband was over there with a woman whom she'd always valued as closer to her than her sister; and she wondered again where all the feelings they'd had for each other had gone, if they'd grown holes in themselves like human colanders, and it had drained out slowly.

'I feel sod all, which is a nice surprise,' said Morton,

attempting to dab off the spot of coffee that had fallen on his tie. 'That woman over there is a taker. And so is Bruce. And we're givers, us, Shay. I don't know if they're happy, but they aren't talking much and they've both got faces on them like wet weekends. She's great with an audience, but whenever it was just her and me out for a night, there wasn't a lot else going on apart from eating. I'd start a conversation about something at work and she'd tell me to shut up because I was boring.'

'Then you deserve better,' said Shay.

'I do. I want someone like you that brings out the best in me. Someone kind, someone that doesn't look at me like sh— . . . poop on their shoe all the time, someone I don't have to buy. We used to have smashing sex after I'd bought her a handbag. You've no idea how many of them she's got.'

Shay laughed. She hoped Morton would find the woman he wanted because she'd be lucky. And very loved.

'What about you, Shay?' asked Morton. 'Do you think you'll ever take the plunge again? We could have one of those pacts where if we haven't met anyone in ten years, we'll give up the ghost and get together.'

'I think you'll be off the shelf sooner than you think,' replied Shay. 'As for me . . . there's someone I used to know from a long time ago who's come back into my life. And . . . I think I'm hiding a little behind all I've had to do recently.'

'Why?'

'Because it feels too right and that makes me suspicious.'

Morton finished off the last of his coffee. 'No guarantee with stuff like love, is there? If you like him, don't muck about, Shay. As you know, life isn't fair, it doesn't stop dolloping out shit when it thinks you've had more than enough, so when the good bits come along, grab them with both hands and make up for some lost time.'

She'd gone out that evening to teach Morton Jagger and ended up being his pupil, thought Shay after he'd dropped her off home with a sweet kiss on her cheek. How absolutely mad was that?

Chapter 48

Two days later, an alert went off on Shay's phone, an assigned ringtone she hadn't expected to hear ever again: a text from Les.

> I think we should meet. Marcel's at 11 a.m. tomorrow. Are you free? Les

A summons, short and to the point. Shay wondered why she'd chosen Marcel's, a bistro on student-trendy Eccleshall Road, since it was *their* place – the three of them – and they hadn't been there since Tan had died, because it wouldn't have felt the same with a man down. Had Les chosen that specific place to whip up some fond memories, mollify Shay's feelings towards her? Like perfume, Shay's thoughts about it were layered: an initial top note of outrage, a heart note of shock, a lasting base note of intrigue. She could ignore it, if she wanted to play Les as she'd been played but curiosity won out, so she replied.

> I'm free. I'll be there.

All the old text messages between them were still showing when she scrolled up, going back yonks: birthday messages, Les overspilling about something Morton had done, jokes, arrangements for Tan's funeral. Shay exited the wistful yesterdays, deleted the conversation, then she put Les out of her mind by bagging up some things in the garage to take to the tip.

She arrived at Marcel's on time with a brick in her stomach, wondering why she was putting herself through this. What could they possibly have to say to each other? And if they had anything, wouldn't it have been better said in a boxing ring than a bistro? She couldn't imagine Les sinking to her knees to beg for forgiveness and apologising until her throat was raw; she wasn't the self-flagellating type. But she was here now, something had guided her to agree to it, so Shay took her best step forward to the front entrance of the restaurant.

Standing outside it was the biggest man Shay had ever seen, smart in a suit and tie and for one ridiculous moment she imagined he was acting as a minder for Les, as if she had the status of a Kardashian. She walked in, saw Les in a far corner and had an immediate flashback to the last time they'd met for lunch, when she'd confided in her best friend about her disastrous anniversary trip without having the foggiest that Les was shafting her husband. There would be no friendly wave across the room today.

Shay had called the dress code correctly, casual – jeans and top, but Les's T-shirt was emblazoned with a massive Chloé logo across the front; a played-down outfit played up at the same time. Her handbag on the table was Mulberry, no doubt her knickers were from Gucci, because Les was that kind of gal these days, thought Shay: rich and wanted you to know it. Tan had loved designer gear too, but she bought pieces for their quality and durability as well as for their look. And she wasn't above teaming up a Dolce and Gabbana top with a pair of trousers from Tesco.

Once upon a time, Les would have greeted her with a squashy hug. Today Shay got, 'I'm just warning you, I have security if you try and attack me.'

Shay swallowed down a ball of disbelief the size of Poland. So Lurch on the door really was a hired guard then. Good god, how had they got here?

Shay sat without comment, reading the menu. She wasn't hungry, but she'd eat, break bread, drink wine, on the altar of their fractured friendship while waiting to find out why Les had asked to see her. The food offering was different from the last time they'd been here, and the prices had shot up considerably, she noticed. Lots of 'pulled' things on the menu, pulled chicken, pulled brisket, pulled pork which seemed appropriate as her husband had had his pork pulled by her best mate. She ordered a Pinot Noir and let Les get nervous that she might fling the red wine all over that pretty white top of hers, and queen scallops in a pea foam with a shoot salad; for Les, a glass of house white and a starter-sized Salade Piemontaise which she ordered with dodgy French pronunciation. Once upon a time, she would never have gone for something she couldn't wrap her tongue around, but that Les was long gone.

'Thank you for coming,' said Les, when the waiter had breezed off to the kitchen. 'I didn't know for sure if you would.'

'Then neither of us knows each other very well any more,' Shay answered. She'd said she would be there, and she had never let Les down yet. Then she wondered how fast that big man outside would get to the table if she reached across and dragged Les over it by her extensions. She should have brought Courtney along as her own minder, complete with her pink boxing gloves.

The waiter brought their drinks; Shay thanked him, Les didn't in that entitled way some people had, expecting service without the need to acknowledge it.

'So?' asked Shay after a period of ensuing silence. She took a sip of wine. It just tasted like wine. It was no longer flavoured with the deliciousness of beloved company. They used to love this place, the little oasis of freedom in their busy lives, where they'd dump their souls and pore over the descriptions of giant puddings on the menu before they'd even looked at the mains.

'Firstly I wanted to apologise,' said Les.

'For?' asked Shay; cheap shot, she knew.

Les looked at her blankly. 'You know what for.'

Shay noticed the security man walking past the window to check all was well. She picked up her glass and swilled the contents slightly to get his adrenaline up.

'Can I ask why?' she asked then.

'Are you seeing Morton?' said Les, as if that somehow answered the question.

'That's none of your business. He's free, I'm free.'

'Huh, like you two are a match,' scoffed Les.

'I don't know about that,' Shay mused, 'he's very gallant, kind . . .' She did toy with adding 'passionate' to stir up the pot a little. After all, Morton did say that Les hankered most after what wasn't available to her.

The waiter returned with the food in double-quick time. Shay noticed he put hers down first and more carefully than he did Les's. All three girls had done waitressing jobs in their late teens and moaned about rude customers and mean tippers.

The scallops were delicious and Shay was only sorry she didn't have a better appetite to appreciate them more.

'I did fight it, you know,' said Les, grinding pepper over her lunch. 'And whatever you might say about it now, you and Bruce haven't exactly been love's young dream.'

'We all moan about our partners occasionally with people we can trust, and about parents and kids and jobs; it's called a valve and it didn't give you the right to just move in,' Shay replied.

'Believe it or not, at the start I was propping up your marriage because he was thinking about leaving you,' said Les, annoyed, but keeping a lid on the volume.

Shay was sure he'd spun her that line, but he wouldn't have left unless he had somewhere else to leap to. He was testing the water and found it lukewarm and welcoming.

'So you were doing me a favour is what you're saying? How kind.'

'You're mocking me but yes, I was actually.' Les plunged her fork into a potato. 'You were never meant to find out. We were only scratching an itch. Then I . . . I . . .'

Shay finished her sentence for her. 'Won twelve million on the lottery.'

She raised her glass, swung it a little in Les's direction and watched her instinctively lean back, and the security guard have a spasm through the window. 'Congratulations. I did wonder what the deciding factor was when my husband left me for a multi-millionaire.' It was a variation on the old Mrs Merton/Paul Daniels line but it worked because it incensed Les.

'It wasn't the money, I knew you'd think that. I was unhappy, he was unhappy, we clicked—'

'So what exactly are you apologising for?' asked Shay, cutting her off.

'The way it happened. It wasn't right. You were my friend.'

Were, past tense.

'Why was our friendship not the same after Tan died?' asked Shay. 'I've been trying to work it out. You were never as available for me as you were when there were three of us.'

'You're imagining things.'

'No, I'm really not, Les. You'd make plans to meet up and cancel them all the time.'

'I must have had too much on, or else it was pure bad timing.'

'No, it wasn't that.' Was the strength of their friendship defined only by there being three of them in it? She'd thought long and hard on this and not come up with a viable answer yet.

Les chewed; Shay could tell she was thinking as she did so, using the fact she couldn't talk with a full mouth to work out a better comeback.

'Okay then, if you must know, you were always more Tan's friend than you were mine, so why should I be instantly available to you when you clicked your fingers after she'd gone. Don't think I don't know about your secret little coffee mornings together that I wasn't invited to.' Her bottom lip curled over as much as it could, like a spoilt child's. Shay stared at her incredulously.

'You mean when she was really ill? When she was in the grip of a crisis and needed someone and I could drop everything and be round at her house in five minutes flat?

She only rang me because you were at work and she knew you wouldn't have been able to talk. What do you think we did, Les? Have some scones and rip you to bits behind your back?'

Les swallowed and Shay hoped it was shame she was swallowing.

'It just felt sneaky,' she said eventually.

'Oh, grow up, Les. Don't you think Tan had a bit more going on in her head than to worry about you tallying up how many more minutes she saw me for than you? What about when you two went to the spa in Leicester together and I didn't go? And when just you and I used to go to the cinema because Tan didn't do thrillers, or doesn't that count?'

But Les was not there to accept blame, she was there to apportion it.

'Did you ever think how patronised I felt when you *pretty girls* volunteered to do my make-up and told me not to wear this and that?'

'Because we bloody cared about you,' said Shay, resisting the urge to shout this at her. 'Would you tell someone they had lipstick on their teeth and risk embarrassing them or keep schtum and let them embarrass themselves in front of loads of people instead?' Shay shook her head in wonder. 'Is that how you really saw us?' Her mum's words whispered in her mind: *Three will always be a crowd where friends are concerned. And the odd one out always knows who she is.*

'We were always you two and me.' Les tossed her long caramel hair over her shoulder. 'I wish Tan were here now because we just might have been a proper three.'

She meant she could have matched them for looks with her new knockers and figure, with her tan and her extensions and Angelina lips.

'We always were a proper three,' said Shay. 'I loved you to bits and so did Tan. This would have broken her heart. Do you know, I always wished I had your sense of humour, Les, the way you could make everyone laugh, how you could mimic people, the way you could tell a tale and hold an audience in the palm of your hand, but I never turned myself inside out with jealousy because I couldn't.'

How long had this unwarranted resentment been gnawing inside Les? Shay couldn't bear to think about it. But Les had finally got her wish, she was the most beautiful of them all on the outside. Stunning. To the victor the spoils.

Shay loaded her fork with a scallop and then put it down; she couldn't have eaten it if Jason Momoa was feeding it to her.

'I think we've said all we need to, don't you? I can't believe how wrong you got it, Les.'

Shay picked up her bag, then Les held up her hand, stalled her.

'I have something for you,' she said, reaching into her own bag, then sliding an envelope across the table.

Shay opened it to find a cheque.

'I want you to have this,' she said. 'From my winnings. I was always going to treat you, in case you thought I wouldn't. It would have been wrong not to.'

Ten thousand pounds. It might as well have read thirty pieces of silver. Shay put it back down on the table.

'I hope your money makes you really happy, Les. Good luck.'

Shay left then. Les could pick up the bill. She hoped the waiter would get a tip out of that twelve million, but sadly, somehow she doubted it.

Chapter 49

That weekend, Courtney and Sunny moved into their apartment and set up their office. Luckily Mort was on hand to act as referee when needed, but he reckoned he wouldn't have to blow his whistle as much as predicted. They might row about washing up and tights hanging over radiators, but workwise, they were a perfect combo, both clever adults with skills they were keen to capitalise on. They were a few years off their first Lamborghinis, but they had a couple of clients to start the ball rolling, energy, talent and finally job satisfaction. Shay's chicks had left the nest again and this time their wings looked strong enough to fly.

As for the nest itself, a young couple with a baby on the way had bought it to fill with their own adventures. They'd mark on the side of the wall the height of their children, as Shay had, until she'd had to get a chair to stand on to record it. They'd paint rooms in their choice of colours, knock walls down, make it their own. They'd wanted to move quickly so they could be settled in for Christmas. Shay cleaned it from top to bottom for them so they'd walk in to polished woodwork and shiny surfaces, paying forward the kindness the previous owners had paid her. On her last afternoon in the house Shay walked around it, remembering the years she was content in here, the Christmas days when the kids still believed in Santa and their joy at finding the piles of presents under the tree; seeing them crash into the kitchen in their school uniforms starving for fish fingers. The girly evenings she had with Tanya and Les, a Chinese banquet and gin. They had laughed until they cried together, and sometimes they'd cried until they laughed.

She missed Tan, and she also crazily missed Les. Their friendship could never be repaired, not after that level of duplicity, but it had been long and good for so many years, or so she'd thought. She sat for a while at the kitchen table that she was leaving for the new occupants, and let herself grieve for the end of an era, for when she was a daughter juggling her parents' needs and a mother worrying how she was ever going to knock up a Florence Nightingale outfit for the morning, because Courtney had forgotten to tell her about Victorian Day at school. It was amazing what you could do with an old black curtain, a white sheet and a shower cap at the eleventh hour. Part of her missed the mayhem, being a filling in the middle of the sandwich, feeling the squash of family tight against her.

The furniture was all gone, Courtney and Sunny had taken bits to start them off: their old beds, sofa, drawers, spare TV. Bruce didn't want anything – but why would he, living in a mansion. Morton was storing some pieces for her in one of his outbuildings; the rest was picked up by the Heart Foundation van. There were just a few boxes of stuff left that would fit easily in her car.

She didn't expect any visitors, least of all her soon-to-be

ex-husband. It was odd that he'd knock on the door, wait for admittance like a vampire who couldn't enter without permission. Odd and dangerous, not the same as seeing him across a crowded restaurant. The house was *theirs*, the ghosts of their shared life swirling around them at a time when she felt at her most vulnerable, unsure, adrift.

'Hi,' Bruce said, his shoulders jerking with nerves. 'I wondered if you had a minute.'

Shay stood aside to let him pass.

'Blimey,' he said, looking up and around. 'Takes me back to us moving in.' His voice was echoey, bouncing off the walls. 'Do you remember?'

Of course she did, she'd been seven months pregnant with Sunny and her nest-building hormones were cranked up to the max. There was a lot of house for their money, but it had needed so much doing to it, which was reflected in the price they'd paid. And they'd done it all. She, mostly.

She poured him a glass of cherryade from the bottle she'd opened. They'd drunk it on their first night in the house, used it to toast their new life. She'd bought some for old times' sake, to drink on her last night in it.

'So, how are you? How are the kids?' he asked, taking a seat at the table.

'I'm okay, and you can always ask the kids how they are.'

'Do they want to talk to me?'

'Of course,' she answered. 'It may surprise you to know that they've worked out you're not perfect. But you're their father. It's never too late to try and get close to them. They're not that hard to understand if you make the effort.'

He took a drink from the glass, a long one and then put it down on the table with his customary heavy-handedness as if he'd misjudged the distance. He looked like a man with a lot to say and no idea of where to start. Eventually he bumbled his way in.

'There's no easy ... proper ... Look, Shay, I don't want to throw away twenty-four years of marriage over a daft mistake.' He held his hand up to fend off any response she might make to that. 'I know this is more than a daft mistake, but if there's any way we can ... start again, well, that's what we'll have to chalk it up to – a mistake. I don't know what I was thinking.'

She let that settle into her brain.

'Okay,' she said, which wasn't an outright no, and gave him hope.

'We have two children between us and we'll be grandparents one day. What we had worked for so long, and every road has a blip in it. And sometimes you need to step out of something before you realise how comfortable it is. The grass wasn't as green as I thought it was. In fact it was blue. You don't see perspective when you're stood right next to it.'

She let him get to the end of his Bluffer's Guide to Idioms, waiting for 'Sorry seems to be the hardest word' to come out. She took a sip of the cherryade and let it slide down her throat.

'Not going too well with Les then?'

'I cocked up ...'

She could have made a really sarcastic comment there but fought it, let him continue.

Bruce wiped a slick of nervous sweat from his forehead. 'It was exciting at first, new, strange, bit naughty. She made me feel like a man, not a dad or a husband. It was only meant to be a fling, then she won that money and we got a bit drunk with it all.' He sighed. 'Then the hangover happened. When I saw you with Morton, it made me realise it's you I love.

You looked so . . . so beautiful. You *are* so beautiful. I know I'm asking a lot, but can't we pretend this madness never happened? I'll do anything to put it right. You're everything I could ever want.'

It would be so much easier to fall back into the familiar rather than forge forward into the unknown, she thought.

'I've stayed away because I was ashamed. We could get that villa in the sun now, just take off, wherever you want to go – you choose. I want to look after you, like a proper husband. It'll be easier now there's just you and me.' Then he said decisively, 'I'm going to pull out of the divorce.'

'Wow,' was all she said to that.

'Is that a yes?' The corners of Bruce's mouth twitched upwards with expectancy.

They could grow old together and the family would stay intact, the easy choice like her mum and dad had taken. She knew what she'd get with him, no need to worry about the unknown that presently shimmered in front of her with rainbow colours but offered no sureties . . .

'It's a no, I'm sorry,' replied Shay, not really taking any pleasure in popping his balloon. 'If only you'd put as much effort into your family as you did into your affair.' It was what stung more than anything, when she'd had time to process it, the energy he'd never spent on them when he'd so obviously had it to give.

'I know, I know. But I can change,' he pleaded.

'I've already changed, Bruce, and I don't fit in this marriage any more.'

She was so much bigger than it now, it was a too-tight skin she had shed. She had grown, flowered, strengthened, walked out of the shadows where she had hidden for so long and into the sunshine and it felt flipping marvellous. She had stood up for her loved ones, fought for what was right and was doing a fine job of looking after herself without anyone needing to do it for her. She hadn't a clue what going forwards entailed, but she was heading in that direction only, not backwards.

'Wouldn't you at least give it some thought?' he tried. 'Please.'

She shook her head slowly. Then she stood, indicating their meeting was at an end.

At the door, Bruce bent, kissed her cheek and it would have been churlish of her not to let him hold her, one last time, the person he had thrown away. The person who had been outweighed on the scales by a brand new Audi and a row of Armani shirts, the trappings of luxury that had turned out to be a Farrow and Ball-painted prison.

Bruce looked up at the 'sold' sign.

'Where will you go?' he asked her.

'Home,' she replied.

When her car pulled up in front of the barn that night, Jonah was waiting for her. He'd been on tenterhooks since she rang to say she was coming over and could they talk? He ran out into the dark November air, sparkly with the first snow of winter, Christmas come early to his heart.

'Here you are,' he said, his lips aching with the smile that stretched them.

'Here I am,' she replied, fear fluttering like a trapped bird inside her. She'd been driving around for the best part of an hour, scared that the magic between them would have melted like these snow flurries in the air, that nostalgia had blinded him, that the rose-coloured euphoria spun by their reunion had, in the space he had granted her, faded; that too many years had passed by for them to be bridged by anything other than fond friendship. But the look in his eyes told her everything she needed to know.

'I've missed you so much,' said Jonah. 'And I've spent too long missing you. No more, Shay Corrigan, no more.'

He held out his hand and she took it, feeling the same thrill she had so many years ago when she was a schoolgirl madly in love with a schoolboy, and together they walked into his house to pick up the past and mould it into a future.

EPILOGUE

Ella Smith died at Christmas and Shay had kept her word. After Ella was buried, she went to the police with the diary that she said had been bequeathed to her. The bones of old Bradley Smith were exhumed and committed to a proper resting place, though no one went to the funeral. The local newspaper did a piece about the historic story which the nationals picked up. It couldn't bring Denny back, but it could right the injustice that had been done to his two young friends. It highlighted the new charity, 'Denny's Circle', which would grow and go on to help many teenagers who felt they had nowhere to turn for help and support. Denny's name would live on, because his friends valued him as too precious to be forgotten.

Les and Bruce didn't last the course. He bought a small villa and moved to Spain to test out a slower pace of life and be king of his own one-bedroomed castle rather than being a slave in someone else's country pile. He Zoomed his children regularly, amazed at their mature capacity for forgiveness. He couldn't make up for the years he'd been there with them but not *for* them, but going forward, he was determined to strengthen their relationship and he realised, not too late, what a brilliant pair of kids he had. He gave their mother full credit for that.

Sandwich went from strength to strength. The brother and sister power combo earned their stripes and took over from JoMint for Colin Parks-Davis's company, managed some very lucrative influencer contracts and handled all the social media and design needs for Yorkshire Crumble cheese. They were busy as Terri and Amanda's bees – and loving it.

Morton wasn't greedy in his divorce settlement, he was quite happy keeping his farmhouse and his savings and he left Les to bathe in asses' milk and buy even bigger lips because he'd discovered the sort of happiness that money couldn't buy. Armed with his new silky-smooth dating skills, Morton Jagger found a cracking woman on Tinder. An owner of twelve bodegas in the north of England, she had plenty of money of her own, so she didn't need his. She had been about to give up trawling for love when Morton landed on her radar. She liked his kind heart and his gentlemanly manners, and she hooted at his anecdotes and repertoire of fart jokes. Also she loved sex. Morton was as happy as a cat in a bath of clotted cream. And when Les texted him asking if he'd be interested in some no-strings fun for old times' sake, he didn't even dignify it with a response.

Paula took umbrage that her father had left the family cuckoo in the nest a portion of inheritance equal to that which he'd left her – his true and only daughter. She wrote to tell Shay she was cutting her and hers out of her life for good. Courtney volunteered to deliver a response, but her mother told her to leave well alone.

Little Mort proposed to Courtney in Bran Castle in Transylvania; he thought she'd appreciate it more than if he did it at the top of the Eiffel tower or the Empire State Building – he knew his girl so well. Shay knew she wouldn't need to take her daughter aside before the wedding and ask if she wanted to run off, no questions asked, but she did joke that she might pull Mort to one side and ask him instead.

Sunny went to a school reunion and met up with a girl he'd fancied from afar in his teenage years. It turned out that she'd fancied him from afar too. So they started fancying each other from much nearer. Courtney had no desire to smash her face in, which was considered the ultimate seal of approval.

The pensioners of Merriment Close were delighted with the new additions – a bit of young blood, Errol and wife in number 2, and Errol was renting out 1A to a young couple with twin toddlers. They joined the residents' association and the neighbourhood watch, sent Christmas cards and said hello in passing. Order was restored.

As for Shay, she would always be integral to the family sandwich, even if it was more of an open construction these days. Her children were flying happily and high, they didn't need her but she'd always be there for them if that changed. And as much as she sometimes, in wistful moments, missed the manic days of eleventh-hour fancy dress costume-making, homework-helping, fish finger-frying and bridegroom-rescuing, she was enjoying the peace and contentment she'd found in the future she should always have had. Life, as Morton Jagger had once wisely said, was for grabbing with both hands when the good bits came along and making up for lost time, and that's exactly what she and Jonah Wells were doing.

She knew who she was and that made her strong. She never had to choose between being the daughter of Harry Corrigan or Ammon Habib because she was both. Her identity was the sum of her experiences and her values, her battles and achievements; she was made of everything she had been and thought she was: Italian throwback, Egyptian love-child, worker, wrecker of weddings, estranged sister, daughter, mother, wife, friend, lover, survivor, fighter, sandwich filling. But more than the labels, she belonged to the people she loved, and they belonged to her and that, above it all, made her everything she wanted to be.

Acknowledgements

There are always so many people to thank because I get to be frontstage, but there's an army backstage all beavering away to get this book on the shelves. And what a fabulous bunch they are.

Thanks to Sally Partington, my copyeditor, whose hair I have turned whiter than Bruce's posh shirt.

My agent is right at the top of my thank-you list as always. Lizzy Kremer is the woman you want in your corner and at your back. I'm lucky to have her in those positions and the wonderful lot at David Higham who are getting me deals all over the globe. Big shout-out to ma boy Brian who dishes out the dosh.

And all the fabulous lot at Simon & Schuster – my work family – Ian, Suzanne, SJ, Hayley, Gill, Joe, Jess, Rich, Maddie, Kat, Dom, Sian, Pip, Francesca and my wonderful editor Clare. What a team you are. How lucky am I? A big shout-out to Alice Rodgers who has gone on to pastures new and our loss is their great gain. I wish this efficient and wonderful young lady all the success and happiness I can fling at her.

Thank you to Emma and Annabelle at ED PR for your sterling work, you are fab. I'm still buzzing over being on Graham Norton's show – like, ME!! Now get me a gig with Jason Momoa. If anyone can – you can.

Adam Appleby is based on a wonder of a gentleman I met when my mum had the same problems as Roberta. Andy Pearson is one of those experts sent from heaven to help people who are ready to tear out their hair or bang their head on their town hall door until they get answers that can make sense. Don't even attempt to understand the Party Wall Act of 1996. Andy saved us thousands of pounds in our fight against the stupid revised planning laws which have caused neighbourhood wars, thanks to Whitehall idiots who don't think things through at all. What Andy doesn't know about planning restrictions and allowances can be written on a very small postage stamp. His consultation service is worth every penny. He can be reached at www.apbuildingdesign.co.uk – tell him I sent you.

Thank you to my family who have supplied me with too much material for this book. I love being a mother but my goodness, what a hard job it is. High-five to all the mums out there, especially the single ones, who have to cover all the bases. Funny how forgiving you become of your own parents when you give birth, isn't it? I miss my dad, I'd give anything to be running around after him but Mum's keeping me busy on that front. Mum, Pete, Tez, George, I love you xxx

Thank you to the bloggers who do so much to support us authors, reading books in their spare time and reviewing them, spreading the word. We love you.

Thank you to the Romantic Novelists' Association – the best thing I ever joined. The support, the friendship, the booze. They work tirelessly to support authors – both old and those new ones trying to break through. Most of them are volunteers and they don't get half the credit they should.

Thank you to my readers who humble me with their loyalty. I am blessed to be so supported – especially by Barnsley, my home town. The library, the Barnsley Book Vault bookshop (across all social media as @thebookvault07 – they do a postal service), Andrew Harrod, the editor of the *Barnsley Chronicle*, Mike's Famous Bookstall in the market and all the people who turn up to my launches. You can't buy that sort of treasure but I wish you could.

Big ta to Stu my website guy as always. He's a wonder. I wish I had his brain. Alas I'll have to make do with this inferior one.

Thank you to Tony and Diane Walker for giving me the character of Dagmara Mitic. They won the opportunity to name a character in my book after someone and chose Diane's mum. Every time I've done this, I've ended up with some blinding characters which were never in the original plans. Most of what I've written about Dagmara's history in this book is true: having to flee Latvia after living a privileged life. And her husband Bozidar running from Yugoslavia after smuggling guns to the partisans, only for them to finally meet in Bognor Regis. Bozidar (or Gordon as he became better known) was likened in looks to Omar Sharif – something I found out AFTER I'd written Omar into my book. How's that for a coincidence?

And thank you to my pals because it's hard having a job like this and you need an understanding bunch who know you aren't making lame excuses on a sunny Saturday night when they're having a barbecue and you're stuck at your desk on an eleventh-hour edit. Traz, Cath, Sue, Kath,

Jackie, Rae, Maggie – big *mwah*. And because of the vagaries of this job, you need your fellow author pals to keep you on the right side of insane – because you'll never achieve true sanity in this profession. A special mention to Debbie Johnson, Cathy Bramley, Veronica Henry and Catherine Isaac, friends and fellow crew members in the stormy sea that is our world. Also my mates in the Shit Book Club (don't ask): Judy Astley, Katie Fforde, Catherine Jones, Bernie Kennedy, Jill Mansell, Janie Millman, AJ Pearce, Jo Thomas, Jane Wenham-Jones. I love 'em all.

For those of you who recognise the name 'Tommy Tanner' – he's based on a real life boxer – Josh 'The Outlaw' Wale, a Barnsley lad who is the ex British Bantamweight champion. A lovely bloke who is dedicated to the sport. Watch out for a lad in his stable called Billy 'The Kid' Allen because we're sponsoring him and wish him all the very best.

And thank you as well to David Charles Gordon who once again appears as super-solicitor David Charles. Who would have thought I'd get this sort of mileage out of our relationship, David, when I came to see you torn and tattered all those years ago. And who would have thought there was such fun to be had in trying to sue a global enterprise.

Our young people are but delicate shoots that we hope will harden into oak trees, but this era is not kind to them. None of them should have nowhere to turn. Help is out there – please use it if you need it: youngminds.org.uk (@youngmindsuk on Twitter).

And if you find yourself in the sandwich generation – it's hard, I know. You have to juggle until your arms ache with the weight, but buckling is not an option. Be kind to yourself, take some time out, learn to delegate, accept all the help offered, tell any guilty feelings to swivel. Hang on to your patience. We do what we can, spreading ourselves like cheap margarine, worry and load ourselves with blame and hope that the best we've done is appreciated a bit. We never quite get it right but we won't go too far wrong if we do some things out of love as well as duty. Family dynamics are – in short – a bugger to balance. And there's always some Brady bunch in your eyeline who is gliding along on a path of scented rose petals as you strain over obstacles, bloodied and battered. Ignore them – they are not the norm. Hang on in there.